HAIL

Books by W.L. Ripley

Storme Warning

Storme Front

Eye of the Storme

Cole Springer Series

Springer's Gambit

Pressing the Bet

Springer's Fortune

HAIL STORME

A WYATT STORME THRILLER

W. L. RIPLEY

The characters and events portrayed in this book are fictitious. Any similarity to real persons, living or dead, is coincidental and not intended by the author.

ISBN: 1941298753
ISBN 13: 9781941298756

Published by Brash Books, LLC
12120 State Line #253
Leawood, Kansas 66209

www.brash-books.com

For my brother, Jim (badge 826),
of the Missouri State Highway Patrol.

The lion never counts the herd that is about him,
nor weighs how many flocks he has to scatter.

—Aaron Hill (1685–1750)

ONE

The afternoon sun hung like a bruised peach in the autumn sky when I stepped over the sagging, rusted fence into the biggest marijuana field I'd ever seen.

It was enormous. A field of a thousand hazy daydreams stretching like a Kansas cornfield and disappearing into the tree-lined ridge rising up behind it. A breeze from the west washed across my neck and by my face, rustling the spiked plants. Golden-orange leaves from the overhead trees drifted and danced, then settled among the green cannabis stalks.

It was the deer, killed and butchered, that had brought me here.

I had been bowhunting the public-use land of the Missouri Ozarks when I discovered the dead buck. Its antlers had been sawed off at the base of the skull and removed, the carcass left to rot. Two hundred pounds of wasted meat. It was a fresh kill. The wet sheen of scarlet blood glistened against the dull fur. It smelled like a fistful of dirty pennies.

There were five bullet entries. Three in the gut. Smell of dirty pennies and three in the gut. Gun season was still a month away. Poacher. The ground around the corpse was fouled with man-prints, smooth-soled boots heading east, deeper into the timber. I followed them. As I did I nocked an arrow and secured the arrow's shaft with the flexible holder on the compound bow. I wanted to find the man who would kill a buck for its rack and then leave it to rot. Wanted to look at him. See what kind of man would do that. Maybe shake him a little.

I slipped through the October woods, the damp soil soft under my boots. Smelled the heavy aroma of decaying leaves. I found one of those miniature liquor bottles like the airlines serve. Jim Beam. Found a cigarette butt. Marlboro Light. Drinks whiskey, smokes cigarettes, litters the countryside, and shoots deer for kicks. Had to be a real man. I crossed a creek that cut like a vein through the forest, while the sun pulsed and spat yellow-orange rays through the crooked fingers of the timber. Shadows reached for me. A squirrel skittered through the leaves, then scampered up a tree, his claws clicking and scraping against the bark. He sat on a limb, chattering excitedly, scolding me. Two hours of light left.

I crossed the brown-crusted fence and saw the marijuana then. The stalks were head-high. Enough grass to keep Paradise County blurred and mellow for a month. There was raw stubble for a few rows where the plants had been harvested. I was three miles in, and most hunters wouldn't come this far before turning back. Besides, this area didn't get much traffic until the November gun season, by which time the crop would be gone and rolled into Zig-Zag papers.

I stepped into the stubble. On one side of the field was a small garbage pile of Miller beer cans, Maxwell House coffee cans, various tins from beans, soups, and other canned items. The gray-speckled blackness of an old campfire spotted the edge of the field like a scab. Thoughtful of them to bring garbage. Made it more like civilization. Just bring your own. From the amount of debris it looked as if several men tended the crop. There were more cigarette butts, none of which looked fresh. I heard a rustling noise in the marijuana stalks. Another deer? Or the poacher?

Then I heard something I'd never heard in the woods. A sound that sent an electric chill along the back of my neck. I was gripped by an ancient, paralyzing fear. Older than bullets and steel. It was the low, guttural snarl of carnivore, an animal rumble followed by the quickening whisper of slapping weeds.

Getting closer. Coming toward me.

I saw the low shadow first; then the black, triangle face and red mouth appeared through the spiked plants. There are few terrors to equal that caused by a huge hound, especially a Doberman pinscher. The lean, black body and viperlike head are the child nightmares of fiendish monsters and shadowy terrors grabbing at you out of the night. Fetid breath and dripping yellow fangs, snapping and tearing at you.

Years ago, in Vietnam, a Saigon pimp had burned a couple of Marines. Had his girls roll them. One of the Marines was a dog handler for the military police. I was on a three-day pass when I came across the pimp, lying in a heap of garbage, flies buzzing around his torn throat. The wound was raw and turning brown, like bad meat. Around the wound the skin was purple, and a flap of shredded dermis hung open like a leather pocket with bad stitching. His eyes were swollen, with the whites showing around the dark brown irises, a look of terror in them like I'd never seen, and I'd seen too much by that point in the war. A disturbing picture I had never fully shaken.

One more memory of Vietnam I didn't need.

The hound snarled, then flattened out in a dead run across the stubble. No tree close enough to climb before he was on me. When the black predator was fifteen yards away and closing, I sighted, allowed for his approach, and released a fluted arrow. The dog made a *whuff* sound as the wicked razor head bit into his shoulder. He faltered only slightly and came purposefully on. I bellowed a war cry of rage and fear and set my feet. He leapt at me, jaws popping, eyes yellow and narrow. I clubbed him with the bow like George Brett slapping a triple off the wall with the bases loaded. Arrows rattled off the quiver and scattered like burnt matches on the ground. The dog bawled in pain when the bow thudded against him. He landed heavily, like a sack of vegetables tossed from a truck, rolled once, then bounded to his feet.

He faced me, blood and saliva dripping from his mouth. The arrow's shaft was bent and the broadhead flashed silver and crimson where it escaped from his ribs. I dropped the bow and retrieved an arrow, ready to use it as a spear. Tore my skinning knife from its sheath. I waited, knees bent, weight evenly distributed, waiting for his rush. I could feel the hairs at the back of my neck, the sweat rolling down the backs of my thighs. My body tingled and the blood roiled in my head and ears; I felt the delicious ache of the anticipation of battle.

If I used the knife or arrow I would have to sustain a bite. I knew that. Accepted it. Not a conscious acceptance, but the acceptance of hundreds of messages streaming furiously through thousands of synapses and buried memories. I tucked my chin to protect my throat. I was wearing light camo. I could fend him off by feeding him one forearm while I stabbed with the knife, or I could stab at his eyes or down his mouth with the arrow. There was no good way.

One would die, the other live.

The hound gathered himself, legs splayed. A liquid growl rattled in his lungs, torn and lacerated by the razor-edged arrow. Reddish froth splashed his dark mouth. A stalactite of scarlet dripped syruplike from his side.

We stood and glared at each other. Man and beast. Ten feet separated us. My forearms began to stiffen and shake. The dog's breath came in shallow grumbles, like a worn bellows. He snuffed loudly, lay down, shuddered, and died.

Only seconds had passed, though it seemed as if we had moved in a slow dance of motion and emotion. My shoulders relaxed. I sank to my knees. Relief flooded me. My breathing came in short gasps, unable to satisfy the urgent thirst in my lungs. I fought the spasms of hyperventilation. Several seconds—or was it minutes?—passed before I gained control of my breathing.

There was a bad taste at the base of my throat. My arms and legs felt as if I'd run a mile carrying a fifty-pound rock. The cool air was delicious. Finally, I was able to stand. I walked to where the dog lay. I looked at his black, shining body and bloody mouth. Then I kicked him. Hard. My boot thudded and sank, gases escaped from the dog, causing a posthumous moan.

I was glad he was dead and I was alive. None of this man's best friend crap. That was for the puppy your father brought home for your birthday or for the Brittany spaniel walking at your side and pointing quail on chilled autumn afternoons. Not for this monster. He would have been more than happy to kill me, shake me by the throat until it came loose in his teeth, then stand over me and howl in triumph.

The hell with him.

I rubbed my forehead with the back of a trembling hand. My skin felt clammy. I gathered the fallen arrows and fixed them to the quiver. I was surprised at how my mind could suppress the fear. Shocked by the businesslike way I'd dispatched the animal. More automatic than calculated.

I'd forgotten about the poacher. Though the exchange between the attack dog and me hadn't been loud or long, it had attracted his attention. I heard the angry sizzle as the bullet zipped by before I heard the crack and rolling echo of a large-caliber rifle. In Vietnam you learned not to worry about the shot you heard—it was the bullet you never heard that put you in a body bag.

I dropped to the ground and belly-crawled to the creek bank. Two more shots buzzed through the brush before I rolled over the edge and down the bank. The barbed wire tore a square of cloth from my shirt and my shoulder struck the branch of a blowdown as I tumbled. I lost my bow briefly, then retrieved it before I scrambled under the fallen tree. The silence of the woods screamed at me.

Where was he? The spacing of the shots suggested one man armed with a bolt- or lever-action rifle. A poor shot, though. Untrained. He tried to make up for his marksmanship by shooting often, as he had with the buck. Or maybe he was just trying to scare me. That part was working.

I had some advantages. I was camouflaged. Though there was sunlight left, the lengthening shadows would make it tough for him if I kept the sun behind me. He probably expected me to run. I expected me to run. But would he expect me to circle him and try to take him? Would he come after me? Could he take a chance of me getting away, now I'd seen the marijuana? People who go to the trouble of posting an attack dog have a lot at stake. The size of the field argued for that. No, my guess was he didn't want me to get out of there alive.

I wanted me out of there. Alive.

The shooting ceased. He couldn't see me now I was down in the creek hollow. If he was any distance he would have a hard time sighting me, then getting off a good shot. The sound of the rifle suggested a shot within 150 yards. I thought about the dead buck, his rack torn from its cape. It didn't always take a good shot. Even a blind hog finds an acorn, and the unlucky die.

If I tried to run I could blunder right into him. Maybe a distraction would give me an edge. I removed an arrow from the quiver, nocked it to the string, placed the sixty-yard pin on a thick oak tree and released the string. The arrow whistled away and struck the ancient tree with a solid *thwok.*

I was moving with the arrow's departure, circling in the direction of the gunshots. A dangerous tactic, but not without logic. If I got behind him I could keep my eye on him, and in a couple of hours it would be too dark for him to find me. I liked my chances after dark. Besides, I didn't want a man with a high-powered rifle dogging my trail. Until sunset, he had the big stick and the black aces.

It took twenty minutes for me to maneuver to a point on the ridge where I could see a good distance. I took careful steps, avoiding sticks and placing my feet on clumps of grass. The key was patience and to move slowly, not allowing panic to hurry you, keeping to the shadows.

I positioned myself behind a forked tree with a stand of second-growth brush at my back to break up my outline and take advantage of my camo. I waited, feeling my body heat, smelling my own scent, the scent of exertion, anticipation, and anxiety. I watched for movement, searching with my eyes before panning with my head to minimize my own movement. A woodpecker tapped on a rotting tree behind me. I smelled crushed evergreen. Thought about the 9-millimeter Browning pistol in the glove box of my Ford Bronco. If I were the Lone Ranger I could've had Tonto circle back to the truck and bring it, or the cavalry. Never a sidekick around when you need one.

I saw the poacher then. Rather, a pair of crows saw him first and told me. Cawing and chiding him, they launched themselves from their perch 125 yards southeast of me. He was at the base of an oak tree examining my arrow buried deep in its trunk. If he was any kind of tracker, he'd notice there were no tracks leading out of the woods. The ground was damp and soft from recent rains—good for moving quietly, but not for concealing footprints. I watched him pause to look around. His movements were unsure, furtive. He stopped, looked up the ridge, then back to the field. He raised the rifle, pointed it, held momentarily, then slowly dropped it to his side. Fear of the unknown is a powerful anxiety. He had seen a man, then that man had disappeared, and now he was wondering where.

He moved toward the field, bent slightly, with the gun sweeping in front of him. Reaching the edge of the field, he paused to light a cigarette, took three quick puffs and looked around quickly. I sat. Silent. The hunter once more.

He found the dog. Bent down to examine the corpse, touched the bent arrow, then looked around. He puffed the cigarette, plucked it from his lips and flicked it away as if it were poison. Reaching under his jacket, he produced a walkie-talkie and spoke into it. I hadn't counted on that. I couldn't make out what he was saying. His eyes searched around him as he spoke. Calling in reinforcements? He put the walkie-talkie away and called out, his voice cutting the stillness.

"Whoever you are, you better come on out. Or you better hope you're gone. People're coming to help me find you." Hated to hear that. I was hardly dressed for company and shy to boot. I fixed an arrow to the string. He was seventy-five yards away and moving in my direction. Too far for a shot. I waited.

"You killed Mr. Roberts's dog. He won't like that. Wouldn't want to be you when he finds out." He kept moving, looking behind him and all around as he did. Sixty-five yards away now. He called back over his shoulder. "Better come out, man. We'll find you soon enough. Might as well make it easy on yourself."

He was still moving in my direction. If he'd seen me and was trying to fool me, he was the best actor alive. If he saw me he would have no trouble hitting me from this distance. He was five ten, midthirties, with long, dirty-blond hair, a droopy Fu Manchu mustache of a darker shade, hangdog eyes, sallow complexion. And he was moving right at me. He must have been making his way to a vehicle. His movement suggested departure, not pursuit. Trying to vacate the woods before whoever killed the dog found him. By some dreadful fluke I had placed myself in his path. My throat was dry, and I fought the impulse to clear it. He was forty yards away now and still coming. I could see the sweat on his forehead and the Spanish leather boots on his feet. Heard his feet crumple the leaves and branches underfoot. No matter how well camouflaged I was he would soon see me.

I raised the bow and placed my fingers on the string.

TWO

Later, when I had a chance to reflect on the situation, I decided there was nothing else I could've done. He was nervous and wired to the gills on cocaine or booze. Or both. Saw it in his eyes. They were glazed. Manic.

"Put the gun down, partner," I said, as calmly and soothingly as I could. "And everything will be fine."

Maybe it was the sight of a camouflaged man rising up from the shadows of the woods, face smudged, only the whites of my eyes to suggest it was just a man and not some dark apparition materializing before him. I raised up behind one of the tree's forks, where little of me showed except the bow and the nasty razor-tipped shaft. I was off to his right, so he would have to turn slightly to shoot at me. I wasn't going to make it easy for him.

Maybe it was the unreality of the situation. Or the memory of the dog, now cold and stiff. Whatever caused it, he panicked. He didn't hesitate when he heard my voice, just swung the rifle quickly, snapping off a shot before he was ready.

The roar of the gun was deafening, filling my head and ears as if I were closeted in a small, soundless room. The bullet smacked into the tree as I relaxed my string fingers and sent the shaft away. The noise and flash of muzzle caused me to flinch slightly, but the arrow punched into the hollow of his right shoulder, then disappeared as if it had never touched him. The sixty-pound pull of the Browning compound powered the arrow through his shoulder and out the back. Cleanly. Five yards farther back and I might've missed him.

An arrow has no shock power like a bullet. An arrow kills by severing vital organs, without smashed tissue and splintered bones. I'd heard other bowhunters tell of arrows bouncing off bones or passing through the deer exactly like the arrow I'd just released. Sometimes, if the blades were sharp, the animal didn't feel it. My blades were honed to a shaving edge with a fine-grained whetstone. I didn't think the rifleman felt it pass through. He hardly seemed to notice at first. That is, he hardly noticed until he tried to raise the rifle again and found he couldn't. His right hand dangled uselessly, the fingers twitching electrically, as if a wire had been severed inside him with tin snips.

His eyes were wild with fear and chemicals. He looked at the convulsive hand, then at me. His lips trembled. The rifle fell to the ground.

"Take it easy," I said. "I don't want to hurt you."

He reached into his jacket pocket with his good hand. He posed no threat now. With considerable effort he pulled out a small plastic medicine vial, which fell to the ground. He started to pick it up when I stepped from behind the tree with another arrow ready. I didn't remember pulling it from the quiver or fitting it to the string. He turned and ran. I raised the bow, pulled the string to anchor point, held on the middle of his back, allowed for his movement, then slowly, as slowly as you can let off a compound bow, I relaxed the string. Didn't shoot. Didn't need to kill him. Didn't want to. I was uneasy about my instinct to do so.

I watched him crash through the woods, then up the hill. He was no outdoorsman. No gunman, either. When I examined his rifle, a Marlin lever-action, it was dirty and ring-wormed with patches of rust. Oil had congealed like rancid pudding at the seams of the receiver, the stock pocked with scratches and long, pale scars. No hunter would neglect his piece in such a manner.

I reached down and picked up the prescription bottle he'd dropped. Inside the unlabeled vial were two milky crystals that looked like rock candy. I opened the top and sniffed it. No smell.

I thought about tasting it, then remembered the wire-tight look in the poacher's eyes. Drugs? But it didn't look like anything I'd seen before, and I'd seen about everything while in Vietnam, except a solution. I replaced the lid and put it in my pocket.

I hiked out of the woods. I was fatigued. Something deep within me ached and pulled. Reaching the Bronco, I placed the Browning X-Cellerator bow in its rack, started the truck, floored the pedal, and bumped down the rough, gravel-scrubbed road. And I thought—about what I'd done, about what had just occurred. About myself. Two miles down the road I stopped the Ford in a sideways spray of rock, threw open the door, and dry-heaved as the dust swirled around me. There were no other vehicles around. No other sounds. It was a lonely road I was on.

I drove back to town and thought about what I should do. First, I needed to report the marijuana without their knowing who I was. I could call it in. Involvement didn't bother me, calling attention to myself did.

Second, I was supposed to meet a man named Chick Easton. Easton was a friend of a friend. My friend's name was Matt Jenkins. Easton was returning a vehicle that had been stolen in Missouri and dumped in Colorado. Jenkins had asked if I would give Easton a ride back to Colorado. Said Easton was "colorful." I owed Matt Jenkins. Not for anything he'd done, or for the reasons most people feel they owe another, but because I liked him and could trust him and trust is a tough thing to come by anymore.

As I neared town I passed a sign announcing:

PARADISE
City Limits
Pop. 37,523

Black letters on a white background. Paradise was a small city perched on the northern edge of the Ozarks. It was big enough for some big-town troubles and too small to have the solutions. It was spackled with the usual strip of chain restaurants and motels, convenience stores and gas stations, the mom-and-pop businesses linking them like a cheap lavaliere: too tired to keep going, too late to quit trying. Traffic was thick, but manageable. I parked at an open-air phone booth, lit the electronic bells with a quarter, and dialed 911. My quarter returned.

"Emergency 911," said the answering male voice after the sixth ring.

"How many times does it ring when it isn't an emergency?"

"Who the hell is this?"

"I know where there is a field of marijuana the size of Busch Stadium. Somebody took a shot at me, also."

"This is an emergency line, buddy. A field of marijuana isn't gonna pick up and move. And you sound pretty calm for a guy who's been shot at. We don't take anonymous tips and crank calls on this line."

"It's out on Farm Road H. Twelve miles south of Highway 24, then three miles west of the gravel, back on public-use ground," I said, ignoring him. We're a society of cynics. You dial 911 about drug activity and attempted homicide and it's not considered an emergency.

"Dial 555-COPS," said the voice. "Ask for Sheriff Kennedy." He hung up before I could commend his compassion and courtesy.

I dialed the number and a female voice answered. My quarter didn't come back this time. The cops and Ma Bell were in this together. I asked for Kennedy and she put me on hold. A male voice came on the line and said, "Sheriff Kennedy."

"Twelve miles south of Highway 24 on Farm Road H, back on public-use land, there's a twenty-acre field of marijuana that's been partially harvested."

"What's your name?"

"I had to kill a guard dog. Doberman. Somebody shot at me. I wounded him with an arrow, but he ran off. I've got his rifle. Send somebody to look. Better send a couple of guys. I'll leave the rifle where you can find it. I don't think they leave the field unattended long."

"Why don't you come in and make a report?"

"Told you where it is."

"What were you doing out there?"

"Looking for Jimmy Hoffa."

There was a pause. But it wasn't for laughter. "Look, sir. Why not come in and make a report in person? How much trouble could that be?"

"I'm terminally bashful. How much trouble would it be for you to go and look without me coming in?"

The other end was silent again. "You say you wounded him with an arrow? Where did you wound him?"

"Right shoulder."

"What were you aiming at?"

"Well, you see, he had this apple on his head and I bet him I could shoot it without—"

"We need a description," he said, interrupting me. Humor is dead. "We've had a lot of drug activity in this county. It's getting dangerous. You could be one of them, drawing us off on a coon hunt while you move drugs from some other place. Happened before."

I wanted a cup of coffee and a shower. I said, "If I come in, you keep my name out of it and I only meet with you. Nobody else. Deal?"

"Too thin. I want to see you face-to-face without conditions."

"You must think I'm pretty stupid. You don't have any bargaining chips. You don't know me, and I don't need you or this. My way or no way."

"Okay," he said. "Come on in. You only talk to me and you're out of it."

"How do I know I can trust you?"

"Because I said you can. And because this is the first solid lead I've had on the drug traffic around here in a while and I'm not gonna stick my pecker in it. Savvy?"

I did. He told me how to get there, and I told him I'd be in as soon as I picked up someone. Chick Easton.

Chick Easton wasn't at the place I was to meet him, but I was running a little late. I found him at a saloon across the street called the Silver Spur. "If you don't find him," Matt Jenkins had said, "look in the closest bar. He'll be there."

That's where he was, drinking Wild Turkey and chasing it with Budweiser. Drunk. At least, I thought he was. I would be, if the number of bottles and shot glasses was any indication.

"You Easton?" I asked. He fit the description. Slim build with shoulders like a middleweight boxer, forearms like Popeye's. Couple inches shorter than me, sandy hair, sky-blue eyes, age indeterminate, between thirtysomething and forty-five, like the gun. "Don't let the skinny hips fool you," Matt said. "Boy's strong as a logger."

"Haven't seen 'im," he said, sipping off the whiskey. "You must be the guy Jenks said was coming."

"I'm Wyatt Storme," I said. "I'm supposed to take you to Colorado with me." I looked at him. "He didn't tell me you were a drunk."

He laughed. "He didn't tell me you were Sir Galahad, either. But that's Matt. He's not very judgmental. Sit down, I'll buy you a beer."

"No thanks," I said. But I pulled out a chair and sat.

"Wouldn't hurt you any."

"Done wonders for you."

"Thought all you big-time football players were big drinkers."

"Another myth shattered."

"Matt didn't tell me it was you that was coming. I'm honored."

"You'll get over it."

A leggy waitress bustled over. Nice figure, too much makeup, too little covering the nice figure. "Get you something, good-lookin'?"

"You have coffee?" I asked.

"I can make you some."

"Fine. I take it black."

"Do you like it slow and easy?" she said, flashing me a smile marred by one crooked tooth, but still nice teeth.

"Just black, thank you," I said, smiling. She shrugged. I said, "Bring him some coffee, too."

Easton laughed. "Coffee messes up my alcohol system." The waitress looked uneasy. "It's okay," Chick said to the waitress. "Coffee's fine."

"Cream and sugar?"

Easton looked at me, giving me a bent smile. "I want cream 'n' sugar, daddy?" he asked. I looked back at him. Then he said, "I'll take mine black, too, like my hero and bestest buddy here. He's a legitimate American hero, ya know? Caught three touchdown passes in the Super Bowl. Beat the Raiders with the last one. Fucked up the economy. For me, anyway. The Cowboys were a nine-point underdog. I had two bills on the Raiders. You caught that last pass and broke my heart, Storme." The waitress was looking at me.

"He telling the truth?" she asked. Patted her hair.

"I look like a pro football player to you?"

"Some. Don't know for sure what one looks like. You're cute. Got nice shoulders. Could be." She smiled. Nice-looking working girl.

"He's drunk," I said. "Never touched a football in my life."

She sighed, then shrugged. Left to get the coffee.

"I may drink too much," Easton said, a big grin on his face. "But I ain't no liar. What's the matter? You ashamed of it?"

"No. Doesn't mean anything, though. Just a game."

"There're people who'd disagree with that. Like that waitress. She's extra deadly. Rodeo beautiful."

"So, what do you do?" I asked.

"Mostly, I drink," he said. "Though it isn't widely known." When he smiled, little wrinkles appeared at the corners of his eyes. He was going to be difficult to avoid liking. "I show off some. Hire out some."

"Hire out?"

"Bodyguard. Bounty hunter. Somebody skips with your bail money down, I find 'em, drag 'em back. But I'm only wonderful at it."

I considered him. He was twenty pounds lighter than me, rangy and lean like a Montana cowboy. Most bodyguards are steroid-bloated freaks with twenty-inch necks and screaming-eagle tattoos, their eyes dark and hooded under thick foreheads. Easton didn't fit the mold. He seemed too affable, too relaxed. Too drunk. "You don't look like a bodyguard."

"I eat fire and shit ice cubes," he said. "I'm jumping Arnold Schwarzenegger's wife and he knows it. Chick T. Easton is the name, danger is the game. The *T* stands for Terrific." I grinned. Very difficult not to like him. He drained his beer, then asked, "So, what does the man with the best hands in the NFL do when he quits playing games?"

Good question. I was still working on the answer. "Semi-retired, more or less. Hunt and fish. Race the moon. You know, you don't look like a bounty hunter, either."

"Got a rubber hose, a pair of handcuffs, and an autographed picture of Steve McQueen." The waitress brought the coffee.

"Thanks," I said. She smiled. I said, "He says you're rodeo beautiful."

She leaned back at the waist and looked at Chick. "Rodeo beautiful? I never heard such a thing. What does it mean?"

Easton stirred his coffee with a swizzle stick that had a little spur on top, looked into the whirlpool he'd made in the coffee, a half-smile on his face. He looked up and said, "Means if I were to bust out the gate with you, darlin', I'd ride the full eight seconds, jump off, and take a bow."

She laughed. "You ornery thing." She slapped him on the shoulder. "You better behave."

"No offense meant," he said.

"None taken," she said. "Just let me know if you need anything." She smiled at us and walked away.

I sipped my coffee; its warmth spread through me. I was still a little spooked by my encounter in the woods.

He said, "So, why'd you do it? Why'd you quit?"

"I grew up," I said.

"It'll happen, unless you're careful. You were the first white boy since Lance Alworth who could go uptown for it."

"Meanwhile, babies were born, people went to work at real jobs, got married, sent the kids to school. Me, I was catching footballs. Everybody acting like it gave me significance."

"Pretty cynical."

"Sorry. Don't mean to be. After a while it didn't mean what it did at first. Money got in the way of the fun. Besides, it's not exactly real life."

"Life is a tale told by an idiot, full of sound and fury, signifying nothing," he said, then sipped his coffee. "Or something like that." He shrugged.

"Well," I said, "you're the most lyrical bounty hunter I've ever known."

"Not just another pretty face."

"Look. I've got to run over to the sheriff's office. Think you can sit here without drinking the place dry and propositioning the waitress with your cracker-barrel wise guy routine?"

"Too much temptation. Besides, I need to go with you. Check wanted posters like us bounty hunters do. See if anybody's wanted—dead or alive. The dead ones are easier to catch."

"My truck's parked in back," I said.

"Good. I'll drive. I'm in no condition to be walking."

It was 6:30. We stepped over red-and-white Budweiser cans and broken pavement, grass peeking through the concrete like the last hairs on a balding man's head. Twilight swallowed the opaque light from the sun, which was an angry orange blister on the western horizon. Easton smelled of cigarettes and whiskey, yet his gait was sure and his step had a spring to it.

We turned the corner and saw the Bronco. Three men leaned against it. They were laughing roughly and sharing a bottle of Jack Daniel's, a six-pack of Olympia on top of the hood. I thought I heard Easton chuckle low in his chest. I didn't see anything funny.

"What's up, guys?" I said. I didn't want trouble, just my vehicle. They were in their late twenties. Cowboy boots and baseball caps with seed company names on the crown. One of the hats said Shit Happens! Perfect.

They leaned against the Bronco, passing the bottle around, tilting it to their lips, then wiping their mouths on their sleeves. I felt very tired. The only other car in the lot was an aging copper-colored Mark IV with a torn vinyl roof, its glory days a memory. Two of the men were over six feet tall—one slender and one much heavier than the others, looked to go about 260. The heavy guy had a full beard like Charlie Daniels. Didn't look like a fiddle player, though. Mr. Shit Happens was a small, ferretlike guy with a three-day-old beard. Been watching *Miami Vice* reruns.

"Evenin'," said the third man, a lean cowboy with a long jawline. "This your car, boy?"

Two tours of Indochina, seven years in the NFL, and I'm still a boy. Oh, well. Dignity in the face of ignorance is difficult, but attainable. I nodded. Smiled. I was saving my searing Clint Eastwood squint.

"Nice ride," said the fat guy.

"Hope you don't mind us using it," said Shit Happens, leaning against the door. "Not that we give a big shit." Since he was so incredibly witty, they all laughed. Guffawed, in fact. If there is anything I hate, it's being guffawed at by people with room temperature IQs.

I tried to get around the ferret to open the door. "Excuse me," I said, trying for affable. He didn't move. Odd. My affable is generally infallible. Must've had a hole in his upbringing. "May I get in my truck?"

"When we're done," he said, hooking a thumb in a belt loop and passing the whiskey bottle to Jawline.

I exhaled through my mouth. Rubbed my face with a hand. "Well," I said, low, to Easton, "I've heard you talk and I know you can drink, but now I could use some of that Terrific stuff."

"Showtime," he said. Cleared his throat. Smiled. "Fellas. We don't want to interrupt the fun. Just want to take the truck. We're late for piano lessons. No problems, huh?"

Half the whiskey was gone. Enough distilled courage to keep them from moving. Local toughs. Probably roughed up drunks once in a while. Terrorized the college kids. Something to brag about on the night shift at the canning factory. Jawline looked the toughest of the three, though Fatbeard would be the hardest to put down. Jawline was lean, flinty—a couple yards of angles and bones. He unfolded his arms and eyed Chick. Ferret Face leaned nonchalantly against the truck, a nasty smile on his face. He was the least of our worries unless he was radioactive.

"When we're done, asshole," said Fatbeard. "Come back later."

"You tell him I was an asshole?" Chick asked me.

"No," I said, keeping my eyes on them. "Maybe he's intuitive."

Jawline had the whiskey bottle. We could just walk away and come back later, but I was tired and it was my truck. And I wanted to drive it. Now. Personality quirk.

"He don't look intuitive to me," said Chick. "Just another fat drunk. Plenty of those."

"One more time," I said. "No trouble. Just want to get in the truck, then we'll drive away. That's all."

"Who's he callin' fat?" asked Fatbeard, jerking his head in Chick's direction. "Who you callin' fat, boy?"

"Certainly not you, Twiggy. When you go to the movies do you stand at the back, or do they knock out an armrest?"

"What're you guys doing here, anyway?" asked the ferret.

"We're from the EPA," I said. "We're checking reports of creeping slime. You need to turn yourselves in. Go easier for you if you do."

Jawline lifted the bottle to his lips as Shit Happens reached into his jacket. Fatso started toward Chick. "You boys want some shit—" he began before he was interrupted by a left hand that snaked from Chick Easton, catching the bearded man in the throat. With the heel of my hand I smacked the bottom of the tilted whiskey bottle, ramming the hard glass into Jawline's mouth. The glass cracked against the cowboy's teeth, a sickening sound, and his head snapped back. He yelped, dropping the bottle, and it shattered on the asphalt. I kicked him in the shin and he screamed. Chick jumped up and kicked Ferret Face below the left shoulder, where the man was reaching into his jacket. The kick pinned the hand inside the jacket. There was a distinct pop, like marbles clacking together. The little man screamed and bent over, cradling the damaged arm.

Before Jawline could straighten, I brought an elbow up alongside his jaw, a big target. He staggered back but didn't go down. He was tough. I aimed a left jab at his throat, which missed and bounced off his shoulder. He rolled away, tried to cover with his arms, and set himself. I shot another left at his head and caught him on the ear. He shook his head, sending droplets of blood flying from his mouth. There was a half-moon cut out of his upper lip, and his teeth were pink with blood. He came at me, bony fists flailing. I took the blows on my arms and shoulders, but they still hurt. He was no boxer, but he'd been in plenty of street fights.

The kind of guy willing to take punishment in order to get in his licks and hurt you. But he had too much booze in him. His feet and body rhythm were out of sync, betraying him. I kept him away with jabs and body shots.

Finally, I faked to his midsection with a left, which caused him to drop his arms to cover, then I looped a left hook over his arms that caught him on the point of the chin. It spun him a quarter turn, and I drove a right uppercut into his solar plexus. It felt as good as a three-hundred-yard tee shot. His breath exploded from him in a shower of saliva and blood and he sat down hard on the pavement, blood running from his mouth and nose. He held up a hand. "No more," he said, wheezing through split and swollen lips. " 'Nuff."

I stepped away from him, and he scrambled to his feet and ran away. He was smarter than his fat friend. The heavy drunk swung wildly at Chick, who leaned away from the impotent punches and slapped him—once, then again. The fat man winced, shook his head, and swung again. Slow learner. Chick slapped his hand away absently, then cuffed him on the ears, left, right, left, right. "Quit," Chick said. "I can do this all day."

The ferret tried to get behind Chick, but I grabbed him by the collar and kicked him behind the knee. He didn't weigh much, and I had him off his feet, using the momentum of his collapse to drive him against the fender of the Bronco. He thudded into the unforgiving metal and slumped to the pavement, moaning.

Chick finished off the big man with a jump kick, the impact snapping his head back. His legs folded under him like paper, and the back of his head cracked against the pavement.

Chick dropped his hands to his sides. Wasn't even breathing hard. "These are some tough guys," he said, fishing in his shirt pocket for a cigarette. "Need to be more careful where we hang out."

I grabbed the ferret by the front of his jacket and sat him against the tire. "Can you walk?" I asked him.

His face was puckered up in a grimace. "My hand. It's broke. Motherfucker broke my hand."

"Dirty names," said Chick, shaking his head. "And I don't even know your mother. Quit whining and give it to me." Chick held out his hand, palm up, flexed his fingers as if calling for something. "Come on, let's have it."

"What?" said the ferret. His hat was sideways on his head. His eyes were furtive.

"Don't play games with me. You still got one hand left. Want a matched set? I want what's in the jacket."

"Who are you guys?" He was perplexed. One minute he was drinking whiskey, talking tough, terrorizing the parking lot, and the next thing he knows he's sitting in the chat with a broken hand, his day screwed up, and two strangers standing over him.

"I'm Butch Cassidy, and this here's the Sundance Kid. Now gimme. Everything in your pocket. Pronto."

The ferret reached into his jacket with his good hand, mumbling to himself. His right hand had an obscene knot on it. He didn't look Chick in the eye when he handed him the wheel-shaped disk and the small lump of aluminum foil. The disk was a Japanese throwing star. Chick looked at it and smiled, then his shoulders began to bounce up and down merrily. He held the star up and squinted at it.

"We were in serious danger here," Chick said. "This man has been trained in the martial arts." He looked at the man on the ground, whose face was turning red. "Where'd you get it, shit-for-brains? Comic book ad? And what's this?" He rustled the tinfoil. "Ex-Lax? Looks like rock candy. What do you think, Storme?" He handed me the tinfoil, and I looked at the crystal, the cousin to the ones I'd recovered in the woods where a dog lay dead and a man with an arrow wound had run away from a million-dollar field of dreams.

"It ain't nothin'," the man said, licking his lips with a sharp tongue. "Give it back."

I shook my head and closed my fist around the rock. "Believe we'll keep it." The ferret started to protest, changed his mind, then started again.

"You're pissing on the wrong guy, buddy," he said. "I got friends'll fuck up your life."

"I doubt you have all that many friends," I said, helping him to his feet. "So peddle that crap somewhere else." I straightened his hat on his head and made sure he could walk on his own. He forgot to thank me. We got into the Bronco and left him and Fatso to lick their wounds. He gave us the finger as we drove away. Another new friend.

"Let's get something to eat," Chick said. "Slapping creeps around always gives me an appetite."

"It'll wait." My hands hurt. The left one was swelling. "Have to stop by the sheriff's office first."

"What's in the foil?"

"I don't know." I didn't. But it wasn't rock candy.

THREE

The Paradise County sheriff's office was a new building. Gray brick and aluminum and glass. Landscaped lawn. No pot-bellied stove with a speckled coffeepot on top. No oak racks of Winchesters on the wall or skeleton keys on a big iron ring. No hardwood floors bleached with use and spur-pocked. No character. No ambience. Progress. Antiseptic and way overrated. A deputy with corporal's stripes manned the desk. The name on his pocket nametag was Simmons. I asked to see the sheriff.

"He's out. We got a call from the Silver Spur, a bar. Fight or something. He should be back soon. Can I help you?"

I looked at Chick. He shrugged his shoulders. "No," I said. "We'll wait. He said to ask for him."

Corporal Simmons led us to a small waiting lounge. There was an instant coffee machine, a Coca-Cola machine, and a large windowed snack-and-candy machine, the kind with the cork-screw dispensers to push the candy out. I put two quarters in the big red Coke machine and a scarlet-and-white can clattered out onto the silver lip. Chick shook his head at the offered can and lit a cigarette. I sat on an aluminum-framed davenport with cheap cushions. Drank my Coke. Read a year-old copy of *Sports Afield*. Black cigarette burn marks pocked the sofa, and the air was rank with the soaked-in aroma of stale tobacco. After a few minutes I closed the magazine.

"Where'd you learn that stuff?" I asked Chick.

"What stuff?"

"Karate."

"Oh, that. I watch a lot of television."

I waited for more, but there was no more forthcoming. Okay, so he wasn't going to say. Fine with me. He had his reasons. I had mine. Been a long time since I'd seen anyone move so quickly, so fluidly. Not since I quit playing football, anyway. Maybe it was the unexpectedness of it. Thought he was a burnout. The boilermakers he'd knocked back hardly affected him. The guy had instincts. I had bruises all over my upper body, swollen hands, and a cut along my neck. They hadn't laid a finger on him.

He was intuitive and likable and had that strange smile—a world-weary smile that seemed to speak of thousands of miles of knowing that life was, at best, a tough bargain entered into by fools and madmen.

A big deputy with sergeant's stripes and a beechwood-aged gut hanging over a tooled-leather belt stepped into the room. He wore cowboy boots and had a Colt .45 Government Model strapped to his side. His shirt collar was open and his pants pockets were smudged. His nametag, which said BAXTER, was crooked over his shirt pocket. All he needed was a pair of mirrored sunglasses or a bulge of chewing tobacco in his cheek to complete the picture.

"Bet he's got a pouch of Red Man in his desk drawer," Chick said, reading my thoughts.

"You the guys waiting for Sheriff Kennedy?" asked Deputy Baxter. He dug at a back molar with a finger.

"Not me," Chick said. "I'm just here to study crime-stopper techniques."

The deputy's jaw tightened. "You think you're some kind of comic? You look like you been drinking, too."

"Never touch the stuff, officer," Chick said, flashing his disarming smile. "Drink the crap out of it, but I never touch it."

This wasn't going too well. Easton was not a first-impression kind of guy. I said, "We're here to see Kennedy."

The big county cop gave Chick one more look, then said, "The sheriff ain't here, so you can talk to me. My office is just down the hall. C'mon along." He jerked his head in the direction of the doors down the hall.

"Thanks anyway. We'll wait for the sheriff."

"You look familiar." He cocked his head to look at me. The look was reptilian. Greasy. One eye didn't track as well as the other, as though a nerve or a tendon had been damaged. His nose had been broken before. Often. The knuckles of his right hand were gnarled and misshapen. Probably a thumper. "I seen you before?"

I shook my head.

"You two come along with me and I'll get your statements," he said, ignoring my preference to talk with the sheriff.

"Sorry. The sheriff said to ask for him."

"Well, he ain't here right now, is he?" He was used to getting his way. Move too slowly getting into the patrol car on a lonely road and you got a knee in the gut. I didn't like him. "So I guess you'll just have to talk to me."

I said, "No."

His hand rested on the butt of the .45. "You got somethin' in your ears? I said for you to come along, and you damn well better."

"Dale Carnegie grad, right?" said Chick.

He turned his gaze to Chick. "What's your name, fella?"

"Randolph Scott," said Chick. "You've probably seen my movies."

"Funny guy, huh? Had 'em in here before. You ever hear of obstruction of justice?"

"Wasn't Steven Seagal in that?"

Baxter's face turned crimson, then purple. The bad eye went blotchy, like the eye of a vulture. If he had any molars left they were superbly enameled. It was time to leave. A good plan. I stood to do so just as a tall man whose nametag said KENNEDY entered the waiting room. He looked at the three of us, sized up the situation, then spoke to me. "You the guy?" he asked. "One that called?"

I nodded. To Easton, he said, "You with him?" Easton nodded also. The reticence twins. Kennedy was taller than me, slightly overweight, but with a formidable pair of shoulders. Early fifties, some scar tissue along his right eye. Somewhere along the line he had forced his will upon someone—or resisted someone else's. I was glad we weren't still in the parking lot when he answered the call. He led us into his office. Deputy Baxter didn't look very happy. Maybe I'd send him a Christmas card. Make it up to him.

In the sheriff's office we sat in aluminum chairs padded with vinyl, similar to those in the lounge only without the cigarette burns. Probably not wise to burn holes in Kennedy's furniture. On the walls were pictures of other officers—fresh-faced deputies with square jaws and bright eyes, older-looking constables with weathered jowls and straw cowboy hats, men who looked like they meant what they said. There were other pictures. A teen-aged boy in a football uniform. The same boy-face in a Marine uniform. Had his father's eyes. A picture of a girl with neither her father's eyes nor bulk—teenaged and slender in a cheerleader's outfit. She had straight teeth and a melt-your-heart smile. Apple of Daddy's eye. No wife pictures. A diploma from the University of Missouri—criminal justice. They didn't give those things away for cereal box tops. The guy was no rube. His desk was large, neat. Everything in its place, though it spoke of great activity.

"I'm Sheriff Kennedy," he said, sitting down. "What'd you say your name was again?"

He was good. "I didn't," I said.

He turned his attention to Chick. "You got a name?"

"Clayton Moore."

"You give that name to Baxter?"

"No, I gave him my stage name."

He looked us over. "I could book you both on suspicion. Make you ID yourselves."

"You've got more important things to do," I said.

"Or, I could arrest you for disturbing the peace. Better get some ice on that hand. You slam a door on it?" He picked a pipe out of a round walnut pipe rack and settled back in his chair. He didn't light it, just stuck it between his teeth and chewed on the stem. "Wonder if I call Citizens Memorial if they'll tell me if they've had anyone in the ER the past hour with bruises, lacerations, loose teeth? That kind of thing. Like they'd been in a fight." He took the pipe from his lips and pointed the bit at me. "How'd you get that cut on your neck?"

"I could say the dog did it." He was *very* good. We each knew what the other was thinking.

He filled the pipe from a leather-covered humidor. "Tell you what I've got, gentlemen. Coming in I got a report of three guys at ER. One broken hand. One with a concussion. All had multiple cuts and lacerations. Three local punks. I've had 'em all in our little hotel for one thing or another. Assault, public intoxication, pimping out at the truck stop, possession of controlled substances. Solid citizens. Lawyer, name of Winston, always manages to get them off or reduce the penalty. Frustration runs high in this job. These three guys imagine themselves tough. Some people around here would agree with them. Can't imagine anyone around here that could bounce 'em around like that. Doc Collins said they look like they fell in a blender." He'd bitten down hard on the pipestem when he mentioned the lawyer, but smiled when he related the condition of our three buddies.

He continued. "Funny thing, there was nobody at the Silver Spur who saw anything. There's blood all over the parking lot. Some on you two, also. I've got an anonymous phone caller says he took out a rifleman and a Doberman with a bow and arrow like he was Robin Hood…" Chick looked at me and raised his eyebrows. "Then, I got a skip-tracker with a fat federal dossier, but I can't look at it and the feds aren't sharing. Why are the feds keeping a tab on you, Easton?"

If Chick was surprised, he didn't show it. "I tore one of those tags off my mattress."

"Made you a couple days ago," Kennedy said. He lighted the pipe with a wooden kitchen match. Folksy. Taking his time. Letting us think about it. "Checked on you. You got some papers on a skip named Prescott. Then the suits show up. For some reason they're interested in you, Easton." He shook the match out. "Why?"

Chick shrugged. "They think I'm the lost Lindbergh baby."

They looked at each other across the desk. Kennedy's eyes burned a hole through the plume of blue smoke hanging in the air between them. Easton looked amused. Calm. "Long as you don't screw up in my county I got no problem with you." The county badge turned his attention back to me. "Who are you?"

I didn't say anything.

"I'll leave your name out of this," he said. "Yours, too, Easton." He didn't say anything hokey like he promised or "word of honor." Just looked at us with intense, whiskey-brown eyes and said it.

"Storme," I said. "Wyatt Storme."

"The football player?" He settled back in his chair, appraising me. I wasn't going to help him out. "Yeah. You're him. Walked out, didn't you? Didn't hold a press conference. Just called in and told them you weren't coming. They thought it was a holdout trick. Press beat the bushes for months. No drumroll. No interviews. Just faded away. I like that. Now, here you sit in my office."

I waited.

"Tell me about the marijuana field."

I told him. About the field, about the dog, about the rifle in my truck and the guy with the arrow wound. Told him about our parking lot prayer meeting with his three friends. Gave him exact directions to the field of *Cannabis sativa*. He didn't interrupt.

Occasionally nodded. Smiled when I told him how Chick broke Shit Happens's hand.

"Luke Hanson," Kennedy said, when I'd finished. "That's the guy with the broken hand. The other two are Jerry Caswell and Large Michael Moore. Caswell's not a bad sort. Went through a bad divorce. Drinks too much. Shouldn't hang around with those two. Large Michael's the fat guy with the beard. He's the night manager of the Truck Hangar out by the interstate. 'Manager' isn't descriptive enough. He's the muscle for a string of prostitutes they run in a motel next to the truck stop. A motel conveniently over the county line, where I can't touch it and can't get any cooperation from the sheriff of Ford County, a nice guy who used to own a junkyard. No lawman, but smart enough to know what to leave alone. Guy named Willie Boy Roberts owns the Truck Hangar and about everything else around Paradise."

"The shooter said the dog belonged to a Mr. Roberts."

He paused to draw on the pipe; the room smelled of maple tobacco. "Interesting. I'll check on that. The guy shot at you sounds like a man I know. Doper named Killian. He used to mule drugs into the county. Disappear 'on vacation' for a few days, then he'd come back spending money and suddenly there'd be cocaine back in the county. Used to be we were too remote for such sophisticated drugs. But it's a new day." The last part came grudgingly. "That field is way back in there. That far back you could hide the Chinese army and a herd of elephants for them to ride. They probably figured nobody'd ever wander back in there."

"Somebody did."

"Yeah," he agreed, nodding his head. "Fellas, you've managed to scrape the hide off most of the county's criminal element. In one day. But Roberts is the big gun. He's the one I want to turn the key on. But he's damn near untouchable. But, I find Killian, maybe I can squeeze him a little. Most people don't realize that Roberts—"

The door to the office opened and Deputy Baxter stepped in, his bulk darkening the doorway. He had a lump in his cheek this time. Chick bulged out his own cheek, then nodded at Baxter.

"What do you need, Les?" asked the sheriff.

"Thought you might need me."

"I don't. And where's your tie? You look like a spavined goat. This is a professional police force, not a Burt Reynolds movie."

"Simmons said these guys know something about a marijuana field."

Kennedy's whiskey eyes clouded over. He bit down on his pipe. I said, "Thanks for keeping this quiet. Let's go, Chick." Chick stood up. Kennedy's face looked like a building summer storm.

"Just hold it a minute," Kennedy said, holding a hand up to stop us. "Goddammit, Les! I've had enough of this shit. This is none of your business. These men have information pertinent to an investigation and I've agreed to keep it quiet. Do you understand? Now, get your well-padded ass out of here until I ask for you."

"These are the two guys assaulted Luke and Large Michael," Baxter said, looking us over as if cataloging us for future reference. I didn't like it. "They fit the description Hanson gave me at—"

"Les, I don't care if Hanson and Moore get beat up every day. In fact, I'd prefer it. I may make it department policy. I was about to give these men community service medals when you barged in. And why did Hanson give you a description? He didn't know anything when I talked to him. He want to file charges?"

"Well…no."

"That's amazing, isn't it? Doesn't want to press charges, but he gives you a description anyway. And why're you talking to Hanson? I don't want a deputy of mine consorting with known dogshit like Hanson, you understand? Now get out, and from now on when the door's shut you stay out. Go."

Les was either thicker through the forehead than he looked or didn't want to listen, or thought he didn't have to listen. "Where'd you guys come across a marijuana field?" he asked.

"I'd tell you," I said, "but you look like you'd just forget."

Baxter's bad eye filled with blood and his neck colored. "You get crossways with me, boy, and I'll make you wish—"

"Les!" The sheriff's voice cracked like thunder. "If you don't get the hell outta here in the next five seconds, you're fired."

"But these guys—"

"Four seconds."

Baxter glared at me.

"Three."

Baxter left the room, quickly. But not before he gave me another tough-guy look as he shut the door. I didn't even have time to shudder with terror.

"Sheriff's going to keep this quiet," I said to Chick.

"No leaks here," Chick said. "Very tight lipped."

"Simmons took the first call you made. On the 911 line. Baxter was close by when it came in. Sorry. Couldn't be helped. I should've let Baxter go a long time ago."

"Why haven't you?"

"He's got experience. A good man to have in a situation where your back's against the wall and a handicap everywhere else. He was an all-state defensive tackle here fifteen years ago. Next month he's going to run against me for sheriff. Willie Boy Roberts has his money behind him. I fire him now it'll look personal." His pipe had gone out. He paused to relight it. "But I'll fire him if it comes to that."

I believed him.

The sheriff walked us out to the parking lot, shook hands with us. I liked him. "Best place to eat supper around here is the Raintree Inn," he said. Gave us directions. I gave him the rifle. He thanked me for coming in and went back inside. As I backed the Bronco out of the parking lot, I saw Baxter's face at the window. Chick waved at him.

"You know he's taking your plate numbers, don't you?" Chick said.

"Yeah."

"As a trained bodyguard I would recommend you watch your ass."

Sounded like good advice.

FOUR

The Raintree Inn was a nice place, too dark, but the food was excellent. Chick had a steak and I had rainbow trout. Chick had Wild Turkey on the rocks. I drank ice water and coffee. We didn't ask about each other's past.

I did find out he was a bowhunter and had brought his bow and tackle with him. Since he was still looking for Prescott, the bail jumper, he couldn't go hunting in the morning. We made plans to go the morning after next. After supper I drove him out to the Best Western, where he'd already paid for another night. I told him I'd come by to get him and his things the next evening. Told him to stay at my cabin until we left for Colorado.

The dream.

It came again. It came less often as the years went by. Each time with a different wrinkle. I was humping through the rice paddies, mud sucking at my boots as if alive. My helmet was gone, but I didn't know where or why. Through the mist I saw a phalanx of NVA regulars moving toward me. With my M16 on rock-and-roll I swept their ranks—some fell, but they kept coming, their numbers unchanged, seeming to move no closer, as if they were on a treadmill. Then they disappeared. Out of the quagmire came VC in black pajamas. The swamp under me became solid and raised, leaving me on a small hill, alone. Raining now. Forms leaped at me from the fog. Steel knives flashed. My gun jammed, so I swung it like a club, sweat rolling into my eyes, its saltiness stinging and blinding. One of the black forms stabbed me in the chest. I felt the coldness of the knife, sharp, like an icicle in my heart, but I didn't die. Continued to fight.

Then the face came.

The face I couldn't forget, the chin and jaw flayed back, leaving a skeletal smile. The last smile. I fired, my gun working now. She stopped and her hair fell loose from the band tied around her head. She had looked like a man. I had thought she was a man. She had *looked like a man!* She fell to the ground in slow motion, her arms flapping like a rag doll's. The black pajamas stopped attacking, stood in the swamp, the mist wrapping around their heads like a smoky shroud. They were faceless. She was a girl. Looked fourteen. What was she doing here? This was a man's work. A man's fight. She wasn't pretty. Just a child carrying a gun. A child facing eternity with the bottom of her face missing, the teeth sunk back in her mouth.

I wiped a hand across my face. The hand felt sticky. It was. Sticky and red.

She was a child.

She wasn't pretty.

She was dead.

I didn't know.

Why was she here?

Why, God?

Suddenly she sat up, a skeletal leer on her face. I screamed. A man in black pajamas leapt at me, changing into a horrible black hound, mouth frothing, jaws popping…

I sat up in bed, mouth open, sweating. The darkness of the room pressed in on me.

I was on my deer stand by 5:30 a.m. Saw two does and a spike buck. Didn't shoot. I was waiting on a ten-point patriarch I'd seen a week ago. The woods were cool and quiet. There had been a skin of frost on the ground, but the sun melted it away. Very cold for this time of the year. Unseasonably so.

I thought about Sandy as I sat in the tree, my body heat rising from my collar and warming my neck and chin. Thinking about Sandy tied my brain in Gordian knots. It had been three months now. Three months since she'd taken the job in Denver. I didn't blame her. I couldn't hold her back, didn't want to. But that wasn't all of it. Something about our relationship bothered her. Right now, there was no relationship. She said it wasn't me. Said it was her, but that was all she would say. Whether it was her or me, I was still denied her—her laughter, her face, her eyes sparkling with life, my reflection in those eyes.

I kept up two cabins—one in Missouri and another in Colorado. I moved back and forth between them. Missouri was my childhood home, but Missouri summers drove me into the Rockies. I had played football at Colorado State before turning pro and had fallen in love with the mountains. Denver was three hours away from my Colorado cabin. Three hours away geographically and light years away socially. She went places I no longer wanted to walk. Did things I no longer wanted to do. No more concrete canyons and smog. No more hermetically sealed, freeze-dried, one-size-fits-all lifestyle. No more shopping mall lemmings rushing to the edge of their gold cards. No more fitness clubs. No more elevator Muzak nightclubs and foreign luxury wheels. No more insurance salesmen piecing off my life. No more acrylic suits in BMWs rushing off to take another bite of American fabric.

No. No more. Farewell to all that. Good riddance to all that.

Was I just hiding? Or fooling myself? Hiding from what? A nineties dropout. Too late for existential posing. Maybe I was socially retarded. Hated crowds. Liked people. Maybe I was afraid. I had seen what civilization had to offer, had briefly reached for its definition of success, then, just as I was about to snatch it, I pulled my hand back and fled. Society was too lupine, too vicious and unrelenting for me.

Freedom. How I love her. Sandy. How I love her. How to have both? Or, settle for only one? But perhaps I couldn't have both and half was somehow less than half.

Back at the cabin, I cut up a cantaloupe and brewed coffee. Sliced turkey breast from a block I'd bought at a deli two days ago. Noticed I was out of milk and flour. I put the turkey between two slices of wheat bread, not white. The last two pieces. I turned the stereo to an oldies station. The Byrds sang "I Wasn't Born to Follow." The phone rang. Startled me. It didn't ring often. Only a handful of people had the number.

"Storme's all-night Chinese laundry and fortune-cookie factory." I was expecting to hear Matt Jenkins's voice.

"Is Grizzly Storme there?" said a female voice. A voice like a silver bell in my head. Sandy's voice. Lovely. I hadn't expected it. There was a catch in my chest, a dull pang.

"I don't know," I said. "Maybe if you describe him, I'll recognize him."

"He's a broken-down wide receiver. Six two, maybe six three, gray eyes. Bad knees, worse attitude. Conceited chauvinist smirk on his perpetually boyish face. Loves John Wayne and Bob Dylan and beautiful newswomen. He can't polka, but has excellent taste in women."

"Nobody like that here. There's a guy who kinda resembles Robert Redford, but his taste in women runs to media snobs with strange sexual appetites."

"Mmmmm," she purred. An electric shiver raced down my neck. "Sounds more interesting than the guy I had in mind. Maybe I'd like to meet him."

"I can arrange it," I said. "Anytime."

"How about this weekend? She really needs to get away from the city for a while. Like maybe forever."

"I think he's told her that before."

"Highway runs both ways, cowboy," she said.

"My guy rides a one-way horse."

"Sounds like the guy I'm talking about."

"The Redford look-alike?"

"No. The stubborn has-been with the great hands and bad knees."

"Oh. Him. He waits for you. Always will. When can you get away?"

"Saturday. I'll have to do the six o'clock news, but Karen can cover me on the late broadcast. Do you watch the news?"

"Only the sports."

"Liar. You probably tape the shows and dream of my sun-kissed hair and laughing eyes."

"Self-assured TV snob," I said. "Actually, I only think of your milky-white teeth and tanned legs."

"I miss you, Wyatt."

I admitted missing her. How long had I waited to hear those words. Three months. Seemed longer. She had called Matt when she couldn't reach me in Colorado. He told her where to find me. Thank God, I hadn't removed the phone as I'd thought about so many times. We talked. Good, fluid conversation, playing off each other. Filling in where it was needed, saying nothing when it wasn't. Hearing what was not being said as well as what was. Her voice was a sunbeam, her laughter the west wind, warming me. Thawing me. Hearing it created an ache I couldn't rub.

"Can you get back this weekend?" she asked.

I had planned to hunt for another week or so before returning. To get back by Saturday left me four days to hunt and one day to travel.

Reluctantly, I said good-bye. The phone clicked but didn't break the spell. On the stereo Bob Dylan was singing "Forever Young" backed up by J. Robbie Robertson and The Band. The best version. The right version. The words wrenched from Dylan's lips and the horns soared and Robertson's guitar buzzed and cried. I tasted some coffee. Just right.

Forever young.

I showered, shaved, put on a pair of Levi's, smoothed by time and memory, and a Colorado State University sweatshirt. Pulled on a pair of Adidas basketball shoes and drove to town. It was a beautiful day. Harvest autumn in Missouri. Cornstalks in fields stretching across the horizon. Trees blazing gold and orange. Leaves drifting and the wind sighing at summer's passing.

I bought a cup of coffee, "made fresh every twenty minutes," at a convenience store. Must've been nineteen minutes old. I stopped at a mom-and-pop supermarket in town. I don't shop chains and conglomerates. A small rebellion, but we strike where we can. I parked the Bronco at the back of the hot-top parking lot. When I got out of the truck a slender, attractive young woman with chestnut hair and matching eyes stopped me. She had a bag slung over her shoulder that wasn't a purse.

"You're Wyatt Storme, aren't you?" she asked, without preamble. She looked confident, assured, as if she were revealing something I wouldn't know.

"He's much taller," I said, walking on. I smelled media. The lowest form of life. After lawyers. But I make exceptions. Sandy was one. The only one.

"Wait," she said. I heard her low heels clack on the asphalt. I stopped. She said, "You're the guy tipped the sheriff about the marijuana field."

I looked at her. Wondered about the sheriff's promise of anonymity. Maybe I'd misjudged him. No, I hadn't. Somebody else had clued her in. Probably Baxter. But why? "You've got the wrong person. I'm just passing through."

"I'd like to interview you."

"No."

"What are you afraid of?" Her eyes were defiant.

"Lots of things. What are you afraid of?"

"I'll ask the questions."

I smiled. "Maybe you can supply the answers, too."

"How did you discover the field?"

"I looked under the letter *F* in the dictionary. It was right across the page from 'fiasco' and 'fiction.' "

"My, my," she said, cocking her head to one side. "How glib we are. How did you manage to kill the guard dog?" She was beginning to annoy me. An old prejudice. Old memories of microphones in my face. Cheap aftershave and cheaper cigar smoke in my nostrils, and the same tired questions and pat answers. "League policy, Storme," I was told. "You will talk to those people or be fined again." And again. But her perfume smelled good and she didn't look the cigar type.

She said, "That's quite a story. Man bites dog. A classic."

I walked on. She trailed me. Followed me across the parking lot, through the whoosh of electric door and warm air. Down the aisles. I am irresistible to female journalists.

"You can't get rid of me that easily," she said. I selected a can of Campbell's chunky clam chowder. Yummy.

"That's okay. Are you housebroken? Maybe I can teach you to fetch my slippers, bring in the paper—"

"Where are you from?"

I pushed my cart. Somehow it's difficult to feel supremely manly while pushing a shopping cart. But I thought manly thoughts. Hoped that would help.

"Why are you here?" she asked. "Where are you staying? Where have you been since the Super Bowl? What do you know about yesterday's events?" People, women mostly, stared at us as we paraded through the frozen food section, through the produce. I paid at the register and she followed me to the parking lot.

"I'm going to get this interview," she said, as I put the groceries in the Bronco. "One way or another."

"Good luck," I said. A young guy with a camera scooted quickly up and pointed the camera at me. I turned my head away before the shutter clicked. Years of practice.

"You get it?" she asked.

"No," he said. "Sorry, Jill."

"Try again."

"No," I said.

"Do it," she said.

I looked at him as he raised the camera. "Don't," I said. I wasn't kidding. I'd put up with this nonsense for too long not many years ago. Some guy with a camera in your face—in restaurants, while you were shopping—all because I could run a Z-out and catch a football. Kinda silly when you think about it.

Something in my expression or my voice convinced him I was serious. Different in small towns. In the city you could hold a gun to their head and they'd still snap it. Cities made for social mutants with no sense of propriety. It was better here. "C'mon, mister," he said. "It's my job." He started to raise the camera again. I reached out and gently put my hand on it. He stopped and looked at her.

"Take the picture, Andy," she said, her teeth clenched. "Either you're a photographer or you're not. Take the damn picture."

I felt sorry for the kid. Probably started out taking pictures of kittens and old farmhouses. "That's right, Andy," I said. "She's not the one going to the hospital with a camera up her nose. What does she care?"

"He's bluffing," she said.

"Look at me, Andy. I look like I need to bluff?"

Andy chewed his lower lip, and his eyes slipped off me and trailed to the girl, asking for a reprieve. She blew out a puff of air, probably pure nitro, in anger. The muscles in her throat tightened. "All right," she said. "If you'll answer a few questions, then we won't take any pictures."

"No pictures," I said. "No interview. No film at eleven. No kidding."

Her eyes were hot. "This is a mistake."

I shrugged. "Made 'em before."

"Human life has no value to you, does it, mister hot-shit jock?"

I looked at her. She was serious. Human life? "What are you talking about?"

Her expression softened. She'd read something in my face, something she hadn't expected. "You really don't know," she said, "do you?"

"Know what?"

"You don't know about Sheriff Kennedy. I assumed you knew that's what I was talking about."

"What about him?"

"They found him this morning," she said. "They wouldn't tell me what happened, but I know they found him in his car. Early this morning. Nobody had seen him since last night. He's dead."

FIVE

"Where did they find him?" I asked her.

"You show me yours and I'll show you mine," she said.

I didn't have time for word games. I was uneasy. The sheriff was dead, and he didn't look easy to kill. Yesterday he was alive, smoking his pipe. Pictures of his children on his desk. Yesterday I told him about a marijuana field. Now he was dead. Maybe a coincidence. But I don't believe in them. A man was dead, a good man, perhaps because of something I'd told him. But that was the job, wasn't it? Like walking point in the bush and seeing the muzzle flash at the same instant your legs went out from under you. Sheriff Kennedy knew it was dangerous. Part of the job, right? Sure it was.

Then just walk away, Storme.

But could I?

When I was still playing in the NFL, the Eagles had a cornerback named Solomon "Slasher" Jones, a vicious D-back with a deserved reputation as a cheap-shot artist. He led the league in interceptions and sports page quotes. He loved to run with the ball, often giving up yardage to make another move, gain another second of attention. When he tackled you or broke up a pass, he would point at you. Talk at you. Constantly. It bothered some wide-outs. Messed them up. I ignored him.

In one game, Murphy Chandler, our quarterback and my best friend, was flushed from the pocket on a broken play when one of the offensive linemen missed his blocking assignment. Murphy, anything but a classic scrambler, managed to get out-of-bounds.

In fact he was five yards out-of-bounds on the Eagle sideline when Slasher stuck his helmet in Chandler's silver number sixteen. Then Slasher stood over Murph, talking his trash and pointing down at him. There was some shoving around, some names called, some facemask grabbing by both teams.

The Eagles were penalized fifteen yards for unsportsmanlike conduct and Jones was ejected. Didn't do much for Murph, who spent several minutes on the ground trying to get his breath and several days recovering from bruised ribs. Nothing worse than the hit you think you're safe from.

I was on the other side of the field when it happened.

I had suggested the play that got Murphy hurt. Wasn't my fault the tackle missed his blocking assignment, but I had called the play. And Murphy Chandler was my partner.

In a postgame interview, Slasher said, "If Chandler don't wanna get hit he can get his Texas ass out of the NFL. Football is for men." Chandler laughed at the comment, rubbed his sore ribs. I remembered that comment. Remembered I suggested the play.

Later in the season the Eagles came to Texas. Chandler threw a deep route to Jackson Carlyle, our other wide-out. Slasher picked it off and began his dance—bobbing, weaving, high-stepping—a superb athlete.

I started running, hard as I could. Dodged a blocker, fought by another one. I had gained full speed when I drove my shoulder into Slasher's solar plexus. It was a full-out, Brahma bull goring. I heard him grunt as the wind exploded from his lungs. His feet went straight up and I drove him to the ground. The ball popped loose and was recovered by Murphy Chandler. Who says there isn't a God? I stood over Slasher, watching him writhe on the ground. Enjoyed it.

I didn't point at him. "Clean hit," I said. "In the open field. Not out-of-bounds. Straight up and in your face, clown. You don't want to get hit, then get out of the NFL. Football is for men." Then I walked away, the crowd noise swelling in my helmet.

"Damn, hoss," said Murphy Chandler, in his West Texas drawl. "You hit ol' Slash so hard you near separated him from his personality."

I liked Sheriff Kennedy. Though I'd just met him. He was a straight shooter, tough and honest. He was dead, and that wasn't right. It wasn't my side of the field, but I had suggested the play.

"What is your connection to this incident?" asked the girl reporter as I opened the door to the Bronco. I stepped up and sat down. "Do you think the sheriff's death is connected to the marijuana field?" I shut the door. She ran around to the other side and opened the passenger door and got in. Sat in the passenger seat. "You may as well tell me what I want to know."

"Get out or I'll throw you out," I said, without emotion. I'd do it.

She sat there, her chin up, hands on her nice hips. "Try it," she said.

I opened my door, got out, walked around the truck, opened the passenger door. "What's it going to be?" I asked.

"You'd really do it, wouldn't you?"

"Yes, ma'am."

"You big bully."

"Maybe," I said. "But a bully who'll toss your narrow tail in the street."

She got out. I got back into the Bronco. She snatched the camera from Andy. I averted my face as she raised it. I heard her yell an obscenity as I drove away. Wyatt Storme, media darling.

The parking area around the Paradise County sheriff's office looked like Christmas Eve at Wal-Mart—highway patrol units, local police cars, a couple of plain-brown-wrapper state cars, along with a KCMO news truck and a K.C. *Star* vehicle, were there. I wasn't in the mood for an afternoon of badges and official questions, but I wanted to tell somebody what I knew. I parked a block away and walked to the station. Inside, the building swarmed with cops of all kinds and colors. The sheriff's office door was closed and sealed with yellow tape.

Nobody paid attention to me. I could've done pretty much as I pleased. At least, that's what I thought until I turned around and a state trooper with a square jaw and a military-clean uniform stepped in front of me. He was six feet tall and looked like a highway patrol recruiting poster.

"I'm Trooper Browne," he said. "Can I help you?"

"Gee whiz," I said, in my best rube-from-the-sticks accent. "I just dropped by to see my old buddy Bill Kennedy, and boy-howdy, this looks like the policeman's ball. Where is Bill, anyway?"

He searched my face momentarily. "I'm sorry," he said. "I'm afraid the sheriff is…" His eyes swept me, up and down. "Unfortunately, Sheriff Kennedy is dead."

Another trooper stepped into the foyer and said, "Hey, Sam, we need you in here."

"In a minute," Browne answered. He looked back at me.

I put a hand to the side of my face. "Bill's dead? I can't believe it. How'd it happen? Car wreck?"

"What was your relationship to Sheriff Kennedy?" Oh-oh, I thought. He sounded like a cop with questions instead of one consoling a crash victim's old friend. His eyes never left my face. Not a good guy to fool around with, perhaps. But what the heck.

"Sam Browne?" I said. "Great name for a trooper."

"I've heard all the jokes. By the way, I've known Sheriff Kennedy for several years. Been fishing with him a few times. He never went by William or Bill. Everybody called him T.W., for Thomas William. But you wouldn't know that, would you? How long have you known Kennedy?"

"Counting today? Oh, I'd say about thirty-two hours, give or take a few minutes."

"What's your name?"

"Wyatt Storme. With an *e* on the end, like Browne. Maybe we're related."

"Let's see some ID, Mr. Storme." Official.

I showed him my Colorado driver's license. He pulled a pad from a pocket and wrote something on it. "What do you do for a living, Mr. Storme?"

"A little of this. Little of that."

He didn't like the answer. Can't say I blame him. Few did. "Mr. Storme," he said, politely. "I don't have time to be jerked around by some off-the-street wiseass. What is your interest in this investigation?"

"I thought the place needed some comedy relief."

His eyes narrowed. "Either answer the questions straight, or I can place you under arrest for interfering with a felony investigation."

"He *was* murdered, then."

The look on his face was almost worth being arrested, if it came to that. He knew he'd been had. For a moment I thought he was going to cuff me, that is, unless he Maced me or just popped me in the mouth. Instead, he smiled, then nodded his head.

"That's pretty good, Storme. Now, once more without the folksy accent. What's your interest?"

"It's possible I gave Kennedy information that may have caused his death." He looked back over his shoulder and then back at me.

"Okay," he said. "Shoot."

I started to tell him about the marijuana field, about the little rocks in my pocket. Started to tell him several things, when Deputy Les Baxter spotted me. He took three strides and pointed a sausagelike finger at my nose. His face was red and agitated and his breath stank of Red Man and stale coffee.

"What the hell are you doin' here?" he said, spitting a little when he did. No breeding at all.

"Don't point your finger at me," I said.

"You're not outta here in thirty seconds, I'll throw your ass in the can."

"For what? You're the one doing the overweight Barney Fife routine." I screwed up my face. "And what have you been eating? You own a toothbrush?"

"That's it, mister big-shit football player." Who told Baxter I'd played football? "One more smart crack from you and—" He started to poke me in the chest to punctuate his speech, but on the first poke I slapped his hand away.

"Don't do that," I said. Serious.

He went ballistic. "You son of a bitch! You're going to jail. When you get out they'll be driving rocket cars."

The activity in the cop station ceased. Baxter pulled a sap from a leather holster. Trooper Browne stepped between us. "Take it easy, Deputy," he said. "I was interviewing this man when you interrupted."

"*I'm* running this investigation," Baxter said. The veins in his neck were swollen and white against the red flesh. His bad eye had filled with purple-black blood, and the other eye was bloodshot and his complexion sallow. Obviously hung over. "As acting sheriff I'll decide who's interviewed and who's locked up in my county. We don't need you state boys to direct us."

I took a step back. Didn't want in the middle of this. Baxter was fifty pounds heavier than Browne, but I wouldn't bet he could take the trooper. Browne was chiseled from quartz, hard-edged. But Baxter was too loutish to know better. He was used to using his bulk to intimidate. I didn't think anyone intimidated Browne.

"Look, Deputy," Browne said evenly but firmly. "We're here to assist one another. It's not my intention to step on your authority, but if you don't modulate your voice when you talk to me, I'll jack your ass in front of everybody. You understand?"

"You won't always be wearing the Smokey the Bear hat."

"You're right. I won't. I'll give you my address and duty schedule if you'd like to look me up so we can get this all hashed out."

I love it when cops fight over me. I was wondering if I should blush, when a big trooper with sergeant's stripes intervened.

"Browne!" he said. The name McKinley was embossed upon his pocket nametag. "You back off!"

Browne took one step back without his eyes leaving Baxter.

"Now what's going on here?" asked Sergeant McKinley.

"Your boy here's interfering with my job," Baxter said. Stupidity never takes a vacation.

"The deputy was attempting to physically roust me when Trooper Browne interceded, sir," I said helpfully. "Trooper Browne was conducting himself with professionalism and dignity when—"

"You shut up," said the sergeant. I did. I adopted a cooperative-citizen pose. Maybe they'd give me an honorary highway patrol badge. Maybe not, too.

"What happened here, Sam?"

"I was questioning Mr. Storme. He has information pertinent to this investigation. Baxter interrupted and began to insult Storme. Storme objected when Baxter poked him in the chest."

"Sonofabitch slapped my hand," Baxter said. A stream of tobacco juice rolled like a tear from the corner of his mouth. He ignored it. Not only a colossal bore, he was also the king of slobs.

McKinley looked at me with raised eyebrows. Probably wanted to slap Baxter's hand himself. "Why are you here, Storme?"

"I wanted to find out what happened to the sheriff."

"What's your interest?"

I nodded in Baxter's direction. "Not in front of the children."

"His interest is he's a smartass with a big nose," said Baxter. "Wouldna poked him if he wasn't a wiseass."

"You a wiseass, Storme?" McKinley asked.

I shrugged. "It's a gift."

"Well," said McKinley, "you try it with me and I'll do more than poke you in the chest. Savvy?" I nodded. "Now, what is it you have?"

"He don't know nothin'," said Baxter, ever the poet.

"He's not alone in that respect," McKinley said. "You know, Baxter, I heard you were a jackass, but had no idea how big a one you are. Now, I'm going to ask you not to interrupt again." McKinley and Baxter looked at each other, then McKinley said, "Browne, take Storme out to your unit, interview him, then use your discretion whether to release him or not."

We exited. As we left I stuck my tongue out at Baxter. He looked like he might froth at the mouth at any moment.

In the patrol car, Browne pulled a clipboard from the passenger-side visor. The transmission hump was a collage of radios and scanners. Intermittently, one or more of them would crackle and hiss with an electronic rasp, spitting numbers and call letters. I told him about the marijuana field and my visit to the sheriff's office, leaving out the rifleman and the rocks for now. I related my encounter with the local media also.

"Brown-haired girl?" he asked. "Five five? Hundred and eighteen pounds? Attractive with a heart-shaped chin? Pushy?"

"That's her. How'd she know about me?"

"I don't know. We don't talk to the press. Not permitted. McKinley is media officer. But Baxter talked to her anyway. Pissed Mac off. This isn't the first problem we've had with Baxter. Baxter didn't tell her Kennedy was murdered, and I doubt he told her about you." He put the clipboard back on the visor. "Kennedy was close to firing him. McKinley will try to get Baxter off the case, if he can. But Baxter is a local and it will be a problem, so you'd better steer clear of him for now. He's a nasty asshole. Roughs up people he arrests."

"What about the marijuana field?"

"I don't know. Nothing in the log. Kennedy went to check it but never reported it. Whether he was killed going to it or returning, we don't know. However, you're right. The information you gave him may have had something to do with his death."

"What if Baxter killed him so he could become sheriff?"

He laughed. "You watch too much television. When a cop goes down it's usually some lightweight little puke with a gun and a bellyful of whiskey or a head full of dope. Forget about Baxter. He's a bad cop, not a killer."

I fished in my pocket and brought out one of the rocks. "Here. I found this. Guy that shot at me dropped it. Don't know what it is."

He turned over the crystallike rock in his hand. "Something else, Storme. How did you take out the Doberman with a bow and arrow?"

"Lucky."

"Uh-huh," he said. "I'll run a check on this." He hefted the rock and put it in his shirt pocket. "And you stay away from this investigation."

"Let me know what you find out."

"Can't do that. Only the major case squad has access. Best thing for you is to stay out and read the papers. Get you a buck. Go back to Colorado."

"Give me the rock candy, then," I said. I held out my hand.

He patted his pocket. "No way."

"There's more," I said. "But I'm rapidly developing selective amnesia."

"What do you mean, there's more?"

I put the back of my wrist to my forehead. "It's slipping away from me even as we talk. Everything's cloudy. I see a man with an arrow wound. He looks like...wait, he's gone."

"I could hold you as a material witness."

"I could get laryngitis."

He sighed. Rubbed his face with a hand. "All right. I'll let you know what's happening. But what you have had better be bottled-in-bond, grade-A info. And if you leak anything, I'll drop-kick you around Paradise County."

I couldn't turn down an offer like that. I described the rifleman. Gave the location of his wound. Asked how they could get away with planting that large a field of marijuana on public ground.

"Happens all the time in Missouri," he answered. He pronounced Missouri like it had an "uh" on the end. "They find a place way back and plant. Booby-trap the fields or, like they did here, they use guard dogs—Dobermans, Rottweilers, pit bulls. There was a place down in the bootheel where they posted a fucking jaguar. Guy had been given the cat by his Central American drug connection. One of our guys killed it with a shotgun. Pumped the entire load into the animal before it stopped coming. Animal rights people went crazy. Okay if a trooper gets torn to pieces, but don't hurt the little animals. We've come across bear traps, pungi sticks, fishhooks at eye level; you can expect about anything. Getting dangerous. The conservation department has been warning hunters about public-use land. Big money involved. Domestic grass, even Missouri Mud, packs a big jolt. More potent than the imports. Midwest agriculture at its best." He paused, as if remembering something, then said:

"I didn't recognize you back at the station. Not at first, anyway. Wyatt Storme. Fastest hands in the West. Used to be one of my favorite players. Where have you been all these years? Why'd you give it up?"

SIX

"So, Fatty Baxter may or may not have leaked your name to the press?" said Chick Easton, between bites of prime rib, rare. One of the best things about Missouri is the quality of the beef. It's like getting seafood in San Francisco or New Orleans—you're right next to the source, and it's fresh. The restaurant was McNaughton's, a steak-and-seafood restaurant with dark wood beams, thick mocha-colored carpet, and a large fireplace and hearth. It was connected to the Best Western motel where Chick was staying. Waiters in short tartan waistcoats and waitresses in tasseled knee socks and tartan kilts bustled about. Pretty nice for a Midwest cow town. "That doesn't tell you much."

I said, "I'm heading out by the end of the week. Can you be ready by Friday?"

"Thought you wanted to hunt another week or so."

"Something's come up in Colorado." I meant Sandy.

"Like what?"

"Unfinished business."

"Woman, ain't it?" he said, then continued as if not requiring confirmation from me. "Might be ready. Got unfinished business here myself. I might have it done by Friday. If not, go on back. I'll catch another ride. Don't wait up for me."

"I'll wait until you're ready." I had promised Matt Jenkins I'd bring Easton back. I would do so.

He chuckled. Took a bite of steak. Chewed it, slowly. Swallowed. "Jenkins said you felt like you had to accomplish everything you set out to do. Climb every mountain. Swim every stream.

Said you could trust your wife or girlfriend with you even if she looked like Christie Brinkley and was a nymphomaniac who'd been living in a convent."

A Scottish lassie brought him another drink, Cutty Sark, his third. I was on my third drink also. Coffee. Black.

"You drink too much," I said. He looked at me, squinting with one eye. He looked bemused, as usual. It was somewhat irritating. "An observation," I said. "Not a criticism."

"What about you? Notice you don't drink."

"Didn't know I needed a reason not to."

He laughed. It was laughter with a hint of pain, but only a flash, like summer lightning. The laugh turned into the type that invited you to join in. Bite on the bullet and don't let them think you are afraid. I could accept him on the basis of what I'd seen. But something was eating away at him. Not taking big bites, just nibbling, but it was there.

"You want to go hunting in the morning?" I asked.

"Sure. Where?"

"I know a place."

"You sure you want to go back there?" he asked, reading between the lines.

"Have to," I said.

"Figured it that way," he said.

Easton slept in the guest room of my cabin. I fixed pancakes and sausage for breakfast. Ground coffee. I gave him an extra pair of camo coveralls. They were new and had been given to me by a friend. I preferred my old ones. Chick had brought his bow because Jenkins told him I would be hunting. We checked our tackle. Fresh strings. Broadheads tight and sharp. Fletching undamaged. I cut a ten-foot length of nylon rope from a spool I kept, gave it to Chick. He would need it to drag out a deer if he took one. He rolled it into a ball around his hand and put it in his pocket. I poured coffee into a steel-lined thermos. I also took something I never take when bowhunting unless I'm in grizzly country—my Browning 9-millimeter semiauto pistol. Easton packed a .357 Colt Python.

There are no bears in Missouri.

It was Halloween dark when we arrived at the road I'd parked on the day I'd killed the dog. The moon was a sliver in the mattered sky, the air smelled of the loamy decay of autumn. All sound and movement was amplified, and there was a damp snap in the air, which lay cold against my exposed face. Before leaving the truck we agreed to meet at 10:30 a.m. to investigate the marijuana field. I used a small pocket flashlight to lead us through the woods.

We were intruders as we moved through the woods, and the silence spread before us like a stain, dozens of unseen eyes watching, dozens of ears straining to hear. Easier to hear me than Chick Easton. I had never known anyone who could move as stealthily as he could. He was a whispering shadow behind me. Spooky. Ethereal. More than once I stopped to see I hadn't lost him. Each time he was close by, within a few feet, sometimes mere inches away.

Who was this man? And where had he acquired such unusual talents? He was an enigma to me. A puzzle with parts withheld.

I led him to the base of a forked tree and pointed up to a natural seat in the lee of the fork. I don't nail boards into trees. God got it right the first time. Chick nodded, handed me his bow, then scaled the tree, soundlessly, as if he were a lizard rather than a 190-pound man. When he was seated, I handed up his bow and left him there, silent and motionless in his perch like a huge bird of prey.

I kept the wind in my face and worked my way to another tree I'd marked on an earlier scouting foray. At the base of the tree, I used nylon cord to tie a slipknot at one end of the bow. I tied the other end of the cord around my left wrist and climbed. Once situated, I pulled the bow up hand-over-hand into the tree with me. Waited.

The sun peeked over the horizon as I nocked the arrow. It had black fletching. All my arrows had black fletching. Real feathers rather than plastic vanes. Many of my friends told me plastic vanes were more accurate and durable, citing test reports in sporting publications. I would nod at them and continue to use my black feathers. Always the last to learn.

I thought about Sandy. Sandy Collingsworth. I loved her. Always had. Always would. She was the only media person I'd ever granted a personal interview. She had crystal-blue eyes and a face-lighting smile. She possessed dignity and intelligence. Honest. Never posed or preened. "You'll never make it big in this business," I had told her, "unless you get over this vicious streak of honesty."

"Maybe," she'd said. "But I get to be me."

Good trade.

I was hard in love with her. We shared thoughts. Hopes. She understood things without my having to say them. And she loved me. At one point we had agreed to marry. Then one day it changed. She changed her mind. "I love you," she said. I didn't understand. She would explain it, later, she said. Just needed time. So I gave her time. And distance. And my trust. I believed in her. When the time came, she would tell me. I understood about time and didn't ask much from it, just enough to warm my memories when needed. I waited. It was a dry trail. A lonely one. And now the time neared. The weekend looked far away but would come. Soon I would know. Soon I would see her. Fill my eyes with her. Fill my mind. And my heart.

Soon.

At 8:00 a.m. two does wandered by my stand. They were alert, testing the air, watching with their 180-degree vision, moving silently, wraithlike, then passing on.

Within the half hour, the ten-point buck came by. The buck I'd been waiting for, the buck I'd passed up lesser animals for. The trophy I'd made the trip for. He was a beauty. Magnificent.

He sniffed at the trail of the does. They say the rut doesn't come until November, and then only after the first hard freeze. But I'd witnessed rutting behavior at earlier times. Like now. His neck was swollen with the blood of his libido. His rack was majestic and symmetrical. Slowly I raised the bow, putting the thirty-yard pin high on his shoulder, allowing for the height and angle of entry. I pulled the black-feathered shaft to anchor at the corner of my mouth, let out half a breath. He was mine. It would be clean, a classic shot, one that didn't come along often. No obstructions, no twisting of my body to shoot. Almost two weeks of waiting was over.

Then I slowly let down the arrow without releasing the string. Not today.

In a low voice, just above a whisper, I spoke to the big deer, "Get out of here, big guy. Not your day to die. Go find your girlfriends." I tipped my cap to him. A little corny maybe, but sincere.

He snorted at the sound of my voice, tossed his head, then bounded on. At the top of a rise he stopped, raised his splendid head to its full height, the prince of the woods, and looked back in my direction—did he see me?—then walked away.

I leaned back against a limb and smiled. Wyatt Storme, hopeless dipzoid romantic, talking to animals. A terminally goofy case, and not without precedent. When I was in-country, someone kept hitting the company goodies stash—beer, whiskey, candy bars, cigars, cigarettes. The person didn't take much, so we didn't think it was for black market purposes. The guy was slick, we couldn't catch him at it, but whenever something was taken, he would leave something in its place—cheap jewelry, miniature Buddhas, some rice, something. The guy was trading with us. But this was Nam, where justice was quick, sure, and brutal, and quite often forever.

One night it was my turn on guard duty. Most of the men in my unit were from metropolitan areas, unaccustomed to watching for movement in poor light, in shadows, or in the dark. More often than not, due to the nightmare of the war and the carnage we attended daily, we saw things that were not there, heard voices that were not there. I was waiting for him when he came into the tent where we kept our special stuff stashed. He was reaching for a box of Butterfinger candy bars when I clicked back the hammer of my contraband Colt .45 Government Model.

His eyes were bright and wide, cognizant of his situation. Being a native, he had seen and heard much violence from both sides. Still, he stood quietly, his eyes locked on mine. I let the hammer down, slowly, on the cocked pistol. In his hand was an Archie comic book he'd brought to exchange. Where he'd gotten it I had no idea. Saying nothing, I picked out a six-pack of beer and carton of cigarettes, handing both items to him. That done, I pointed to the comic book in his hand, then to myself. He handed it to me, still unsure and frightened. I indicated the outside with a nod of my head, then held up my hand like Tonto to the Lone Ranger. He nodded, then left.

The next day my comrades dogged me unmercifully. "Got more in one hit than he ever had, Storme," they said. "Where were you, Storme? Asleep? Some guard. Big deer hunter. Country boy." I smiled, ignored them, and read my comic book.

I never saw him again. Never came back. But he left more than he'd ever taken. He made me feel human, which was a difficult feeling to come by in that inhumane time.

And so it was with the buck. Penance for the dog.

It was 10:29 by my watch when Chick materialized at the base of my tree. I had neither seen nor heard his approach. It startled me. I handed him my bow and shimmied down the trunk. He was smiling.

"How'd you do that?" I asked.

"Do what?"

"Get here without me hearing you? Find this tree? You've never been here before."

"Knew you'd keep your face in the wind and the sun at your back, even though it was dark when you walked in. You're a good hunter. A broken twig here, an overturned leaf there, and here I am."

"Doesn't explain not being able to see or hear you."

"Came up behind you."

"It's quiet. The breeze is light. I was listening for deer. I didn't hear you."

"I'm Captain Midnight," he said. "My feet don't touch the ground." His smile was white against his camo-smudged face. "You gonna show me the field, or what? May want to smoke some of it. For research purposes only, of course."

The curtain had come down. That was all I was going to get, for now. It dawned on me he had no reason to trust me, other than the testimony of Matt Jenkins. "This way," I said.

We walked through the woods, the broken orange sunlight slanting through the trees, altering landmarks from my afternoon discovery. I looked for landmarks that cast no shadows—blow-downs, rocks, hollows. The woods are a kaleidoscope of shifting shadows and hues, never looking quite the same twice.

"Why'd you pass up the shot on the buck?" he asked as we walked through the woods.

"How'd you know?" This was spooky.

"Why didn't you take the shot? You could hunt ten more years and not get another chance like that. His rack was perfect."

I looked at him. Stopped walking. I shrugged. "Wasn't his day to die, I guess." He looked at me, and for the first time his eyes lost their bemused cast. He nodded, satisfied, and I knew he understood.

"Why I didn't shoot, either," he said. I could swear he was choking back something else, something he wouldn't, or couldn't, say. Now I knew who he was. As if I'd known him for twenty years instead of two days. Just a matter of meeting him. He knew what it was. Without me having to explain.

We walked through the brilliantly colored forest, the dew dripping from golden leaves. Some leaves fluttered and danced in the breath of the woods. We crossed the ancient fence, second time for me, and passed on. The same fence bordering the field of a thousand blurry daydreams.

But, now the marijuana was gone.

It had been plowed under and the ground was pocked with charred pits of black where something had been burned. The woods stank of the burnt-rope smell. No guard dogs. No tall, spiked stalks of cannabis.

Just a plowed field in the middle of the forest.

We walked on the turned earth. There were a few sprigs of marijuana on the ground; they would soon curl at the edges and turn brown. I found a fresh cigarette butt. Marlboro Lights. I leaned over to pick it up when the rolling crack of a rifle creased the silence. Chick hit the ground, slapping my legs out from under me as he did.

"Get down, dammit."

I hit the dirt, rolled, then ran in a low crouch to the edge of the field and ducked behind a blowdown as the second shot rang out. This was not my favorite place. Chick was up and running after the report echoed through the trees. "I got the flash," he said from behind a low bank. "Up there." He pointed to the rise on the west slope with his Colt. "About a hundred and fifty yards up that rise."

My heart raced and my breathing was irregular. I did not enjoy being shot at. Never adjusted to it. It was the same horrible slap of apprehension each time. The same racing, icy, stinging fear, grabbing at you and starting the involuntary responses—dry mouth, shallow breathing, determined survival mode. You are never so alive as when death is one hammer-snap away.

Chick discarded his bow. I already had. "We take him?" he asked. "Or do you want to get out of here?" His eyes were hot. Intense. The eyes of a warrior. Born to it.

"He's got a rifle and the better position."

"You go outside to the south. If we can get close we'll have—There he goes!"

I saw a flash of white up the hill. We broke from cover, then zigzagged along opposite sides of the field. Branches snapped at me as I crashed through the woods. My gun was holstered. At this distance it was worthless. Nearing the end of the field we slowed, and I unsheathed the Browning. We became more deliberate now, moving slowly and watching up the hill. My breath was harsh and dry in my throat. I was behind a tree, searching the tree line, when Chick hollered out.

"Wyatt! Don't move! Wherever you are, for God's sake, don't move!"

SEVEN

A crow cackled. An engine was gunned to life over the ridge. Too late now. They would be long gone before we got there.

"What's up?" I yelled across to Chick.

"Booby traps. Stay where you are and I'll work your way."

I holstered the Browning. Booby traps and killer dogs. It fit the pattern Trooper Browne talked about. But why had the sniper been here? He couldn't have known we were coming. Unless he followed us. Or maybe he was expecting someone else. Who? Or maybe he was a she. Why guard an empty field? Did he follow us in? No headlights behind us when we drove in this morning.

It took Chick several minutes to work his way back to me. "Let me show you something," he said.

Twenty-five feet away Chick pointed at a spot where a mat of leaves had been placed, concealing something. He picked up a heavy branch and stuck it in the center of the leaves. Steel jaws exploded from the leaves like a largemouth bass with a popping bug caught in its mouth. It snapped shut with a metallic clang, wrenching the branch from Chick's hand. Splinters from the shattered wood pinwheeled away. I whistled low and thought about my shins. Bear trap. Like I said, there are no bears in Missouri.

Chick lighted a cigarette. "Wonder how many of these things we've managed to miss," he said. "I found another one over on the other side. Also a couple of trip wires. Claymores or bouncing Bettys. This ain't Disneyland, partner. Need to be careful walking out." Then he smiled and said, "After you."

"What about our sniper buddy?"

"Not a pro. Or we'd be dead. Also, I'm beginning to think you lack local appeal."

"Not possible."

"Of course not."

"They couldn't be worried about discovery now. Field's plowed under and harvested. Couldn't know we were coming."

"Mistook us for somebody, maybe?" he said. "Or maybe they decided to ace us."

"Why here, then? Killing us here would call attention to this place."

"So, what's here? A plowed field? And who'd miss us? Couple of out-of-towners. Maybe they wouldn't bother to look for us. And how would they know to look here?" I thought about that. Sam Browne would look. He knew the location. Chick extinguished his cigarette against the bottom of his boot and put it in his pocket, then said, "Check this. You find this field, you report it to the sheriff, who promises to keep you out of it. And I think he kept that promise. Then, somebody whacks the sheriff, cuts the grass, plows it under, then somebody else, or maybe the same somebody, tries to blow you away."

"Or you," I said.

He tapped another Camel from the crumpled pack and stuck it between his lips, squinted as he struck a wooden kitchen match and touched it to the end of the cigarette. Nodded.

"Or me," he said.

EIGHT

The offices of the *Paradise Herald-Examiner* were sterile and antiseptic. More like a hospital than what I imagined a newsroom to look like. I imagined cigar smoke floating in the air, roll-top desks, Remington manual typewriters, and reporters with loosened ties and rolled-up sleeves. Instead, there were computer terminals and No Smoking signs.

I asked for a reporter named Jill, and a girl at the information desk led Chick and me to a city room desk and asked us to wait. There was an ashtray filled with Virginia Slims butts, a coffee mug smudged with pale lipstick, and a little desk sign that said, "I only had one nerve left when I got up and you're getting on it." A triangular walnut nameplate said JILL MAXWELL.

Jill Maxwell came out of a back room with a Styrofoam cup of coffee and a cigarette. Maybe she didn't want to clean the mug on her desk. Maybe it would be sexist to ask her to wash it out. Maybe I would ask. Break the ice. She stopped when she saw me. "Well," she said, "if it isn't the camera-shy dog killer. What brings you here? And who's your friend?"

"This is Chick Easton," I said. "Sign says no smoking."

"You do everything by the rules?" she asked. She sat down, gave me a flash of leg. Nice legs, too. She smiled and nodded at Chick. Cocked her head at me in challenge and took a slow drag on the cigarette, blew the smoke in my direction. I think I was falling in love. Wondered whether we could find someplace private where she could flog me with her nameplate.

"I want to know who gave you my name and how you knew about the marijuana field."

"Been doing a little research on you," she said, ignoring me. She hadn't improved at providing information. "An old *Sports Illustrated* article said you had the best hands in the NFL. What do you do with your hands nowadays?"

"I keep them to myself," I said. Chick lit a cigarette and settled back in his chair. "And 'nowadays' is not a word, it's a colloquialism. I'd think a professional wordsmith would know better. Now, I want to know how you knew about me and the marijuana, and I haven't got time for games."

"What're you gonna do if I don't tell?" she said. She sat back and clicked her fingernails. "Beat me up? Big, strong guy like you."

I heard Easton chuckle beside me. I frowned at him, then looked back at her. "There's a story in this, a big one, if you help us. Otherwise, I'm walking out of here and you get squat."

"Already got a story. First, I've got the murder of the sheriff. And I have a little sidebar of a reclusive ex-pro going mano-a-mano with a Doberman pinscher. A football player who disappeared from the public eye years ago. A mystery man who resurfaces in the middle of the biggest murder in Paradise County history. What else do I need?"

"It's bigger than that," I said. "Besides, without me you have nothing to corroborate your story. You've only got half of it."

She put her cigarette down and leaned forward in her chair. "What do you have?" she said, shifting gears. She wet her lips and lifted her chin, exposing her lovely neck. I wondered how many guys had spilled headlines to her when she did that? But I was too strong for that. She'd have to show me the legs again or my lips were sealed.

"Unh-uh," I said. "First, you tell me where you got my name and give me your word you'll leave me out of any story you write."

"No good," she said. "The guys from K.C. and St. Louis are already filtering into town. First, you tell me what you got, then I decide if it's worth it."

"Maybe this is too big for you. It's not the Rotary Club picnic or a new bank opening."

It stung her. A cheap shot maybe, but I needed her help. Her eyes slitted and she bristled like a cat. "I work damn hard at this job," she said. "I'm good at it. I don't need some has-been ex-jock telling me how to do it."

"Has-been," said Chick, chuckling.

"Ex-jock," I said to him.

"Pegged you immediately," he said.

"Must be the cleat marks on my forehead."

"Or the way you slur your words and say 'duh.' "

She said, "How do I know you've got anything I need?" She gave me the once-over with her eyes, smiling. "Or, at least, anything I don't already know?"

"Somebody just took target practice at us," I said. "Less than an hour ago."

"Where? Who was it? What were the circumstances? You shoot back?" She shoved papers out of the way and pulled a notepad in front of her and clicked a pen into readiness. I could hear the drag sing on the reel as she took the bait and pulled it down.

"No," I said. "Not yet. First, you agree not to use my name in anything you write. Nobody likes to read about us old has-beens anyway. Boring stuff. Second, we need information."

"How do I write an article and leave your name out of this?"

"Use an alias," I said. "Or say, 'informed sources' told you. Something like that."

"Not as effective. Story has more power and validity if I use your name. Just you showing up here after all these years is a story in itself."

"I'm not the story." I never was the story, but they never seemed to accept that. "There's more. Much more."

She looked at both of us. Chewed the end of her pen. Her cigarette had burned a long ash in the ashtray. "Okay," she said, finally. "I leave you out. I can pull it off. But you give me everything."

"First you answer some questions," I said. "Then I'll tell you what you want to know."

"Maybe I can't trust you."

"Maybe you can't."

She exhaled. Shrugged her shoulders. "What do you want to know?"

"Who told you about me and the marijuana field and the dog?"

"Anonymous tip," she said. I made a face and leaned back in my chair. She offered a palms-up gesture of resignation. "It's the truth. I can't help it. They called my recorder at home. I was sleeping when the phone rang. I heard it ring, but I'd been up most of the night so I let the machine answer. When I heard the message, I reached to pick it up, but he'd already hung up. That was yesterday morning. He just said there was a former football player who killed an attack dog in a marijuana field.

"I have an informant at the sheriff's office. Got a description of you and the guy with you yesterday. I ran those by the sports editor, and he said one of them sounded like Wyatt Storme. I said, 'Who?' " She looked at me. Coy. I didn't react. "He said he'd heard you had a cabin in the area. So I went through the microfiche files, confirmed your description, checked your background. It was vaguely interesting."

"You recognize the voice on your machine?"

"No. I've got the tape if you want to hear it."

"Doesn't explain how you tracked me to the grocery store. Even with the description that'd be tough."

"Traced you through motor vehicle. I have a couple of cop friends who owe me." She smiled wickedly. "Gave them your name and birthdate, which I got from an old football program.

You have three vehicles registered with Colorado plates. A '91 Bronco, a 1969 Mustang Mach I, and a '66 T-bird. I offered a twenty-dollar reward to some kids who work in different jobs—grocery stores, fast-food places, gas stations, convenience stores—places I figured you might turn up if you were around."

"Pretty resourceful."

"I have my moments," she said. I'd managed to duck the national press for years only to be found by a small-town reporter. Hadn't figured on that. Someday they'd make her editor of this paper if management had any sense. She lighted another cigarette, then offered her light to Easton. He accepted it and joined her. I had more questions.

"Who has the voltage to get Baxter named interim sheriff in the middle of a murder investigation when the murder victim was the man he was going to run against for sheriff? Especially when Baxter is so unlikable?"

"Seemed odd to me, too," she agreed. "Baxter is slime. Makes perverse suggestions when he's around me. His idea of flirting. He's gross. There're a few people who could get him the position. Evan Sullivan, the county commissioner, for one. Mark Bannister is another. He's president of the Chemical Bank. Sullivan can't stand Baxter, and Bannister was a close friend of Kennedy's. That leaves Alan Winston, a local attorney with a big family name. And Willie Boy Roberts." I sat up when I heard Roberts's name again. She continued. "Winston didn't like Kennedy. And the feeling was mutual. Kennedy thought Winston fixed cases. He also thought Alan was trying to hit on his daughter. Kennedy once threatened to whip Winston if he spoke to his daughter again. In front of some of Winston's friends. Something Alan wouldn't forget. As for Roberts, he has the most power behind the scenes in the county. He can do about what he wants around Paradise, and does, but he's slick about it. Subtle."

"Tell me about Roberts."

She took a drag on her cigarette. "He's a contemptible snake." She shuddered as if something crawly and multilegged had landed on her shoulder. "He came here a few years back from somewhere down south. Louisiana or Alabama. Somewhere. Has that drawl and plays with a Cajun accent now and then like he thinks it's clever. He owns Starr Industries. They make aluminum casters, conveyor belts, and other materials for assembly-line work. He also owns a trucking line and the Truck Hangar, which is this monster truck stop out on the interstate. There are people around here who think his money is dirty."

"Those businesses sound legitimate."

"Six months after he took over Starr Industries, the workers went on strike. Things got ugly. Somebody burned down a shed on Starr property. Shot through the window of the personnel office after hours. Tires were slashed. That kind of thing. Then a couple of the most vocal workers got the shit kicked out of them. They were big guys, too. Broken bones, lacerations. Then some of the strike organizers were fired, but they didn't complain. Two union stewards just up and moved away one weekend. Nobody knew why. Suddenly, the strike was over and things went on like before." She jammed her cigarette out in the crowded ashtray.

"People are afraid of Willie Boy Roberts. Oh, he'll give you the big smile, clap you on the back, buy you lunch, but there is something...I don't know, this all sounds trite, but there is something insidious about that man. Something evil."

"Is he involved in drug traffic?"

"Haven't heard that," she said. "But he's careful to stay above things. There are people who think he has out-of-town money behind him. Illegal money. I've heard people say, whispering when they say it, that he's involved in some custom prostitution. High-dollar girls for important people like senators, contractors. Gets the whores out of the city. They help him make the deal he wants. They say he recruits local women—some of them wives of local businessmen. But it may just be talk. You men are good at keeping things like that secret."

"We're tight-lipped about our concubines," said Chick.

"They run some girls out at the Truck Hangar. Some of them young. Work the truckers. Knock on their sleeper compartments. Quite a wake-up call, huh? There's a small motel next to the truck stop. Truck Hangar is in this county, but the motel is conveniently just over the line or Kennedy would've shut it down."

"Roberts slips a couple bucks into the Ford County sheriff's campaign fund and he gets left alone. That the way it works?" She nodded. "So you think Willie Boy would be a good place to start?"

"If you want broken bones. No, stay away from him. You won't get anywhere. If Roberts is involved in this, it'll be a waste of time. Nobody will say anything about or against him. Baxter is a complete moron. Unless the major case squad can bring an indictment, nobody will ever be caught. If Baxter arrests someone it'll be a scapegoat—some local crud he's had trouble with in the past. If Roberts had anything to do with it, he'll never take the fall."

"You think Baxter's in the bag?"

She looked into her coffee cup as if the answer were in there. Shook her head. "No. I really don't think so. I think Baxter's just dumb—and mean. Kennedy was making inroads into the drug traffic. Put some guys away over the years, burned some fields. Then came the upscale drugs—cocaine, crack, speed—easier to carry, harder to detect. Most of the grass around here is sold by small-timers working the fast-food places out of their cars. Hustling the teenagers."

I told her the size of the marijuana field I'd found, then the rest of it. I kept back a few things—the little rocks for one. If they were publicized Baxter could demand them as evidence. She thought he was dumb, but I wasn't ready to dismiss him so easily. He was cunning enough to find out my name though the sheriff wouldn't give it to him. Sly enough to get himself appointed interim sheriff. He didn't appear to be afraid of anyone or anything—including the highway patrol. Besides, I knew it was bad practice to underestimate people. That's when you got hurt—ran your patterns a little sloppier, didn't finish out your blocks. That's when you got a helmet in the ribs, a forearm under your chinstrap, or a potential big gain got stuffed for three yards. It was the difference between being a thoroughbred and an also-ran.

Near the end of my narrative, we were interrupted by a slender man, five seven, 135 pounds, slender wrists, delicate hands. Stylish tie and styled hair.

"You know you're not supposed to smoke here, Maxwell," he said. He was irritated. The backs of his wrists were against his hips like an angry baby-sitter's.

"Go away, Horton." She waved the back of her hand at him as if shooing a fly. "I'm busy."

"You know the rules," he said. "No smoking in the city room." His voice rose half an octave. "And that goes for visitors, too." He looked at Chick, who looked back, smiled his disarming smile, then blew a lazy cloud of blue smoke at the ceiling.

"Go shit in your hat, Horton," she said. "At least I don't shove things up my nose and other orifices."

His face reddened and his eyes flamed up. "You bitch."

"Don't be vulgar, sweet-pants," she said.

"Journalistic camaraderie," said Chick.

"Warms the heart," I said.

"I don't know why Marvin allows a little slut like you to—"

"That's enough," I said.

Horton pursed his lips and looked at me. "And *who* are *you?* And what makes you think I have to listen to you?"

"I'm Miss Manners's nephew," I said. "And I'm here to tell you that it is bad manners to speak to women like that."

"Not to mention a health risk," Chick said. "Did you realize most accidents occur within twenty-five miles of home?"

Horton's face became blotchy. He glared at us, then stomped off, stiff-legged.

"I think we angered him," Chick said.

"Ignore Horton," Jill said. "I'm twice the woman he is. And I can handle him without your help."

"They just don't make damsels in distress like they used to," said Chick.

"What was that all about?" I asked.

"Horton's jealous, that's all."

"What's his job here?"

"Besides being a loathsome slug, he's the lifestyle editor. What you might think of as the society pages. Garden club. Country club dances. Features about which wine to drink with what cheese. He's not too bad at it, really. He's the publisher's nephew besides being an asshole and a coke freak. Sometimes I smoke just to piss him off."

"Can he get you in trouble?"

She shrugged. "He'll tattle like a third-grader, but they'll just bitch at me. I work sixty hours a week and I'm reliable. They know that. Besides, his uncle doesn't like him, either. Who could?" She flicked ash off her cigarette.

"How does he afford cocaine on a journalist's salary?"

"Deals a little. But because of his uncle and Alan Winston, the little turd doesn't get hassled, except by Kennedy. But now he's gone."

"What about Winston? What does he have to do with Horton?"

"Horton's got a crush on Alan."

"Winston's gay?"

"Nobody believes it," she said. "He lifts every skirt he can. One of the reasons Kennedy threatened him. At most, he's bisexual. But I don't know how anyone can be friends with Horton without being a little twisted."

"Winston ever try to hit on you?"

"That's one of the reasons Horton hates me. Yeah, Alan's come on to me. He's a good-looking guy, but I've got no interest in him. I think he's a phony." She sipped her coffee. "I'd steer clear of Alan Winston if I were you. His family are the blue bloods of Paradise County. They've got streets named after their children and pets. Run the Chamber of Commerce and the Presbyterian church. Alan's done a lot for Paradise. Donates a lot of money to civic causes. Member of everything. Kind of a hero around here. He's also vindictive. Even petty. Bad things happen when people cross Alan Winston."

"Like what?"

"I know he had a neighbor whose dog killed Alan's Siamese cat. The guy apologized. Offered to pay for another cat. Alan wouldn't talk to him. Slammed the door in the guy's face. A week later the dog was found hung with barbed wire from a tree in his owner's backyard."

"Nice town," I said.

"Yeah," Chick said. "Nice place to live, but you wouldn't want to visit here."

NINE

We were back in the Silver Spur Lounge. Chick said he needed his engine revved. He was revving it with Canadian Club and Moosehead. The talk with Jill Maxwell left a faint lassitude thrumming against the back of my brain. The more I learned of the politics of Paradise and the county named for it, the less I liked the place and the more I wished to return to Colorado and to Sandy. The sooner we left, the sooner I could leave all this behind me.

Except the sheriff was dead. Back to that. It would always be there and would keep bubbling back to the surface of that little chamber of awareness where I kept all the near misses and failed opportunities stored to be released in the early morning dreams that troubled me. Dreams that would not stop. Dreams that I could not control. Dreams that kept me here and other places I wished to leave. One more thing to separate me from Sandy. Always something.

"Gotta pick up Prescott sometime," said Chick, talking about the bail jumper he had to return to Colorado. Prescott had stolen chemicals from a lab at Colorado University, he told me.

"Not much of a crime," I said.

"Chemicals were rare. High-dollar. Guy's some kind of chemist. Couple drug busts. Cooking crack. China white. Some ice. All the little pretties that go pop in your head. No convictions, except the chemical theft. But he sapped the night security man when he took the chemicals, put the guy in the hospital. The state of Colorado thinks the guy's a bad actor, so they set bail at fifty large. I get five grand to bring him back."

"How long will it take to find him?"

"Already know where he is." He sipped the beer.

"Why haven't you picked him up, then?"

"Waiting on you," he said. "See how long you want to stay around and play detective. Besides, what'm I gonna do with the guy? Can't drag him around on a leash. I'll pick him up just before we leave. You don't like what happened to the sheriff. Wanna do something about it, like you were the Lone Ranger or something." He finished off the shot of Canadian Club and swallowed some Moosehead to follow it down. "What's one more lost cause, anyway?"

"You like that stuff?" I said, pointing at the beer.

"It's all right."

"Just all right? Why drink it, then?"

"I'm Canadian."

"You're not Canadian."

He looked at the green bottle, took another sip. "Hmmm," he said, pondering it. "Must be some other reason."

"We keep poking around, things could get nasty."

He nodded.

"No use getting involved in this," I said.

"None."

"The police can handle it."

"Of course they can," he agreed. Smiled. We sat for a moment. Quiet. The jukebox changed tunes. Chick lighted another cigarette and drained the bottle of beer.

"So," he said. "Which one do you want? Roberts or the lawyer?"

I called Alan Winston's office. He was in court and unavailable. Then I called the motel where Trooper Sam Browne was staying. He wasn't in. I wanted to tell him about the shooting and the harvested marijuana. The courthouse was two blocks away, so Chick went over to watch Alan Winston in action while I checked out

Willie Boy Roberts. Information gave me the office number of Starr Industries. I punched the numbers and a receptionist transferred me to his secretary.

"Starr Industries," said the female voice. "Mr. Roberts's office."

"My name's Wyatt Dark," I said. "Is Mr. Roberts in? Friend of mine, Alan Winston, said I should get hold of Mr. Roberts. I'm looking for work and Alan said Mr. Roberts was hiring."

"Could you hold, please?" I did. There was a brief wait. If he tried to call Winston while I was waiting, I knew he would be unable to get hold of him as Winston was in court. If he had me come in, then I had a connection, however slight, between Roberts and Winston. Although that might have no meaning, it was a start. She came back on the line.

"Mr. Roberts said if you could come in within the next hour he will be glad to talk with you."

Forty-five minutes later I drove to Starr Industries and walked in through a door marked Personnel. I was wearing a Harris tweed jacket, oxblood loafers, eggshell-blue oxford cloth shirt, a pair of blue-gray Haggar slacks, and an actual paisley tie—detective work requires many sacrifices. The salesman at Thomas's Men's Wear was a little surprised when I told him I'd wear all the items out of the store and put my jeans and other clothes in the boxes. The shirt was still creased from being folded in the plastic packaging.

Roberts's secretary was an auburn-haired beauty with light gold streaks that looked like the real item. Her gold highlights shone in the sunlight slanting through a large picture window. The office was warm—soft brown carpet and exotic plants.

The nameplate on her desk said TEMPESTT FINESTRA. "May I help you?" she asked. Up close I saw emerald-green eyes and smooth cheekbones. She looked more like a John Wayne heroine than a secretary. I was becoming more impressed with Willie Boy Roberts by the minute.

"I'm here to see Mr. Roberts," I said. "I'm the guy who telephoned earlier."

"Mr. Dark," she said, searching with her eyes, like a high school principal. "Of course. He's expecting you." She punched numbers into the black AT&T business phone. She spoke straight, without deference, nor was she overly formal. She cradled the phone and folded her arms under her breast and leaned forward on the cherry-wood desk. "If you can wait a few minutes, Mr. Dark, Mr. Roberts will see you."

"That's fine." Patience is my middle name. I looked through the magazines on the coffee table in the waiting area. It was the same selection as at the sheriff's office with the exception they were current issues—fresh and uncreased. I watched Tempestt walk over to a file cabinet. She walked in the leggy way tall women have. She was tightly muscled and firm like a dancer or a swimmer. She might require further investigation. She was suspiciously beautiful. Maybe I could set up a second appointment, come an hour early. Keep an eye on her. Surveillance was important. I saw a button light up on her phone. Roberts was calling someone. Winston?

"Tempestt," I said to her, as she sat down. "That's an unusual name."

"Tem-*pestt*," she said, gently correcting me. Friendly. "The accent is on the second syllable."

"Nice name. Sounds good when you say it."

"Thank you." She smiled. I took the brunt of it. Withstood it. "You're not trying to put the move on me now, are you, Mr. Dark?"

"No," I said. "Just like the name."

"Didn't say I'd mind. Just wanted to know if you were going to." Straight out, just like that. No posturing. No word games. Bang.

"If I were looking, you'd be someone I'd want to get to know."

"Thank you," she said. Her green eyes sparkled. "That's the nicest letdown I've ever received."

"Bet you don't get many."

"You have a lady?"

I nodded. Nothing dazzles women like a tight-lipped guy.

"You don't find many men who aren't on the prowl. Looking for strays." Her face was open. Bright. We could have been discussing the weather. Always nice to meet one of the real ones. The comfortable ones. The phone on her desk buzzed. She picked it up, listened, then put it down.

"You can go in now. Good luck." I thanked her. Offered to buy her a cup of coffee sometime.

"I'd like that," she said. "She won't mind?"

"She knows me. There's nothing says we can't be friends."

"What's her name?"

"Sandy."

"Is she pretty?"

I nodded. "And gentle and intelligent."

"You have any brothers?" she asked.

Willie Boy Roberts was a big man, with a big smile. Tailored suit, western cut, beige with a yellow-and-brown tie. Huge diamond on his right hand. His eyes were crinkly and friendly. He looked like somebody's favorite uncle, the one with the funny stories of life as a roughneck or ranch hand. The biggest thing was the smile. A radiant, come-along grin that put you at ease and made you want him to like you. I thought about what Jill Maxwell had said, then I thought about Chick Easton's smile, also disarming and warm, hiding a side I knew little of. I remembered something else Jill had said, just before we left her office. "It's Willie Boy's town now. He just lets us live in it."

"William Roberts," he said, beaming, and engulfing my hand with his wide paw. The diamond band bit into my knuckles when he squeezed. "Friends call me Willie Boy."

"Wyatt Dark," I said, and sat in the chair he indicated.

"You like something to drink, you?" he said. "Got some New Orleans chicory I just had ground. Extra fine."

"Sounds good."

He turned and poured black liquid from a Bunn coffee maker behind him. "Cream or sugar?"

"Black."

"Only way to drink it. Putting shit in it's for women. I like a man who takes life straight," he said, giving me a funny look when he did. "Drink whiskey the same way. How you take your whiskey, you?"

I don't take it at all, I thought, but didn't say that. "Straight up or with water," I said. "I don't put candy in anything."

He chuckled, winking at me. A good old boy. Maxwell was right, he liked to toy with the Cajun accent, mixed it with a Deep South drawl. And yet there was a hint of something gritty and hard. Something from the streets and back alleys. "You 'n' me gonna get along just fine." He handed me the chicory. It smelled strong, but good. Reminded me of New Orleans. Accordion players and street dancers in multicolored suits at Mardi Gras. Cypress trees and iron gates.

"You a vet?" he asked, taking his seat behind the mile-wide walnut desk. When he sat he was framed by a dark walnut bookcase, looking like a portrait of a senator from a southern state. A man of taste and singularity. But something was wrong with the picture. He was playing a part. Playing it well, but playing one nonetheless.

"Yeah," I said. "First Air Cav. Able Company. Made corporal." Actually I was recon, and made lieutenant before I mustered out.

"Damn," he said. He smacked a palm down on the desk top. "Small world. I was First Air Cav, too." We were becoming buddies already. Maybe later we'd go out and beat up some union stewards together. "I was in Saigon during Tet in '68. Caught a piece of shrapnel in the back of my shoulder." He slapped the back of his shoulder, in a self-congratulatory pat, to indicate the spot. “Tore out a chunk size of a Ping-Pong ball. Had the medic stitch it up and ordered him to keep his mouth shut. Our kill ratio was seventeen to one in my unit. Fire-eaters.” His face went dreamy. Wistful. “Shit, we killed a lot of gooks that day. Press made it look like we lost. We kicked their yella butts.”

One of those, I thought. He was there but missed the lesson. Vietnam wasn’t a Richard Widmark movie, it was a spidery-legged demon crawling up your leg with a razor in its teeth and then slithering into your nightmares. It was mud-slogging, mind-raping madness without the benefit of a heroic soundtrack. And yet…and yet, there was still an uneasy sensation, a rush of excitement, of being alive, of surviving the horror, riding the beast to the end. Of being there and living through it. A masculine feeling. Establishing and riveting for all time what you were and what you might become. No apologies. No denials.

“Media screwed it up for us, too,” I said, adopting the character of disillusioned vet. Wasn’t hard to do, either. “We’d go into a ‘safe’ village and the tail guy’d catch a bullet, then we’d sweep back through and the rear’d get popped again. We’d pull up the village chief and he never knew nothing, so we’d torch the village and find a cache of weapons and supplies. Then some newspaper liberal would make us out to be mad-dog killers.”

“You need a job?” he asked.

“Yessir, I do.”

“What talents you got?”

“Same’s I had in Nam. I’m not afraid, and I do what I’m told and what I have to.”

He sat back in his chair and considered me. “Pretty good-sized fella, you. Nose has been broken. Couple time, in fact. Scar tissue in your eyebrows and ‘long your chin. Sports or fightin’?”

“Football,” I said. He was sharp. Picked up on things. I didn’t want to pursue the football thing in too much depth. “Some fighting, I guess.”

"You been outside a lot," he said. "It's in your face. Little lines around your eyes from squinting at the sun. Skin is tanned. You work construction, you? Or something like it?"

This wasn't going the way I wanted. I came for information and was giving it instead. He was keeping me on the dodge. "Worked the rigs in Oklahoma. Around Bartlesville. Some road work in Wyoming." That would keep him busy running that down, if he decided to check it.

"Your hands look strong and you got the forearms and shoulders for it. But your hands aren't callused. Fingernails are straight, not broken. No nicks or scars on your fingers, although you broke a couple of them at different times. 'Specially the little one on the left hand."

"Been out of work for six months," I said. I thought about my store-fresh outfit. Sure he noticed it. "Tried selling real estate. Haven't done any heavy work for over a year."

"Any hobbies?"

"Fishing," I said. He'd caught me off guard with the good-old-boy routine. I hadn't underestimated him, but he was so good at it you were caught up in it before you knew it.

"Me, too," he said. "Like to hunt, also. Some good turkey hunting around here. Lot of deer, too. You like to hunt?"

"Some. Not very good at it, though."

He laughed. "Probably better than you let on. You bowhunt any?"

There it was. Smiling at me now. Friendly. Eased me right into it. Willie Boy was either a very smart businessman or a very dangerous one. I thought about what Jill Maxwell said about the custom call-girl ring. I could see him talking to some bored, upscale local wife, easing her into it with his rich Cajun baritone. "Looka here, darlin'. Nothin' to it. Be excitin' and y'all make some real money for yourself, yessir. Beats watchin' the soaps, gar-on-tee…"

Yeah, he could pull it off. Then he could use it to get business favors. Paradise was at the tip of the Bible belt. Sexual adventures were still taboo here. Not good for a local to have people talking about what his wife did on her free time. He could leverage the husband with the emotional extortion, get a favorable zoning, have an unsavory business practice overlooked.

"Love to bowhunt," I said. Shine it back at him. See where he took it. Sometimes you had to run up the middle to establish the deep patterns. "I use a Browning compound."

"Nice rig."

"Hit where I aim, too."

"You do for a fact," he said. "Why'd you come here, you? You're not the kind does wage work. Too smart. Too pretty. You need to stick to what you know." His eyes flashed briefly, like a cat's eyes in the beam of your headlights.

"Good advice. Heard you hired muscle. Thought you could use me." Go for it all. Nothing to lose. Take a chance.

He laughed. A booming laugh. Like he was laughing at a personal joke. "What makes you think I need muscle? You think I'm some kind of gangster?" He was still laughing as he reached across his desk and opened a teakwood box. I smelled the rosy-sweet scent of cedar. He brought out two long, dark brown cigars, handed them to me. I accepted them. They had a silver band on them.

"Cuban?"

"Hell no. Don't smoke that shit. Tampa. Hand-rolled. Aged domestic. Good a leaf as you'll ever burn. Gar-on-tee. I get 'em special from a war buddy down there. Three dollars each. Hundred of them a month. You'll find ol' Willie Boy takes care of his own. You good to me, you'll be in tall grass"—smiling now when he said it, missing the irony of the statement. Then the smile faded and his mouth firmed into a straight line. "Or, I got a load of shit for those folks that mess with me." Then, as quickly as it had appeared, the dark look passed from his face and was replaced by the open, convivial one. A mask. A prop to be wheeled out and used to fit the scene. We were buddies again. He could turn it on and off like an electric fence.

“Now you get out there, boy, and see that thoroughbred filly out front. Ain’t she fine. Get you an application.”

Time for me to throw a high hard one.

“You want my real name on the application?” I asked, searching his face for surprise. There was none.

The phony accent disappeared and so did the smile. “What is it you really want, Mr. Storme?”

TEN

"I've been shot at—twice," I said. "Attacked by a dog. And I don't like it. I want it to stop."

"Right to it, huh?" Roberts said. He got up and walked to a wet bar. "Drink?" He held up a bottle of Wild Turkey. I shook my head. "Don't drink, do you?"

"No."

"What else did you lie about?"

"Nearly everything," I said.

He poured two fingers into a thick lowball glass. Added ice. He returned to his desk and sat. "What if I have you tossed out?" He said it offhand, as if it didn't matter either way.

"I'm heavy. Maybe I wouldn't toss."

"Sound pretty sure of yourself. You tough, Storme?"

"Purposeful. You own a dog? Doberman with a bad attitude?"

His cheek twitched as if a fly had landed there. "I'm not very happy about that," he said. "I understand a man has to protect himself, but don't throw it in my face. Very dangerous."

"Somebody popped Sheriff Kennedy. I'm not happy about that. What do you know about it? Why was your dog guarding a field of marijuana?"

"I notice you haven't shown a badge."

"That's because you're a good noticer."

"You a private detective?"

I shook my head. Drank some chicory. "Just a good citizen like yourself."

He threw back his head and laughed his raucous, booming laugh. "You've got cojones, podna. I'll give you that. You come in, ask me about a murder I know little of, then you sit here sipping my chicory. You're in the wrong place, boy. You have no official capacity and no idea who you're fucking around with."

"And who would that be?"

"Ask around."

"I have."

He cocked his head to one side and eyed me like a cobra would eye a mongoose. "And what do they say?"

"That you run whores out at your truck stop. That you're a ruthless businessman and you pretty much have your way around Paradise. That everybody is afraid of you but they're not sure exactly why."

He elevated his chin two inches, pointed it at me. "And what do you say?"

"That you're the bull goose in a mud puddle. You run drugs, bully the locals, and you got reason and ability to whack the sheriff. That, and you've got this cheap carny act working with the Deep South, coon-ass routine."

His lips thinned to a straight line, and I saw a tightening at his temples where a blood vessel rose like a worm against the skin. Though his facial expression changed little, the force of his anger was palpable. Sentient, yet crackling in the air between us. "Well, Storme. We know how it lays, now. You're an interesting man. Interesting, if not smart. I don't like your conversation. Be nice to talk with you some more, but," he said, slipping in the Cajun accent, "ol' Willie Boy don't tole you all things, him. So get lost, cowboy."

I stood up. Met his eyes with mine. Two gunfighters backing away from the table. Each wary of the other.

A door opened at the back of the office and two men—a blond surfer type and a darker, hairy guy—stepped in. They had weight-machine muscles and steroid-soaked eyes. "This is Vance and Breck," said Roberts. "Boys, this is Mr. Storme. He's leaving now." They crossed their large forearms in front of their forty-eight-inch chests simultaneously. Synchronized bulging. Maybe it was a new Olympic event. They certainly looked big enough to toss me out, and I was wearing new threads, but I wondered if they realized I possessed the secret knowledge of how to cloud men's minds. Probably didn't care. Their minds looked clouded enough already.

"They do any tricks?" I asked Roberts, keeping my eye on the beef. "Roll over? Speak? Play dead?"

"Shut up, wiseass," said Vance, the darker man.

"Is 'speak' the only command you respond to?"

"Just come along with us, Mr. Storme," said Breck, the blond guy. "Please. No trouble." A polite bone breaker.

I was thinking of another snappy rejoinder when the sky darkened and a man only half the size of a station wagon stepped into the office. He was bald as Mr. Clean and had a wicked red Fu Manchu. He looked like a pirate. A really big pirate. I tried to remember if I'd thought to bring an antitank mine. Darn. Changed clothes. "You need something, Willie?" asked the giant. He was six nine and had to weigh close to three hundred pounds.

Roberts looked at me. He smiled. Smug. In control. "Do I need Mr. Cugat for anything, Storme?" he asked. With a little luck I might have been able to handle the salt-and-pepper twins. However, the mountainoid was another matter.

"No," I said. "Not yet, anyway."

"Y'all come back," said Roberts.

"Love to," I said. I left. And did so with as much dignity as the situation would allow. At least I didn't let them kick sand in my face. I didn't let them tweak my nose, either. What a man. Tempestt said good-bye as I was leaving.

"How did it go?" she asked.

"Swimmingly," I said. "I should make vice president by Christmas."

"Call me for coffee."

"Looking forward to it."

"So am I."

She was standing at the picture window when I pulled out of the parking lot.

So, I'd made one friend. Out of five. Not bad for me.

ELEVEN

So, I'd met Willie Boy Roberts. Hadn't accomplished much by it. He'd played me like a catfish in shallow water. Controlled the interview. Called the shots. I was small change to him.

No doubt about it. Willie Boy Roberts was a dangerous man.

I knew he was involved in something the local Kiwanis Club wouldn't approve of. Unless there was more to the caster-and-conveyor-belt business than I knew, there was no reason to keep that much hired beef around.

Chick Easton was back at the Silver Spur, knocking back Carta Blanca when I came in.

"I thought you were Canadian," I said, sitting on the chair he'd kicked out from the table for me.

"No habla englisa," he said, then added, "gringo."

The waitress brought coffee without being asked. It was fresh. Willie Boy's chicory had been bitter. Fresh coffee in the late afternoon in a blue-collar bar could only mean Chick had clued the waitress in. I thanked him.

"No problem. You owe the waitress an autograph."

Though not an autograph person, I said, "Okay."

"Wait 'til you hear where she wants it. Ah, sweet bird of youth ever thou were't. Or is it thou never were't? These are hard questions for us Mexican-Canadians. How'd you make out with Roberts?"

"Pretty good. They didn't fold me up in a packing crate and mail me back to Colorado." I related my meeting with Roberts and the hired help. Chick nodded occasionally, didn't interrupt. I told him about Tempestt.

"Maybe she can give us some inside information," I said.

He raised an eyebrow. When he did, I noticed part of the left one was missing. Hadn't noticed before because his dark, weathered skin had obscured it. Now I could see the dull blush of scar tissue. The eyebrow looked like an apostrophe. "No other interest?"

I ignored him. "What about the lawyer? Winston."

"You didn't answer my question. What about the girl?"

"What about her?"

"Dark hair with gold highlights, long legs, muscular? Sounds like we should go back and lean on her a little. Or at least you should. I'll hold your coat."

"The lawyer."

He smiled, sipped the Carta Blanca. Leaned back in his chair. "He's quite the boy, our Alan. Brooks Brothers suit. Rep tie. Capped teeth. Got a salon tan. Has that dull green cast to it. Five ten, 165 pounds. Smokes imported cigarettes. Works out some, but he's not athletic. Left-handed. Been to an eastern university. Maybe even Ivy League. Smart. Cool. Can look you straight in the face and lie his ass off, but has a nervous habit of straightening his tie when he does." He stopped and drank more beer. Smiled at me. Proud of himself.

"That all you could get?"

"It's the Mex beer. Messes up my head. He also likes to fast dance and drinks vodka."

I sipped my coffee, smiling into it when I did. Easton was pretty sharp. "Okay," I said, "how do you know all that?"

"I lied about the dancing. He was a little tipsy in court, but not worried about breathing in anybody's face. Vodka drinkers can get away with that. Got a little New England accent that slips in with the midwest drawl. Lays off his *r*'s some. But it isn't often and seems practiced. Held the cigarette in his left hand. It had a gold circle above the filter and is thinner than domestic. He's slim-waisted, but he dropped a pen and the bailiff tossed it to him and he slapped at it with two hands. Not athletic."

"Anything else?"

"Thinks he's cute. Girl reporter may be right. He may swing both ways. Likes being in the center ring. Primps and preens. Mugs. Bullies. He worked the female judge. Gave her the eye, cocked his head at her. Pouted a little. At first she didn't like it, probably seen it before, but by the end of the session he was making points with it. Lawyers. Living proof that snakes fuck cockroaches. He patted the male bailiff's hand, rubbed his shoulder. Subtle androgyny is an advantage for him in court. He tries to seduce the entire room. And loves it."

He lit up a cigarette. Continued. "Another thing. He ain't above fixing it so he wins. You can see it's all that matters. Winning. I wouldn't be surprised to hear he breaks down in tears when he loses. He's got something on the prosecutor. Either that or the PA is superdumb. He let Winston get away with murder. Several times he didn't object when he should have, let Winston introduce testimony that was full of holes. Even the judge got annoyed with the prosecutor's performance. This is a good county to get arrested in. Just hire Winston. Something else. More than once Winston looked at me without looking at me. It was funny. Like he didn't think I noticed it."

"Maybe he thought you were cute."

"I am."

"You think he's involved in any of this? The drugs? The sheriff?"

"I think he's capable of anything," Chick said. "There's probably little happens around Paradise he's not at least aware of. Highly intelligent. Brilliant even. Well thought of around town. He's involved in a campaign to save the downtown area. A unique guy. Knows a lot of people, but probably has few close friends, though there are people who would like to have him in their corner."

"There's Horton," I said, reminding him of the lifestyle editor with the bad manners.

"You find Horton attractive?"

"Mesmerizing," I said.

"Probably not a lot to choose from in a community like this. Being gay is dangerous work in this part of the country. They may march in the streets and hold political office in San Francisco, but around here they get the crap beat out of 'em, and that's when the locals are feeling generous. Still, I'm having trouble buying Horton and Winston. Winston has money and mobility. He can go other places for it."

"Maybe Horton provides information for Winston. He does work for a newspaper. Besides, between the two of them it doubles the contacts they have."

"Pimp for each other? We're guessing. But I'll bet my Josh Logan fan club button he's involved in this, either directly or peripherally. He likes this stuff. He's attracted to the wild side. When he left the courtroom he finally looked at me. At first he just glanced, then he looked again and there was something else in it."

"Recognition?"

Chick shook his head. "Anger. Even hatred."

"So, what have we got so far? We kicked over some rocks and found a couple of snakes. I didn't really get anything from Roberts except a bad feeling about my longevity and a warning to keep out of his business. He didn't seem particularly worried about me." A door slammed and I heard the sound of a stool flushing.

"This is a nasty place," said Chick. "I know. I've been in nasty places before, and this is one of them. Something ain't right. The whole feel is wrong. Community betterment signs and a businessman with head-knockers on the payroll. Then, you got this honest sheriff in the middle of all this corruption and everybody says he was honest and he gets bumped. Now you got a moron in his place and all the little snakes don't have to crawl under rocks anymore. They can come right out and play in the sunshine like they were real people. Oh, here's something interesting. Guess who Winston was defending in court? Our buddy Luke. The little weasel with the Shit Happens hat."

"Small world."

"Tiny."

I paid Chick's tab. He was good at this work. In fact, he was good at many things. Unusual things. Talents one didn't acquire at the Acme Bounty Hunter's School. Where had he learned them, then? As for Winston and Roberts, I was sure they were involved in most of the dirty doings around the county, but would they kill the sheriff? Winston had his own reasons to hate Kennedy. But kill him? Winston had the big family name. Money. Position. Still, he was a strange one. Roberts was a better candidate. Willie Boy would benefit from having a bonehead like Baxter as sheriff. But killing the sheriff brought in the heat—state bulls and out-of-town suits with names to make. Killing the sheriff was stupid, something Roberts wasn't.

Unless there was no other choice.

Chick bought a six-pack of Carta Blanca and a pint of Mezcal. "Never know when Villa might ride by," he said.

We walked outside into the cool, fading light of Ozark autumn. As we neared the Bronco, a county car pulled up and Baxter got out. Deputy Simmons, whom I remembered from my first visit to the sheriff's office, got out on the passenger side.

"Charles Easton?" Baxter said, trying for official.

"Too many cop shows," said Chick, to me.

Baxter said, "You're under arrest."

TWELVE

"What's the charge?" I asked.

"Shut up," Baxter said. "Or I'll run you in with him. I'd like that. You might even resist arrest." He smiled. "I'd like that even more. A night in the jug might cool that mouth of yours."

Chick looked cool and unworried. He had an amused look on his face, as if the sheriff's fly were unzipped. "What'd I do this time?" he asked.

"I'll think of something. Just get in the car."

"Nah," said Chick. "You know how it works. Play fair. Just tell me what heinous crime I committed. You know, like aggravated assault, public drunkenness. Using polysyllables in front of a known imbecile."

Baxter reached into the police unit and pulled out a nightstick, one of those black clubs with a T-handle. A nasty weapon. "I'm taking you in for questioning in the murder of Sheriff Kennedy."

"Waste of time," said Chick. "I know less about it than you know about fifth-grade math. If I knew who killed the sheriff they'd already be in jail." He paused for a moment, stuck his cigarette in the corner of his mouth. "Or worse."

Baxter placed the barrel of the stick in his free hand. "I've been trained with this, Easton."

"That mean you won't mess your diapers when I take it from you?" Chick said. Baxter's face reddened. The light at the intersection turned amber then crimson behind him. Deputy Simmons was nervous. Baxter wanted to use the stick.

"You dealt it, boy," Baxter said.

Chick handed me the booze and calmly said, "We don't need this silliness. I'll go with you. Quietly, even."

Baxter relaxed his grip on the nightstick. "Cuff him, Simmons," he said. Chick held his arms out and allowed him to place the bracelets on his wrists.

"You got anything in a yellow gold?" asked Chick.

"No more smart shit," said Baxter.

"Mind if I chuckle to myself if I think of something funny?" Chick said. "Like your ACT scores?"

"Get in the car, asshole."

"I love it when you talk dirty."

The deputy escorted Chick to the unit. Held the top of Chick's head as he helped him into the back of the unit. There was a screen between the backseat and the front.

The sheriff moved closer to me, leaned into my face. "You watching this, hotshot?" His breath was hot on my face. "Learn something from it. This is my county now, and you're stinking it up."

"You're so lyrical," I said.

"Don't fuck with me, Storme."

"That cuts both ways, Leslie."

We stared at each other for a long moment, like two high school kids in a schoolyard. His eyes were bloodshot and mean, the bad eye, malevolent and dark. Finally, he backed away.

"I'll follow you down, Chick," I said.

"Do what you like," said Baxter. "But nobody talks to or sees him 'til tomorrow afternoon."

"That's crap."

He smiled at my rising anger, spat tobacco on my shoes, and got in his car. They drove away, leaving me on the sidewalk with a bottle of Mezcal and some Mexican beer I wasn't going to drink. Tobacco spit on my shoes. I felt impotent and stupid.

I put the beverages in the Bronco and walked to an open-air pay phone. The street was quiet and deserted. I thought of the old joke about pulling the streets up after dark, but didn't laugh. Downtown Paradise was almost gone. Drained of its life by shopping malls, corporate discount chain stores, dual-lane highways, and recession. No jobs and few businesses. The American Dream. Gone without even leaving a high-water mark on the buildings. Mortgaged tomorrows for today. Then tomorrow came.

There was a sadness to it and no joy in its realization.

If Alan Winston could restore the downtown, then more power to him.

I called information and got Jill Maxwell's number. Called it. Her recorder answered and I hung up. A few blocks away I heard a horn honk and echo. I called information again and got the number of the newspaper. I dialed that number and asked for her.

"I'm sorry," said a female voice. "Jill's on vacation."

I asked when she would return and the voice said two weeks. That made no sense. I hung up and dialed the Days Inn and asked for Sam Browne. Finally, something went right. He answered.

"What's up, Storme?"

"Chick's been arrested," I said.

"Who?"

"Friend of mine. Chick Easton. Baxter cuffed him, said he wanted to question him about the sheriff's murder. What do you know about it?"

"Nothing. The name never came up. I got a message you called earlier. What did you need?"

I told him about the vanished marijuana. Being shot at. He said they hadn't had time to get out to the field yet. He asked why I hadn't reported it.

"I don't trust Baxter. The last time I made a report someone was killed. And my name leaked out despite assurances from the murder victim." I told him of my visit to the newspaper and my talk with Jill Maxwell. I told him about her sudden vacation. "Somebody's damming the swamp. I've been shot at, Chick's been arrested, and Jill takes an unscheduled vacation. Bad things are happening to people I talk to, including the sheriff."

"Maybe the girl planned the vacation."

"No way. She'd never let go of something like this. Too hungry. Too good a reporter." I told him of my visit with Willie Boy Roberts and Chick's observation of Alan Winston. It failed to make him happy.

"What the hell are you doing? You stay out of this investigation."

"What did we do? I can't apply for a job, and Chick can't visit a public courtroom?"

There was a silence at the other end. I was beginning to think he'd hung up when he said, "You amateurs are going to stir up a hornet's nest. You can't go around burning the locals."

"So, what have you got?" I asked.

"That information is privileged. You know that."

"You've got squat. I know Roberts is linked to the marijuana field because of the dog."

"Doesn't do me any good. Where's the dog now? Your word against his. We know Roberts is a bad actor, but he's never been arrested or indicted for anything. Not even a speeding ticket. His sheet is clean. We can't move on him until we've got something solid. The information you've given me is interesting, but you don't just jump on a guy like Roberts without everything in place."

"Roberts is going to run you in circles. Eventually, you'll leave town. He knows that. Or whoever shot Kennedy knows that, too. You guys leave and it'll be back to business as usual."

"I should arrest you for interfering in a homicide investigation," he said, then there was another pause. "But…there *is* something to what you're saying. Roberts smells of something. Something familiar and out of place here. He doesn't seem like a businessman. We're running into blocks when we try to run Roberts's background. Federal blocks. They won't tell us why.

Look, I'll check on the girl and the big goon, Cugat, and try to get out to the marijuana site. But you back off. Do you understand?"

I agreed to. Better off in his hands. I thought about Sandy. Bail Chick out, grab the chemist and head back to Colorado, and let the wheels of justice turn. I could always come back. Then I thought about Jill Maxwell. What if she never turned up? What if I couldn't get Chick out of jail? Or, if I could, would they let him leave town? I asked Browne if he could do something to cut Chick loose.

"You *are* crazy," he said. "McKinley will fry my butt if I stick my nose in…" He paused. I heard him sigh. "What the hell. See what I can do. Maybe I can find something out. I didn't want to make sergeant anyway. What would I do with the extra money? Easton may have done things you know nothing about, you know."

No doubt about that, I thought.

"Meanwhile," he said, "get him a lawyer and keep out of this. As for Roberts, I've heard some things. He isn't anybody to push. You could end up with a permanent limp."

"You think he's capable of that?"

"Yes."

"Murder?"

"Damn," he said. "You don't listen, do you? That's all you get. Head back to the mountains. You're a pain in the butt." He hung up, loudly.

As he did, I noticed a brown Chevrolet pickup making its third circuit of the block. It had tinted windows. Couldn't see inside. I memorized the license number and filed it away. Was I becoming paranoid? Like the comedian says, "Just because you're paranoid, doesn't mean everybody's not really out to get you."

I dialed Jill's number again. The electric voice of the answering machine started up and I broke the connection. I didn't want to leave my voice and name on tape at this point. While trying to think what to do next I'd forgotten about the pickup. A mistake.

I felt a hand, a big one, on the back of my neck. It squeezed and my head exploded into little spiders of pain. Another hand gripped my belt and I felt myself being lifted. He grabbed my collar and hustled me down the sidewalk, my feet touching the ground intermittently. I weigh over two hundred pounds and he was handling me like a sack of feed. I struggled, reaching back to break the hand loose from my jacket, but couldn't. He was too strong. I kicked back with my heel and caught a leg, but it was a glancing blow and did little damage.

He shoved me into a darkened doorway and slammed me into the wall. The feeling of helplessness was pervasive. I was at the mercy of this powerful force behind me. I felt the rough contour of brick scrape my face. He drove a meaty fist into my kidneys, and for a brief moment I was afraid I would wet my pants like a child. He cuffed me with an open hand and the inside of my head erupted into a nightfall of diamonds. Consciousness pinwheeled away from me. As my head cleared I saw the face of the giant from Roberts's office. He said something that bounced puttylike in my ears. My head was hazy, as if clouds of steel wool were clogging my thought processes.

"...where you're not wanted," he said. "Smartasses can get stomped and shoved in a culvert around here." He picked me up and slammed me down roughly on my feet. My teeth clacked together and my damaged knees felt like glass had shattered within them. My head smacked against the wall again. I couldn't take much more. There was no fear, just the realization I had to stop this.

His breath was on my face now, and it smelled of beer and tomato sauce. He had me by the front of my jacket with both hands. A voice behind him said, "Fuck 'im up, Cugie. S'matter, shithead? Nothin' funny to say?"

My head cleared. In the bigs you played with pain. Played through the pain. It was irrelevant to the task. I raised both arms and brought them down heavily against his forearms, which brought his face close to mine. Then I drove my forehead into his mouth and nose. I heard something crunch and pop like stepping on popcorn. I lifted my hands from his arms and lashed out with the back of my right hand, catching him on the mouth. I followed that with my left elbow, driving it hard against the side of his chin.

He bellowed, letting go of my jacket to put his hand to his face. I felt something warm and damp on my forehead. I fought the fog drifting into my brain and staggered from the doorway. There was a form in front of me. Much smaller than the other man. Felt raw knuckles on my shoulder. I drove on through the man as if breaking a tackle. I needed to get away. The small man crumpled before me like a card castle. Must be near the goal line, I thought. I staggered three steps and fell against a parked car.

I slid down. Down…

THIRTEEN

"We're concerned about your conduct with the media," said the voice of Richmond Butler, vice president of the Dallas Cowboys. His voice came at me from somewhere behind the too-large desk as he smoked a too-big Jamaican cigar.

"I don't conduct myself with them," I heard my voice say. It was disembodied and hovering somewhere above me. "I don't talk to them. I nod. I grunt. I take my shower."

"That's the problem, son," Butler said. He leaned forward. His face grew. Too much nose. Not enough chin. "You won't talk to them. Why the mystery? What does it hurt to talk to them? It's league policy and it's good PR. As a Cowboy, you are part of this organization, and as part of this family it is your responsibility to promote the Dallas Cowboys."

"I do promote them. Every Sunday afternoon."

His face was warping, twisting out of shape. "We pay you a hell of a salary. You owe us."

"No," I said, rising to leave. "I owe you nothing. You didn't buy me. You rent my skills. Nothing else. You don't get me. I belong to Christ and myself and I can walk out of here anytime."

Butler laughed and his too-large diamond winked in the artificial light. "Where are you gonna make the kind of money we pay you?"

I laughed back at him, and it felt good. "You think I do it for the money."

"What other reasons you got?"

"If you have to ask," I said, quoting Louis Armstrong, "you'll never know."

He gestured with the cigar, and it flamed at the end like a torch. "You made a deal with us. You are what we say you are. That's your job."

"I don't have a job. I play a part. And whatever part I try to play, it's obvious that the person who plays that part never suited up for the game."

Richmond Butler's office dissolved into the hard pavement of a Paradise sidewalk. A female voice spoke and I felt soft hands against my face. I was in a movie and the heroine was kneeling over me, asking if I was all right. I forgot my lines and looked into the wonderful bone structure of Tempestt Finestra. Her eyes were large and green and soft. I reached up and touched her cheek and she kissed my palm. Despite my condition I felt stirrings inside. Not good. Sandy.

"My God," she said, and her voice resonated inside my head, bouncing off jagged peaks and canyons that hadn't been there before. "Are you all right?"

"You ready for that cup of coffee now?" I said, then laughed, which made my head hurt. Always on. Ever the performer.

"You've got blood all over you," she said.

"Is it mine?"

"Whose should it be? We need to get you to a hospital."

"No. Wait." I sat up and took inventory. Moved my arms and torso. Took a deep breath. Dull pain in the ribs. Probably bruised. One ear hurt, and there was soreness in my back. I put a hand to my head and felt a sticky substance. Blood. Not mine, though. At least I didn't think it was mine. "You see any cuts on my head?" I asked.

She examined my hairline and looked closely at my face. "Some small cuts. Some abrasions. Nothing deep. But you need to see a doctor to make sure. The hospit—"

"No," I said. "No hospital." I wasn't being stubborn. Well, maybe a little. But I knew when I was hurt badly enough to need a doctor. I'd been hit harder and more often on several occasions. But it had been some time since anyone had handled me so easily. They were teaching me. Little demonstrations. First Chick, then me. I didn't like it but didn't know what I could do about it. "I'm okay. Nothing broken. No major cuts. I'll be sore in the morning, that's all."

She helped me stand. There was a roaring in my ears, like the sea in a conch shell, and I sucked in my breath at the pain in my ribs. It was annoying, not intolerable.

"You see a big guy?" I asked. "Bald head?"

"There were two of them. He was one of them."

"What did the other one look like?"

"Skinny guy. Needed a shave. Arm in a cast." Had to be my buddy Luke.

"You recognize either of them?"

"Yes. They work for Mr. Roberts."

"Why would an upstanding businessman like Roberts employ so many thugs?"

"I don't know what their job description is. I'm just a secretary. I don't know everything that's going on."

I let that pass. "Was the big guy bleeding?"

"Yes."

"Good."

She gave me a severe look. Even in the weak light the cheekbones were wonderful. "That make you happy?"

"It'll do," I said. "For now. How did you get here?"

She looked blank for a moment. "What?" she asked, balking. She'd heard the question. I repeated it.

"I was driving by and saw you fall against the car. Why were those men beating you up?"

"I voted for McGovern in '72."

"I ought to leave you here in the street," she said.

"But you didn't."

"No." Her eyes softened. "I didn't. We need to get you home if you're not going to the hospital. Where do you live?"

"I'm all right." I took a couple of steps, swaying as I did. "Maybe not."

"I'll take you home," she said.

"I can drive myself."

"You're stubborn."

"But I'm very clean."

"I'll follow you."

"It's a long way." She turned on her heat-vision eyes. Not going to win this one. "Okay," I said. "Good idea."

It was dark when we arrived at the cabin. She helped me out of the truck and into the house. I didn't fight it. I was exhausted. My ribs were on fire, and my face was scraped raw and it hurt. I had some Percodan I used occasionally for my knees and an old shoulder injury. Football players are the biggest prescription junkies in the world. Couple of tabs and I'd be copacetic. I didn't usually use drugs, but it would stop the pain and help me sleep.

She helped me to the couch, and her perfume filled my head. She was beautiful. Glorious. I felt the tug of her. Steady, Wyatt. She walked behind the kitchen bar and made a couple of drinks. I smelled the heady wood aroma of bourbon. On the rocks. She brought them over, and I shook my head. A mistake. "Just water," I said.

She drank part of her drink, then poured mine into her glass and walked to the kitchen to get a glass of water. While she did that I walked to the bathroom. I opened the medicine cabinet, reached inside it to get a brown, opaque bottle, shook two tablets into my hand, and returned to the den.

"What are those?" she asked.

"Painkillers. I couldn't find a bullet to bite."

"You said you were okay."

"I am. Big day tomorrow."

She brushed back the hair from my forehead. "Why were they trying to hurt you?"

Back to that question. You're getting suspicious in your old age, Storme. "I'm not sure," I said, being evasive. It didn't make me feel gallant, lying to her, but I didn't really know her, though I liked what I had seen so far.

"People don't get mugged for no reason. You must've done something."

"Can't think what it might be."

"You don't trust me," she said.

"Do you trust me?"

She considered me with her emerald eyes. A smile grew in them. "You're very evasive."

"And you're very inquisitive. And intelligent. I like intelligent. You've also done work besides secretarial." For a brief moment her eyes looked panicked. Maybe my imagination. Why did it seem as if everyone I met had something to keep back? Or maybe everybody does have something to keep back and I didn't realize it. Things like girls dressed like men, but who could make you just as dead as a man could. Little girls with guns, on another planet, in another dimension, gnawing at my dreams, at my conscience.

"Most people fall apart when they see blood, or men running from the scene of an assault. Not you." And why had they run away? I wondered. "You were composed. Checked me for injuries. Knew what to look for. Followed me home."

"So I could seduce you," she said. She smiled, then searched my eyes.

"Flattering, but I don't think that's your entire motivation. You knew there was a possibility I was injured worse than I thought. But how could you know I am two hundred pounds of tungsten steel? Or that I still have a hundred thousand miles left on my warranty?"

"Stay away from them," she said. She reached out and took my hand in hers. Then she sat on the couch, pulling me lightly down with her. The touch of her hand had the warmth of friendship yet the heat of an effortless sexuality. Smooth, dark skin. Health that radiated like a highly tuned engine. Chopin's "Heroic" was playing on the stereo. "Stay away from Starr Industries. You don't know what you're getting into. They are evil men."

"What's going on at Starr? Do you know something you're not saying?"

"No. I just know you should avoid them."

"Who is the big guy?"

"If I tell you, how do I know you won't go looking for him?"

"I'm going to look up a guy big as a rhino?"

"Yes. I believe you would."

"I've already met him. Even know his name. But why is he working for Roberts?"

"I guess I could ask why you're so interested in Starr Industries."

"You could ask," I said.

She smiled. "You may remember Cugat as the Sultan. Sultan Cugat. Real name is Faron Cugat. Pro wrestler. Had to quit when he nearly killed a promoter who owed him money."

Faron Cugat. He'd been with Atlanta for a couple of years. I remembered him now, because he was big even by NFL standards. Six feet nine inches and 325 pounds of bad attitude. Drummed out of the league for testing positive—steroids, cocaine, booze—anything he could inject, absorb, or swallow. A huge pharmaceutical test animal. During a preseason game he'd instigated a brawl with our offensive line. It took several minutes to subdue him. None of his teammates came to his rescue. Gerald Robinson, a friend of mine who played for Atlanta, told me after the game, "Cugie so full of Peres and 'roids, babe, you coulda performed eye surgery on him at halftime and he wouldn't even blink."

After leaving the NFL he'd wrestled as the Sultan. Turban on his shaved head and a harem of girl attendants. Silly stuff. But it is a mistake to underestimate pro wrestlers. The wrestling is fake, but they are still amazing athletes.

"Why were you driving down that street?" I asked Tempestt. "Nothing there but closed shops and bars. Not exactly on your way home."

"Time for you to get some sleep," she said.

Then we were quiet two beats too long. An awkward two beats. Chopin was building in the background. A man and a woman alone. Miles alone, and aware of each other. Feeling the presence of one another. She touched my cheek. Her hand was light and healing against my raw skin. She kissed me. I let her. I fell for miles into her scent, her soul, felt her firmness against me. We parted and I held her at arm's length, where I could look at her. She said, "I'll help you to bed."

I didn't argue. I could've navigated it by myself but enjoyed being babied by this beautiful woman. She walked me to my room. I sat on the bed and she sat beside me. Kissed me again, and again I allowed it. Pulled her to me. The Percodan and events of the day started to work on me. I lay down. She put her head on my chest, and I fell asleep with the scent of her buzzing in my head.

But I dreamed of Sandy.

FOURTEEN

I woke to the smell of bacon and coffee. The crimson digits of the clock radio read 6:47. The residue of the Percodan had settled into my joints, creating a drugged lethargy. Still had my clothes on, but she must have removed my shoes. I wandered into the front room. Tempestt had set the table for two. Scrambled eggs, bacon, and pancakes on the table. It looked and smelled wonderful. There was a dull ache in my ribs and head.

"Good morning," she said. "I hope you didn't mind me staying overnight." She was wearing one of my sweatshirts and a smile. Her long, smooth-muscled legs disappeared into the ribbed border of the sweatshirt. It made her appear smaller, lighter. Never looked that good on me.

"Good cooks and people who save my life are always welcome," I said. I was a little uncomfortable. The morning light made me think of Sandy. "I…a…where did you—"

"In the guest bedroom, prudence," she said, but smiled. "Your virtue is intact. Darn it. Maybe you won't be so lucky next time."

I sat down at the table. I was famished. Hadn't eaten for eighteen hours. She was a good cook. Knew how to make good coffee, also. Not too strong, not too weak. Just right. She was just right, too. Maybe I would marry her, though that might hamper my relationship with Sandy. I liked her. I don't shop for women. I looked for people. I'm no feminist sympathizer. There were few of the good ones of either sex; people with the right combination of courage, compassion, and morality. Intelligence.

And intelligence is more than acquired facts and knowledge. Intelligence comes from insight, from inner courage, experience, and conviction. People talk about what they want and who they are; few are concerned with duty and responsibility—the things we must do to be what we are. The things that separate us from animal instincts and lust and greed, that make us human, flawed though we all may be.

"You're a good cook," I said, between bites. She had great legs. Magnificent legs. I tried not to wolf my food. Maybe if I could distract her momentarily, I could stick it all in my mouth at once. I made a conscious effort not to smack my lips. The essence of her was powerful.

"Thank you. I do several things well, but I'm getting no offers around here." She smiled a brilliantly wicked smile. Dazzling. She took a nibble of bacon. So much girl, such small bites.

"The best things shouldn't be rushed," I said. "Are you free this evening?"

"What did you have in mind?"

"Dinner. Stimulating conversation. Dancing 'til dawn. Maybe a little more Chopin by the fireplace."

"A little wine, maybe?"

"I don't partake."

"Maybe you should."

I looked into her jeweled irises. I really liked her. She was special. I enjoyed her company. There was something wrong with a business where someone with her talent was only a secretary, which made me wonder about something else. So I asked.

"What's a nice girl like you doing—"

"Working for scum like Roberts?" she finished for me. I nodded. "Won't be for much longer. I'll be leaving soon."

"He know that?"

"No. I hope not, anyway." Strange answer. "Not yet, anyway. You finish eating. Eat all you want. I've got to get to work." She walked over and wriggled into my lap, leaving no room for appetite, though I was still hungry. She kissed my eyes and then my mouth, then stood up. Always leave 'em wanting more, I guess. I grabbed her wrist and pulled her back. Kissed her again. What to do with her?

She leaned back. "Tonight," she said. "I have to go now." She left me to change clothes. I didn't know how she expected me to eat if I couldn't swallow. There was a knot in my throat and a larger one in my chest. I was confused, uncertain.

I finished breakfast and was rinsing the dishes when she came out of the guest room, wearing last night's clothing. She walked over to me. She smelled of soap and musk.

"God, you're cute when you do domestic chores," she said.

"I have a varied repertoire. Oughta see me unclog a pipe. Pure artistry."

"Gotta go, slugger," she said. "You need to get something on that scrape. Stay out of street fights. Please take care of yourself." She was telling me something or trying to tell me something, but it lay between the lines of what she was saying. Obscure, yet plaintive. She was worried about something. Something about me. It was in her voice and eyes.

"I'm a big boy," I said.

"And I'm a big girl." She touched my face. "This seems a little foolish, but sometimes people aren't what they seem or what they wish."

"And sometimes they are more than what is seen." I thought about it. Like Sandy, Tempestt wasn't telling me everything. I said, "What are you holding back from me?"

We looked at each other. "Maybe nothing," she said. "What are you holding back from me?"

"I'm in love with someone," I said. "There's nothing I can do about that."

"I know." She reached up and adjusted my collar. "And there's nothing I can do about what you can't know."

"I like you," I said.

She smiled, then kissed me on the cheek and said, "Until tonight, then."

She opened the door and left, and the room diminished with her departure. I looked at the door and the finality of its closing. For three months my heart had lain dormant, cobwebbed and echoing the hurt of each beat. I felt something for Tempestt. But I had no illusions about being what she was looking for. I wasn't. But maybe I could survive without Sandy. I didn't want to and hoped I would never have to, but it was a comfort to have hope that I could. I was uncertain of the direction of my relationship with Tempestt. I knew where the stop sign was, but not where the curves would be leading to it, or if I would see them in time.

Nothing is for sure.

I cleaned the dishes and thought about Chick's predicament. I wasn't worried about him but was ill at ease with my inability to help. I called a lawyer I knew. George Fairchild. George did some legal work for the Kansas City Chiefs. He was a friend. He'd helped me negotiate my first pro contract. Pointed out where I was selling myself short. I was young and eager to sign anything. Trusting. I grew out of it soon enough. They were good at teaching you that. "I just want to play football," I told George.

"And you will," said George. "But cheaply gained is cheaply prized. The more they invest initially, the greater will be their desire to see you succeed. Nobody likes to think they got a bad deal. And you're not a used car."

George Fairchild was a straight shooter in a profession where his colleagues shot from around corners and hid behind the law and used "the law" as a sick synonym for the word "justice." I liked him. And he owed me a favor. George had a daughter who lived in Boulder. She was pretty. And smart. And talented in the area of business acumen. She was a loan officer at a bank. A man she had turned down for a loan was annoying her, following her to work, calling her at work and at home. Sitting in his car outside her apartment at night. The police said they could do nothing until he did something. George asked me to help. I turned it around on the guy. I started following him. Calling him. Sitting in my car outside *his* apartment. Finally, I convinced him. He became cooperative. I'm a convincing guy. George appreciated it.

When I called Fairchild and explained the situation he was glad to help. "I'll drive down," he said. George was a busy man. He could have sent one of the young lawyers who worked for him and I would've been satisfied. But George was from the old school. "Should be there by late morning. Unless he murdered the governor's daughter I'll have him out by early afternoon. If he murdered the governor's daughter it'll be early evening."

I thanked him and hung up, feeling a little better.

I called Jill Maxwell again and got the recorder again. Didn't leave a message. The police didn't have a thing, yet every time I turned around, someone threw an obstacle in my path, or, as it turned out, in Chick's path.

Who shot at us? And why? Roberts? I didn't think so. If Roberts had sent someone they would have been better marksmen. It was sloppy and amateurish.

I finished the dishes and showered. Did some household chores. I was pulling on a pair of boots when the phone rang. I picked it up.

"It's me," I said. "Start talking."

"Need to talk to you, Storme," said a voice. It was reedy and smothered as if the caller were talking through a straw. How did he get this number?

"Who is this?"

"I know about the marijuana field."

"What do you know?" I asked.

"Not on the phone. I'll meet you."

"When and where?"

"Got a pen?"

"I'll remember," I said.

"1405 East Twelfth Street. Two o'clock this afternoon. It's unlocked. Let yourself in and wait."

"For what? A bullet in my back?"

"You're in no danger," said the voice. "At least, not from me." The accent was familiar, but I couldn't place it. Voice was disguised. "There's some bad shit going down, though. I have to talk to you. You're my last hope."

"How'd you get my number?"

He broke the connection.

I looked at the clock. It was 10:30. Plenty of time to phone Sandy, then get to town and spring Chick. I wanted to call Sandy, to help assuage some of the guilt I was beginning to feel, but I called Sam Browne first.

"This is Browne," he said, answering.

"Storme," I said. "What did you find out about Easton?"

"Held for questioning, like you said. It's bogus, though. Easton's not connected to the murder. I couldn't get much from Baxter. But I expected that. Said he was operating on a tip. I think he brought Easton in to make it look like he's doing something. Said he didn't have to report to me like a high school kid. He's a joy to work with. I tried to connect with Sergeant McKinley, but he'd already headed back to Troop A. Pulled out."

"What do you mean, pulled out?"

"We had a warrant out for a guy named Killian. Local dealer. The warrant was for the murder of Sheriff Kennedy. We found Killian in a two-ton truck loaded with marijuana. Bullet hole behind the ear. It was your buddy from the field. He had a wound in his right shoulder. Like an arrow wound. We think he killed Kennedy because he'd discovered the field and was going to shut it down. Killian had a partner named Dexter. Dexter murdered Killian and took off. That's the official line, anyway."

My ribs hurt. "How'd you find out about Killian and Dexter?"

"Anonymous tip. If you can get Easton out of jail, you can head back to Colorado anytime."

"Where's the rest of the crop? There was a lot more marijuana than a truck that size could handle. Why would Dexter ace Killian?"

"The theory is they tried to double-cross each other."

"What kind of gun did Dexter use to do Killian?"

"Twenty-two caliber. Close range. Right behind the ear. Quick. Clean."

"What kind of gun killed the sheriff?"

"You writing a book?"

"Make you the hero of it if you tell me how they did the sheriff."

"Shotgun. Pellets were number-two buckshot. There was a twelve-gauge Remington pump in the truck with Killian, along with a box of number twos."

"Surprised you didn't get a videotape and a signed confession from both of them. Pretty convenient. Was the truck automatic or stick shift?"

"Stick. What are you getting at, Storme?"

"Twenty-two caliber at close range is a pro job. You know that. And then you find a shotgun and the proper-sized buckshot in the truck with a dead suspect. Guess he won't be saying much in his own behalf. You ever drive a two-ton truck with a stick shift? How does a guy with a shoulder wound drive a rig like that? Why did his partner run? If he dropped the gun off a bridge there would be nothing to connect him. Why not just blast him with a shotgun, make sure? How does he know anybody's coming after him? Almost a sure thing now. You think he had an audience when he shot the guy?

"Another thing," I said. "No burnout with a shotgun could take Kennedy. I saw the drug dealer eye to eye. He wasn't a shooter. Kennedy was a pro, a hard man who'd survived in this sewer of a town for a long time. You ever fire a shotgun with a deep wound in your shoulder? Ever shoot one with your weak hand? Killian couldn't even hold a gun after I stuck him."

"Here's what I know," said Browne, a little exasperated. "I'm out. They, somebody, has tied this up in a neat little package with a pretty bow and mailed it special delivery to us. I've been ordered to vacate by noon today. We've got pressure on us from above. A state senator named Hobbs. You're right. This is too pat. Too sweet. McKinley didn't like it, either. He bitched to the head shed in Jeff City, not something we do much if we want to go far. We're trying to get back on this thing, but right now we've been ordered to back off. And you've got an attitude problem. We just do what we're told. But I'm not done yet. In a week or so, we'll start pushing back."

I told him about being assaulted by Cugat. About the call from the mystery man.

"Storme, get out of this. This is dangerous shit. Give it to the authorities and get out."

"I am. I'm giving it to you. But to you only. Anybody else asks me, I won't talk."

"All right. We'll play it your way. All I can do. Another thing. The guy you're hanging around with. Easton? I ran some background on him. Got a strange report. We don't have a thing on him before 1976. Not even a driver's license. It's like he landed here on a spaceship for the Bicentennial. Hell, we can't even get his social security number. The guy doesn't exist before then. Everything's classified. If I were you I'd clear town…and without Easton. He's bad news."

"I disagree."

"Suit yourself. Watch your ass."

I thanked him. I dialed Sandy's number and there was no answer. Called the television station and they said she hadn't come in yet. I felt a small rush of relief. I thought about Tempestt. Could still smell her perfume.

Somehow, I needed to uncomplicate my life.

I had just poured myself a fresh cup of coffee when two guys with short haircuts, suits, and London Fog raincoats knocked on my door.

"We'd like to speak with you, Mr. Storme," said the taller of the pair.

"No thanks. I don't want to be a Mormon."

"We're not Mormons," he said. "I'm Special Agent Morrison of the FBI. May we come in?"

FIFTEEN

"You guys got membership cards?" I asked.

They flashed photostats. Tall, dark, and boring was FBI like he said, but didn't look like Efrem Zimbalist, Jr. Life is one disappointment after another. The other guy was blond, early thirties. Capped teeth. DEA. Looked like he belonged to a fitness club. One with a tanning bed. He lifted weights, too. I had weights of my own, back in Colorado. They were gathering dust in my basement but weren't costing me two hundred a month to do so. Of course, it was tough to meet single girls in your basement. And it wasn't very chic.

I let them in. Always was a sucker for handsome government men. They sat in the den and looked around the room, searching with their eyes for foreign spies or secret panels, not realizing I'd had all the secret panels nailed shut only the week before. I offered them coffee, which the tall guy, Morrison, accepted. Agent Candless, the only beachboy in Missouri, asked if it was decaffeinated.

"No," I said. "It's not. No sugarless gum, either."

"I don't do caffeine."

"Would you care to see a menu?"

They looked at each other. I waited for one of them to say, "Just the facts, ma'am." Didn't happen. I poured a cup of coffee for Morrison and brought it back to him. He wasn't as persnickety as his partner, even spooning sugar into it. Caffeine and sugar. Born to be wild. I sat down with my coffee. Leaned back and smiled, winningly. The perfect host.

"Mr. Storme—" began the FBI man.

"Please," I said. "Call me Wyatt. All the other G-men do." I didn't know why they were here. They didn't have a warrant. My place. Hadn't asked them to come.

Morrison smiled and drank some coffee. Cool. He looked like a coffee advertisement. However, Candless pursed his lips and frowned as if I were a boring child they had to watch until its parents came home from bowling. They looked at each other again. Maybe they were telepathic. You never knew what advances the government was making.

"Why are you in Missouri at this time, Mr. Storme?"

"Bowhunting. Whitetail deer."

"Do you know Chick Easton?"

"I know him."

"How well?"

"Just met him. He's going back to Colorado with me."

"When?"

"Soon."

"We'd like precise answers," Candless said, breaking in.

"Okay. It's none of your business, that's when we're leaving." I didn't like being questioned without knowing why.

Candless's jaw worked, and I saw a knot of muscle at the juncture of his mandible. "We know you met him in the Silver Spur Lounge three days ago. The day Sheriff Kennedy was killed." He pulled a small black leather notebook from his coat pocket. A large diamond winked from a ring on his right hand. He was wearing a Rolex watch. DEA must pay pretty well, I thought. "4:03 p.m. Subject enters Silver Spur Lounge, Paradise, Missouri. 5:47. A man enters lounge and sits down with subject. The second man is Wyatt Storme, a former—"

"That got your initials on it?" I asked, meaning the notebook. He gave me a pained look. "Nice," I said. "Why are you checking on Easton?"

"We know you were the last people to talk to Kennedy before he was killed," Candless said, ignoring my question. I hate a one-way street.

"You deduce that from your notes?" I said.

"Maybe you killed him."

"Was there a zodiac sign carved in his stomach?"

"What?" Candless said, rather sharply, I thought. A rude man.

"I always carve a zodiac sign in their stomach with a Bowie knife when I do somebody. My trademark."

"Funny guy, aren't you?" He glared at me with hot eyes. Since there was little else to do, I glared back at him. It was kind of fun to work out on a manic-depressive who unwisely soaked his flesh in ultraviolet rays.

"Take it easy, Candless," Morrison said. "Listen, Storme, we're not getting anywhere like this. There's nothing to be gained by baiting Agent Candless."

"It has some recreational value," I said.

"We have a few concerns about you, Storme," Candless said. He smiled as if he had just moved his knight into a fork position. "For one, how are you able to afford the place in Colorado, plus this place, when you have no visible means of support? What you have in your bank account won't last forever. For another, how did you manage to come across that marijuana field? Why are you hanging around with a skip-tracer with a dossier like Easton's?"

I shrugged in response. Probably wouldn't be considered a precise answer. Candless leaned forward and gave me a tough cop look. When I forgot to clap my hands to my face and fall to pieces, he said, "We know everything about you, Storme."

"Yeah? What's my favorite color? Do I sleep on my stomach or my back? Who did I take to the junior prom?"

"We know you broke a guy's ribs two years ago with a baseball bat but he wouldn't file charges."

The guy didn't file charges because he couldn't. He was running a protection racket. Tried to squeeze a friend of mine. I talked with the guy and hammered out a mutually beneficial deal. I wanted him to lay off my buddy, and he didn't want shattered kneecaps. Compromise, the keystone of industry.

"You make a hobby of little incidents like that. You have a masked-avenger mentality. We also know you talked to a local reporter who has subsequently disappeared. You got a lot to answer for, Storme. Everybody you come into contact with suddenly meets misfortune. That, and your relationship with Easton is suspect. You come to town, the sheriff is killed, then you think you're Travis McGee, asking questions and annoying people in the community."

"Aw, shucks. It was nothing."

"Your presence here and your activities are highly suspicious. You reported the marijuana field to Sheriff Kennedy, yet you were suspected of smoking marijuana while in Vietnam."

"I didn't inhale. You see, there was this guy from Arkansas who taught me how to—"

"Can it," said Candless. "Maybe we need to arrest you and make you answer—"

"Now, Dan," Morrison said, using his best Fred MacMurray voice. "There's no reason to badger Mr. Storme. We just need to talk with him, that's all. No need to threaten. We can do this without having to take him in."

Aw, gee, I thought, Bad Cop—Good Cop. This was comical, except for the fact they knew quite a bit. Several things, in fact. What else did they know?

"We're not here to pump you about the sheriff's homicide," Morrison said, setting down his coffee cup. "We know you're not involved in that. The highway patrol has a suspect—who's been found murdered himself, by the way. The reason we're here is to warn you off interfering with this investigation. We are closing in on a large-scale drug trafficking operation, and your free-lancing is ill advised and poorly timed. We must ask you to shy away from our investigation of Starr Industries."

"And to leave Alan Winston alone," said Candless.

"Who?" I said, playing coy. I can play coy with the best.

"We know Easton has been bird-dogging him."

"I forgot you knew everything about me."

Morrison seemed confused by Candless's statement. Why leave Winston alone? And why was Candless interested in Winston? Did it have anything to do with Browne's warning about people in high places? How much power did Alan Winston have? And what had I stumbled onto? Morrison continued:

"We have an agent inside Roberts's organization. We know he is running a crooked game and that he is the key to an interstate drug-distribution network. Sort of a way station. We also think he is building up to a big score, and you could jeopardize the whole operation."

"Yours," I said. "Or his?"

"You're small change for Roberts," said Candless. "A bump in the road, nothing more."

"What about the sheriff's murder?"

"A problem for the local authorities," said Morrison. "Not really our concern. We're familiar with their suspect. Name is Killian, a hard-core dealer whom we've been aware of for some time. We're happy to find him making such a big mistake and then getting himself removed from the board."

"Yeah, lucky you. Good thing he killed the sheriff when he did—if he did."

Morrison looked uncomfortable. "That was an unfortunate choice of words. I apologize."

"We're not the bad guys here," said Candless.

"Neither am I."

"Are you sure about Easton, though?"

"Yes."

Candless chuckled. There was no end to his irritating qualities. "There are people who'd disagree with your assessment."

"Didn't ask them," I said. "Didn't ask you, either."

"Mr. Storme…er, Wyatt," Morrison said. "As I was saying, we have someone under cover and the…ah…operation is at a delicate juncture. Your presence could create problems for our undercover agent, possibly to the point of compromising their cover."

"We've been working on this for six months," said Candless. "And we don't need some self-appointed vigilante messing it up."

What a sweetheart. Probably a Redskins fan. "Would you like some more coffee?" I asked Morrison. I didn't point out that "self-appointed vigilante" was redundant.

Morrison said, "Please." I rose and took his cup.

"Anything I can get you?" I said to Candless. "Carrot juice? Rubber hose? A personality?" He scowled at me. I poured the coffee and brought it back and sat down. Candless pulled a cigarette from a package of Trues. Hah! Couldn't drink anything with caffeine in it. Morrison continued:

"We've talked with a highway patrolman named Sam Browne. Quite a name for a trooper, actually. You see, the belt across—"

"It's called a Sam Browne."

"Ah…yes. Anyway, we talked with him and also conversed with a Colorado trooper named Younger who is familiar with you. Both said you were capable and resourceful—for a civilian. Younger said you were highly stubborn. Nevertheless, he said you were often, to quote him, a 'human hemorrhoid.' Browne said you were in over your head on this thing, and I must concur with his assessment. With Easton in the picture, especially. Something I had not foreseen. By now, you must have concluded that Easton possesses some rather peculiar, even remarkable, talents."

"What peculiar talents?"

The two government men looked at each other. Candless drew on his low-tar, caffeine-free, low-cal cigarette. Almost hadn't caught it in time. They were sharper than I had given them credit for. They were trying to squeeze me for information about Chick. It was Chick they were interested in.

"We checked you out thoroughly," said Morrison. "You keep to yourself. Decorated in Vietnam. Pro football player. You avoided the media. Very independent. Several run-ins with the front office, particularly a Mr. Richmond Butler. And now you have made enemies of some very influential people in Paradise."

"People not involved in the sheriff's homicide," said Candless. "Or in drug traffic."

"Like who?" I asked.

Candless looked at Morrison. "It's not important. But I'll tell you something, hot rod. You shouldn't associate with a spook like Easton. He's a juicer and a coward."

Spook. The word conjured up an image from Vietnam. It was what the grunts called CIA operatives. They were snake-eaters and crazies like the Green Berets. Was the word being used in some other connotation, or was that what Chick was or had been? It would explain many things. But, regardless, I didn't like Candless calling him a coward. Chick was anything but.

And he was a friend.

"Don't say anything else about Chick."

He laughed. "What'll happen if I do?"

"I'll be forced to make you desist."

His face reddened and he shot up from his seat. A hothead. "Go ahead, cowboy," he said. "Take a shot."

"Sit down, Dan!" Morrison said. This wasn't part of the script.

Candless pointed his finger at my face. I love that so much. "Keep talking, bigmouth, and I'll show you why you're out of your league. This isn't some country shit you're dealing with now. The referees won't be around to break it up, either. I'll mess up your whole day."

"*Sit down!*" shouted Morrison. I smiled at Danny-boy. He was bulled up like a gander. Something about me got under his skin. Couldn't understand it. I'd offered him coffee. No decaf, that must be it.

"Maybe he's not through scaring me," I said, standing.

"I've had enough of you, Storme."

"Use your head," I said. "I outweigh you thirty pounds and almost never microwave my flesh. So give it a rest, huh? Save it for the secretaries at the health club."

He went into a crouch. Fluid. Some kind of martial arts thing. These guys are overtrained. Nothing better to do than go around and beat up on ex-athletes with bad knees. What a waste. Probably took the whole course; could handle guys with knives, clubs, broken bottles, things like that. Probably wasn't any training regimen for hot coffee, though, so I pitched the contents of my cup into his eyes. Wasn't very sporting of me, but if he wanted a fair fight he could try someone else. He bellowed in pain and fell over his chair and tumbled onto the floor. I kept the coffee mug in hand, in case I had to throw it at him. Morrison jumped up and got between us.

"That's enough," said Morrison.

"Up to him," I said. Coffee dripped from Candless's face and clothes. "Don't get any on the furniture."

"Fuck you," he said. Maybe obscenity was part of the training, like a karate yell or something.

"Both of you need to get out of here," I said.

"I'm sorry about this, Storme," said Morrison. "We just wanted—"

"No. Game's over. You haven't been shooting me straight. I know things you want to know, but you're playing it like I was some brain-dead jock. You want to know about Chick Easton, but you're missing the big picture. Two men are dead and maybe a girl reporter, and Chick is in jail for no reason. If I'd been on this thing as long as you say you have and people were still running around killing people, I wouldn't tell anyone else how to handle it. Now, I know things you don't. Things you want to know. If you want it, then you'll have to tell me what I want to know and not just the abridged version. Otherwise, get Kung Fu cleaned up and leave. I've got no time for this crap."

Morrison's hands relaxed in resignation. I kind of liked him. Just doing his job. Candless, on the other hand, was just another bully with an expensive suit and a badge who'd seen too many Chuck Norris movies.

"Look," Morrison said. "Roberts is a ruthless sociopath, and there are others involved you don't know about. People you can't begin to imagine. People with political clout whom we might not be able to touch."

I thought a moment. Might be nice to have Morrison in my corner. Might be able to keep Baxter off my back. "I've got something you could use. Really use. But I give it to you it'll cost, and I'm not talking money. Information's what I want." I walked over to my desk, opened the drawer, and brought out the last little rock. I held it up for them. "Sheriff Kennedy had one like it, and now Sam Browne and the highway patrol have one."

Morrison's face changed, looking at me as if I'd just told him I'd memorized the formula for a secret rocket fuel. He moved so he was between me and Candless. "Where did you get this?"

"I had three. Got two off Killian, the guy they think killed the sheriff, and one off a local puke named Luke Hanson."

"Do you know what it is?" he asked.

"No."

"If it's what I think it is," he said, his eyes on the rock, "then it's the first sample we've managed to get our hands on."

"First sample of what?" I asked.

"Dreamsicle."

SIXTEEN

Danny-boy decided to be civil in exchange for information. I got him a damp towel from the bathroom and he dabbed at his suit with it. Then I broke the seal on a bottle of J&B scotch, the chosen beverage of Billy Clyde Puckett and Shake Tiller, and poured some over ice for both men. Peace offering. They accepted, as they were not on company time, an unspoken token to the urgency of their visit. I poured coffee for myself.

"You're not drinking with us?" asked Morrison.

"Gave it up for Lent," I said.

Morrison tasted the whiskey and studied me over the rim of the glass. He expressed satisfaction at its flavor, then said, "You're an interesting study, Storme."

"What is dreamsicle?" I asked.

They looked at each other. I really wanted them to stop that.

"On the West Coast and particularly in Hawaii the big-ticket item is a drug called ice. More potent than crack, with a higher street value, and as addictive. An individual addicted to ice becomes unpredictable, even dangerous. Crack is scary, but ice is worse." He paused, as if gathering wind. I waited.

"There has been a street rumor circulating that an outlaw chemist has developed a compound that is more addictive than either crack or ice, has a longer duration of effect, and is cheaper to manufacture." I thought about the guy Chick was trying to corral, the guy who had stolen the chemicals from the university. "Unlike crack, dreamsicle requires no paraphernalia, such as a pipe, to use it. Detection is tougher. It's so new we weren't even sure what form it would be used in. Then we got a break. One of our agents made a felony arrest. Interstate transportation of stolen goods. When he was bringing the perpetrator in, the guy kept complaining of a cough and dipping into his pockets for what he called 'cough drops.' The more cough drops he ate, the happier he became. He was flying by the time the agent figured out what was happening. When our agent asked for the cough drops, he swallowed the last one. The thing is, the guy was sucking on the things just like they *were* cough drops."

"Getting high off the vapors?"

"It appears so. At least initially. This guy has figured out how to make dreamsicle palatable and nearly undetectable, if that was a sample. They get an initial rush from the vapors. And then they milk the rush for several minutes. If you catch them with it, they just swallow. Once in the stomach, the drug is absorbed into the bloodstream through the stomach lining. There is nothing else like it. But most of what we know is conjecture and rumor. But if even part of it is reality, the person controlling the supply could become a multimillionaire virtually overnight. Unlike marijuana, which is large and bulky, dreamsicle could be carried like candy. Worse, we don't even know if the ingredients could be transported in their base form to mix at the site of distribution. This stuff is the fantasy of every punk on the street. It would replace crack as the drug of choice on the streets within a matter of weeks. Even days."

I sat back in my chair and chewed on it. Thought about Willie Boy Roberts. The way he heaped only the best things around him. Special coffee. Special cigars. A former pro wrestler–NFL lineman for protection, even though in a place like Paradise, Sultan Cugat was superfluous. Breck and Vance, the salt-and-pepper thugs, could handle anything around here. But having money and being the most powerful man in Paradise County meant little to Roberts. His businesses and holdings generated enough income to keep him in chicory and handmade cigars for a long time. Maybe it wasn't enough.

"Besides the money," I said, "how powerful would a man be who had control of such a product, its distribution and supply?"

"It's conceivable such a person could become one of the most powerful men in the country," answered Morrison thoughtfully. "Certainly, one of the most powerful criminals. But it would be difficult to keep out the Sicilians, the Colombians, the Chinese, and the Jamaicans. You would have to fight off the wolves."

"But if somebody could pull it off?"

"Then we have a nightmare scenario. We have one immediately if this stuff hits the streets, but one person controlling it might, by sheer force of the revenue generated, be able to pull together some of these factions. And if that happened…" He let it trail off. His eyes dropped, and his mouth constricted.

"So how does a guy like Roberts come across something like this?" I asked.

"I'm afraid I don't follow," said Morrison. "I didn't say Roberts had anything to do with this."

I looked at him and then at Candless. Their faces were impassive, blank with the mask that all feds learn to utilize. "Come on. You want me to stay away from Starr Industries. You've got a DEA man in tow, and I picked up three of these rocks, which by your account are rare, in a matter of days. This is your first sample, so this is the place they're coming from. Roberts has trucks, money, and muscle. It was his dog I killed in the marijuana field. Has to be Roberts. So we're back to the original question, the one you're dancing around: How does Willie Boy come across something like this? He wouldn't have the contacts or the knowledge to go big time. Willie is a big dog around Paradise, but so what? Unless there is more to Willie Boy Roberts than you want to say, and you think I know more than I want to say. So if we're going to trade, I want the straight skinny."

Morrison appeared lost in thought. He looked at Candless. The DEA man shrugged, said, "What difference does it make?"

"I agree," said Morrison, then he looked at me. "Willie Boy Roberts is an alias."

"Who is he, then?"

"Roberts is actually Max Beauchamps, a hired hitter from New Orleans, one of the best around in the late seventies. He came back from Vietnam and hired himself out to the loan sharks. Come up short on the vig and Max comes to see you."

"Leg breaker."

"Right. He graduated to mechanic work. Took a couple of out-of-town contracts, then he was arrested, ironically for a crime he didn't commit. The real perpetrator was a connected guy. Max kept his mouth shut and was prepared to take the fall, but a high-dollar lawyer showed up. A mob lawyer. Max got off. The Sicilians like a man who can take the heat, so they set Max up, even let him be a little independent. Let him have his quirks."

"What quirks?"

"They say he won't take a contract on a vet. And he likes it dangerous. Even dramatic. Likes to take it right to the edge, like it was the Old West. He especially liked to hit the Colombians and blacks. Max is more than a little of a racist. He liked shooting Colombians because of their reputation for violent retaliation. Legend has it he invited three brothers of a Colombian he killed to try to take him out. He even named a time and place. The brothers came, along with two soldiers—"

"And Max is still around," I said.

"But the brothers and the shooters aren't. They say he took out all five. Alone. Nobody knows how, but after that they left him alone. Supposedly, he didn't get a contract he wanted and offered to shoot it out with the hired man, the winner getting the contract."

"So what's he doing here? Sounds like he had it made in New Orleans. Why change his name?"

"In 1981 Max took a contract on William Boswell Roberts, but that isn't what precipitated the identity switch. Not directly, anyway. This is where the story gets interesting." Morrison pulled a pipe from his suit pocket, tamped some tobacco into it. A commercial interruption. "The real William Roberts was shot in front of an eyewitness." Morrison paused to light his pipe with a silver butane lighter. He sat back, took a puff. He was enjoying himself. The storyteller. He was waiting for me to ask, so I did.

"So why didn't they arrest Roberts, or Beauchamps, or whatever his name is?"

Morrison smiled. "The eyewitness was the wife of a key foreign diplomat."

I thought about that for a moment. "The diplomat hired Max to take out his wife's lover?"

Morrison nodded. "The government hushed it up, and we couldn't burn the diplomat because of his immunity. Nor could we go after Beauchamps for killing Roberts. Beauchamps outsmarted us."

Beauchamps had killed Roberts, and they knew it. And he had taken over Roberts's identity. So how did he get away with that? I asked them how that came about.

"Simple," said Morrison. "There is no William Roberts. He is fictitious."

SEVENTEEN

I had decided talking to these two was like going to the dentist. It was painful and you had to extract everything with pliers. "Who is Roberts, then? A cartoon character? A ventriloquist's dummy? Stop talking in riddles and get to it."

Morrison took a deep breath. He sipped his scotch. "Sorry. I am being a little obscure. The so-called real William Roberts was actually a former mob lieutenant named Mickey 'the Rodent' Scullzinni. Scullzinni rolled over on some of his former employers in exchange for immunity and a new identity in the witness protection program."

"So, Beauchamps shot a man who didn't exist in front of a witness who wasn't there on behalf of a man who couldn't be prosecuted, and now he's walking around with a spic-and-span ID provided by the government." I smiled, considering it.

"Not to mention," said Morrison, "he gets paid by the diplomat—and probably the mob as well—for killing one man with two names."

"Two contracts, one bullet? It has a certain symmetry when you think about it. Why doesn't the government just turn him out?"

Morrison massaged a spot between his eyebrows. "The witness protection program is under the jurisdiction of the U.S. Marshal's service. They have no love for the Bureau. Scullzinni's identity was brand-new when Beauchamps took him out. None of their people knew what Mickey the Rodent looked like. So Beauchamps just took Scullzinni's papers and reported to the

U.S. marshal in charge. By the time we sorted it out, it was too late. To the marshal's service, it's a reality that Beauchamps is Roberts and they must protect his identity. So now Roberts has two identities. Two sets of papers. We have no choice but to play along. Scullzinni was no loss. However, the whole episode is a little embarrassing."

"You're not worried I might let this story out? Why not?"

"First, there is your known dislike of the media. Also, no one would believe you if you were to tell. Besides, there is no way to connect Beauchamps to Roberts to Scullzinni, since Mickey no longer exists. A phony death certificate was arranged, along with a bogus autopsy report. I'm telling you for the sake of your safety and because you have helped us in your own…ah…singular fashion."

Candless added, "He means you haven't screwed it up too badly—yet."

I ignored him. "How long have you been following Roberts?"

Morrison explained that he hadn't really followed him here. Morrison had been stationed in New Orleans at the time Beauchamps made the identity switch. Two years ago Morrison had been promoted and transferred to Kansas City. He accidentally stumbled across Beauchamps-cum-Roberts while doing a check of a former special forces operative.

Click. "Chick Easton," I said.

"Yes."

"Why are you checking on him?"

"That's classified," Candless said.

"Agent Candless means it is not within our province to reveal the nature of the government's…ah…interest in Mr. Easton."

I set my coffee mug down. It was empty and clunked hollowly. "Why not just arrest him?"

"He has committed no crime," said Morrison. "None of which the Bureau is aware, that is."

I sat back and looked at them, smug and businesslike in their button-down suits, two federal agents who, on their day off, thought it necessary to drive twenty miles back to find out what I knew about Chick Easton. And about a strange new drug. What had I stumbled across? "If he's committed no crime, then why don't you back off?"

"We just do what we're told," said Morrison. "That's our job."

"Just good Germans, huh?" I searched his eyes. He blinked and looked away, uncomfortable.

"I don't expect you to understand," Morrison said apologetically. I was beginning to suspect he was human. "However, Easton possesses certain knowledge, information that could prove…ah…embarrassing. He worked for the government for a time and will not allow himself to be debriefed regarding his final mission."

"You mean Vietnam? Or something else?"

"I'm afraid I can't make that distinction for you."

"What is it about Chick that makes the federal government afraid?"

"There are certain organizations within the umbrella of the federal government that thrive on paranoia. They are not afraid of Easton, the man. They are afraid of Easton, the maverick."

"How long has this been going on?"

"Several years. Since 1975, in fact."

"Your tax dollars at work," I said, then thought about the absurdity of spending nearly two decades following a man who had committed no crime. Then I remembered the chemist.

"What if Chick could do something for the government? For the Bureau and the DEA? What if he could give you something you wanted? Would you back off?"

"Possibly," said Morrison. He studied me, as if trying to determine if I was bluffing. "Depends upon the nature of the information. However, I can't be the spokesman for all the agencies."

"But would you be willing to try to get the CIA off his back?"

Morrison's eyes widened. "Nobody mentioned them."

"You're right. But if the IRS was after him they and the Treasury Department would be all over him. Neither of you appears particularly interested, and I doubt if ATF cares. He's committed no crime, yet he's been shadowed since 1975. You mentioned paranoia, and the *p* is silent in CIA. Get them off Chick's back and I'll try to get him to hand you a career arrest." He looked as if he was trying to decide something. I said, "What's the CIA done for you lately?"

Morrison smiled and shrugged. "Not a thing. What kind of deal are we talking about?"

"We give you something that makes you look good. Real good. Allows you to wrap up this whole thing. Maybe even turn the key on Willie Boy Beauchamps or whatever his name is this week. For a long time. Promotions for both of you."

"How could you do that?" asked Candless. "What have you got that we don't already have or know? And why are you interested in getting Easton clear?"

I thought about Chick passing up the shot on the buck, how he tried to talk three guys in a parking lot out of a fight when he knew he could take them without breaking a sweat. Thought about his ever-present grin, then about the world-weary hurt that flickered like a silent movie behind the laughing eyes. I didn't owe these guys an explanation. "We got a deal or not?" I asked.

Candless looked at Morrison. Morrison said, "If it's good enough. And you can deliver. I'll see what I can do."

"But it had better be good," said Candless. "Or all bets are off. Now, what have you got?"

"Chick knows where the dreamsicle chemist is."

EIGHTEEN

Special agent Morrison of the FBI used my phone to make a couple of calls to his superiors. His people were satisfied. If we produced the chemist, the Bureau would do what it could to reduce its monitoring of Chick Easton. The CIA wouldn't like it and would probably conduct unauthorized surveillance of Chick, but it would do so without the assistance of the FBI. Morrison admitted there was a certain amount of tension, even jealousy, between the two agencies. As for the DEA, it had not been participating but was aware of the arrangement.

They left and I drove into town to see about Chick. I stopped at a fast-food restaurant and bought four sandwiches. They smelled great. I figured Chick would be hungry. Thirsty, too. I bought a bag of ice and put it into a cooler along with the six bottles of Carta Blanca Chick had purchased.

I got into the Bronco and pointed it to the highway. Sandy had called before I left the cabin for town. The station told her I'd phoned.

"I can get off a couple of days early," she had said. "Karen can cover me. How about starting our reconciliation a little early?"

I wanted to see her. But I couldn't help feeling a twinge of resentment. Three months I'd waited. Three months in limbo, wondering. Then she decides it's time to reconcile. I loved Sandra Collingsworth, of that there was no doubt. But I'd started something I'd have to see through. Make sure Chick turned in the chemist. Then there was Tempestt. Where did she fit in my feelings? First, get Chick loose of the CIA, then figure out my next step. Soon, though. Colorado called.

"Sounds good to me," I said, careful to conceal my irritation. "Got something to do, then I'll head back."

"What have you got that could keep you away from me?"

Good question. "Something that has to be done."

"Not the Red Ryder thing again," she said. "Where you right some wrong that makes no difference in the overall scheme of things."

"Makes a difference to me."

"There it is," she said. "The thing that confuses me and makes me feel alone. And yet, I know it's part of you. It fascinates me, but it puts me on the outside. You can't fix everything, Wyatt. When are you going to learn that? It's not a perfect world."

"Darn," I said. "I was afraid of that."

"You're being evasive. You won't allow yourself to be touched in certain places. Won't let anyone in. Not even me, sometimes."

"I'm sorry." Guilt over Tempestt tugged at me. "That's not my intention."

"I know you mean that. But at the same time maybe you'll never be able to control it. I'm just selfish and jealous. When the quest becomes more important than me."

"Sometimes I feel the same way about your job," I said. "Sometimes I become every cliché about machismo, and goofy romanticism. I'm not fair when I protect you from the things I see and am involved in. It's condescending. I know that. But I'm drawn to things I should avoid. I wouldn't call it a quest. It's more a need to finish things before moving on. Don't know what to do about it. It's just the way I am. It's not much, but it's me."

"And," she said, "if you weren't that way, you wouldn't be the man I love."

"Marry me, Sandy."

She was quiet, then said, "Come home so we can talk about it. It can't be done over the phone."

"That's not an answer."

"My heart is ready. But, I'm...afraid, I guess. Maybe I can't live up to your standards. To your expectations."

"You exceed them."

"I'll bet you say that to every girl who has beautiful golden tresses and a sunbeam smile." I detected a catch in her voice.

"Brunettes with dusky jewels for eyes, too," I said, my voice husky.

"Damn you, Storme. You get your rickety old bones back here soon, or I'm going to return some of Robert Redford's calls."

"Nobody likes a pushy broad, sweetheart," I said, in a pretty good Bogart impression.

"Nobody except you, anyway," she said. "You require direction. And keep working on the Bogie, you're getting closer. At least, now you sound like Bacall instead of Glen Campbell with a lisp." She laughed, pleased with herself, then became serious again.

"I need you, Wyatt. Things aren't going so well for me right now. It seems as if there is always something that comes between us. My career, your aversion to society..."

"I don't object to society, it's society's definition of civilization I have problems with. But if I have to put up with civilization to have you, I'll do it." I noticed I was pacing the hardwood floor.

"I can't ask you to do that. I can't lock you in a cage."

"It isn't that bad," I said.

"Are you kidding? You're like a dog on a short chain. You pace back and forth"—I stopped pacing—"become moody and reticent. Knowing you'll make that sacrifice makes it harder to decide. You think too highly of me."

"No. I see you as you are. And what I see I like. I don't have you on a pedestal or in an ivory tower. I'm not the White Knight, and I'm not some hormone-crazed teenager. I don't have any illusions about commitment."

"But I do. I need my illusions. You're so sure of things. I'm not like that. Sometimes I am like a young girl and things frighten me. I want to see things, experience things, and sometimes I get the feeling you've seen too much. Things I wish you hadn't seen. Things you need to share, but won't. I need you. Your understanding. Your love."

"You have it."

"You say it too easily."

"I mean it. You know that."

"Yes. I know it. It's frightening how much you mean it," she said. "Come quickly, Red Ryder."

I told her I would and hung up. Hung up without mentioning Tempestt, which didn't make me feel better about myself. I didn't understand her reluctance, though I knew she wanted to be with me. I loved her. Needed to be with her. I wanted to go back, knew I was risking separation if I stayed, but was torn by wanting to see this thing through. A good man had died, maybe Jill Maxwell, too, and Chick was in jail and being shadowed by the CIA. I had a chance to help him out of that situation.

My sense of order was offended by the intrigues of Paradise County. I hated to let go. I hate to fail. Hate to quit before it is finished. Win or lose, I was going to get in a last lick, a final attempt, regardless. That stubbornness had saved me in Nam, made me in the pros, but at times it was almost a curse, when it would gnaw at me and whip me on. Sandy thought I wouldn't let go, but the truth was I couldn't let go. It was, perhaps, beyond me.

En route to the jailhouse I ate one of Chick's sandwiches. He wouldn't miss it. I debated whether he would miss two, but by then I had arrived at my destination. Another opportunity lost due to indecision.

I parked the Bronco in the lot and walked into the Paradise County sheriff's office. George Fairchild was already there, in a striking gray suit with a subtle glen plaid design, rep tie, and a burgundy pocket handkerchief. His hair was ivory white and his strong chin and slim waist made him appear younger than his sixty years. I was glad to see him.

"Hello, George," I said.

"Wyatt," he said, turning to greet me. We shook hands. "You look like you could still be playing."

"And you look like you could still beat me at tennis."

"That's not much of an accomplishment, the way you play." He smiled, but then his mouth shrank to a thin line and he shook his head. "You're not going to like this, Wyatt."

"Couldn't you get him out?"

"That part was easy enough. The whole arrest is a sham. Ridiculous. They have nothing on him. But you didn't tell me about the sheriff."

"A jewel, isn't he?"

"His ignorance of constitutional procedure is unsurpassed. I'm afraid I was too late to prevent…that is, when you see your friend, you will—" I didn't have to wait. We were interrupted by the entrance of Sheriff Baxter and Chick. Deputy Simmons had Chick in tow.

I didn't like what I saw.

Chick had a bruise over one eye. The eye with the apostrophe eyebrow. The right corner of his mouth was cut and swollen. The left ear was an angry red. Still, he smiled when he saw me, the swollen corner making it a lopsided grin, as if he were a kid returning from the dentist.

"Wyatt," he said. "Good to see you. Knew you'd ride to the rescue. Couldn't resist, could you? Had a little problem at the senior prom, though, as you can see."

My stomach knotted and I felt heat up the back of my neck. "You do that, Baxter?" I asked.

"Had to," he answered, unconcerned. He picked at his back molars with a toothpick. "He was drunk and got outta hand. A shame."

"He was handcuffed and cooperative when you brought him in."

"Got violent," said Baxter, looking at the toothpick. "Ain't that right, Deputy Simmons?"

Simmons looked at me, then down at the floor. "Yeah," he said, not looking up. "That's what happened." He didn't seem eager to agree. The heat in my neck welled into a boiling knot.

"Two minutes with the badge off, Baxter," I said. "All I want. All I'll need."

"Sounds like a threat to me, Storme. Better watch that. End up in jail yourself."

Fairchild put a hand on my chest. "Let me handle this, Wyatt. I know you're angry, and you have every right to be. But right now that won't help anything." I swallowed my anger, but it burned in my gut like bad whiskey. Fairchild turned to Baxter.

"You have abused the powers of your office, Baxter. In all the years I have been practicing law I have never witnessed anything so clumsily brutal and actionable. Your Gestapo tactics will not be tolerated. I will advise Mr. Easton to file charges and to litigate for damages. Unbelievable! Where have you been during the past century?"

"Look here," Baxter said. "Your client, as you call 'im, resisted arrest, and I had to restrain him. So I don't have to listen to this shit."

"You do have to listen and, by God, you will listen." George's Wasp chin was thrust forward and a vein stood out on his temple. "I am unimpressed by your pathetic backwoods lawman act. This episode will cause you more legal trouble than you will ever have time with which to deal." Fairchild turned to Chick. "Mr. Easton, you should file charges."

"Naw," Chick said, eyeing the sheriff. "Me and the sheriff, we understand each other. Isn't that right, Lester? Just doing your job, weren't you?"

"Just doing what I had to do," Baxter said.

"See? You do what you gotta do, and I do what I gotta do. Y'know?"

"You're free to go," Baxter said. "So hurry up and move on. I've got more important things to do."

There was no reason to stay, so we left. As we pushed the door open to leave, Chick hollered back to Baxter, "See you around campus."

Outside, Chick thanked Fairchild. "Appreciate you coming down. What do I owe you?"

"There will be no charge," said Fairchild. "Glad to do it. But you should follow my advice and litigate. I'd be more than happy to represent you. He should not be allowed to get away with this."

"You're probably right," Chick said, smiling. "Maybe he won't. But thanks for the offer. I'm hungry, Storme. Let's go throw down."

"Got something in the truck," I said.

"You're my boy, Stormey."

I thanked George, and he drove off in a red Lincoln. "Who was that masked man?" asked Chick. I told him. "You had the Chiefs' legal rep shake me loose? For free? How'd you manage that?"

I told him about George's daughter and the guy who'd been annoying her.

"And you asked him to stop," said Chick.

"Politely, though."

"Occurs to me I don't know what it is you do besides hunt."

"Lot of that going around," I said.

He smiled.

Back in the Bronco, Chick wolfed down the sandwiches. "You should see the crap they serve for breakfast. I think they scrape it off the floor of the drunk tank."

"Got something else for you," I said. "In the cooler. Much as I hate to contribute to your vices."

He reached into the backseat and opened the blue-and-white cooler. He pulled one of the bottles from the ice and opened it with the seat belt clasp. "Storme, you are a beautiful person."

"You get violent last night?"

He tilted the dark brown bottle and swallowed, then said, "The day I can't take the Baxters of the world with both hands tied, or cuffed, behind my back, I'll turn in my Hulk Hogan tear-jersey. Besides, it's bad business to tag a lawman in his own lockup. Even if the cop's dirty like Baxter. It's okay, though. Every dog has his day."

"What happened, then?"

"He was taking me back to the lockup and I asked to see the honeymoon suite. He didn't laugh. Didn't even smile. I said I thought fat guys were supposed to be jolly and he sapped me. Turned my knees to Jell-O and I couldn't focus. Grabbed me by the hair and smacked me around. Wasn't expecting it. My fault. I know better. The deputy, Simmons, stopped it. Good thing, too, because I was just getting ready to snap my handcuffs and show him the red S on my T-shirt."

"You okay?"

"Been hit harder."

"What did he ask you?"

"The usual crap. What was I doing in Paradise? How long did I know the sheriff? How long have I known you? What did you tell me about the marijuana field?"

"I thought they were satisfied about the marijuana. That they had suspects. One of them dead." I told him about my conversation with Browne.

"Interesting that Baxter was asking, then."

"You think he's involved in any of this?"

"Maybe," Chick said, fishing in his pocket for a cigarette. "Son of a gun. Baxter copped some of my Camels. Can't trust anybody." He pushed in the car lighter. "If I was running a pet shop I wouldn't let Baxter clean the pens. Sooner or later he'd have shit on everything and everybody. He's a biological stain with arms and legs. Smart operator like Roberts wouldn't let him inside. But he might use him. Which is what may be going on. He's mean and stupid, but I don't think he's in on anything big. They may slip him a few bucks now and then."

I related all the things that had transpired in the last eighteen hours—waltzing with the Sultan, the calls to Browne, and the visit from the feds. I left out the part about Tempestt. I also mentioned the call from the mystery man and my two o'clock appointment.

"Boy," he said. "Leave you alone for a few minutes…I'll go with you. Watch your back."

"He said alone."

"Never know I'm there. It's a sucker move to go in without backup. You're not exactly a favorite son around Paradise."

"Hasn't been for lack of trying," I said. "Okay. Be good to have you watching me. But try to arrive in the nick of time if I need you."

"Always. So, they think the guy you wounded did the sheriff, then his partner dusted him and hit the road?"

"That's the way they read it."

"You believe that?"

"I will if you will."

"Neither do I. So, who do you like for it?"

"There are three people with different reasons to want the sheriff dead. Roberts is poised for a big move. Be nice to have an honest sheriff out of the way and a buffoon in his place. Winston hated Kennedy for burning him in public, and he's not the type to take it lightly. We haven't really considered the third man. Baxter. Sheriff's dead, and he runs unopposed for county sheriff."

"What a prize."

"Does seem pretty weak," I agreed.

"Then there's the fourth possibility," said Chick. "Maybe the druggie really did smoke the sheriff."

"No. I saw the guy. No way he takes the sheriff."

"You think the other three are connected to each other?"

"Paradise is small enough. But I don't know. You're right about Roberts. He's too smart to let Baxter in on anything big. But your arrest was arranged for some reason."

I fumbled with the radio dial. Couldn't find anything. Switched it off. "The government guys told me some interesting things about Roberts." I explained the convoluted events by which Beauchamps became Roberts. "They also told me what the rocks I had may be." I told him about dreamsicle and its implications.

"Which explains why Dr. Drugenstein is here."

"Who?"

"The skip I'm looking for. Prescott. The feds know he's here?"

"No. They just know there's a chemist involved. Somebody to cook the junk."

"Anything else?"

A traffic light suspended by cable turned red and swayed in the autumn breeze. I stopped the truck. "Told them we could deliver the chemist to them."

"Why'd you do—" He stopped, looked at me, took a drag on his cigarette. "Had to, didn't you?"

I looked straight ahead. "Yeah."

He chugged the beer and got another one from the cooler. He opened it and took a long pull. The light turned green and I pulled into the midday traffic, cars going different places with different people inside them. Regular people. Going to the supermarket, to the weight-loss center, to lunch with old friends, to doctor appointments, to pick up the kids. People with normal lives. Married. Home by five for a cup of coffee and the evening news with Peter Jennings. Real life. Domestic life gets a bad rap. I wished I was with Sandy going somewhere, anywhere. Or nowhere. I wanted a peaceful life. Wanted to be anywhere but Paradise chasing shadows and murderers. I searched the console and found a Jimmy Buffett tape. I put it in and Buffett sang about a cowboy in the jungle.

"So, don't you want to know what it's all about?" he asked.

"You'll tell me when you're ready. Or you won't. Up to you. I know what I need to know."

He looked tired and drained, as if the air were slowly leaking from him. "I used to work for the CIA," he said, talking to the windshield. "Which stands for Collectively Ignorant Assholes. In Vietnam. I was an infiltrator." He laughed. "Infiltrate, terminate, then evaporate. Gotta learn the words, man, or you can't dance the dance. Shit, I was a fucking assassin. No better, I guess, than Roberts or Beauchamps, or whatever."

"Phoenix program?"

"No. Something like it, though. I was even good at it." He looked out his window, the back of his head to me. "Hell of a thing to be good at. Some people are good at math, or skiing, or golf. Or football. Me, I'm good at killing people. The Duke of Death. The Prince of Perish. Killing is our business," he said. His jaw tensed. "And business is good."

"You're not like Roberts," I said. "Roberts would have killed the buck, then put his head on the wall for everybody to see. You'll never be like him."

"Thanks," he said.

"What's their interest? Langley's boys, I mean."

"There's a manuscript. A journal of my time in Nam," he said. "Even if there weren't, it makes no difference. They think there is, and that's all that matters. As long as they think it exists they won't let me rest. But if they thought there wasn't a record, then I become a target. It's an insurance policy as well as a burden. A ridiculous way to live, man."

"What's in it? What are they afraid of?"

"What are they afraid of?" He grunted. It was an exhalation of disgust. "Everything. They're afraid of their own twisted imaginations. They're afraid they don't know everything. But mostly, they're afraid somebody might know what the truth was and tell it to someone else. Remember the CIA report regarding Iraq before they invaded Kuwait? CIA reported there wasn't anything brewing in Iraq. Everything was A-J squared away. No problem. But whether they didn't know, or knew and *wanted* Saddam to invade Kuwait, is irrelevant. It happened and they were criticized. Heads rolled on that one, because even if they did know, they wouldn't want to look bad in the press, and somebody leaked and has to take a fall. Whoever did leak it is probably shadowing penguins in Antarctica."

"What do they think you know?"

"Too much. What my mission was. Who I was assigned to make, in their choice of semantics, 'inoperative.' "

"People die in wars," I said.

"Wish it was that simple. Living with it is the hard part." He explained that the agency had tried to buy the journal even though they weren't sure it existed. Even when he denied its existence.

"But that's the way it works. You don't tell them anything directly. You disavow it, they think that confirms its existence. To lie to the spooks, you just tell them the truth. A completely unnatural way to live. They can't dust me or frame me because they're afraid the manuscript will become public knowledge if anything happens to me."

"Will it become public knowledge?"

"Sure. I look stupid to you? These guys don't fuck around, and I ain't no cherry. They gonna get me, they're going to have to work at it. Day and night."

NINETEEN

"Okay, we give them Prescott, even though you got a lot more faith in those guys than I do," said Chick.

"I trust Morrison," I said. "He'll do what he says."

"How do you know?"

"What have you lost if he doesn't?"

The city blocks clicked by under the wheels of the Bronco. I headed east, then turned south. I crossed Ninth Street. Then Tenth. Eleventh.

"You've got a lot to learn about the feds. First, they're like cockroaches. You see one when you turn on the light, you know there's a hundred more in the woodwork. Roberts knows that, too. Where there's drug traffic, there's gonna be feds sniffing around." He paused to light another cigarette. "He'll have bought off the right people. Put the arm on the others. The girl reporter said people were afraid of him, but wasn't sure why. Roberts will also know it's a matter of time before the heavy hitters move in to soak the take when he starts moving dreamsicle. He's probably got a contingency plan already. Dreamsicle will be too big for Paradise. It'll explode outta here like a Roman candle, then the Sicilians and the Colombians will be on this place like wolves. They'll bust this town's cherry. Willie Boy knows that. The feds know it, too. Guys like Baxter and Winston don't."

"Why not just kill us instead of all this crap?" I asked.

"Not enough reason, maybe. Roberts is a pro. He'd have to get a good return on your death. An edge. There's already plenty of humidity with the sheriff getting killed; he doesn't want to turn it up some more with another killing. We're just annoying right now. Ordinarily, he might try to buy you off, but like I said, he's smart. Smart enough to figure you aren't for sale and won't go to the cops with anything since you don't like Baxter. He's got somebody inside the sheriff's office, maybe even Baxter. Besides, it's one thing to pop a local sheriff in the middle of nowhere or even a drug dealer that everybody, including his friends, won't miss. It's another thing to whack out a former pro football star. That'd bring in the national media."

"Which may explain why they roughed me up," I said. "And maybe why they had you locked up."

"They want us out of the way because something's going down. And soon. I can smell it."

"Or already has. They probably figured me for a couple of days R and R in the hospital and about the same time for you in the tank."

He nodded. "Which means we have to move quickly."

"Then let's grab the chemist," I said. He made a face. "You know where he is, don't you?"

"If I didn't lose him when they put me in jail. If they thought enough of me to set me up, they know I'm here to get Prescott. They might have moved him. But I'll find him. It's all rock 'n' roll to me."

1405 East Twelfth Street was a run-down frame house in a matching neighborhood several blocks from the town square. The house had rusty screens on paint-curled doors and weeds growing up around the turn-of-the-century siding. Termites lunched on the wooden spindles of the front porch. A narrow alley ran behind the house. There was a weedy vacant lot next door with a realty sign peeking out of the weeds. I drove by to get a feel for the layout.

"He'll come in through the alley," said Chick, on our second pass. "Might bring somebody in behind you, or they got somebody inside, waiting. But it's not a hit. There's easier ways and better places. They could have pulled it off already if they were going to. Good idea to get in ahead of them and wait." It was nearly an hour before the agreed-upon time. "Let me out a couple of blocks away, and I'll work my way back. Park the truck in front and go inside. Nobody followed us."

I let Chick out in front of an old church that had been converted into apartments. It had a forlorn look, as if it mourned its fall from grace. Before opening the door, Chick took a .380 Colt from the glove box and put it under his jacket. He changed guns like other people changed ties. One for every occasion. I drove back to the house, parked the Bronco on the street, and walked up to the house as if I were an interested buyer. I opened the ancient screen door and it screeched in protest. There was no doorknob on the inner door. I pushed it and it scraped against the floor. I walked inside.

I was met by the musty smell of old dirt, older plaster, and poor waterproofing. Damp. Cold. Lonely. The windows were so smudged it was difficult to see out and impossible to see in. There was a three-legged couch covered with a dirty bedspread and a wooden chair with a broken back. I walked through the house, boards creaking under my feet. I checked the other rooms, expecting Peter Lorre or Bela Lugosi to pop out. Instead, I found mice and spiders. I returned to the living room, satisfied I was alone. For now. I pulled out a Macanudo Portofino cigar and lit it. I held the Browning 9-millimeter in my lap and waited. I had a round chambered. No sense going for subtle. If they came in shooting, I didn't want to be fumbling with the slide when they do.

I thought about Sandy. Couldn't wait to see her. Maybe this time it would work out. The city and her career had come between us before. Or maybe the mountains and my selfishness. Hard to be objective. I couldn't live in the city. Not very long, anyway. I became claustrophobic in its constricted streets, choked with cars, its air stale with concrete dust and unleaded smog. It just sat there gobbling meadows and hills, belching fumes. An ugly, neon monster.

Could I have her and allow her to stay there? Better, could she allow me to live in the mountains? I wanted her near. So why was I here, sitting in a musty, broken-down house, waiting for somebody to either enlighten me or blow large holes in my body? She wanted me there, and I wanted to be there; with all my heart I wanted that. But here I stayed. We are complex creatures. Sometimes we don't know what motivates us, pulls us to do the things we do. The things we are driven to do. Things we can't stop. I should be there in Colorado with Sandy. Right now.

Here I sat, though.

I paced the floor. Didn't remember getting up. Mr. Alert. They wouldn't need guns, they could bulldoze the place. Not good. I came to a loose board lying in a pile of dirt and rubbish. I kicked at it and it clattered over to reveal a swarming, squirming mass of those tiny bugs that look like they have armor on. Roly-poly little bugs scurrying around in the dirt.

I heard a door creak and shut at the rear of the house. A shiver ran along my neck. I moved to a spot at the left side of the door they would have to enter. If they had a gun and if they were right-handed, they would have to come all the way into the room to get a shot at me. If. If. If...

Shoes scuffed the ancient boards, proceeding at a clip that couldn't be described as stealthy. I pushed myself against the wall and raised the Browning. Slipped off the safety...

I heard "Storme?" in a familiar, female voice. "You in here?" Jill Maxwell stepped into the room. "Where are—" She sucked in her breath and squealed when she saw me. Saw the gun. "Jesus. Don't scare me like that."

I put the gun down, though shooting her wasn't such a bad idea. "What are you doing here?" I said. "I thought you were on vacation. Or worse."

"Almost was. Worse, that is." She rubbed her hands together. "After you and your friend came by, I got a call telling me to back off printing anything you told me or I'd find out what happened to little girls who didn't do what they were told. You imagine that? 'Little girls who don't do what they're told.' Just like that."

"That's the way it'd be, too. Just like that. Good thing you killed the story and took off." I put the gun away.

"I didn't kill it. I turned it in. Marvin, the editor, wouldn't print it. Said it was supposition and unsubstantiated. But he knows a good story. I watched him read it. He read it all. If it was like he said, he wouldn't have bothered."

"You think they got to him?"

"Marvin's pretty tough. Korean vet. Even at a small-town paper there are people, influential people, who try to pressure him, but he hangs tough. Has a sincere belief in the First Amendment. Yeah, I think somebody got to him. But he wouldn't be scared for himself. They probably threatened to get me."

There was a lot of pressure coming from all directions. Pressure to wrap up the murder case with a convenient suspect. Pressure for the highway patrol to leave town. Pressure for me and Chick to disappear.

"How'd you know to come here?" I asked.

"After the nasty call I told Marvin I was going on vacation, then I figured I'd be able to check on things without being bothered. Maybe they'd think I was scared. I listened to the tape over and over, trying to see if I could recognize the voice. No luck. He was disguising it. Then I got a break when he called again."

"Who is it?"

"He'll be here any minute. I'll let him tell you himself."

Her answer didn't please me. "Listen, I've been shot at, beaten up, and threatened by everyone in the Paradise County phone book. Now I'm sitting in a smelly house, ten blocks from anywhere, waiting for a guy I don't know anything about. I want to know who it is, and I want to know now. So cut the Alfred Hitchcock junk."

"Come on," she said. "Don't you like some mystery in your life?"

"Not even a little."

"He's scared."

"*He's* scared? And you think I'm not, right? You're going to tell me. Who is it?"

"What're you going to do?" she said, with a bad-little-girl smile. "Beat me up?"

"You've had worse ideas."

"Or maybe you could force yourself upon me," she said. "I might not be able to stop you. May not even want to." Just what I needed, a reporter with an overactive libido.

"Get serious," I said.

"I am."

I waited.

"Party pooper," she said. She stuck out her lower lip in a mock pout. She was pretty, but annoying. "You sure you were a football player? Thought all you guys were the rutting stag type."

"Another myth disintegrates. We rutting stag types must occasionally rest from our life of ceaseless debauchery, or we get in a rut. Who's meeting us, Jill?"

Before she could answer, the rear door shut and I heard footsteps scuffle through the cluttered rooms. We waited. A man walked into the room with a gun in his hand. He pointed it at me.

I recognized the face behind the gun.

TWENTY

The face belonged to Deputy Simmons. The deputy who'd helped Baxter arrest Chick. The deputy who didn't look happy to go along with Baxter's resisting-arrest story. Still, he had a gun pointed at my heart, and his hand was unwavering.

" 'He's scared,' " I said, mimicking Jill. Then, to Simmons I said, "Look. No need for the gun. We're on the same side." At least I hoped we were.

"Put it away, Cal," Jill said.

"Not yet," said Simmons. He was dressed in civvies. Light blue chamois shirt and jeans. Levi's jacket with shearling lining and a blue cap with scrambled eggs, the military type, on the bill. The cap said Law Enforcement Academy on the crown.

"Listen," I said. "I'm tired of people threatening me. You're not even the first one today. So put the gun away and let's talk. You're the one asked me here." He kept the gun pointed at me. Pessimist. "Besides, if you don't put it down you may get hurt, because right now there's a gun pointed at you."

I didn't see Chick. Hadn't heard him come in. But I was willing to bet my Creedence Clearwater Revival collection he was zoning in on Simmons right now.

Simmons chuckled. Scoffed, actually. Everybody's a cynic anymore. "Oldest trick in the book," he said.

"But still effective," said Chick, as he stepped into the room with his Colt pointed at the deputy's head. "Traditions are always best. Like arriving in the nick of time."

"A couple of seconds after the nick of time," I said.

"Bitch, bitch, bitch," said Chick. Then, to Simmons, he said, "How about you coming down with a mild attack of good sense and putting the piece away. I hardly ever miss at this range, and I haven't killed anything today and it's already past noon."

Simmons let the gun relax to his side. "You guys DEA? Or FBI?"

"I'm a Methodist," Chick said. "And Wyatt here's a Baptist and a Bob Dylan fan, and that's about it as far as affiliation goes."

Simmons looked crestfallen. "Then everything I've done has been a waste of time."

"What do you mean?" I asked. I started to sit on the wooden chair, remembered my manners, and offered it to Jill. She declined with a shake of her head. I sat, and then she sat on my lap. I frowned at her, but she smiled in triumph.

"I'm the guy took the shots at you. That day in the field where the marijuana used to be. I had to do something after nothing came of you finding it. I thought you were working under cover."

"Oooh, undercover work," cooed Jill. I ignored her.

"Well," I said. "You missed. How would shooting us solve anything?"

"I wasn't shooting at you. Just shooting. If I'd wanted to hit you, you wouldn't be here. I was just trying to call attention to the field. Keep the investigation alive. They're going to shuffle it under the rug. Killian didn't kill the sheriff. He wasn't man enough. And I don't think Dexter shot Killian. I think someone spooked Dexter so he'd run. Either that, or Dexter's dead, too."

"So, if you don't think Killian did it and you knew about the grass, why not investigate it yourself? Why make anonymous calls and meet me in this place?"

He put his hands on his hips, then looked at the ceiling as if deciding something. It was embarrassing to talk to him with the girl on my lap, but I was afraid she'd make a big thing if I tried to stand up. Besides, it wasn't exactly unpleasant. Maybe I needed to reconsider her offer.

Simmons took a deep breath. "About three months ago," he began, "Christa, that's my sister, got into trouble over in Ford County. Got arrested with some friends on a possession charge. Marijuana and booze. She's underage. Our parents are dead, so I'm her only family." He chewed on his lower lip and shook his head. "A teenaged girl raised by an older brother who works sixty hours a week. Shit, law enforcement's easier. She thinks I'm too strict because I make her have a curfew and won't let her go out with certain guys. Guys that just want to get into her pants." His face reddened. "Sorry, Jill," he said.

"It's okay, Cal," she said. She looped her arms around my neck as if we were going steady, enjoying herself. She was funny, if nothing else. Another time, different circumstances. Too late for that now. I had enough problems.

Simmons said, "Anyway, they picked her up and took her to the courthouse. She didn't want to call me. She's a little spoiled. She was always Dad's little girl. He sure loved her, but he's gone now and it's my job to watch after her." I watched him struggle with his narrative. He was a cop, a young cop, but he was also an orphan with a teenaged sister to watch after and it weighed heavy on him. But he looked to be the type raised to accept trial. Or maybe he was beginning to accept his manhood and what went with it. I liked Deputy Simmons. "I guess she didn't want to call me because she was scared I'd chew her out."

"It's called respect," Jill said.

His eyes glistened. "Thanks," he said. "So, instead of calling me she called Alan Winston, and he got her off. Pulled some strings. No bail, no record of the arrest. He covered it pretty good."

"You could've gotten the same things done yourself. Your badge would've helped."

"Maybe. I think I could've. Even told her that. They're pretty good guys over there." I remembered what I'd heard about Ford County and the rumored "arrangement" Ford County had with

Willie Boy Roberts and his truck stop. I wondered if his sister was set up. Roberts could pull it off. But why? We needed to visit the Truck Hangar in the near future. Like maybe today. Simmons continued:

"Now Winston has me and Christa over a barrel. Wouldn't take money to represent her. Instead, he wanted a couple of"—he made a face as if he had something distasteful in his mouth—" 'favors,' he called them"

"Blackmail."

"Yeah. Like that. Wanted information about what Kennedy was doing. Little things, he said. Inside stuff. Didn't want to get off any real criminals, he said, just some of the 'good' people of Paradise."

"Good people meaning the ones he selected."

"Yeah, but I told him to go piss up a rope. Then he said, be a shame if it got out the deputy sheriff's little sister had been arrested. Might mess her up as far as scholarship money went. I can't afford to send her, and Dad would like it if she got a college degree, so I had to give in."

"He ever mention Willie Boy Roberts?"

"Not directly. But I'll let you guys in on something. There ain't nothing going down in this county that Roberts hasn't got a part of. He's a piece of shit in a five-hundred-dollar suit."

"So did you give Winston what he wanted?"

"Little things. Things that didn't amount to much. Couple inside tips on some liquor licenses, things like that. I didn't give him anything big, but I had to play it up so he'd lay off Christa. Then he started pumping me about the sheriff. Wanted to know if he ever cut corners on things. Budget. Expenses. Wanted to know what investigations he was interested in."

"Did he cut corners?"

"No way. Kennedy was the last of the straight shooters. A real man. Never did anything wrong his whole life. Came by the house himself after Dad and Mom were killed in the auto accident. Could tell it was hard on him. He could have sent a deputy, but he did it himself." His voice became a little hoarse. "That's why I don't want the investigation to end. I want the bastard that killed him to pay up."

"Why didn't you go to Kennedy when Winston started leaning on you?"

He looked uncomfortable, rubbed his hands on his jeans. He was a good-looking kid. Square jaw, slim waist, big shoulders. He looked like a cop. But he also looked like the young man that he was. "I wanted to. I should have. But…shit…there's something else. Something personal." I waited. He looked around as if he wanted to avoid it, but he wasn't the type and I couldn't afford him that luxury anyway. Too much had happened.

"Sheriff's got a daughter. Elaine. Beautiful girl." I remembered the photograph in Kennedy's office. The cheerleader with the nice teeth. Also the daughter Winston had tried to put the move on. "Goes to the university. We used to go together." He wouldn't look at Jill when he said the next thing. "She got pregnant. I wanted to marry her. I loved her, but she said she wasn't ready. She got an abortion. I tried to talk her out of it, but what can you do? Her dad didn't know about it, and I couldn't tell him because she said it would kill him if he found out. I didn't want to tell him, anyway. Not after all he'd done for me. But somehow Baxter found out, and he and Winston have become big buddies since Les filed for sheriff." There was an interesting statement. Now I had a link between Baxter and Winston, the defense attorney who hated Kennedy.

"Baxter used it against me. Said I'd better go along with Winston or the sheriff would find out about our 'little bundle of joy' that never was." Simmons was breathing hard now as he rid himself of the weight of guilty secrets too heavy for any man to bear, especially one as young as he was. The room was quiet.

"That Baxter," Chick said, breaking the silence. "He's a peach, ain't he?"

"I was in a bad spot," said Simmons. "So I played along."

"Anybody would've done the same."

"No way I could win. So I tried to get some leverage. Get Baxter and Winston, or at least one of them, off my back. Did some checking around. Found out who sold the dope to Christa and looked him up. A puke named Frankie Crisp. Sells a lot of grief to the teenagers around here. I punched him in the mouth to introduce myself. By then, I wanted to punch somebody and I couldn't punch myself.

"I asked Crisp where he got his stuff. He wouldn't tell me, so I hit him again. Hurt my hand. He was scared of them, he said. Said if he narked they'd kill him. I kicked him then. Not proud of it." He paused to look at us. "Not sorry, either. I felt like killing him for selling dope to my sister." His jaw was set and his eyes narrowed as if defying us to disagree. We didn't. Winston and Baxter made a mistake with Simmons. He wasn't a good patsy. Too much backbone. "Finally, he said he didn't know my sister was going to be one of the people he sold the grass to that night and that he'd never do it again. But he did say he'd been pointed in her direction by some big people. But that's all he was going to tell me even if I beat the hide off him."

"You were set up," I said. "They used your sister. Winston probably knew about it all the way. Baxter, too."

He nodded and chewed his lip. "Way I got it figured, too. Probably tipped off Ford County, too. But knowing it doesn't do a thing for me."

"Whose marijuana is it?"

"I don't know," he said. "Just know Killian and some other guys tended it. See, I'd heard that Roberts was out of the pot business. That, and I think there's more to it."

"Why do you say that?" asked Chick.

"Same reason I know Killian didn't do the sheriff. Guy was a cinder. His brain was fried. He couldn't run a big operation. The money end of it would be too much for him. He was a gofer and a user, not a player."

I looked at Chick, then at Simmons. "Where's Crisp now?"

"You can usually find him hanging out at Fast Eddie's."

"That old drive-in on the main drag?" I'd seen it.

"That's it. Kids drive around there. Hang out. That's where he makes most of his sales. We've arrested him before, but Winston gets him off." It was interesting who was on Winston's protected list.

"Maybe we can help you," I said.

"How?" he asked. I pushed Jill off my lap and stood. She wiggled a little as she slid off. Chick had a big smile on his face.

"I want to help, too," she said.

"You can," I said. "By getting out of town until this thing is over. There's too much going on, and you'll be in the way."

"You sweet-talker, you," Chick said.

"I'm going to get this story," she said, jutting her nice chin out and up. "You don't tell me what to do."

"This time I do. When it's over I'll give you the whole thing. Things the police won't. But you have to play it like I say or you get squat. All you'll get is the press release like the other hacks. That is, you'll get what they let you know and leave out the meat. You're a better reporter than that or I've misjudged you. Nothing to me, though. Either way. You call it."

She crossed her arms and pursed her lips tightly. She looked as if she was struggling not to hit me. She didn't respond well to being told what to do, regardless of its practicality. Simmons shuffled uncomfortably. Chick kept smiling, enjoying the scene, but I'd already decided what I was going to do. "Okay," she said, finally. "But you stiff me and I'll splash your name all over the paper."

I nodded. I turned to Simmons. "You just need to keep on like nothing happened. When we find something out, we'll get in touch. But both of you stay clear for a couple of days."

"Why a couple of days?" she asked.

"Because," said Chick, "by then it'll all be over. Either we eat the bear or the bear eats us."

TWENTY-ONE

Fast Eddie's Drive-in was a time warp—a piece of fifties Americana with a face-lift. Red-and-yellow neon. Carhops in letter sweaters. Speed bumps. I half expected Frankie and Annette to drive up in a two-seater T-bird.

I pulled into a parking slab and a girl with braces, hair pulled back in a ponytail, stuck a card with the number 7 under my wiper blade. She wore a satin-sheen jacket with *Fast Eddie's* scripted across the back. Chantilly lace. The autumn air was cool but not cold. I ordered a chocolate shake and a double cheeseburger. Wasn't really hungry but the atmosphere demanded it. Chick ordered a cherry 7-up. That is, a 7-up with cherry syrup poured in it and not mixed at the factory. We were too cool to school.

"This I like," Chick said.

"You see anybody looks like a puke drug dealer?" I asked.

"Only suspicious-looking people I see are you and me."

We waited. A carload of teenagers pulled up in an old Camaro, its rear fenders crusted with rust and a large decal emblazoned across the rear window—AC/DC. Heavy metal music belched from the car at a decibel level to stir dust on the moon.

There were four of them. All males in their late teens, smoking cigarettes and wearing denim jackets with the names of quasi-satanic rock groups on them. They got out of the car and sat on its hood.

"Aha, Watson," I said. "A lead. Slip your Wembley into your pocket, old chum, these are deep waters."

Chick groaned. "We're not going to talk to these zombies, are we?"

"Life is experiential."

We got out of the Bronco. The Camaro was parked on Chick's side. They were bopping their heads in time to the music and talking loudly so everyone would know they were there. As we walked toward them, they stopped talking and glared at us. I tried not to drop dead with terror. A long way from Frankie and Annette.

"Hey, fellas," I said, having to yell it to be heard. "Got a minute? I need to ask you a couple of questions."

"Whatchu want, man?" said the biggest of the group, a sandy-haired kid with an earring through his nose. Very chic. He had a John Cougar Mellencamp haircut, a leather jacket, and black Levi's over scuffed shit-kicker cowboy boots. I think he was attempting some sort of fashion statement. Either that, or his other clothes had been destroyed in a fire.

"You know a guy named Frankie Crisp?" I asked, still yelling.

"Maybe," he said. His cigarette, which was stuck to his lower lip, dangled as he spoke. I wondered how long it had taken him to get that down. "What's it to ya? You a narc?"

I looked at Chick. He was leaning against the Camaro. "It's your wardrobe," Chick said. "You look like one."

"I'm not a cop," I said. "And…could I get you to turn that down? I can hardly hear what I think I'm saying."

"Tough fuckin' shit," he slurred at me.

"Country charm," I said to Chick. "Love it."

"Can't get enough of it," Chick said. He reached into the Camaro and shut the key off. The silence was immediate and wonderful.

"Hey, asshole," said Ringnose, the trained baboon. "Get the fuck away from my sled, man." Then, turning to one of his lieutenants, he said, "Joe, turn that shit back on."

Chick straightened back out of the car. "Whoops," he said. "Look at this." The keys dangled from his fingers. "Must've got stuck to my hands. Guess you'll need these to turn it on again, huh?" Joe looked at Chick and hesitated. He was smarter than he looked. He had to be. "You can have 'em in a minute, junior. Soon as you answer my associate's question."

"Whadda we do, Chet?" Joe asked the guy with the ring in his nose. Chet got off the hood and unfolded his arms. I forgot to faint when he did.

"Man, I don't gotta tell you nothin'," he said to me.

"That's a double negative, Chet," I said. "Can't believe a classy uptown guy like you wouldn't know better. Good grammar is the cornerstone of polite society."

"There's four of us," said Chet, obstinate.

"We can wait while you get reinforcements," offered Chick.

"We don't want any trouble," I said. "Just ask you a couple of questions, that's all. Then we'll go on our way and you can go back to scratching your pelts and picking fleas off each other."

"I don't have to take any shit off you, old man."

I was tired of his dirty mouth, but I didn't want to get into a physical altercation with a bunch of kids, no matter how big they were, and they were plenty big enough. The waitress bustled over to us with our order. I told her to put it on the hood of the Bronco. I gave her five dollars and told her to keep the change. She smiled and thanked me, then started to walk away. Before she could, though, Chet reached out and pinched her cute little bottom.

"Stop it, Chet," she said, her face red.

"Just checking the groceries," he said. "Got something else for you, too." He patted his zipper. "Right here." Mr. Enchantment.

"Ah, youth," said Chick.

"Wasted on the young, I've heard," I said. Chet didn't know when to quit. He reached out and grabbed the girl by her arm and cupped one of her breasts with a hand. She tried to pull away, but he was too strong.

"Whadda you say, sweet stuff? Gimme a little of it. Do you right. You just let—"

I reached out and grabbed his nose between my thumb and forefinger, getting the ring in there also. I pinched and squeezed, twisting downward as I did, pulling his face down to the hood of his car. The hood was warm under my hand. He squawked in pain and surprise, arms flailing at the air.

"Don't move, guys," Chick said to the other three.

I had Chet's ugly face sideways on the hood, his arms down along his sides. He was unable to get any leverage to move. He tried to move his right arm and wrench away, but I dug a palm above the back of his left elbow, pinning that arm to the car. I gave his nose another squeeze. A hard one. I was enjoying it, which made me worry about myself.

"I've had about enough of your crummy behavior," I said. "So let's make a deal. Let's say I don't want any more bad language and rough treatment of this girl, and let's say you don't become Rudolph, the red-nosed hood ornament."

"Muthah fuck—" I twisted the nose, once more interrupting him. This time the scream was pain, exploding from his mouth.

"You're not listening. This is the part of being a tough guy you don't know anything about. Sooner or later somebody comes along who is tougher than you. That someone is there for all of us. Don't go looking for him."

"By doze," he said, nasally. "You're hurdig by doze."

"Where's Frankie?"

"Let go, I'll tell you."

I released my hold and he stood up, rubbing his nose. "Shit, my nose hurts."

"Sorry. You dealt it." I was a real tough guy, beating up on teenagers at a burger hangout. Maybe Archie and Jughead would swing by later and I could bang their heads together. "You haven't answered me yet."

He looked at his buddies, then at the ground. Rubbed his nose some more. The sneer was gone from his face. I had emasculated him in front of his disciples. No way to tell this one where he would look good. Probably some poor high school kid would suffer some indignity so Chet could restore his lost honor in front of his disciples. Didn't help me much, though. I still felt like a bully.

"He's s'posed to meet us here," he said, his eyes avoiding his friends. He sniffed. A dollop of blood retreated back into his nostrils.

"When?"

"Three o'clock." I looked at my watch. Two-fifty. "Don't tell 'im I told," he said. He put his hand to his nose and then looked at the blood on his hand.

"You be nice to the girl." I indicated the carhop with a nod. "From now on you're Prince Valiant around her. Got it? I'll be back to check it out. Now, saddle up and get out of here."

Chick surrendered the keys and they piled into the Camaro without a word. They limped out of the parking lot. Even forgot to peel rubber when they did. They just don't make juvenile delinquents like they used to. Can't learn attitude playing Nintendo.

We watched them drive away. Chick said, "Feel bad 'cause you roughed up the punk?"

"They were kids."

"Yeah. Some kids. Three of 'em were packing knives. There was booze and dope in the car. They were sweethearts. Probably friends of Wally and the Beaver. Boy Scouts." He paused to light a cigarette. "They were abusing the girl, Wyatt. Somebody's daughter. Y'think if you asked nice he'd have stopped?" He shook his head. "Forget 'em. They weren't the Osmond Brothers."

"Not the Manson family, either."

"He had it coming."

"It doesn't bother me that I did it," I said. "It bothers me that I enjoyed it."

"You're too hard on yourself. Something we can't afford with people like Willie Boy Roberts. You can't play fair with these guys. You're not Gary Cooper, and this ain't the movies. Sooner or later you get your armor smudged." His voice became low and strained. Something inside him, long buried, had extinguished the sparkle in his eyes. "I know. You can want it to be just and true. But you play by the rules and the pukes bend 'em. Hell, sometimes the good guys bend 'em. Hard to tell the difference sometimes. Can't keep up if you don't give 'em what they deserve once in a while."

I picked up my chocolate shake. Didn't taste like it did when I was a kid.

Chick said, "That's why you quit playing football, wasn't it?"

I swished the straw around in the ice cream. "Part of it, maybe."

He smoked his cigarette, and I brushed dust from the hood of the Camaro off my jacket sleeve. He looked down the street.

He said, "The errors of a wise man make the rules for a fool."

"Shakespeare again?"

"J. Robbie Robertson."

"Oh."

"The white hat shit don't play in the sewer, Wyatt. If you're gonna play it that way, then leave it alone. Go home."

"Too late for that," I said.

"What I figured," he said.

TWENTY-TWO

Frankie Crisp arrived fashionably late. He was driving a blood-red Trans-Am financed by the youth of Paradise County. Crisp pulled across two parking slots, squealing his brakes, his stereo rumbling from within the sanctuary of crimson paint and tinted glass. The vanity plate, CRISPY 1, gave him away.

"Subtle, isn't he?" said Chick.

"Maybe 'I'm a lowlife drug dealer' wouldn't fit on the license plate," I said. Crisp rolled down a tinted window to talk to the carhop, the same one who'd waited on us. We opened our doors and strolled over to his car. As we neared, the carhop looked at us. I smelled raw gasoline and hot grease in the air.

"You two again?" the girl said. "Now what?"

"We're gonna clean up this one-horse town, little missy," Chick said.

She smiled and walked past us, bounced up onto the walkway and back into the restaurant. Back to her short orders and hamburger daydreams.

We walked up to the Trans-Am. Chick knocked on the top of the car and said, "Hey, Frankie, what's happening?"

Frankie looked up. I saw the faint snatches of yellow-green under his left eye and lower lip, a fading reminder not to sell drugs to Cal Simmons's sister. Frankie was a better-looking guy than I'd expected. Like Rob Lowe, only creepier. Longish, wispy hair. Crucifix earring dangling from an ear. He was dressed expensively, if not well. Rolex watch, leather bomber jacket, and a big diamond on a pinkie ring. Who says crime doesn't pay?

Fast Eddie, whoever he was, had to know what was going on at his drive-in, which is part of the problem. We look the other way. Rationalize. Not our problem. Maybe Frankie made a contribution to the Fast Eddie slow-pitch softball team. Knew there was something wrong with the shake. Shame, too, because the place looked great. And it wasn't another McDonald's. Or Hardee's. Or Burger King...

"The fuck're you guys?" he said. Does everybody talk that way anymore? It lacks poetry. I don't like it. His voice was high-pitched and didn't fit his face.

"FBI," Chick said, in a monotone. "Special Agent Parker and this is Special Agent Longbaugh. Please step out of your vehicle, sir. We'd like to ask some questions, if we could."

"I ain't done nothing," Crisp said, his eyes shifting from Chick to me, then back to Chick. "I don't know nothing, either." Probably the understatement of the year. He started to open the door, then hesitated. I saw expensive cowboy boots with silver-filigreed toes. "Hey! I wanta see a shield, man."

Chick reached into his back pocket, flipped open his wallet, and there was a photostat with the letters FBI printed against the seal. It was Chick's picture. Now, where did he get that?

"Oh. Okay," Frankie said, chuckling nervously. He was our friend now, just another misunderstood guy who sold dope to the teenyboppers. "You don't dress like feds." He got out of the car.

"Television," said Chick. "Portrays us like that. Actually helpful in undercover situations." Frankie nodded his head. He seemed to understand. "We've talked to some people. Understand you sold controlled substances to a..." Chick paused, checked his wallet as if looking for her name. "...Let's see...yes, a Christa Simmons." He snapped the wallet shut. "Is that correct, Mr. Crisp?"

"Hunh-unh. No way, man," he said, shaking his head. The earring slapped against his neck. "Did not happen, man. Her brother, he's a deputy, come up and starts doing a Sugar Ray

Leonard number on me. Didn't know what he was talking about. He is not a right dude. Got stuff loose in his head or something. I don't do drugs, man. Just say no, huh?"

"You won't mind, then, if we check you and your vehicle for drugs, or..." Chick looked into the Pontiac. There was an Arturo Fuente cigar box on the passenger seat. "...or for ill-gotten gains. You smoke cigars, Frankie? My partner here smokes a good cigar now and then. That a good brand, Longbaugh?"

"One of the best," I said. "Certainly one of the most expensive."

"Gee," said Chick. "Wonder what they'll cost him? You familiar with the RICO Act, Frankie?" Frankie shook his head. "It says any money that can't be accounted for is subject to seizure by law enforcement officers. That connect for you?"

Frankie wet his lips with his tongue. "You got a search warrant?" He was going for defiant but fell short. Nervous eyes.

"Over in the car, Frankie," Chick said. "Judge signed it this morning. You're not well liked around here. Lots of guys dumping on you, junior. So if you'll just step aside, we can clear you of all wrongdoing. We didn't want to do it this way, but—"

"Hey, c'mon, man," Frankie said. "No reason for that. C'mon. Chill a little. Let me buy you a Coke or—"

"You attempting to bribe a federal officer?"

"What? With a Coke? No! Hey...look." He spread his arms, showing his palms. "I ain't nobody. Whadda you want with me, huh?"

"We don't want you," Chick said. "We want information. A lot of it. And fast."

"What kinds?" Frankie said, shifting uneasily from one foot to the other. But he looked relieved, which made me wonder how much product he kept in the car, how much dirty money was in the cigar box. Chick looked around the parking lot, conspiratorially, then leaned toward Crisp.

"Who's your source?"

Frankie's eyes grew. He looked like a cartoon character with a big firecracker in its hands. "No way. I'm not dropping a dime on nobody." He reached into the pocket of the bomber jacket and pulled out a pack of cigarettes. His hand trembled. Camel Lights. Everybody smoking low tar and nicotine. Hedging their bet. Never had any desire to smoke them myself, but it seems like you might as well smoke the real thing if you're going to poison yourself anyway. "I ain't no snitch. Fuck that noise."

Chick looked at me and said, "And they say there's no honor among thieves." He looked back to Crisp. "Well, Frankie, I admire you. You're willing to take the fall to spare your source. That's kind of touching. Drug dealing. Conspiracy. Homicide."

"Hey! I got nothin' to do with clipping the badge. Wasn't me, man. They already got somebody for that." His mouth snapped shut when he realized what he had done. He wished he could take it back. You could see it in his eyes.

"How did you know that, Frankie? That information hasn't been released."

"Street talk. You know. Gets around quick."

"Street talk, Frankie? This is Hickville, not Detroit. I'll ask again. Who is your source?"

"Man, what I gotta tell you? I don't shuffle no flake."

"That's not what we hear from Killian."

"That fuck? He's a raging crank freak. Overamped all the time. You can't believe him." He knew him, then.

"Killian's dead, Frankie. Somebody unplugged him."

Frankie looked sick, rubbed a hand across his mouth. "Shit, man."

"One more time, then we're laying paper on you. Tell me who supplies you."

"Can't do it. They'll croak my ass."

"And we'll just fry it," said Chick. "You'll do okay in the pen, though. Good-lookin' kid like you. The cons up at Jeff City'll love your act. Have it made. Big guys with tattoos and spoon shivs fighting over your tender cheeks. Gotta be careful in the shower, though. Watch it when you bend over to pick up the soap. Somebody might give you a free ride home."

Frankie was, by now, shaking like a palsied rodent. The smoke trail from his cigarette wavered as he held it. "You ain't scaring me, man."

"Sure I am, Frankie. I'm scaring you with the damn truth. You're going down. I got a bureau chief breathing fire down my neck, and I'm going to throw him somebody. You're as good as I got, now that Killian's gone and Dexter's on the lam. You're dirty, anyway. I open that cigar box I'll bet I don't find cigars. What do you think? But there is a way out." Chick paused to let Frankie consider the way out. Frankie swallowed and leaned closer. Chick continued. "A way out of prison and a way to protect you from the people that helped you plant the marijuana."

Crisp looked perplexed. He stopped trembling, leaned away from us, and turned his head sideways to look at us. "Marijuana?" He looked offended, as if we'd just offered a light beer to a wine connoisseur. "I look like the department of agriculture? That's husbandry work, man. Fucking farmers grow that shit." He chuckled. "Man, I may do a number now and then, socially. I even sell a lid or two, now and then, for a favored customer. But no volume work. Grass planter? Me? That's a hoot."

Chick played it off. Calm. Implacable. "So where do you get your other stuff?"

"What other stuff?" The cocky look was back. He drew on his cigarette, letting the smoke roll from his mouth, slowly.

"You know. Crack, blow..." Chick hesitated before he hit him with, "dreamsicle."

The cigarette was halfway back to Crisp's mouth when it just stopped, suspended in midmotion. His facial muscles went slack before he could recover. "What's that?"

"Too late, Frankie. Too late to pretend you don't know, too late to say you do. Too late to save your ass. Too late for everything." Chick gave me a bored look, as if he were tired of arresting low-echelon criminals. "Get the warrant, Harry, and let's get this over with." Without hesitation I started for the Bronco, playing the part, though if he didn't buy it I had no idea what our next move would be.

"No! Wait. Please," said Frankie. I kept walking. "I'll tell you some stuff." I stopped and turned around. "But not here. They got this big guy, he'll tear me to pieces. They're not anybody to be fuckin' with. They're hooked up with some connected guys."

"Right here," Chick said. "Right now. I'm out of patience. One more try and then we check the car and you go directly to jail, do not pass go, and do not collect two hundred dollars. Capisce? I'll give you some names, and you nod your head if they're involved. You won't have to say anything. You'll just be confirming, not pointing the finger at anybody. We'll leave you out of it, get you some protection. High-level stuff. New identity. Guarantee you'll never have to testify, but you have to promise never to deal drugs in Paradise County again. You'll have to move. Deal?"

Frankie nodded. Chick smiled, then said, "Sheriff Baxter?" Frankie shook his head. Negative. I thought it odd that Chick started with Baxter.

"A little guy named Luke?"

Nod.

"Alan Winston?"

Frankie shrugged. Screwed up his face.

"You're not sure?"

Nod.

"But he may be involved?"

Nod.

"Sultan Cugat?"

Crisp swallowed, looked around, then nodded, slightly.

"Willie Boy Roberts?"

He paled and his mouth worked like a beached fish's. A pink tongue licked his upper lip. Shook his head no.

"Don't lie to me, Crisp," said Chick. "Cugat keeps the troops in line, right?" Crisp nodded. "Cugat works for Roberts, right?" We already knew the answer, but Frankie hesitated. He was genuinely frightened. "I'm not asking if he is your boss, I'm asking if Cugat works for him. Does Cugat work for Roberts?"

He nodded.

Chick patted him on the shoulder. He had him back on track. Chick was working him, setting him up, asking questions with known answers to see if he would lie, then calling him on it so he could ask the questions we didn't know the answers to. "You're all right, Crispy. Almost there."

"You said—"

"Don't interrupt. We're gonna let you slide. But if you know anything else, you better spill now, because if you don't, I'll be right back and you'll go down with the rest. Not to mention the fact I'll let it be known you copped on Roberts." Chick smiled.

"Fuckin' shitass fed," Frankie said. "Shoulda known I couldn't—" Chick reached out with his hand and put it over Frankie's mouth.

"Shhhh. Shhhh," he hissed, shaking his head. "Watch your mouth. See, you're stupid. You confirmed Roberts just now. Thanks. It's a pleasure doing business with a bright guy like you. Something else. I don't like drug dealers much. But I'll keep my word. You're gonna walk. You just better not be holding out on me. We're going to drop the net, and I want to be able to report to my superiors that you were cooperative and that we'll be justified in letting you fly. Blink if you understand." Frankie blinked, and Chick removed his hand.

"Okay, okay," Frankie said, breathing as if he'd just remembered how. "I got something."

"Well?"

"They found out about your undercover agent. The one inside Starr Industries."

I remembered Morrison mentioning an inside man.

"When did they find out?" asked Chick.

"This morning. Caught her trying to call out on—"

"Wait," I said, interrupting. "You said her."

"Yeah. Good-lookin' piece, too. Pretty smart of you guys using a gash and sticking her under Willie Boy's nose like that. Funny name, though. Tempest something..."

TWENTY-THREE

Chick told Frankie Crisp to drive to Springfield and check into a motel and stay there for one week until Chick contacted him. Then Chick relieved him of the cigar box. Frankie protested, but Chick was persuasive. Inside the box, instead of the imported long filler handmades, there was $2,700, cash, in various denominations. Chick let Crisp keep five bills for expenses. He even gave Crisp a receipt.

"Nice touch, huh?" Chick asked me, when we were back in the Bronco. I was anxious to find a phone.

"Where'd you get FBI credentials?"

"Little place outside Boulder. Guy runs a gas station–convenience store. Liquor store in the rear. It's in the middle of nowhere. Guy makes stuff so good it'll break your heart. An artiste."

I drove to the nearest pay phone and dialed Starr Industries. I asked for Tempestt.

"I'm sorry," said the female voice that answered. "Miss Finestra did not come to work this morning." I broke the connection and called the number Agent Morrison had given me. He answered on the seventh ring.

"Morrison," he said.

"This is Storme. Tempestt's cover is blown. Get her out of there."

"Who? Tempestt who?"

"Don't play games, Morrison." I squeezed the phone. "I know Tempestt is the agent at Starr Industries and so does Roberts."

"How do I know this is Storme?"

"Okay. I'll play your silly secret agent games. Candless doesn't like coffee with caffeine, and he especially doesn't like it tossed in his face."

"When did you find out?" Morrison asked, satisfied.

"Ten minutes ago. Dealer named Frankie Crisp just told us. Told us a lot of things. He's involved with Roberts and maybe Winston."

"Alan Winston? The attorney?"

"That's him."

"That is difficult to believe."

"I don't have time to convince you. You've got to move and get Tempestt out of there. Now."

"That's not possible. The investigation is at a sensitive point and we can't extricate her."

"What if they kill her?" I said. He was frightening me. I felt ineffectual, helpless. They probably made her when she helped me. She had come along at just the right moment when Sultan was tattooing me on the bricks. No coincidence. She had been evasive about how she had happened along at that time. She had compromised her assignment and safety to help me. Something Morrison and Candless wouldn't have done. But something I would now do for her. If I wasn't too late.

"Agent Taylor was apprised of the risks going in," Morrison said.

"You ass. We're talking about her life. You do something or I will personally saw your head off."

"I appreciate your concern, Storme. I am also concerned for her. But we can't let them off the hook now by tipping our hand."

I rapped the receiver against the side of the booth in frustration, then I placed it back against my ear. "Are you listening to me? There's more. But unless you get her out of there you get nothing."

"Dammit, Storme," he said, exploding, which was a departure from his usual calm demeanor. "You have got to quit messing around in this affair. You're complicating things. Can't you see that?"

"I don't care about your investigation. I don't care about your procedure. I don't care about protocol. I don't care about you. The only thing that matters is Tempestt, or Agent Taylor, or whatever her name is."

"You could end up in front of a federal judge."

"Make me laugh, Morrison," I said. "That's crap and you know it. I spend fifteen seconds in court or jail and I start talking about the witness protection scam with Beauchamps and how he got away from you guys. I talk about dreamsicle. About how you guys have mucked around with this and let an agent be compromised. How you managed to allow the sheriff to get murdered on your watch."

"That was not our fault—"

"Shut up. How you allowed a Mafia hit man to operate with a free rein and take over an entire community. How you sat back while the locals railroaded a homicide investigation. How you kept the highway patrol in the dark while you—"

"All right!" Morrison said, interrupting. "All right. What else have you got?"

"Get her out of there."

I could hear him breathing, heavily. "I can't do that."

"Then I'm on my own. I'll get her out."

"Storme. Let me caution you. Do not attempt anything heroic. Agent Taylor will not appreciate your sabotaging this investigation. Then her sacrifice, if it comes to that, will be for naught."

I wasn't listening to him. How can you take someone seriously who says things like "for naught." I had another thought. "Don't say anything about this to Candless."

"Why not?"

"I don't trust him. I've got a feeling, nothing more, that he's leaking information. Everybody is one step ahead of me. Roberts knew who I was. Somebody tipped them about Tempestt. Crisp indicated that Winston may be indirectly involved, and Candless seems to be afraid somebody is going to disturb Winston. And how did he know Chick was checking on Winston? Why would he even care? Ask yourself that."

"We are cooperating with the DEA in this investigation and they are privy to any—"

"Doggonit, Morrison. Get your head out of the dark, smelly place and think. Anything happens to her and I'm going to look you up."

"You'll accomplish nothing threatening me."

"All I'm asking for is forty-eight hours. Just hold back telling him anything for that period of time. Please." I was pleading with him now. If begging would save Tempestt's life, then that's what I would do. "That's all. He won't know that I know. Not yet, anyway. What have you got to lose?"

There was a pause. "All right," he said. "Forty-eight hours. That's all you get. But you'll have to promise to stay out of it."

"No good. My neck's already stretched out. So's hers. I can't sit still when I know that. If you want to tell Candless, go ahead. But do it knowing you may be killing her. I'm not a sideline guy, I'm a player. No matter what happens, even if I go to jail, I'm still going to try to get her out."

"You can't have it all, Storme."

"I'll turn the chemist. To you and you alone. If Candless is involved the deal is off."

"You're a hardheaded son of a bitch."

"Scots-Irish. Goes with the heritage."

"I give up," he said. "I'll say nothing to Candless for the agreed upon time. But this conversation never occurred. And, I caution you. You are placing yourself in a highly charged situation. If something goes awry, I may be unable to guarantee immunity if you are prosecuted. I give you my word I will not personally initiate prosecution. You are a damned nuisance. Get me the chemist and I'll see what I can do. You are dealing with people who are ruthless and without conscience. Some of them are powerful and dangerous beyond your imagination."

"It's okay. I'm wearing my lucky socks."

"This is not a game, Storme."

"And I'm not playing around," I said. He hung up.

I hung the phone on the hook and Chick said, "So what's the drill?"

"He says we're sticking our noses in where they'll get cut off. Along with some other things."

"Whew. For a minute there, I thought we might be in trouble. Well, this looks like a job for Super Chick and his rusty-trusty sidekick, Wyatt, the Boy Wonder. Do we get to wear the white hats this time?"

I called the offices of Alan Winston, attorney-at-law. A female voice, very efficient, very proper, answered on the fourth ring. No hurry. "Mr. Winston is unavailable at the moment. May he return the call?"

"Tell him it's Wyatt Storme. He'll want to talk to me."

"He's unavailable."

"I heard you say that. Tell him anyway."

She started to protest, gave up. Elevator music swelled electronically from the phone. Two minutes passed. The voice returned. "Mr. Winston seems to be unfamiliar with you. I'm sorry, but you'll have to make an appointment."

"Okay," I said. "Make it for four this afternoon."

"That's only fifteen minutes from now."

"Sorry. I can't make it any sooner."

"He's busy all afternoon."

"Tell him to shake loose."

"But, I—"

"I know the secret password."

"I'm afraid I don't understand," she said.

"Dreamsicle. Tell him that." I hung up.

"Well," said Chick, "that was easy enough."

"I have a nice telephone manner."

"Courtesy is everything."

TWENTY-FOUR

The law offices of Winston & Bedford, est. 1947, were situated in a brown brick colonial-style building in a trendy business park on the east side of town. Very upscale. There were late-blooming flowers and evergreens growing in a garden that sat in the middle of the common.

"Very soothing," Chick said. We entered the building. The office was hushed, with golden-brown carpet and a tasteful wall-paper pattern. Walls were hung with expensive prints—Neiman, Picasso, some impressionists. At a desk was a nice-looking brunette wearing a red blazer, dark sweater underneath, and large glasses, which set off her large hazel eyes. Walnut furniture adorned the office. Decorating the door to Winston's office were two gorillas of the species *Thickus moronus*. It was Breck and Vance, my favorite muscleheads. Click, again. One more connection between Winston and Roberts. The secretary, Ellen Fontaine, by the nameplate on her desk, was uncomfortable.

Chick spoke to the goons guarding the door. "Look, it's Heckle and Jeckle."

"May...may I help you gentlemen?" asked Miss Fontaine. We didn't look like we required help with a speeding ticket.

"We have an appointment with Mr. Winston," I said. "I'm the guy who called, Wyatt Storme. This is my associate, Mr. Easton."

Chick smiled. "Darn," he said, looking at Breck and Vance. "Forgot to bring our appointment card."

Ellen Fontaine said, "I'm sorry, but...but there seems to be a...a mistake."

"Are we early?" I asked, politely. "Clock says four o'clock."

"Mr. Winston is busy," said Vance, the darker of the musclemen. He had a black mustache and wiry black hair on thick forearms, which were crossed in front of his chest. He was wearing short sleeves in the middle of autumn so we could see the muscles he'd grown. Probably considered himself menacing. He wasn't far wrong. "Come back some other time."

"Shouldn't you guys be out front?" Chick said. "With a headdress and a handful of cigars?"

"If you're looking for trouble," Vance said, "then you're in the right place." He measured each syllable in the best B movie tough-guy tradition.

"Clichés," said Chick. "Real men don't use 'em."

"We need to speak with Mr. Winston," I said. "Just talk, that's all. We're not going to rough him up, and we're not going to kidnap him."

"Besides, we need legal advice," said Chick. "We've been charged with assault and battery."

"Oh, yeah?" Vance said, with a sneer, ever the straight man. "Who'd you two lightweights assault? Coupla junior high kids?"

Chick's smile spread broadly across his face. The apostrophe eyebrow raised. He said, "Couple of guys who mumbled in monosyllables and wouldn't let us go where we wanted to."

The blond guy stepped forward. "You can't see him. He doesn't want to see you. He gave us a call, told us to keep everyone out, and you two specifically. So that's what we have to do. Nothing personal. That's the job." Formal and courteous. Service with a smile. Vance, on the other hand, looked as if he wanted to bite us. Breck was the guy to watch. He was calm, the kind of calm that came with experience. He wasn't looking for trouble. Trouble would come.

"I appreciate your position," I said. "But we're going in. That's the way it is. Sorry." Breck's eyes had a tired look, as if he had to discipline a precocious child. His partner moved to bar our way.

"No way, all-star," he said. "It ends right here. You and Mr. Mouth can turn around and blow."

" 'Turn around and blow?' " Chick said, his smile wider than before.

"Hard to believe he says things like that, isn't it?"

"I like it," Chick said. "You go on in, while I hang around here and see if he comes up with another gem."

"That right? I think you're leaving. Soon." Vance reached into his back pocket, and with a flip of his wrist he produced a leather sap, one of those with the flat piece of lead in the end like the police carry. He began flopping it in his hand. Without warning, Chick snaked out a hand and rapped Vance sharply on the wrist. Vance yelped in surprise, then Chick swept the blackjack from the dark man's hand, flipped it into the air, and caught it, teasing Vance. The whole action had transpired in seconds. It had been quick, dreamlike. It was as if the sap had materialized in Chick's hand.

"Will you look at this," Chick said, brandishing the blackjack. "A horrible weapon of destruction. Good thing I was able to get it before you hurt yourself. Maybe you oughta try one with training wheels first. Course it's not as exotic as a Japanese throwing star, but it has a certain atavistic appeal."

The blond guy, Breck, made a funny little move; he loosened his shoulders and shuffled right. Chick relaxed his arms and bent his knees slightly, facing Breck. "Whoa there, blondie. You don't want none of this."

"It's what they pay me for," Breck said.

"They don't pay you enough for this. Nothing personal."

The door to Winston's office opened suddenly and Alan Winston appeared. He wore a dark blue suit with a faint chalk stripe running through it. Hand-painted tie like the uptown guys in New York wore. Florsheim wing-tipped tasseled loafers in oxblood. Very *GQ*. His face was drawn tight.

"What's going on here?" he demanded.

"We're playing who's got the blackjack," said Chick. "And, as so often happens, I'm winning."

"Call the police, Ellen," said Winston.

"Sure you want to do that?" I said. "Nothing to me. I'll be glad to talk to them. Got nothing else to do. You call them, I call the paper. They'll hear the call on the scanner, anyway. They'll get a reporter over here quicker than you can say 'dreamsicle.' I'll tell them about a wounded man with a new wonder drug in a plastic container." Ellen Fontaine was punching numbers on the phone. "I'll also tell them about a local lawyer trying to extort information from the sheriff's office to help himself in court."

"Hang up, Ellen," Winston said, his eyes hot on me. Miss Fontaine kept the phone to her ear. "I said hang up, dammit!" She jumped, as if stung, and put the phone on the hook.

"Sorry, Mr. Winston," said Breck. His eyes were still on Chick. "You're pretty good," he said to Chick. "Vance is usually pretty hard to take."

"Too eager," said Chick. "Too slow, too."

"Quick enough for most."

"Not enough once you've seen the best."

"This ain't over, motherfucker," said Vance.

"Do you eat with that mouth?" said Chick "There's a lady present. You have no background at all, do you?"

"I'm gonna kick your—"

"Shut up, Vance," Winston said. His courtroom voice was a whipcrack. "Breck, get him out of my sight."

"Yes, sir," said Breck. "You want these guys to stay out?"

"We're going in," I said.

"Mr. Winston?" Breck said.

Winston looked angry but said, "Let them in." He turned and walked back into the office, ignoring us but leaving the door open.

"Your lucky day," Breck said.

"Yours, too," said Chick, as we went in. Two men stood as we entered. The office was thickly carpeted and large, furnished with chrome and glass. The downfall of twentieth-century man. Chrome and glass. Cold and antiseptic. The two men who stood at our entrance were doing so near a low table, papers and folders strewn on top of that. The older of the two men immediately closed one of the folders, which made me want to look at it even more. The other man, late twenties, early thirties, was dressed similarly to Winston, though he was taller and looked athletic. He also looked angry at our barging in. He had a fist on a hip, pushing back his expensive jacket.

Winston introduced us, then sat down behind his desk. He didn't offer us a chair and nobody shook hands, which was okay since we weren't there to sell Amway or life insurance. The younger, athletic-looking man's name was Gary Bedford. He was the junior partner.

"What are these men doing here, Alan?" asked Bedford, as if we weren't in the room.

"We're here to spread love and goodwill to people everywhere," said Chick, looking at the older man, a Mr. Campbell. He was dressed differently from Bedford and Winston. He had on a suit, but it looked rumpled, and his tie was askew. His hair was unruly, as if he'd slept on it.

"This is a private meeting," said Bedford. "You two will have to leave."

"We're not leaving," I said.

"Maybe you'll have to," Bedford said, putting both hands on his hips.

"Maybe that's already been tried."

"The noise outside," Winston said, "was Breck and Vance attempting to deny them entrance. They took a blackjack from Vance. It wasn't an accident."

Bedford considered this momentarily. He was a good-sized man. Probably a quarterback or tight end in high school. Maybe even college. His posture was the best in high school locker-room intimidation. Unfortunately, there was never a high school kid around when you needed one.

"I can hold my own with this pair of morons," he said, glaring at me. Chick continued watching the older man at the table. Alan Winston looked amused.

"Now, Gary," Winston said, soothingly. "I already know of one man who has suffered a broken nose this week." He took his index finger and pushed his aquiline nose to one side for emphasis. "And I like your nose the way it is."

As if on cue a door opened at the rear of the office and a huge form stepped into the room. Sultan Cugat. He wore an aluminum-and-foam-rubber splint splayed across his face like a shiny octopus, making him appear gladiatorial and malevolent. As if he needed that. Willie Boy Roberts stepped from behind him. Winston had probably called him when he heard we were coming. No doubt about the connection now.

"Hello, boys," said Roberts, with his affected drawl. "Good to see you again, Storme." Cugat stood behind Roberts, outlining his boss with his huge body, thick forearms folded across his rain-barrel chest. His slick bald head reflected the overhead light.

"Come in," said Winston, looking at me and smiling confidently. "Sit down, I'll fix you a drink. We'll find out what these gentlemen want, and then we will get back to the business at hand. I'm sure they won't stay long." He raised a questioning brow at me. "Would you like something to drink, Mr. Storme?"

"No."

"Mr. Easton?"

"Wild Turkey, straight up," Chick said, without removing his eyes from the man in the rumpled suit. Roberts took a seat at Winston's desk. At home. Winston poured bourbon into a square rocks glass from a chiseled crystal decanter that had a chrome spigot on top. The man in the rumpled suit who had been introduced as Mr. Campbell was becoming agitated by Chick's gaze.

"What are you looking at?" Campbell asked.

"You look familiar," said Chick. "Ever been to Colorado?"

"What?...No, of course not," he said, but his quick eyes darted nervously about the room.

"California?"

"You don't know me and I don't know you," he spat, his upper lip curling back to expose his gums. Chick pinned him with his eyes.

"Sure look familiar," said Chick as he accepted the drink from Winston. "I'm usually pretty good with faces."

"Well, you've made a mistake this time."

Chick shrugged, took a swallow of his drink. "Possible," he said. His free hand reached into his jacket. "But I don't think so."

Chick's hand reappeared from beneath his jacket. There was a flash of metal, then a hard click as a handcuff locked on Campbell's wrist.

TWENTY-FIVE

The handcuffs snapped shut before anyone could react. Too late, Campbell pulled back like a frightened animal.

"Hey!" he cried. "Let go!" He tried to jerk his arm away, but Chick pulled the chain and the struggling man to him, all the while balancing his drink with the other hand. Then he forced the manacled man toward a chrome-and-leather chair and locked the second loop to the chair arm.

Campbell looked at the arm chained to the chair and cursed. "You son of a bitch."

"Maybe," said Chick. "But a son of a bitch with a pair of handcuffs. Good whiskey, Alan, but not Wild Turkey."

"Maker's Mark, actually," said the attorney. "Hope you don't mind."

"No. I don't mind."

"What the hell's going on?" said Bedford. Campbell was obviously Prescott, the renegade chemist who had jumped bail in Colorado. Had to be. "These two clowns come waltzing in here, cuff one of our clients, and you apologize for the brand of bourbon you're serving."

"Clowns?" said Chick, to me.

"It's your boorish manner," I said. "Gives you away every time."

"Release him," said Bedford, his face taut. "Now!"

Chick made a show of patting his pockets. "Darn. How do you like that?" He smiled at Bedford. "Forgot the key. Besides, you forgot to say, 'Mother may I?' "

"Who are these guys?" asked Bedford.

"A couple of low-rent pests with an attitude problem," answered Winston.

"Pests? Maybe," Chick said. "But low-rent? Never. Mr. Campbell, as you call him, is a bail jumper. Real name is Prescott. But you already knew that, didn't you?" He directed the question at Roberts, who shrugged and put a cigar between his teeth. Unperturbed. Something was wrong here, but I couldn't put my finger on it.

"You're crazy," said Campbell. "You've confused me with somebody else."

Chick sipped his whiskey but watched Sultan Cugat over the rim of the glass. "I'll let the state of Colorado decide that."

"Do you have a warrant or extradition papers in your possession?" asked Winston, remembering he was a lawyer.

"No. Only a resolute heart and pure thoughts. Also, Vance's blackjack."

"And yet, you are only one man," said Winston.

"Two," I said, correcting him.

"Which, in this case," Chick said, as he scanned the room, "I think, will be sufficient." Cugat's face clouded and his mustache worked.

"Long way back to Colorado," said Roberts.

"But we know the way by heart," I said. "Like you know the way to New Orleans." Roberts's face twitched like the blink of an eye, then quickly composed itself. He was a cool one, no doubt about that. Roberts made a show of lighting his cigar, rolling it between his fingers and touching the flame of a silver-cased lighter to its tip. He looked at Cugat.

"Cugie, have Easton release our friend Mr. Campbell."

The huge man stepped from behind his boss and moved toward Chick. "Okay, partner," he said, in a rich baritone. "Let him go or I'll have to bend you a little."

"No," said Chick. "I found him fair and square, and I think I'll have to ask you to back up." Cugat continued to advance, and

Chick whipped the .380 Colt from his jacket and pointed it at the big man's forehead. "Unless you want me to drill for brains."

Cugat stopped. "You won't shoot."

"Oh, yes," said Roberts. "He will, you betcha. In fact, after he shoots you, he'll shoot every one of us. Without a moment's hesitation, I'd say. Without batting an eye. Isn't that right, Easton?"

Chick nodded. "Everybody but Storme," he said, his eyes and gun rock-solid on Sultan Cugat. "Without batting an eye. I'll even enjoy it a little." His voice, devoid of humor or emotion, sent a chill down my neck. He meant every word.

"Why would he do that?" asked Bedford, the smugness gone from his voice.

Roberts answered. "Because that's what he's good at. Ain't that right, you?"

Chick didn't speak.

Roberts kept talking. "Heard you was the best. Had the gooks scared shitless. They say you killed over twenty VC. Some of 'em big shots past the DMZ. Deep in Ho Chi Minh's pasture."

Chick ignored Roberts. "Back up, baldy," Chick said to Cugat. "You've got three seconds before we find out if you're made of snails and puppy dog tails."

Cugat's eyebrows knitted. Slowly, he stepped back and said, "Maybe we'll have us a rematch someday. Without the gun."

"Don't wish for things that're bad for you, ugly. These things aren't choreographed in real life. I won't take a fall, and you won't be able to tag out."

"I'll break you."

"Now, don't take Easton too lightly," said Willie Boy. "He used to be something special. That is, before he lost his nerve." Chick's face didn't change expression. "Started thinking about it too much, maybe. Got himself a conscience. Or maybe he just turned coward? Bad thing in a professional."

"Where's Tempestt?" I asked.

Willie Boy drew on his cigar before answering. "Miss Finestra? Believe she quit this morning. All of a sudden. Can't understand it. Treated her well, yes I did. No loyalty anymore. Have no idea where she got off to. That what this shit's all about?"

"Some of it, Max," I said, using his real name. His mouth twitched when I used it. "And while we're talking about past lives, have you told your buddies here about the disposal service you used to run in New Orleans?"

His face lost its amused look. "You're starting to bore me, Storme. Not good to do that."

"You've made too many mistakes, Max. Not good for a pro like you. Too many bush leaguers, like Winston here, involved, and you keep leaving bodies around. The sheriff's killing was stupid. Called attention to you. And you on the verge of a big score."

"This is a litigious monologue," Winston said. "You cannot slander a community leader like Mr. Roberts in front of witnesses."

"See what I mean, Beauchamps? Winston doesn't know what it is when he sees it happening. How about it? You going to sue? Stand up in court and defend yourself and the honor of your good name, or at least your present one? There might even be some publicity. Good for business." Roberts said nothing. I said to Winston, "No, counselor, I don't think Willie Boy, or Max, or whatever he wants to be called, is interested in a civil suit. I'm sure he avoids the courtroom whenever possible. Bad memories."

"What's your point, Storme?" Roberts said, his eyes were slitted in his big face. He jammed the cigar out in a large crystal ashtray.

"Where's Tempestt? I want to see her, and I want to know she is safe."

"I don't know."

"You're a liar."

He didn't like that. For the first time he was showing emotion. And it was anger. Malevolent anger. "You're starting to piss me off, Storme," he said. "Bad things happen to people that do that."

"Such as?"

"You could end up dead."

"Maybe I won't die." Our eyes locked.

"How does he know these things?" asked Gary Bedford, reacting as if he'd just stuck his finger in an electric socket. "This was supposed to be kept quiet."

"Shut up, Gary," said Winston. "Quit whining. They can't do anything. They have no official capacity. Storme is blowing smoke. Well, Storme. What is your next brilliant move? You taking us to jail on the basis of your wet-dream fantasies?"

"Which one of you did the sheriff?"

"My God!" said Bedford, jamming his fingers into his styled hair.

"We are all shocked and grieved at the loss of our fine county sheriff," said Winston.

"He hated your guts and threatened to whip you," I said. Winston's face colored. "So save it for court. One of you or all of you are directly or indirectly involved in his death. Somebody's going to pay for that. I don't care who. But somebody will."

"Storme's sense of justice is offended," said Roberts. "Having such high morals is an expensive luxury. And you're right, killing the sheriff was stupid. And I'm not stupid. Gar-on-tee. What do you think, you, that one of us killed him because he found a marijuana field? You are simpleminded. If I wanted the sheriff dead, you would never have been able to trace it to me."

"Why was your dog at the field?"

"I sold him to that fool, Killian. A nobody drug dealer. I owe you no explanation." Then why give me one? I wondered. Something was out of sync. Something just beyond my awareness. Suddenly, Roberts began to laugh, his shoulders jumping up and down. "Quite an imagination you have, you," he said, slipping back into the phony Cajun accent. He rubbed his eyes with his left hand while he held on to his side with his right hand. Instantly, Chick swiveled the gun to point at Roberts's chest.

"Put your hands on the desk," commanded Chick. "Where I can see them. Right now. Do it." Roberts complied. "That's the boy. Now, back away until your weight is on your hands." Cugat tried to take advantage of the moment and stepped forward. Without moving the gun from Roberts, Chick said to Cugat, "Tell you what, fatso. I'll bet I can kneecap your boss and then you with only two shots and do it before you can take another step. To make things sporting, I'll even shoot Roberts first. That'll give you a chance to get at me before I do it. Tough to pick up the ladies when you can't dance. And, it'll hurt like a bitch."

"Get back, Cugie," Roberts said. The giant did so.

"Check Roberts, Wyatt. Back of his belt, under his jacket." I moved behind Roberts, felt along the heat of his back and found it. A .25 Beretta.

"Now why would an honest businessman like yourself need a nasty old gun?" I asked. I hefted the gun.

"Y'all shittin' in your nest," said Roberts, ice in his voice.

"Where's Tempestt?" I said. He didn't say anything, so I clubbed him in the kidneys with the butt of the Beretta. His knees sagged and he coughed. Cugat started to move, but Chick shook his head at him.

"Kill you for that," hissed Roberts.

I moved around in front of him. "One more time," I said. "Where is she?"

He stood up. "Maybe I'll trade her for Campbell over there," he said, as if we were discussing baseball cards. "Besides, she was Sultan's girl last I knew. How was she, Cugie?"

The bald giant smiled, showing capped teeth. "She was just fine, boss. But she wore out after about the third or fourth time. Hard to find a woman with stamina anymore."

The gun became hot in my hand. I swung it up into Roberts's face and snapped back the hammer. "If you've hurt her, I'll kill you both." My teeth were tight, and I had to smother the tremble in my hand.

"Believe you just might want to," said Roberts calmly. "But it's hard to kill an unarmed man when he's looking at you. Don't think you can do that, you. Takes a special kind of man to do that. And you're not the type."

"But I am," said Chick, lazily tracing Roberts with his Colt. "So talk."

"Campbell for the girl," said Roberts. "That's the deal. If not, go ahead and shoot."

"You can't give—" began Winston.

"Shut up, counselor," said Roberts, his face twisted into a mask of anger and annoyance.

I looked at Chick. It was his call. Campbell was his ticket. He nodded his head. "Okay," I said. "It's a deal."

"Much better," said Roberts. "Cugie. Give these boys the key."

Cugat reached into the pocket of his jeans and produced a key with a motel tag attached to it. He placed the metal key between his teeth and bent it. He showed us the bowed key and then placed it between his teeth again and bent it back to its original shape.

"That's nice, ugly," Chick said. "Know any card tricks?"

Cugat tossed the key at my feet. "You can have what's left, superstar," he said, then laughed. I picked up the key. The tag said Rancho Deluxe Motel and had the number 23 on it. Chick uncuffed Campbell and we backed out of the room.

"By the way," Roberts said, "your little darlin' picked up some bad habits since you saw her. Damned shame, too."

Bad habits? What was he talking about? But beyond that, something else was wrong. I could feel it more than I knew it. Roberts and Cugat looked too smug. Bedford looked scared, Winston annoyed.

Something besides Tempestt's plight was bothering me. But what?

We left.

TWENTY-SIX

The Rancho Deluxe was a low-slung motor hotel with crumbling pavement and window-unit air-conditioning. COME STAY WITH US. $19.95 PER NITE, announced the sign in front of the office. Room 23 was the last unit on the west block of rooms. Click slid the Colt from its holster and held it down alongside his leg as I inserted the key into the lock.

We are never really prepared for the shocks of life: The day we catch our boss locked in his office with the girl from the secretarial pool spread-eagled, nylons dangling. When Uncle Bob, the Korean War vet, who used to do tricks with quarters, gets cancer. When the class clown from high school, the guy with the wit and ready smile, sticks a gun in his mouth, ending the fun. For all of us.

So when I opened the wear-scarred metal door to room 23 of the Rancho Deluxe, I wasn't ready for what I saw.

Lying on the bed in a smear of her own excrement, her eyes dark-ringed and her hair tangled, was one of the most beautiful women I had ever known. The John Wayne heroine, crashed and smoldering in the ashes of her marred beauty, in the tossed, seedy comfort of the Rancho Deluxe Motel. Her face had a look of unnatural ecstasy, remote and vacant, as if dreaming with her eyes open. The room smelled of feminine neglect and bowel failure. The television, an old black-and-white portable, was jammed on a neutral channel, tuned into nothing—a blurring, hissing zone of emptiness.

She was naked. Her body, even in tragedy, was lush and beautiful. One handcuff held a bloodless arm to a bedpost. Her free hand reaching toward me and a slow shudder of breast indicated life. I tried to imagine her as I remembered her, vital and exquisite.

I ran to the bed, gripped the bedpost and wrenched it. The cheap wood snapped with a popping, tearing sound, and the handcuffed arm dropped to the side of the bed, the metal jangling. Her hand trembled as the blood returned to it. The effort, or the anxiety, left me panting. I fought off a whimper of anguish, which lay trembling at the back of my throat. Her head lolled and she mumbled something unintelligible. I sat on the side of the bed and hugged her to me. Rocked her in my arms and rubbed her shoulders and back briskly. She was unresponsive. Her skin was cold and rubbery to the touch. I gathered the bedspread about her to cover her nakedness. Chick said nothing. Tempestt said nothing. The room echoed with the sound of it.

I went into the bathroom and ran water into the tub. When the water gushed from the spout, a cockroach scurried from the drain and tried to scramble up the slick porcelain. I killed him and dropped him in the wastebasket.

Returning to the bedroom, I lifted Tempestt from the bed and carried her to the bathroom, placing her into the tub. Some of the excrement got on me when I did. I heard Chick talking on the phone, heard him give the name of the motel.

I washed her with warm, soapy water, then dried her. She couldn't help. I was aware that I was probably washing away rape evidence, but I didn't care. No one needed to see her like that. She had suffered enough indignity, and justice was a cowboy on a fast horse.

I washed her off myself. There were no clothes in the motel room. They had intended for her to stay there. Using an extra towel, I fashioned a crude sarong around her waist, pinning it in place by jamming wire shower curtain hooks through the towel. That done I kneaded her limp body into my jacket. I kissed her. Her breath was sour on my face. I carried her into the bedroom and sat her gently in an easy chair, her arms hanging useless at her sides. I straightened, and rubbed my eyes with the backs of my hands.

"They drugged her," Chick said, his voice low. "Did you see the tracks on her arm? Pinned her up with heroin or morphine, then fed her some barbs or maybe some of the dreamsicle. There's a powdery residue on the nightstand. Even if she came out of it, who would she call? No clothes, and drugs in her system."

"She's been raped," I said, croaking it. "These guys are diseased."

Chick nodded. "Yeah."

It was then it popped into my head, the thing that had been bothering me. "Roberts gave her up too easy," I said. "If she could hurt him, she'd be dead. She probably never saw them, and she was flying when Cugat…" I couldn't say it. "They just wanted her out of the way. Winston was worried about it, but Roberts acted like he could care less. He gets Prescott and we get…this." I felt weak inside. Sick. "Least she's alive."

"They're fucking animals. You knew that, or should have. They're cancerous. Only one way to treat cancer, man. You gotta cut it out."

"Gotta call Browne."

"And tell him what? That we squeezed some street punk by flashing false FBI credentials? That we threatened some of the leading citizens of Paradise at gunpoint? Can't waltz to a rock and roll beat. No way. We gotta smoke their asses."

I looked at Tempestt. "Not yet," I said.

"When, dammit? Your way is too slow and might not work. What do you need? These guys are vampires. You gotta drive a stake through their hearts." His eyes were keen, hard-edged. The eyes behind the mask. "No more Hardy Boys crimebusters crap.

It ain't gettin' it done. We have to go after them. And we go after them hard."

"No," I said. "She'll pull out of this. The feds are closing in on them."

"What if she doesn't? What if she dies? What if she's never right again?"

I looked at her. Touched her hair. "Then," I said, "we go after them. No rules."

TWENTY-SEVEN

The ambulance took Tempestt to Citizens Memorial Hospital, where she was admitted as a Jane Doe. We followed in the Bronco. I hoped they would treat her as an overdose victim and not ask too many questions. I knew the marks on her forearm might raise eyebrows and bring the heat, but I didn't care. Just wanted her to be all right. Nothing else mattered.

Maybe Sam Browne was right. Maybe I *was* in over my head. I hadn't figured on a female agent inside Starr Industries, and now I had put her life in jeopardy because I had no head for intrigue. It was sobering to find out I didn't know everything. And more so to find out I knew almost nothing. Chick was right; you couldn't line up against people like Roberts and expect a fair shuffle. Tempestt was my fault; she'd blown her cover to save me from a bad beating. She'd taken a risk for me, a risk that might still cost her her life. Why? And what could I give in exchange?

I used the pay phone in the hospital waiting room to call Sam Browne. The phone and the room smelled of stale cigarette smoke and failed hope. He didn't answer. I considered calling Agent Morrison for about a millisecond, but I didn't want to hear about missions and sacrifices and procedures. I walked to the floor desk and asked if I could see her yet. Her doctor was at the desk and denied the request.

"Not yet," said the doctor, a young guy with a receding hairline and a nice, crinkly smile. "We're going to put her in intensive care. A precaution. I think she'll be all right, but I've not encountered the substances in her blood test in those concentrations before. There are some strange chemicals I'm unable to account for. Very unusual. She's also been treated rather roughly. Fortunately, she is fit and strong. Whoever did this to her...well, an unprofessional thought comes to mind."

I thanked him and asked when I could see her. He thought perhaps by the next evening, but offered the possibility it could be even longer.

"She's been through a lot," he said. "We treated her for shock. I think you may have spared her some long-term physiological damage by getting her to us."

"There's a couple of guys," I said, "a tall, dark-haired guy looks like an insurance agent with muscles, and a blond guy with a tanning salon complexion, who'll want to see her, but I promise you, they'll just aggravate her. If you could somehow limit their access to her I think it would be helpful."

The young doctor smiled his crinkly smile. "I've already heard from Agent Candless, if that's who you're referring to." That struck me as strange. How did Candless know she was here? "He has already been tossing around the names of senators and congressmen. But I assure you, no one is going to see her. Especially Mr. Candless, if for no other reason than to irritate and annoy him."

I thanked him again and walked down the hall to find Chick. That's when I saw Morrison coming up the hall. His eyes were darkened by the half-moons underlining them. His tie was askew. Still, he smiled when he saw me. I didn't smile back.

"What are you doing here?" I asked.

"You know why," said Morrison, rubbing a hand across his face as if that would wipe away the fatigue. He shut his eyes tight, then reopened them. They were raw, bloodshot. "Where is she?"

"I don't know what you're talking about."

"Look, Storme, I understand your anger, but I need to speak with her."

"How'd you know she was here?"

"Candless. He knew."

"Candless, huh? I thought we had a deal."

Morrison let out a breath. He looked ten years older than the first time I met him. "We do. I didn't call him, he called me. They wouldn't let him see her, so he called me. She's FBI, not DEA."

"How could he know she was here? We called the ambulance under an assumed name. She's here under a Jane Doe. Maybe Candless is clairvoyant. How did he know? Answer that."

Morrison shook his head. "I don't know." He looked uncomfortable. Things weren't in their proper order and he knew it, and he was an orderly man. "How is she?" he asked. He was trying to be human.

"I don't know," I said. "She was pretty rough when we found her. Doctor thinks she'll be all right." I told him about the motel room and how we found her.

Morrison listened, chewing on his lower lip. "I should have listened," he said. "This is my fault."

"Doing your job," I said. "That's all. Too late to do anything when I called you anyway. They already had her."

"Roberts?"

"Yeah."

"How'd you find her?"

"We asked Roberts."

"And he told you where to find her?"

"We asked nicely. How could he resist? We wanted her, and we had something he wanted in return."

"Such as?"

"The chemist," I said, not wanting to use Prescott's name. He was still our trump card. "We traded Tempestt for the chemist."

"Dammit, Storme, you let the chemist go? Do you realize how many people will be hurt by this drug?"

"I won't be using it. People I care about won't use it."

"It's not that simple," he said. "It's not the drugs that cause the problem, it's the network and money involved. People steal and kill to get drugs. Money fuels the big criminals and cartels."

"Too abstract," I said. "I can't deal with everything. I could get Tempestt, so that's what I did."

"You have feelings for her, don't you?"

"Yes."

He chewed on it for a moment. An orderly, who smelled of cheap aftershave and antiseptic, rattled an empty gurney with a bad wheel past us. "I sympathize with you," said Morrison. "But I will not be happy if we cannot salvage this investigation. Do you understand?"

I nodded. "And if Tempestt dies and the sheriff's real killer isn't put away, I won't be happy, either."

"Maybe we can't get everything."

"We can try. I'd rather have you for me than against me."

He nodded and rubbed the back of his neck. "So would I."

"She's on this floor," I said. "But the doctor won't allow her visitors until tomorrow night."

"Thanks," said Morrison. "I'll arrange a guard for her."

"I've got to find Chick," I said.

Morrison cleared his throat. "Ah…I know where to find him. Follow me." I did.

We took the elevator down to the main floor and walked to a conference room, which we entered together. Candless had spotted Chick and hustled him into the room while Morrison looked for me. The conference room was sparsely appointed but comfortable and attractive, with the same hospital smell as the halls. The wallpaper was a light mauve with a flower print. The table was blond wood, and there were six fabric-and-wood chairs around it. Chick was slouched in a chair, his standard bemused look on his face, as if all life were an Ogden Nash poem. Candless was leaning forward and doing most of the talking.

"I'll try again," said Candless, ignoring us. "I want to know how you managed to find her."

"I'm an experienced manhunter," Chick said. "Years in the Canadian Mounties. Wanta hear me sing 'I'm Calling You'?"

"You go out of your way to be a smartass, Easton."

"But well worth the trip."

"Maybe we could do this downtown, in the lockup with a federal prosecutor?"

"No thanks. I've got an aerobics class. Maybe some other time." He fished in his pocket for a cigarette, found one, and put it between his lips.

"Sign says no smoking," said Candless.

"Damn. Knew you guys'd catch me in the act sooner or later. What's it gonna be?" Chick said, then lit the cigarette. "You gonna shoot me, or let me live so I can stand trial?"

"I suppose you think I'm bullshitting you?"

"I think you're a tight-assed neurotic with no juice, so you're jacking me around to make yourself feel good."

"You've got a lot of people interested in you, Easton. Big people."

"The price I pay for my luxurious lifestyle."

I interrupted. "How did you know Tempestt was here, Candless?"

His head swiveled to look at me. "I don't have to answer to you. You have to answer to me."

"Somebody in your orbit has switched sides," I said. I searched Candless's face for a twitch, a touch of fear, anything. Nothing showed. Don't understand it. Always worked for Barnaby Jones. "When Tempestt comes out of it, maybe we'll know who."

"*If* she comes out of it," Candless said.

"She will. She's tough. I'm betting on her."

"Rah, rah, rah," said Candless. "Talking to you two is a waste of time. The chemist is probably several states away by now. If he goes to ground and we lose him and this investigation is beyond saving, you two better grease up, because you're going to take a ride."

"Tough talk," I said. "It's all I ever hear from you. You ready to go, Chick?"

"Where do you think you're going?" asked Candless, as Chick slowly rose from his chair.

"Wherever I want."

"Not until you answer some questions."

"Why? You already think you got the answers."

"You're interfering with a federal investigation."

I said, "How? By saving a girl who's been raped and pumped full of narcotics? This investigation needs to be interfered with as long as you're involved. But I'll give you one tip. Alan Winston is involved. Right up to the Windsor knot in his Dior tie."

"I don't buy that."

"Which amazes me. What's your interest in keeping Winston clear of this?"

He evaded the question. "Where's the chemist?"

"Ask Morrison," I said. "We're going."

Candless jumped up and stepped in front of me. "Don't you dismiss me, Storme."

"Get out of my way."

"Let them go," said Morrison. "I've already got Storme's statement, and I believe what he told me. We've no reason to hold either of these men."

Candless pointed a finger at me. "Watch yourself, Storme. Nothing would make me happier than to take you down."

"Yeah? Maybe I'll turn it around on you," I said.

"What does that mean?"

"It means I think you've got your head up your butt. It means I think it's weird that you turned up here at the hospital, even though nobody knew we were bringing her in except for Chick and myself. But Roberts and Cugat already knew what shape she was in. And so did your buddy, Winston. So you tell me how that adds up."

A strange look flashed across Candless's face, but he recovered. "You're barking up the wrong tree."

"So are you. You're too eager to tie a can to my tail and too hesitant to link Winston to anything to suit me. I don't like the way it lays and if you don't get out of my way you're going to have to use some of those Chinese dance moves you're so proud of to keep me here."

He rolled his shoulders as if his jacket needed adjustment. "You better bring the chemist in. All I've got to say."

"No problem," Chick said. "I feel his vibrations, smell his spoor, hear his heartbeat borne on the night wind…"

"Maybe we'll find him ourselves, smart guy."

"Good luck, darlin'. Wish you only the best. But you better find 'im quick."

"Why do you say that?" Morrison asked.

"Whatever Roberts is going to do he's going to do soon," I said.

"Why do you think that?"

"Roberts's attitude more than anything. He doesn't appear to be worried about what we know, as if it's too late to do anything about him." I paused to let it sink in. The pale white hum of hospital was the only sound. "Another thing. I don't think Roberts killed the sheriff. Maybe the sheriff's death has nothing to do with dreamsicle. The timing of it is inconvenient to Roberts's plans. And I think he's too smart to kill a lawman."

"Maybe he had to," Morrison said.

"Possible," Chick said. "And a man with the balls to whack a guy then assume his identity right under federal eyes is a guy capable of anything. He's a king-hell danger freak. Can smell it on him. Likes it out there on the edge. He could do the sheriff, sure, but I don't see what he's gained from it. Roberts is a guy who thinks under the gun. Got it all covered. You blink and he'll slip between your fingers. He's even got an angle on the girl agent. I just can't see what it is."

"What would you know about it?" Candless said.

"Y'know, I've had about enough of your rude mouth, junior," Chick said. "I heard you called me a coward, like you knew what it was like over there. You don't know anything."

"You ran away."

Chick laughed. "That what they told you? Sounds like them. Tell you what, when this is all over we'll get together and see what you got. But you dial my number, you better do it long distance." His eyes were level. Hard.

Candless glared at him. Morrison said, "This isn't accomplishing anything."

"I can wait," said Chick.

"One thing bothers me," said Morrison. "What makes Roberts so confident? If he's going to move large quantities of product, does he think he's got such a fail-safe hiding place we can't find it?"

That bothered me, also. It made no sense. There was risk involved, yet Roberts turned Tempestt over to us without batting an eye. Knew she was an agent and had to know feds were crawling all over the place. I was missing something. Something right under my nose. But what? He had the trucks and the network to move the stuff, but where was it?

And would we know in time to stop it?

TWENTY-EIGHT

The afternoon had lapsed into early evening by the time we left Agents Morrison and Candless with their badges hanging out. It was one of those incredible Missouri autumn evenings when the sky breaks into colors without names, the sun turns a warm gold, and you think you can live forever and might even want to.

We drove along Truman Trafficway, Chick smoking as I sifted through thoughts, looking for a thread to pull on. Roberts thought—no, Roberts knew he was going to get away with this, even with us watching for it. What made him so smug? It was quiet for several minutes before I broke the silence. "Can you find Prescott again?"

"I can find anybody," Chick said. "They should've put me on Hoffa. I know where Prescott is staying, anyway."

"Where?"

"Out at the Truck Hangar. How do you like that? But as to further revelations, I'll need a beer to stimulate my thought processes. Pull into the Qwik-Trip over there." He indicated the convenience store by gesturing with his cigarette.

I clicked on the indicator, pulled into the asphalt parking lot, and stopped between yellow painted lines. Chick opened his door and asked if I wanted anything. I asked for a Dr Pepper, and he left singing, "I'm a Pepper, you're a Pepper…"

I left the motor running and unwrapped a cigar, using a pocket knife to cut the end of it. I lighted the Jamaican with the dash lighter, and the cab filled with the rich aroma. I rolled down the window to allow the smoke to escape. Something was tumbling around in my mind. I played "what if?" with what I knew so far, as I looked out the window. A large woman in pink sweats, blue-black hair, and too much makeup put a grocery bag in a white Chevrolet Caprice. A little less makeup and easier on the dye and she would be a more attractive woman. She stood up, slapped her forehead with a palm, and hurried back into the store for the thing she'd forgotten.

A string tumbled down from the attic in my brain and I pulled on it. KISS. Keep It Simple, Stupid. Chick returned with a twelve-pack of Budweiser and my Dr Pepper. Shutting the door, he handed me the bruised-purple can, and I backed out of the slot. I said, "If Willie Boy had the formula, would he need Prescott anymore?"

Chick opened the twelve-pack, snapped back a ring-tab on a red-and-white can. "Roberts isn't a chemist. He needs Prescott to turn out a supply for him."

Bingo! I had it. So obvious. So simple it was beautiful, and it fit Roberts's sense of irony. "What if Roberts doesn't intend to market dreamsicle? What if he sells the formula and then slides out from under the whole thing? Takes the money and retires."

Chick sipped from the Budweiser can. He stopped and thought for a moment as I pulled into the traffic. He began to laugh. "It's perfect," he said. "Easier than selling drugs. No risk. He sells Prescott's formula to the highest bidder and is set for life. No muss. No fuss. No picture in the post office. No cops with warrants. He's out of the picture before anyone knows about the stuff. Dreamsicle isn't even illegal yet. It may be the perfect crime."

"Who would he sell it to?"

"The Sicilians. The Colombians. Anybody with a lot of cash and the apparatus to market it. It'd be worth millions to him and more to the people who had a monopoly on it. He could name his price. Ask for a onetime flat rate or get a big advance and then a percentage of the take. Either way it's a beauty."

"It's the kind of thing appeals to someone who thinks like he does, isn't it? Center stage. Feds everywhere. Watch me pull a rabbit out of my hat. Nothing up my sleeve. Presto. He could stay right here and even if it went sour…" I left it open.

"If it went sour," said Chick, "then Roberts could become Max Beauchamps again. First sell Starr Industries, turn everything into cash, then become Max B. or someone new and move his twisted act somewhere else. Interesting thought, isn't it?"

"What if?" Chick said. "While we're playing this game, what if Roberts had a reason to give us the girl?"

"What do you mean?" I changed lanes to pass a red Cadillac.

"He gave us the girl too easy, like you said. Not like him to give anything unless he likes the cards he's holding. You can bet Roberts was nowhere near when they grabbed the girl and sent her to the stars. But maybe he's using the girl to blackmail someone. What if she's got something on someone else in the inner circle? If nothing else, he's got her out of the way for several hours, or maybe even days."

"He keeps a lot of plates spinning."

"Us too." He took another beer from the carton. I thought about Tempestt. I felt like a Jonah. First the sheriff, now Tempestt. Funny how she had become a part of my thoughts and feelings so quickly. The stage fright I'd felt approaching tonight's date with her was now replaced by a sense of loss. I needed to know—about her, about Sandy, about myself. Would I ever know now? Ten years from now I didn't want to be visited by nostalgic vapors of what might have been. I loved Sandy, but I had not been able to pin down what I felt for Tempestt. Friendship? Desire? Love? All of the above? Voltaire said love is a canvas furnished by nature and embroidered by the imagination. Voltaire was right.

The thought of it whistled through my heart and head with gale force.

"So, what's our next step?" asked Chick.

"Not sure. We're running out of time and people who will talk to us. If we knew where to look for their lab, that would help."

"Could be anywhere. At Roberts's factory. His house. Maybe even out at the Truck Hangar, and that's where Prescott is staying."

"Might be interesting," I said. "We haven't checked it out, yet. About the last place to look. If nothing else, maybe Prescott is there."

"What if he's not?"

"We could hang around and be annoying."

"Okay with me. I have an inborn talent for being annoying."

"Yes. I know."

TWENTY-NINE

The Truck Hangar sat at the junction of Interstate 50 and U.S. Highway 61, eleven miles north of Paradise, where it sprawled across the county line into Ford County. Good location. It was a huge complex—restaurant, bar, gift shop, clothing shop, showers for truckers, six-lane bowling alley, thirty-six fuel pumps, twenty-four of which were for eighteen-wheelers, and a ten-unit motel located on the Ford County side, where goodwill was for rent. The motel interested me the most.

We stood momentarily, after getting out of the Bronco, and scanned the mammoth truck stop. "Where's the rest of it?" said Chick.

"Jill said they run prostitutes here. Motel makes it easier. What do you think?"

"Let's grab a road chippie and make her bark like a dog."

"You know which unit Prescott's in?"

"No. Can't ask, either. They'll be watching for me now. I doubt he's still here. But it's worth a look. We could go into the gift shop and buy a T-shirt that says Truckers Do It for the Long Haul. Go native."

"Or," I said, "we could hang around outside the motel and give hard Puritan stares to the truckers as they bring the snuff queens over to the motel."

"Can we cluck our tongues and shake our heads when they walk past?"

"Part of the fun."

We went into the truck stop's restaurant-lounge. It was stainless steel and clean gingham tablecloths and waitresses in white nursing shoes. I bought a cup of coffee, black, to go. They poured it into a large Styrofoam cup; no concern for the environment. A Hank Williams, Jr., song belched from the lounge. Like I said, no concern for the environment. Chick walked into the darkened bar, was gone for several minutes, and reappeared with a longneck Budweiser, which he stuck under his shirt as we left.

"There's an open-container law in this county," he explained.

"There's beer in the truck," I said.

"Where's your sense of adventure? I don't have to sneak those."

"Very childish."

"Keeps me young."

We walked to the motel and took up positions in front. In order to get a room, Chick explained, the john had to get a key in the bar. "The connection is made there," he said. "But no money changes hands. The girls hang around the bar waiting for the truckers to come in. The girls try to get the truckers to buy them a drink and then maneuver them to the motel to do the ultimate naughty. Either way, commerce occurs."

The motel was blue cinder block and clean. Willie Boy was no fool. The nicer it looked, the less likely people were to hassle you. A family could pull into the restaurant, have dinner, bowl a few lines, and be on their way, without disturbance. I sat down on a brick planter and peeled the lid from the coffee cup, tasted its contents. It was fresh and delicious. Roberts was a good businessman. Smart. But he had a wire jammed in his brain. He could make it legitimately, but that wasn't enough for him. Something drove him, whipsawed him to do things in a dark, unnatural way.

We'd only been there a few minutes when an overweight trucker in a well-worn camouflage down vest and a Peterbilt baseball cap walked in our direction, his arm around a nubile miss in a short skirt and a pair of strapless high-heeled shoes. I thought down vests and strapless heels were out of style, along with promiscuous sex. Chick and I stood when they came our way. The girl looked much better than I had expected. Much better.

"Outstanding talent," Chick said. "I may have to get me a Ken-worth and pull in here."

As the amorous couple neared, we moved to block the walkway. They slowed and stopped in front of us.

"We don't want any trouble," the trucker said. He looked uncertain. I noticed a ring on his left hand. Probably had a wife and kids. I didn't like scaring him, but he shouldn't avail himself of the road chippy. The girl was less uncertain.

"What do you guys want?" she said. She looked maybe nineteen, blond, with the kind of slim legs teenagers have, but with a great jawline and lovely sea-green eyes, slim waist.

"We're from the militant branch of the Moral Majority," I said. "And we're here to advise you that paying for sex is a nopey-no and a health hazard."

"Fuck you guys," she said. Charming girl.

"No thanks," Chick said. "I do that and you'll follow me the rest of my life. Besides, I'm all out of penicillin."

"Forget it, Bernice," said the trucker. He was frightened. "Let's just go back to the bar."

"You assholes are screwin' up big time," she said, a fist jammed against a cantilevered hip.

"You shouldn't talk like that," I said. "It's indelicate."

"Bastards," she spat. "We'll see what Large Michael has to say about this."

"Oh, please," Chick said. "Anything but that."

"Fuck you," she said, turning on her heels to stomp away, Down Vest trailing her.

"Girl needs to expand her vocabulary," Chick said.

"I want a master key," I said. I wanted to see the inside of the units.

"Maybe Large What's-his-name will bring us one."

"He also serves who sits and waits."

I drank more coffee. We talked about the Kansas City Chiefs' chances of making the playoffs, talked about whether Clapton was a better guitarist than Hendrix. We both agreed Larry Bird had been the greatest to ever pull on a pair of sneakers, but Jordan might soon prove to be. "Bird, Russell, Jordan, and two warm bodies can whip anyone else," Chick said.

I'd just mentioned Havlicek and Jerry West, my all-time fave, to complete the squad, when a contingent of well-wishers from the Truck Hangar walked in our direction. There were four of them.

"Lookit this," said Chick. "Clubs 'n' everything."

"It's because they think you're Frankenstein."

"Oh yeah? Where're the torches, then?"

The sun had set when they moved into the pale light of the motel sign. I recognized the largest guy from the parking lot of the Silver Spur Lounge.

"Who the hell you guys think—" started Large Michael, then he recognized us. "Aw, shit. You guys again." The other men were carrying short staves and tire irons. No match for two men with goodness as their shield.

"What's happening, guys?" I said, conversational. Always nice to meet new people.

"The fuck you think you're doing here?" asked Large Michael.

"Everybody says that," said Chick.

"No imagination," I said.

Large Michael began rapping his baton in his hand, rhythmically. "You guys are trespassing."

"This from a guy who pimps for teenyboppers," Chick said.

"We want a master key to these units," I said. "Unless you want to tell me which room is Campbell's." They knew Prescott as Campbell.

Large Michael threw back his head and laughed. He turned to the other three and said, "They want a master key." The rest of the all-goon revue laughed with him. Chortled actually. It'd been a long time since I'd heard a good group chortle. They obviously didn't realize we had them surrounded.

I turned to Chick. "I tried polite."

"Nobody can say you didn't do your best."

"So now what?"

"How about Randolph Scott and John Wayne?"

"Sounds good to me."

I pulled the 9-millimeter Browning automatic from its shoulder holster and Chick pulled the .380 Colt about a beat and a half before me. He was so quick I was beginning to suspect he had done this sort of thing before.

"Grab some sky, gents," said Chick.

"Shit!" said Large Michael.

"Of course," said Chick.

"The key," I said. I held a hand out, palm up.

"You don't know who you're messing with," said Large Michael, ever the bearer of news, good and otherwise.

"Neither do you," said Chick, his gun hand seeming to point at nothing in particular, yet everywhere at once. "You got three seconds to put down your little sticks or you get to find out. Ready? One...two..."

Four batons rattled on the asphalt.

"Damn," said Chick. "I never get to shoot anybody anymore."

"Maybe we call the cops," said Large Michael.

"That's even funnier than me not shooting you, you calling the cops. Go ahead. It's a slow night."

"The key," I said, my teeth starting to clench as I thought about Tempestt, left alone in a dirty motel, abused, and pumped full of chemicals. Sheriff Kennedy, father of two, honest lawman, killed for that honesty. I was way past my acceptable limit of crap like that.

"What if I refuse?" said Large Michael.

I slapped the side of the Browning across his cheek. He tried to get his hands up, tried to duck away, but if I wasn't quicker than some fat local tough then I was further past retirement than I thought. The gun whipcracked along his jowls and I felt the scratchy texture of his beard. The trio with him jumped, startled by the sudden violence. The blow staggered him, but he didn't fall.

It didn't suit me.

I followed the backhand with a left-hand swat. Large Michael's eyes widened in amazement. It was the look rookie linemen had the first time one of the moat monsters head-slapped them. You either survived it or quit. Many quit. I stayed.

"The key. Now."

He looked at me in disbelief. Like most bullies, he wasn't used to this. Twice in one week. "Go to hell," he said, trying to regain some of his lost face in front of his comrades.

I looked at Chick. "He's not listening to me," I said. I turned back to the bearded man. "You have no sense of my outrage, fatso. If I have to hospitalize you, I'll do it. You don't matter. Right now, only the key matters. I want it and I will get it, no matter what it takes."

I kicked him between the legs. He dropped to his knees. When he reached for his private parts, I backhanded him. He fell over on the pavement. Not enough. The rage, exacerbated by fatigue and frustration, which had been gurgling beneath the black part of my soul, was rushing to the surface, fueled by adrenaline. Once again, I was startled by that part of me I could not control. The violence that had been so much a part of my life raised its ugly, red-eyed head—the beast within, long suppressed, yet not at bay. I holstered the gun, grabbed Large Michael by his jacket, jerked him erect, and slapped him on both ears with my hands. Then I chopped him on the neck with the side of a fist, followed by a blow from the heel of my hand against his eyebrows. I backhanded him again and saliva flew from his slack mouth.

"Stop," said Large Michael.

"The key," I said. I was panting. Anger, not exhaustion.

"They'll kill me," he said.

"And you think we won't?" Chick said. He put the tip of his gun in Large Michael's mouth. "Make a wish."

Large Michael fumbled in the pocket of his jeans and handed us a ring of keys on a blue plastic tag. He was sweating heavily, and the sour aroma filled my nostrils. I took the key ring from him. "Which room is he in?"

"Seven," he answered, his eyes searching the ground.

"Anybody in number one?"

He shook his head.

"Take them into number one," I said to Chick, "while I see if Prescott is home." Chick nodded, and we hustled the quartet into the room, using one of the keys to open the door.

Chick had them sit down, then asked, "Anybody know any ghost stories? Any songs?"

I pulled on a pair of leather driving gloves so I'd feel like Cary Grant and also so I wouldn't leave any prints. Cary would've been proud, but Bogart would've been smart enough to put them on before roughing up Large Michael. The backs of my hands were sore but were not swelling. The big trucks chugged and droned like metal dinosaurs in the background as I walked to number 7. There were two locks on the door, one on the knob and another one a little higher, probably a dead bolt. None of my keys fit the upper keyhole. I knocked on the door. No answer. I walked back to the first unit. I didn't know how much time we had before somebody called the cops. Now would be a bad time for Baxter to show.

When I opened the door to unit 1, Chick still had the four men sitting on the floor. Their pants were unbuckled and pulled down around their ankles. Their shoes were in a heap by one wall, leaving them barefoot and chagrined.

"Which one you think has the best legs?" asked Chick.

"I need the dead bolt key to number seven," I said, to Large Michael.

"People in hell need ice water, too," said Michael.

"He's such a wit," said Chick.

"Oh yeah?" I said. "Who around here said, 'Grab some sky'?"

"A classic. How about, 'No sense of my outrage'?"

"Okay, Michael," I said. "What's it gonna be? You give me the key, or do I take it from you?"

"I don't have it. Honest. Only the guy, Campbell, and Roberts himself have keys."

I believed him. "We need a crowbar," I said. "Wait here." I left them and walked back to the truck stop and bought a crowbar in the parts store. It was silver and heavy. I hefted it and it felt nice and solid. I walked back to unit 7. The door was hollow-core metal. It took some effort, but I was able to peel the dead bolt. That done, I used the key on the doorknob lock and pushed in. Inside, the room looked like number 1, with the exception of a VCR on the television, a kitchenette, a collection of technical notebooks, and a dead body in the bathtub.

It was Prescott. He hadn't been dead long. There was an open quart bottle of Jack Daniel's black-label bourbon on the floor next to the tub, along with a profusion of pills, caplets, and powders. There were no cuts or bruises on the body. The Magical Mystery Medicine Sleep. Looked like an overdose or a suicide. But I wasn't buying it. Not when the guy was on the brink of the biggest money he'd ever see.

There was the stench of death in the room, but without the rot of long-term death. His face was blotchy, and his arms had begun to stiffen with rigor mortis. His skin was water-puckered. The eyes, glassy, stared at eternity. Died within the last couple of hours. Probably wouldn't have been found for several days if I hadn't gone looking for him.

I walked back into the bedroom, checking under the bed, in the drawers of the cheap veneer nightstand and dresser. I didn't know exactly what I was looking for, but I looked. I searched behind the commode tank in the bathroom. Behind the Kmart pictures on the wall. Under the mattress. In the mattress. Nothing. I rummaged through the collection of videotapes, none of which were hollow. As I was going through them, I knocked one to the floor. It fell and bounced on its edge toward the dresser. When I reached down to pick it up, I noticed an irregularity in the grain of the carpeting. I wouldn't have noticed if I hadn't been looking directly at it. I shoved the dresser aside and saw that someone had apparently cut a two-foot square in the carpet, removed it, and then set it back in. I plucked at a corner of the square, which was glued to a thin metal plate. I lifted it out to reveal a sunken safe with a combination dial on top.

I searched the room again and found what I was looking for taped to the back of the nightstand drawer. Written in blue ink were the numbers 17-75-36-12.

I got the safe open on the second attempt. The handle clicked as I twisted it and the mouth of the safe gaped. Inside were some papers, folded into an envelope and bound with a thick rubber band, a thousand dollars in various denominations, and a short plastic tube containing two dozen rocks of dreamsicle.

Jackpot.

Willie Boy had finally made a mistake.

I rummaged through the papers. It was the dreamsicle formula. Had to be. There were chemical symbols and instructions on how to combine them, along with proper temperatures, cooling time, and measurements. I removed a couple of rocks from the plastic tube and put the tube back in the safe. I pocketed the papers and put the money in my wallet. Prescott wouldn't need it anymore and Chick deserved remuneration for being cheated out of his reward money. The Andy Jacksons, U.S. Grants, and Ben Franklins made a fat bulge in my wallet. I retaped the combination number to the back of the nightstand drawer, returned the carpet square to the correct position, and pushed the dresser back in place over it.

That done, I picked up the phone and dialed the highway patrol to report the murder to Sam Browne.

THIRTY

I called Troop A headquarters in Lee's Summit. Told the dispatcher it was an emergency and I would speak with Browne only. I gave the number on Prescott's phone, hung up, and waited. I knew Chick was alone in the room with our four playmates, but he could handle it. I didn't know how much time we had before other people took an interest in us. But the business of the motel, which was monkey business, probably gave us a good deal of isolation.

Within two minutes the phone jangled. I picked it up and said, "Jerry's Jiggle Joint, where your every dream comes true."

"Cut the shit, Storme," Browne said. "What have you got?"

"A dead body, a safe full of illegal drugs, and a smile that'll make your sister swoon."

"You'd joke at your own funeral."

"I'll send you an invitation."

"Wouldn't miss it. Where are you?" I told him. "The Truck Hangar, huh? Good. You finally did something positive. I'd love to walk through their operation with probable cause. I'll make sergeant by the end of the week."

"Got another problem," I said. "We may have used unique methods to find the dead man."

"Like what?"

"Breaking and entering."

"You crazy—"

"Also assault with a deadly weapon."

"You shoot anybody?"

"No, just kind of pointed it at them and asked for their assistance."

"You didn't rape anybody, did you?"

"They charge for that here. We did manage to lust heavily for one of the chippies, though."

"Let's see. I'm about fifteen minutes away," said Browne. "Okay, here's the drill. You call Baxter and report this."

"You're kidding."

"No. It'll be all right. The motel is out of his jurisdiction. That way it doesn't look like I'm trying to Bogart his territory. Keep the brass off my back, and it'll make you appear cooperative, which'll be a first. How'd you know it was the wrong county when you called? Play dumb and button that smart lip and Baxter won't be able to do anything, and 1-50 is definitely our jurisdiction. I'll call in, get some backup, and be there quicker than you can say Broderick Crawford. Don't tell Baxter anything until I get there."

"Doesn't sound courteous to me."

"Yeah, I'll bet you're dying to help him out."

"Ten-four," I said. "Over and out."

He mumbled an obscenity and I heard the phone clang down on its hook. I walked outside to a pay phone and made an anonymous call to the Paradise County sheriff's office, hung up before they could ask who I was, walked back to the Bronco, put the Browning under the spare tire, and walked to the motel. I dropped the crowbar in a trash can and took off my gloves.

"Hi, kids," I said, when I entered room 1. "Your uncle Wyatt's back."

"Find anything?" Chick asked.

"I gotta piss," said one of the goons.

"Do it in your pants," Chick said. "Whoops, I forgot, you aren't wearing any. Guess you'll have to improvise."

"Is your gun registered?" I asked Chick.

"Some of them."

"This one?"

"Yes."

"Good. The fuzz is coming. Maybe it's the fuzz are coming. Plural. Prescott is in room seven with the worst hangover I've ever seen. The kind they don't make aspirin for."

"How?"

"Got it dressed up to look like an overdose. Or a suicide. Drugs all around. Half-empty bottle of Jack Daniel's. Recent."

"Were you able to save the whiskey?"

"I don't know nothin' about that," said Large Michael.

"That'll be your most convincing defense," I said. "Your ignorance is very believable."

I heard a siren whooping, growing closer, louder, and then the room was bathed in a carousel of red and blue light. Through the window I saw the Paradise County car skid to a halt. Simmons was in the car with Baxter. They got out with drawn weapons. I opened the door and waved at them. A sour expression appeared on the interim sheriff's face, which made the whole thing worthwhile. I left the door open and the county cops stepped inside. Chick's gun had disappeared.

"All right," said Baxter. "What the—?" He stopped when he saw the four men on the floor. "What the hell are you guys doing on the floor like…like that?"

"Sheriff," said Chick, "we've uncovered a vicious depantsing ring and these poor men are victims."

"You shut up," Baxter said to Chick. "You boys pull your pants up. Michael, you look ridiculous." Simmons was smiling.

"It's these guys, Les," said Michael, as he and his comrades shrugged on their jeans. "They made us—"

"Shut up," said Baxter. "Who called about a dead body?"

I shrugged. "You might check room seven," I said.

Baxter said, "Simmons, you stay here and keep an eye on these people while I check this out." He left. Simmons looked at us, said nothing.

The sheriff was gone ten minutes. While he was gone Chick turned on the television and we watched a *Newhart* rerun. Larry, Daryl, and Daryl had just come on the screen when Baxter returned. His gun was drawn, again.

"You're under arrest," he said, waving the gun at Chick and me.

"Must be the depantsing thing," said Chick.

"What are we under arrest for?" I asked.

"Murder."

"Well, you're too clever for us," I said. "What do you think? We pumped the guy full of booze and pills, waited a couple hours for rigor mortis to set in, called you, then sat around in a motel room with four guys with no pants on for you to drop by and arrest us?"

"I'll think of something," said Baxter.

"That'll be another long wait," Chick said.

Just then, there were more dancing lights and the sound of a car pulling up. No siren. No skidding of tires on pavement. Baxter looked out the door and mumbled something. Trooper Browne entered the room. "Put the gun away, Baxter," said Browne.

"What are you doing here?" Baxter said.

"Anonymous tip," said Browne, smiling at me.

"Lot of it going around," said Chick. "Only good, law-abiding folks here in Paradise County."

"This isn't Paradise County," said Browne. "Is it, Baxter?"

The nuance of the situation escaped Baxter. "These two men are under arrest."

"Do you have to be stupid all the time, Baxter?"

"I've been around him quite a bit now," Chick said. "And he has yet to do one smart thing."

"Your memory's a little short, Easton," Baxter said.

"Longer than you think, fats. But I'm patient."

"Who are these people?" Browne asked me, indicating Large Michael and his buddies.

"Four of the seven dwarfs," I said. "Dopey, Sleepy, Grumpy, and Jerky."

"No Doc?" said Chick.

"No Brainy, either. Actually they work here. For Roberts. They pimp for the whores and act as muscle if a John doesn't pay, or if you hang around too much. They're not very good at it, though. They tried to roust us with nasty clubs, but we were able to foil them."

"Foiled the shit out of 'em, in fact," Chick said.

"They pulled guns on us," protested Large Michael.

"There's that, too," I admitted.

"Do you wish to prefer charges against them?" Browne asked me.

"No," I said. "I think they've learned their lesson."

"They got anything to do with the stiff?"

"Probably not. They're too lightweight for that kind of work. They'll be easy to find if you need them. Besides, if they become a problem I could change my mind about the assault charges."

"Okay," Browne said. "Baxter, I'm authorizing you and your deputy to take these four men in for questioning. I'll bring in Storme and Easton after I check the crime scene."

"Bullshit. You don't tell me nothin'. I'm going to—"

Browne took a quick step in Baxter's direction and put his face close to Baxter's. "Do what I say, Baxter. I've got an ME and a lab technician coming in directly. I want them to be able to work without you clomping around and messing it up." The brim of Browne's Smokey the Bear hat was so close to touching Baxter's forehead, that Baxter had to lean away to avoid it. "I've had enough of your crap, Baxter. On the way over I called my captain and briefed him on the situation and the unusual politics of your county, and especially the way you conduct your office. He authorized me to take full responsibility for this investigation, including placing you under arrest if you create problems, since Ford County is out of your jurisdiction. You have no authority here except what I allow. Senator Hobbs, who intervened before, is presently under investigation for illegal use of public funds and sodomy. So you need to shut up and bus your fat tail back to the lockup before I arrest you, too."

"There's six of us and only three of them, Les," said Large Michael.

"There's four of us," said Simmons. "Don't need the job that bad."

"Looks like you're outnumbered, Large," Chick said. "You don't mind if I use your first name, do you?"

Baxter grabbed Large Michael by the front of his jacket and jerked him toward the door. "Let's go, Michael. And if you say one word you're gonna participate in some of that police brutality you hear so much about." He hustled the quartet through the door. As they were leaving, Baxter said, "This ain't the end of it."

"I need to take a look at the body," Browne said, after Baxter was gone. "You two stay out of trouble until I get back."

" 'Bus your fat tail back to the lockup'?" I said.

"Shut up, Storme."

THIRTY-ONE

The medical examiner and the police technician showed up half an hour after Baxter left. In that half hour I updated Browne, leaving out the floor safe and the fact I had a copy of the dreamsicle formula. I needed it for leverage with Roberts.

"You think Roberts killed this guy?" asked Browne.

"Or had it done," I said. "He wasn't counting on anybody checking on Prescott for a couple of days. Guy was an outsider. Didn't know anybody in town."

"What about Baxter's part in all this?"

"Not sure. He was right on top of this place after I called. Like somebody tipped him off. He's dirty, but he's too stupid for Roberts to trust, and he was genuinely surprised by the murder. Still, it doesn't seem right. The murder of Kennedy was too messy. Badly timed. Roberts wouldn't be so inopportune, and the killing of the chemist is a contrast in style. It'll be tough to prove Prescott was murdered. It was well planned and executed."

"Maybe Roberts put a contract on Kennedy," said Browne.

"But why? I've asked myself that a hundred times. He wouldn't kill the sheriff over a field of marijuana. If the heat came down he could just drop the Roberts facade, which, incidentally, would protect him anyway, and become Max Beauchamps again. It's like Chick says, Willie Boy doesn't do anything without a reason. He's too smart. Probably take a legion of federal officers and a dozen U.S. attorneys thirty years to convict him of even driving near that field. I'll bet there's no way to link him to the marijuana even if it is his. Besides, if you were sitting on a deal worth millions, would you run pot?"

"Penny-ante stuff," Browne said. "So now Roberts is the only one with access to the formula."

"That you know of, anyway," I said, hedging on the truth.

"Roberts can market it without cutting Prescott in and maybe hold it over his partners' heads."

"Or sell the formula to the highest bidder," said Chick.

"Your turn," I said to Browne.

"Okay. You were right about the drug dealer. Killian couldn't have killed the sheriff. The ME said the shoulder wound would have prevented him from shouldering the shotgun, much less pulling the trigger. There is some evidence the sheriff was unprepared for the blast even though it came from the front. Death was immediate and the muscles were relaxed in the corpse. Usually, if the shot comes from in front of the victim, the muscles are tensed at the moment of death. Generally, the muscles are relaxed only if the shot comes from beyond the victim's awareness."

"Such as a shot in the back."

"Right. Killian couldn't have driven the truck with the shoulder wound. Manual steering and stick shift."

"Meaning," said Chick, "that someone put him in the truck. Before or after shooting him?"

"After. There was very little blood in the truck. But it threw us because it's the type of wound that does little bleeding. Well placed. Right at the base of the neck with a .22-caliber solid point."

"A pro."

Browne nodded. "Like a former hit man. You cleared up one mystery for me. When we ran a check on William Roberts through NCIC we got nothing. The information was withheld. A mystery man. The witness protection scam explains that. Before, it was like he didn't exist." He looked at Chick. "Kind of like somebody else."

"So why trust me?" Chick said.

"The DA in Boulder is a friend of my captain's. We called. The DA said you were beyond a pain in the ass but a man of your word and the best skip-tracer in Colorado."

"In the universe," Chick said, correcting him.

"Said you always land on your feet. Always around when things are happening and nowhere to be found when they're over. Said you think you can whip Mike Tyson and Steven Seagal at the same time."

"Plus their brothers and sisters."

"Said you *thought* it."

"Half the battle."

"We also found out who was pulling our string." Chick got out a pack of cigarettes, offered them to Browne, who shook his head, then continued. "Senator Hobbs, a state senator from Clearmont, is a close friend of the Winston family. Apparently, Baxter complained to Winston that we were taking over the investigation. Winston complained to Hobbs, who passed it on to our colonel or someone at Jeff. The patrol is a good organization, the best of its kind, but we have some people at the top who are more politician than cop. When the wind blows, they fold."

"I'm shocked to hear such a thing," Chick said, lighting his cigarette.

Browne smiled. "It ain't all dodging bullets and driving fast. Anyway, it turns out Senator Hobbs has a taste for teenaged boys and state funds that aren't earmarked. The guys on the patrol are saying he got caught with his hand in the cookie jar and his meat in the produce section. Which is too bad, really. Except for this, Hobbs had been good to law enforcement."

"So where do we go from here?" I asked.

"I'm going to investigate this homicide, or suicide, or whatever it turns out to be, and you're being instructed, officially, to back off, a warning that you're sure to ignore. But it gets me off the hook if anybody asks you later. Do you understand what I'm saying?"

I nodded. Chick nodded. We understood.

"You've stirred up a hornet's nest, but it's one that needed stirring. You need to understand that because of the witness protection net we will be unable to touch Roberts unless he makes a major mistake. You've got your own agenda. You can do things and go places we can't. That's off the record. I'll run interference for you where I can, unofficially, but the best I may be able to do is keep you out of jail for some of your lesser crimes. With three murders and the abduction of the FBI agent, we will become more involved and Baxter less so." He paused, looked at Chick. "That gun under your jacket registered?"

"Yes."

"How about the one in the ankle holster?"

"You've got a good eye."

"You didn't answer my question."

"No I didn't," said Chick. "Really want to know?"

"Hell no," said Browne. "I don't want to know anything you guys are up to, not even what you held back when you were telling me 'everything.' There's a lot of dirty money involved and you guys aren't as cute as you think, so be careful. These people will not be nice."

"This isn't about money," I said. "Roberts has money. Winston has money. They're only interested in the money so they can accumulate power. Power is what Willie Boy Roberts is all about. Winston, too."

"You may be right," said Browne. "I've got work to do, so get out of here and stay out of my hair."

"You mean you're not going to take us downtown and beat us with rolled newspapers?" said Chick.

"I've got your statements," said Browne. "But, like they say in the movies, don't leave town without telling us. Another thing. Watch yourselves. A couple of K.C. guys, wise guys, are in town.

May be shooters. Hope you aren't the target. They may have done Prescott. This is the major leagues, boys. Now, go polish your comedy routine somewhere."

We left him to his reports. There were two more patrol units outside the motel when we left him, and a Ford County car, too. People were standing outside the truck stop. We walked through the parking lot to the Bronco and got in, and I eased the Bronco through the tangle of official cars and curious onlookers. We headed back to Paradise on Highway 61. Yes, it could be easily done. Out there on Highway 61.

Chick retrieved a beer from the cooler. "Got a present for you," I said. I dug the wad of bills out of my wallet and handed them to him. "Finder's fee you got cheated out of. Compliments of the dear departed. It's only one-fifth of what you had coming, but we do what we can."

"Where'd you get this?"

I told him what I hadn't told Browne, including the part about the dreamsicle formula.

He looked at me, the apostrophe eyebrow raised, and said, "And all this time I thought you were just another dumb jock. How do you know Prescott didn't make this money teaching ghetto children how to read?"

"A chance I'll have to take." I watched him flip through the money. He counted out five hundred and handed it back to me. "No thanks," I said. "Already peeled off a grand for myself." A lie, of course.

"Really? Where is it? There's no lump in your jacket, and the one under your zipper's very small." He opened the glove box, put the money in it, shut it, and said, "Equal partners—fifty-fifty."

"What if I said I don't need it?"

"What if I said I don't care? I'm not a charity case, and you're not Robin Hood."

"And you're stubborn."

"How can we fail? What's our next move?"

"We deal ourselves in. We put the dreamsicle formula on the market. But because we're good people with a sense of fair play, we give Willie Boy first shot at it."

"You got a plan?"

"Always," I said.

THIRTY-TWO

"I've got a copy of the formula," I said, into the pay phone at the back of the Silver Spur Lounge, where my freewheeling associate, Charles Easton, and myself were dining on giant cheeseburgers and onion rings, having shunned the cuisine and clientele of the Truck Hangar. One must draw the line somewhere or risk being taken for a lout. "Want to buy it back? Only fifty-three shopping days 'til Christmas."

"Who is this?" said the voice of Willie Boy Roberts, aka Max Beauchamps.

"I want two hundred and fifty thousand in the usual small denominations, like on television cop shows. If you're not interested, I'll peddle it elsewhere."

Roberts laughed his throaty, good-old-boy-from-the-bayou laugh. He was good. "I don't know what you're talking about, me."

"Dreamsicle."

"That means nothing to me," he said, but hesitated a beat before saying it.

"Guess you won't mind if I sell it to someone else, then."

"Do as you wish, you. You have the wrong person."

"Wonder what the guys with the vowels at the ends of their names will say when they find out they don't have an exclusive."

"There is no formula."

"A moment ago, you didn't know what I was talking about. I know about Prescott. He's dead in his motel room. Phony overdose. A little sloppy, Willie Boy. Prescott kept a floor safe your goons didn't find. The police are already investigating. Your hourglass has a hole in it and the sand is running out. You want to deal, or do I go door-to-door like a Fuller Brush man?"

Chick was flirting with a young lady at a nearby table. He had a Busch long-neck by the throat, leaning it against his hip like in the commercials. She was deciding if she was interested. Nice blonde, late twenties, green eyes, freckles sprinkled across her nose.

"You have nothing that interests me, podna," said Roberts.

Chick winked at the blond. She smiled, then looked away. Smoke from several cigarettes hovered and drifted. Speaking into the phone, I read a couple of the ingredients from the paper in my hand so the customer would know I was sincere. It was quiet on the other end. Chick mimicked a fisherman setting the hook. Then Roberts said, "I would be glad to discuss any business proposition that would be mutually beneficial. If you will tell me where you are, I'll have an employee pick you up—"

It was my turn to laugh, so I did. "Nice try, but my mom told me never to accept rides from strangers. No. You and me, tomorrow morning at ten o'clock. I will call you at nine A.M. at your house to give you the location. If you don't answer or you're not home, the deal is off. Get the money together and wait for my call."

"I'll need more time to get the money together."

"You don't have any more time," I said, then hung up.

Chick said, "He ain't buying nothing from you. He'll try to take you out. Make him look bad if you soak him."

"That's the way I've got it figured, too. But he'll have to be home at nine o'clock tomorrow morning for sure."

The blond got up and walked to our table. Chick smiled as she neared. "Excuse me," she said to me. "You look familiar. You a baseball player or something?"

"No," I said. "Too violent. Chess is my game."

The girl joined us. Her name was Melanie, and she soon figured out it wasn't baseball or chess I had played. She was a big football fan. Nice kid. She drank a beer with Chick, then left to keep an appointment with a friend. She gave Chick her phone number.

We finished our cheeseburgers, which were enormous and filling and delicious and fattening. I could almost hear my arteries clogging. When this was over it would be salad and broiled fish. Chick, a walking bad influence, downed another beer, then took to drinking Wild Turkey from shooters, a glass of water beside them. He was actually becoming tipsy for the first time since I'd met him. The weather was changing outside. The evening sky had turned weepy and dark, threatening rain. The waitress brought me coffee and Chick had another knock of the Turkey. We talked about several things. College football, old girlfriends, old friends, Matt Jenkins. Then the conversation turned to Vietnam. At first it was about old war buddies and where we went for R and R. Then Chick's face began to go slack, flushed with the red glow of Kentucky whiskey. He became serious, a departure for him. The thing nibbling at him took another bite.

"I'd just come off a mission," he said. He lighted a cigarette off the nub of the one he'd been smoking. His eyes were swollen and red-rimmed. "One of the guys, a captain, had scored a lid of Cambodian and rolled a J size of a Cuban cigar, cutting the smoke with San Miguel beer and Jack D. There were a couple of Green Berets and a spook there. Spook drank wine, the snake-eaters drank the whiskey straight from the bottle. They were so ripped an air strike on the hootch would've been a reason to get off on the colors..."

He dragged on his cigarette and took another hit from the bourbon. His capacity for alcohol was incredible. And disturbing. I didn't know if he was fanning the flames or trying to quench them.

"Anyway," he said, "I hadda do an NVA colonel who had a thing for B-girls and Dom Perignon champagne. He had a favorite girl. Seventeen years old. Her foster parents were rice farmers." He blinked and looked over my head, as if looking for something he'd lost or left somewhere. "Shit. How could they farm? We were blowing the place up, Charlie was burning and looting it. What a mess..." He rubbed his jaw and chewed the corner of his lower lip.

"I dusted the colonel and the girl saw it, so I brought her back with me. We were supposed to 'neutralize' witnesses, but I couldn't do it. Chick Easton, the assassin with a heart of gold. I didn't finish the guy on the first shot. I was off just a hair and he didn't die right off. Flopped on the floor, digging at his throat with his hands. Looked like a fish thrashing on a boat. She was screaming and crying by the time I put one behind his ear. A beautiful little girl. Some French blood in her. Hair was the color of flax, unusual for a B-girl. Her eyes were Asian dark but round like a Caucasian's. She was prime, grade A, number one, and it made me glad he died hard.

"So I brought her back. God knows why. She spoke little English but spoke French very well. I speak a little French. Got her calmed down. She was afraid the VC would think she killed the colonel and hurt her family." He drank some more bourbon, then placed his forehead against a palm and ran his hand through his hair. Swallowed, then looked around the room. I waited, not knowing what to say. The dinner crowd was gone, leaving the party people and the hard core to breathe in the gray smoke, their ears pelted by the jukebox, seasoned campaigners against the night. The bathroom door swung open and slammed shut.

"There was a guy, VC, a sapper they'd caught and were interrogating with a car battery and a pan of water. Nice guys, huh? Smokin' dope-a-wana and jump-starting gooks. We were for-sure sweethearts. Good thing we were the good guys or I'da got confused and thought we were doing something wrong." He tilted his head back to swallow more whiskey; his Adam's apple bobbed. He pursed his lips and gritted his teeth.

"So, they juiced the guy too much and he died, y'know? 'Hey, I thought this guy came with a three-year warranty,' says one of the snake-eaters. 'That's the trouble with these foreign models, they're all six volt. Hard to charge up.'

"Then they took the guy out and threw 'im in the river. The girl is shakin' and turnin' pale now. A whiter shade of pale, man. She's a B-girl and seen things, but nothin' like this. She's thinking she's next." He turned in his seat and then put his elbows on his knees and stared at the floor. The muscles in his jaws flexed and worked.

"We don't have to do this," I said. "We can go home."

"I couldn't leave," he said, to the floor, "because I was waiting to be debriefed. Also 'cause I was scared. These were hard guys. War, ya know, is bad fuckin' business. I smoked some guys. But I didn't torture nobody. Those bastards juiced the sapper for recreation, man. He didn't know nothin', dig? Totally out of control." His eyes filled with the memory of it. "They came back after they'd tossed the guy in the water and one of 'em said—check this out now, Wyatt—one of these cold mothers says, 'Y'know what you call a gook floating in the delta? Bob,' he says. So, now they're all laughing like it's the funniest thing ever, the dope screwing up their heads. Now, I already got a bad taste from the girl watching two hard killings, and I'm straight, waiting to be debriefed so I can take the girl back to base, get a shower, something to eat. I don't want nothing to do with these twisted assholes, anyway."

It was building inside him, bubbling and simmering, working its way to the top. His eyes were shiny dimes, and his knuckles were bloodless and pale as he clenched the shot glass. The apostrophe eyebrow was the color of bruised cherries. No stopping it now. He'd shaken it loose and it boiled up, spilling over.

"I was trying to keep it together," he said, taking a deep breath. "You know what it was like over there. Ride it out. I'd seen grunts stoned out and riding the dragon before. But I could feel it was wrong this time. Besides the GBs and the spook, there were two grunts and the dope captain. They were treating the Green Berets and the CIA crazoid like they were celebrities. Death groupies. They started eyeing the girl. Talking shit at her. 'How's about a little gook pussy, Blackjack?' they asked me." I reasoned that Blackjack was Chick's code name. " 'Get that little Your-Asian pull a meat train.'

"I got no stomach for that crap. I tried to keep them off her, but a couple of 'em grabbed me and held me while they took turns on her. It was fucking miserable. The worst moment of my life." His breathing was shallow now. "You have no idea what a bad trip is until you watch six guys gang-rape a teenaged girl who can't speak your language. After a while she didn't even cry anymore, just let them have their way. Once in a while she'd look at me. Maybe she thought I'd brought her there to be attacked, I don't know. I'll never forget the way she looked at me. Never. I can't wash it away. No end to it, man. No end.

"Finally, the assholes finished with her and they let me go, laughing the whole time. 'Your turn, Blackjack,' they said. 'C'mon, man, your gash, take a cut.' I said okay, but first I hadda take a leak. I went outside, got my sixteen and a couple grenades, then I went back in, made 'em let the girl go. She ran, still don't know what became of her. Then it was just me and the six rapists. Six American criminals. Seven, counting me. Americans. Shit." He squeezed his eyes shut. I knew the ending.

"They had it coming, Chick," I said. "That's a long time ago. It's over. Let it go."

"I gotta finish," he said, deadpan. "I've never told anybody what happened. So, I held the gun on 'em until she left, and then I pulled the pins on the frags and said, "I'll be outside, waiting. Either way, the war's over for you guys.' I rolled the grenades inside and stepped out. Some of them tried to get out. No fucking way.

"No fucking way," he said again. "Blackjack. Smoke and fire, man. The Black Death. Shit, I was proud of it, man. Why'd I bring that girl in amongst those animals? Why'd I do that?"

“Wasn’t your fault,” I said. I thought about the girl in my dreams, the girl dressed like a man, the one whose face I’d peeled back like onion skin, the face that would never leave me.

“I killed six Americans.”

“They raped the girl. Tortured the sapper to death.”

“War’s different.”

“That’s crap,” I said. “I’ve heard that excuse until I’m sick of it.” I thought of the arguments I’d had with my father, a World War II vet, the alienation between us when I expressed my disgust with Nam and U.S. policy. “It was inside them. The cruelty. You either are what you are or you’re not. War warps the senses. War reveals what we really are. Sometimes what we are isn’t pretty, but it doesn’t change things. We had to kill the enemy, that was our job. It wasn’t our job to torture, murder, or rape the enemy or the populace. It’s the difference between being a soldier and a barbarian. Leave it there, Chick.”

He looked at me for a long moment, as if deciding something.

“Before this thing is over,” he said, “we may have to do things you won’t like. Things that’ll bring the whole thing back. You know that. There may be no way around it.” I nodded. “What Roberts said, about me losing my nerve. He may be right. In my mind I think I just got sick of it. I said I’d never do it again. But when it comes down to it, I’ll do what has to be done. We’re painted into the corner on this one, partner, and I wanted you to know what kind of man you’d hooked up with. I owe you that.”

“I already know what kind of man you are. It comes into the room with you. Your story changes nothing. If anything, it enhances what you are. I trust you.”

He nodded at me. “The rest of the way it gets hard. From here on out, it’s hunting snakes in the dark.”

“I know.”

THIRTY-THREE

The moon was a fingernail in the muddy autumn sky when we pulled onto the lane leading to my cabin. After we left the Silver Spur we had stopped for coffee before heading home. Chick was a little bleary but was convalescing in the passenger seat, a recovery that consisted mostly of snoring like a rutting bull moose with the whooping cough.

I stopped to check my mail—L. L. Bean catalog, *Sports Afield* magazine, fan mail from Ed McMahon, who insisted he wanted to make me rich. How did Ed find me? Some recluse I was. I put the mail on the floorboard and drove up the road. Chick stirred in his seat, rubbed his face, and made a low guttural sound, part grumble, part groan, then said:

"Did I eat a Styrofoam chest filled with gravel tonight?"

I refused to play straight man for him.

"Was afraid of that," he said. "Does this mean the Silver Spur gets a new wing they can name after me?" I nodded, giving in. Then he said, "Explain your plan to me again. I think I may be a little fuzzy on some of the details."

"Which ones?"

"Starting with calling Morrison."

I pulled to a stop in front of the cabin, shut off the engine, then said, "Roberts is pinned at his house until at least nine in the morning, waiting for the call. Can't leave. We call Morrison, give him the info, see where he would like us to set up the exchange, then the feds move in and arrest Roberts."

"Hopefully, before Roberts has us killed."

"Pessimist."

"What if Morrison doesn't like it?"

"He'll like it," I said. "He hasn't got any choice. Besides, I'll take it to Browne and the highway patrol if he doesn't like it." I started to get out of the vehicle.

"Wait a minute," Chick said, putting a hand on my arm. With his other hand he opened the glove box and retrieved his gun.

"What's up?"

"No sense walking into anything. If they zip you they might figure they don't have to worry about buying the formula. Wait here while I check it out," he said, then bailed out of the vehicle.

I rolled down my window, then reached under the seat, grabbed the butt of the Browning, and put it on the dash. I sat in the dark for several minutes, smelled the cold, clean air, and considered the irony of sitting in my own drive in the dark with a loaded gun while a bounty hunter checked my cabin. Not exactly what I'd had in mind all those years ago when I walked away from the NFL.

It came back to me now, settling in my brain like the aftermath of an early morning rain—the day I decided to quit. The day I knew it was enough. The day I woke up with yet another in a series of hangovers that solved nothing except to eclipse the cold-as-metal pain in my left shoulder and right knee. The day I woke up next to the femme du jour, another interchangeable droid, with straight teeth and all the right moves. The day I woke up.

I no longer wanted to be what they were trying to make me. Or what I was allowing myself to become. The concessions I'd made. Lying to myself. Couldn't believe what I had allowed myself to accept. The all-night parties. The drugs. The booze. The pills I took to kill the pain, to put me to sleep, to blur reality into a fuzzy-edged daydream. Just wanted to be me again. My innocence hadn't died, it had been waylaid by misplaced priorities. I wasn't built to be a star. Wasn't born to follow.

God, I was sick of me.

Had not wanted it to be that way. Too late to regain what had been lost, but maybe not too late to reclaim what was left. I was not who I used to be, but I didn't have to be what I was becoming. So I walked away. Walked away. Retreated to the woods. To obscurity.

Slowed down in time to see the long bend in the highway.

I had been sitting for several minutes, thinking about these things, when Chick returned.

"It's okay," he said. "Somebody was here, though. Broke in, tossed the cabin, probably looking for the formula. Must've thought you made the call from here. But be ready. For all we know they could be watching."

I got out of the Bronco, taking the gun with me, and we walked to the cabin, staying a good distance from each other. At the doorstep I saw where they had broken a windowpane and opened the door from the inside. Inside, things were a mess, as if a high wind had swept through. Cushions lay scattered about, drawers were pulled out, cabinets stood open. It was the same in the other rooms.

"Not much of a housekeeper, are you?" said Chick. "Anything missing?" I looked around. Guns were still there, though the glass was broken and the guns in disarray.

"Nothing important," I said. "I don't own anything important. They just went through everything."

"Pro job. Notice all the drawers are open? Means they started with the bottom drawer and worked their way up; that way they don't have to shut a drawer to look at the next one. Bet there isn't a fingerprint in the whole place."

The phone rang. I looked at the clock. Eleven forty-seven. Who would be calling now? I picked it up. It was Morrison. Saved me a call. I could tell him about the trap we'd set for Roberts.

"Storme, glad I caught you. I've been trying to get hold of you for the past hour."

"We've been out. What's up?"

"Bad news, I'm afraid.…Agent Taylor is dead. Murdered."

My knees felt soupy and I rolled my head back, closed my eyes. No. Tempestt was dead. I'd done it again. Somebody else had died because of me. Why? *Why?* No more. "How?"

"Poisoned. Somebody injected what appears to be Liquid-Plumr and cocaine into her IV bag. She was already dead when they found her. Sorry about this, Storme. I know you had feelings for her. That's why I called you. Storme…are you there? Storme, what's—" I hung up the phone.

"They killed her," I said to Chick. "Tempestt is dead."

Chick looked at me for a long moment. He ran a hand along his jaw. "Sorry," he said. I nodded. Then he said, "So what do you want to do?"

"We change tactics," I said. "No more negotiations. No more games. No cops. We storm the castle and cut the cancer out."

THIRTY-FOUR

We entered the woods two miles behind Roberts's estate at 4:30 a.m. The fingernail moon was gone, hidden behind the mattered sky of blue-black clouds, and a cool mist hung in the air. My face was smudged with camo paint. I wore black jeans, a black Eddie Bauer fatigue sweater with elbow patches, and a pair of black driving gloves.

Chick was dressed similarly, with the exception of a midnight-blue navy watch cap. Under his coat he carried a .357 Ruger Black-hawk and a Colt .22 Match pistol. In a rear pocket he carried a cylindrical silencer for the .22 that was as long as the gun itself. Strapped across his back with a nylon sling was a short-barreled Remington pump shotgun. I was carrying a shotgun, also, a 12-gauge Savage/Stevens side-by-side I'd bought at an estate auction only the week before. It was a pretty piece, despite a couple of rust specks. Before we left the cabin I had stuck it in a vise, sawed eight inches off the barrels, then sanded the truncated muzzle with emery paper, transforming it from a gentleman's fowling piece into a short, wicked weapon with two black, demon eyes that could throw a pattern the size of a tractor tire. It was ruined now. It would never again be what it was forged to be. I rigged a holster for it from an old bow quiver, slashing a slit for the trigger guard with a Buck knife, then lashing the whole thing across my back. When I needed it all I would have to do was reach over my shoulder and grab the stock.

I also carried the Browning Hi-Power pistol and my compound bow, four arrows on the quiver.

The night closed around us like a tent flap as we sank into second-growth timber and the dark secret places of nature. The air was chill on my exposed face, and the forest seemed to reach for us with thin, wooden fingers. My feet searched for stability, the ground uncertain and unfamiliar in the darkness.

Chick moved wraithlike ahead of me. This was his territory. If I had not seen his dark shape before me, I wouldn't have known he was around. He seemed to drift through the forest soundlessly, confident, as if his eyes were infrared. About 150 yards from the road we scared up a wild turkey, which exploded from a tree overhead in a flurry of huge, slapping wings, like a pterodactyl rising from its nest. I heard my breathing, heavy in my chest, more from apprehension than fatigue. A dry knot of anxiety balled in my throat.

As a boy in these Ozark woods, I had accompanied my father and my brother, along with uncles and cousins, on coon hunts with a single-shot .22 rifle in my hands and a flashlight bulb on my hat like an Appalachian coal miner, my heart eager and filled with the delight of shared experience. But this was different.

The black dreams of Vietnam were slithering up my neck into my head. Horrible memories of night patrol, slapping through the elephant grass, your hands clammy and fatigues stiff with the salt of the day's sweat, hoping you didn't trip a claymore, eyes straining for shapes in the darkness, straining so hard it gave you a headache, all the while hoping that if something did happen you wouldn't foul your pants or some freshmeat draftee wouldn't accidentally roll a half-clip of M16 ammo up your back.

It started to grab at me before I was ready. It had been years since I'd experienced it. Usually, I could feel it creeping up on me, but this time it clubbed me along the medulla with a magnitude I hadn't endured since I'd first returned from overseas. I slowed up and tried to head it off. Chick, sensing my problem, or smelling my fear, stopped and looked at me. I felt the hair ball of hyperventilation slinking up my throat, along with the sour sensation of nausea. My knees began to shake. I didn't feel pretty. Or brave. Neither was I ashamed. I was almost glad. It reminded me I was a man with feelings about to do an unpleasant job.

Chick stepped back to me and placed a hand on my shoulder. "Hang on, Wyatt," he said, softly. "Ride it out. I'm right here with you." He knew what it was, probably had experienced a taste himself, a souvenir many of us brought back from our little vacation in Indochina. I held up a hand, tried to inhale slowly through my nose, exhale through my mouth. Finally, I was able to regain control. I looked at him. He looked back, his teeth white against his camo-smudged face. Neither of us said anything for a moment, then he said, "I know."

I nodded appreciation and we continued into the dark spiderweb of predawn forest.

It was 4:47 when we reached the edge of the forest line around Roberts's house, a large redwood-and-stone lodge with high-peaked A-frame roofs and a redwood deck running along the second floor. There was a six-car garage and some outbuildings—tack house, machine shed, and a large Kentucky-home horse barn. The whole thing couldn't have cost any more than a B-2 bomber.

We sat at the edge of the timber and looked over the lay of the estate. "Remember what I said," said Chick. "No second thoughts. No moral dilemmas. No hesitation. These guys are killers. They'd as soon cut your throat and pull your tongue through the hole as say good morning. Roberts ain't mob, but he's been around them so much he thinks and smells like them. If he goes out of here upright, you and I will never be safe again. Somewhere, sometime, you catch a bullet or your car gets a C-4 wire job, and there's no guarantee someone you love will not go with you."

Someone like Sandy, I thought. Or Tempestt, already. I knew he was right. Now that I had the formula I would always be a threat to him. Even if I gave him the formula he could never be sure I hadn't kept a copy. After he guaranteed exclusive rights to the wise guys he couldn't afford a competitor. The uptown guys didn't negotiate, they liquidated assets—yours, not theirs. So we had to take him off the board. Roberts was a killer. First the sheriff, now Tempestt.

I had killed in Vietnam. Forced to. In order to stay alive for 365 days I had killed other men. And a girl. In order to return home. I was seldom angry when I killed in those times. I was afraid. Fear was demon and daily bread as well as ally then. Now I just wanted Willie Boy Roberts to cease to exist; wanted comfort in the thought that he was no longer around to hurt anyone ever again. To avenge Tempestt. I wanted to kill him slowly. Piece by piece. With his crimes on his mind and my name on his lips as he expired. Knowing that it went against my Christian upbringing to kill, knowing, in fact, that it was wrong, made no difference. It had to be that way. I needed a monster in order to do what I had to do, and he had provided me one. There was no other choice.

But the knowledge hardly made the task easier.

Chick took out the .22 pistol and fitted the long silencer on the end of the muzzle. We had two plans. We didn't know which we were going to utilize until we got there. Plan A was to arrive early and take them by surprise. Plan B was to wait until 9:00 a.m., when Deputy Simmons would call Roberts to set up the bogus meeting. Since we were sure Roberts had no intention of buying the formula or of allowing us to live, we knew he would send people to meet with us and zap us. He would be somewhere else with an alibi at ten o'clock. If something did happen to us, then Simmons was to notify Sam Browne and let the patrol take it from there. But I knew Roberts would be at the house until nine, waiting for the call. When he sent the muscle out to meet us, we could go in and take him with fewer soldiers around.

A horned owl floated soundlessly overhead, its wingspan monstrous against the blotchy purple-black sky. On the north ridge a coyote yipped a high-pitched cry and was answered by others. Then, from behind the lodge, came the deep-throated complaint of a large hound, then a second one.

"Dogs," said Chick.

I thought about my encounter with the Doberman, which made me uneasy. Wyatt Storme, dog killer. Now I might have to do it again.

"When the time comes," Chick said, "I'll try to take the dogs out with this." He raised the silenced .22. "But you may have to do it with the bow."

I nodded. "If I have to." But I didn't relish the thought.

The big house sat upon a slight rise. A long white rail fence bordered the road on the south property line; the fence became barbed wire on the east and west lines and ran all around the house. There was a ridge about two hundred yards north of the property. We were positioned on the east ridge, the wind rising up in our faces. The long paved drive leading to the house was decorated by red maples. The lawn was vast. Crossing the fence would present little trouble, but crossing it without the dogs sounding an alarm or severely biting my favorite wide receiver was another matter. Fortunately, most guard dogs depend upon their sight and hearing rather than their sense of smell, and well-trained attack guards didn't bay at coyotes. But it didn't matter whether the dog that crushed your femur was trained or not.

We were deciding whether to use plan A or B when a gray Dodge Dynasty stopped at the road gate. A man got out of the car, opened the gate, and drove up to the house. Chick reached into one of his pockets and produced a monocular, one of those small telescopes with a four-power lens like binoculars. A light came on in the house. The car stopped near the garage. Two dogs, a Doberman and a Rottweiler, bounded up happily into the yard light. A man, their handler perhaps, followed the dogs. The driver got out and petted the dogs. Chick put the scope up to an eye.

"In-fucking-credible," he said, softly. He handed me the scope. Looking through its magnified eye, I saw the blond head of Agent Candless of the Drug Enforcement Agency. He and the other man walked back to the house and went inside. Why was Candless here? Because he was dirty. It explained how Roberts was always one step ahead of the game. But why now, before dawn?

All along I had sensed something rotten about Candless, but up to now I thought his connection was with Alan Winston. More lights came on in the house. So much for hitting them while they slept. What event had brought Candless to the house at this particular moment?

"Maybe he's collecting for the heart fund," Chick said.

"Or maybe the sale is going down."

After Candless and the man entered the house a man wearing a parka and carrying a scoped rifle stepped onto the balcony. He stayed back in the shadows, occasionally stepping forward to look in the direction of the road.

"They couldn't have over seven or eight guys with guns and two attack dogs," Chick said. "They don't have a chance."

"I'm surprised they haven't surrendered already."

"Maybe this was a planned meeting."

"Or maybe Candless wants to be around when the call comes in and he's helping them plan a course of action. I don't like the odds." I didn't. But there was no way to pull back now.

We settled down to wait. I thought about Sandy, or at least I tried to, but the more immediate problem was on my mind.

Chick looked through the scoping glass. He was watching the sentry. "The guy on the balcony sees something," he said.

"Where is he?" I asked. Chick handed the glass to me.

"There," he said, "against the wall." I looked at the man. He was casting quick glances around one corner of an alcove. He had a walkie-talkie to his mouth.

"He's talking to somebody on a radio," I said. I followed the line of the sentry's sight. One hundred and fifty yards southwest of the lodge I saw a shadow moving through the edge of the timber. "Somebody is over on the west ridge. Moving in the direction of the house."

"Place is getting crowded."

The man who had met Candless came out of the house carrying a shotgun and something thin and supple, like rope, in one hand. He gave a low whistle and the two dogs ran to him. The thing in his hand was a pair of leashes. He tethered the dogs and moved over by the tack house, in the shadows of one side of it. I saw the red glow of a cigarette as he lighted it. The distant figure on the opposite ridge made its way slowly across the open field.

"He's coming in from the wrong side," I said. "Wind's at his back and the shadows are wrong."

"Can you tell who it is?"

"No." I hoped it wasn't Simmons. He had expressed a desire to do more than make one phone call, but I had vetoed it. If it was Simmons, he had made a dumb move that could screw up everything. My heart thumped in my chest. If it was Simmons, we would have to abandon our plans in order to rescue him. An iffy proposition. Unless we could radio in an air strike we would be caught out in the open, outgunned and outnumbered.

"Don't even think it," said Chick, reading my mind. "He shouldn't have come."

"We can't let the dogs eat him," I said.

Chick smiled. "Knew you'd see it that way. What the hell. Okay, we work our way along the north side of the property then down the back side of the house and over to the tack house. There's some cover from that direction. When we get there we have to do the guy and both dogs and do it without alarming the sentry. I can burn both dogs with this." He lifted the .22. "But you'll have to stick the guy."

"From behind?"

"From behind. Aim for the base of the neck. Even if it doesn't kill him right off, which it should, it'll keep him from yelling out. I'll pop the dogs, and maybe the guy on the balcony will never know. And maybe the Cleveland Indians will win the pennant this year." He looked at me. "Don't want to do the guy, do you? Rather do the dogs, right?" He was right. I respected animals, but wasn't going to go dewy-eyed over a couple of mutts bred to kill. It was much worse, not even in the ballpark, in fact, to kill another human being. Never understood people who equated animal life with human life.

"No," I said. "I don't want to, but I have to. I'm better with the bow than you are, or you'd do it. The dogs are a smaller target, so the gun is better for them."

"Well, I don't know if you shoot better than me, but it is your bow, so maybe you can shoot it a little better than me."

"Much better," I said.

"Uh-huh," he said, grunting. "We'll see."

"You'll probably miss both dogs," I said.

"You can't shoot a bow worth nothing."

"Bounty hunter. Ha!"

"All-pro," he said, derisively. He grinned and I shrugged.

Then we stepped out of the woods and made our way down the ridge.

THIRTY-FIVE

The first ember of dawn glowed faintly on the east horizon as we reached the back of the property. I followed Chick, placing my feet down in the exact spot he'd stepped in. If he thought a spot of ground was safe and quiet, then it was okay with me.

I reslung the sawed-off so it wouldn't clink against the 9-millimeter. I was careful not to allow the barrel of the shotgun to touch anything. We got a lucky break when we got behind the house. Running along the northern fence line was a hard-packed path, worn smooth by vehicles, which allowed us to move more quickly. We wanted to come up behind the man and the dogs. There was a chance the dogs would scent us, but so far the wind was quartering into our faces. Noise was our biggest problem.

We made it to the back of the tack house without incident. I smelled horsehide and manure. A horse nickered softly from within the barn. I saw the back of the man and the semihorned head of the Doberman. The Rottweiler loomed over the black dog like an elephant, huge and wide. The man dropped a cigarette to the ground and stepped on it.

It was Vance. We were behind a large bale of hay, where he couldn't see us even if he turned around. If it had been about fifteen yards closer it would have been perfect. But I didn't want to try to hit that small an area from that distance. I was going to have to step out into the open to get a shot. With my head I indicated we needed to move up. Chick nodded in return, and we stepped out from behind the bale.

We almost made it.

I was nocking the arrow when Chick's foot scraped something on the ground. The Doberman made a rumbling sound down in its throat and Vance turned around. I wasn't going to have time to shoot him. Vance released the traces on the dogs and reached for the rifle leaning against the building.

He never got it up.

Chick shot him at the base of the throat. Vance's hands reached for his throat as he was falling. He was dead within seconds of hitting the ground. The dogs were racing in our direction, eating up the short distance with loping strides. I put a ten-yard pin on the Doberman, figuring it to be the faster of the pair. Besides, an arrow wouldn't stop the bigger dog. It was Chick's worry now. Didn't have time to be scared. I released the arrow and it jumped from the string. The broadhead tore through the dog's cheek and then ripped into its shoulder. The black dog stumbled and then skidded to the ground, bending the shaft of the arrow. It gave a small yip of pain, and then I heard the muffled .22 spit twice. Still the big Rott came on. I readied myself to swat it with the bow. The Colt sneezed again and the dog slid into the dirt. The Doberman was writhing on the ground; Chick shot it between the eyes and it stopped moving. The bigger dog shivered, then lay still. Vance sat against the side of the building, legs splayed out, a look of surprise on his face, one hand on his crotch, a red spot at the base of his throat.

My shoulder shivered and my mouth felt cottony. I realized Chick had purposely stepped on the twig so I wouldn't have to kill a man from behind. That, or he didn't think I could do it. I didn't know if I could have. Better off not knowing.

Chick looked at me and indicated the direction from which Simmons, or whoever it was, would be coming. We ducked behind the structure and watched for him. He was seventy-five yards away, crouched low and moving from behind the old barn. Stupid. Soon he would be out in the open, visible from the house.

"Wait here," said Chick, and then he ran around the back of the tack house. I put the bow down and unsheathed the shotgun, waiting, the blood pumping in my ears. Several seconds passed before I peeked around the corner of the building. When I did I saw the dark figure of Chick Easton grab the intruder, covering the man's mouth with a hand and pulling him into the darkness. I searched the ground around me for any sign of someone coming from the house. No one came.

I looked at the dogs and Vance. They were very quiet. It wasn't easy to stand close to them. Certainly was a good thing drugs didn't hurt anybody but the people who used them.

Chick came back with a man who wasn't Simmons. Wasn't Spider-Man, either. It was Special Agent Morrison of the FBI. He was wearing a dark jumpsuit, a black baseball cap with the letters *FBI* in gold, and a pair of referee shoes, mud caked on them. He looked at the dogs and the dead man. His eyes were large.

"Damn," he said. "I owe you."

"You need to take a remedial sneaking up course," Chick said. "They've been watching you ever since you entered the property."

"I followed Candless here."

I nodded.

"I think he's compromised."

"No shit?" said Chick.

"What are you two doing here?"

"No more talk," I said. I checked the 9-millimeter, slid the action back. Cocked and loaded. "You going in with us, Morrison?"

"We are investigating this affair. There are procedures that—"

"Procedures!" I said, between clenched teeth. It hissed from me like steam. I leaned into his face. "Your adherence to procedure cost Tempestt her life."

"You got nothing on Roberts," said Chick. "The woman agent was your only hope. He's outsmarted you at every turn and your buddy from the DEA's been helping him stay out front. If Roberts walks, the sheriff and your agent die for nothing. And I've had about enough of that. Worse, if he's alive at the end of the day, he'll kill Wyatt. Or have it done. Someday. For sure. And," he paused, his eyes boring in on Morrison, "that ain't happening. I won't let it. You gonna let them get away with killing her?"

Morrison's eyes looked into mine, then back at Chick. Something was going on inside the G-man's head. Something nearly audible as he wrestled with it before it clicked into place.

"No," he said. "I'm not."

I put on Vance's hat and coat. The coat was bloodstained. I reslung the shotgun over the coat. Picked up his radio and keyed the mike. "House," I said, then clicked the mike on and off as if there were interference on the line. "...got one of..." Hit the key. "...two ran into woods north..."

"You're breaking up, Vance," came the answer. "You say there were others?"

"Right, they...into the woods...dogs after them. Send...after them to make sure." I didn't speak directly into the microphone. "I'd go but...got a prisoner."

"You think it was that football player and the other guy?" Chick mouthed the words "the other guy," soundlessly.

"Could be. I'm out."

I tossed the radio on the ground. "I'll take the guy on the balcony," I said. Chick discarded his shotgun.

"Okay," Chick said. "I'll come in from the back side and penetrate...ah...get inside the house." He left. Disappeared, actually.

"What about me?" Morrison asked.

"You're my prisoner. When we get close we either get the guard to let us in or we drop him. His choice." I pulled the collar up on the coat to conceal the shotgun and pulled the hat down over my eyes. Morrison walked in front of me. I followed behind with Vance's rifle pointed at him. Morrison walked with his hands on the back of his head, his .38 revolver shoved down in the collar of his coveralls where he could reach it easily. I marched him up to the house, keeping to the shadows whenever possible.

Two guys carrying shotguns came out of the house. They didn't look at us, just headed for the north woods. They hadn't gone twenty-five yards from the house when I heard the .22 spit. Two shots and both men fell without making a sound. Never saw Chick.

"Your buddy is scary," Morrison said.

When we reached the house, the rifleman on the balcony was gone. Probably back in the house. We were greeted at the door by a smallish man with a shotgun lying across a white-encased arm—my old buddy Luke. Mr. Shit Happens. He was relaxed, not expecting anyone but Vance.

"Hey, Vance," he said. "Let's see what you got there." He took a step forward. "Mr. Roberts sent Breck and Skeeter out to check—" He stopped. "Hey, you're—"

He tried to level the scattergun, but the cast slowed him. Besides, Morrison already had the .38 pointed at him. Not bad.

"FBI!" said Morrison. "Put the gun down or I will shoot you."

"And if he doesn't, I will," I said. "There's already three of you down. Put the piece down, nice and easy. Not a sound." He complied. Maybe I should go into sales. "Now, turn around, with your good hand in your back pocket. If I see your hand at any time, you're dead." I put Vance's rifle down, reached back, grabbed my sawed-off shotgun, and shrugged out of the blood-stained coat.

"Now, open the door with one hand," I said. As he did so I brought the stock of the shotgun down across the back of his skull. He dropped. I eased him to the ground with my free hand and Morrison cuffed him with a pair of plastic throwaway cuffs. I took a handkerchief from my pocket, balled it up, and stuck it in his mouth, securing it with a length of nylon cord. I made sure he was breathing okay.

"Ready?" I whispered, heart pounding. Morrison nodded and we stepped inside. The door opened into a huge, cathedral-peaked living room. No one there. A staircase in the foyer led to the second level. On the far side of the living room was a large entryway leading to a drawing room or den. Guns ready, we walked in the direction of the opening. Morrison watched my back.

We were about a third of the way through the living room when a big guy wearing a shoulder holster over an expensive shirt walked in. He had coal-black hair and eyes and a thick neck. He wasn't expecting company. He saw the shotgun in my hand and quickly tugged at his gun, crouching and moving left as he did. I tripped the trigger on the Savage/Stevens double and he was slammed backward against the wall, like a quarterback jolted by an inside linebacker. I heard the loud report of Morrison's .38 and was moving for cover when I heard the dull thud of a body tumbling down the staircase. I crouched behind a heavy davenport.

Morrison moved under the staircase and trained his gun on the opening. I broke the shotgun open and inserted another shell. I unholstered the 9-millimeter and put it in my right hand. Held the shotgun in my left. The smell of cordite was thick.

The living room was masculine, burled wood and thick carpet. There was a ship's clock on the mantel of the stone fireplace, and there was a leather-padded wet bar. The house was still. A clock somewhere deep within the house chimed six times. The bell tolls for thee, Willie Boy, I thought.

I waited. The hunter's advantage. I watched the entryway. Chick was probably somewhere in the house by this time. I didn't doubt his ability to break in, somehow. Where was Roberts? And Cugat? And Candless? The guy I killed looked like mob. One of the K.C. shooters. He had come to kill me, and now I had done so for him. How many had the guy killed? Never again. I had killed a man now. The first in nearly two decades. But not the one I had come for.

Tempestt was dead. The sheriff was dead. There was blood on the walls and on the coat I had been wearing. I was calm.

Strange to be calm. Strange to be in a foreign house with the stink of cordite in the air, a defiled relic shotgun in one hand, having killed two dogs and a man in less than a week. Blood on the walls.

I waited.

The stillness pressed down on me.

"Storme," yelled a voice from the next room. The voice belonged to Roberts. I said nothing. "I know it's you out there, Storme. Come along in here, boy." I raised the pistol and gripped the shotgun tighter. "Got somebody in here wants to see you." I looked at Morrison. He moved closer to the opening.

"You got that piece of paper we talked about, Storme? Y'all a lot more resourceful than I give you credit for. Not afraid to stick your hand in the gator's mouth." Then he slipped into the Cajun accent. "Dat gator just sit dere, him, with his mouth open and his eyes closed, and you just stick dat fist down his throat."

My thighs ached from squatting. Morrison was at the corner of the entryway. Anybody coming through that opening would be cut to pieces. Roberts spoke again.

" 'Cept this ol' gator, he got bait in his mouth, him. Just wiggle it where you think you can take him and then he snaps dem ol' jaws shut, him." Did he have Chick?

"Got a lil ol' gal here, wants to say something for you." There was a muffled sound and a female cry of pain. "Why don't you come in here, Storme, and say hello to this reporter friend of yours."

Jill Maxwell. Why didn't she ever listen?

"You bring that shooter friend of yours in here, too," said Roberts, confident. "You both welcome. I'm a reasonable man. Businessman. We done business before. I know how you are. How you don't like to see the little girls hurt. Come on in here, now."

I thought about my options. Chick either was in place by now or soon would be. So what? My options stunk. If we didn't go in, Jill died. If we went in, we died.

"Beauchamps, this is Agent Morrison of the FBI. Give yourself up." Well, great. Efrem Zimbalist, Jr. Just what the situation needed. "Let the girl go and walk into the living room with your hands behind your head."

Roberts's laugh boomed from the next room. "You have it wrong, podna. I'm a friend of the federal government. Protected witness. And I got a friend of yours with me." Then the friendliness left his voice and the bayou accent went with it. "Both of you get in here—now! You have ten seconds, then we start working on the girl. If you want a war I'll give you one. Time starting now."

"You'll kill her anyway," I said. "First let her go, then we'll come in."

"You come in and I'll let her go," he answered. "You have my word."

"What good is the word of a man without an identity? A cop killer and a poisoner of women? The word of a man without honor?"

I heard mumbled voices and then a familiar voice.

"Ollie, Ollie, in free," said Chick, from the other room. "C'mon in, Stormey. I got 'em covered." I stood up and walked around the couch. I heard Chick again. "God. Got 'em covered. That's great. Always wanted to say that."

THIRTY-SIX

Chick was waiting for us in a large library that doubled as an office. There were wing-backed chairs and low coffee tables. Decanters of bourbon on a large bar with a giant mirror behind it. The room smelled of pipe tobacco. Besides Roberts, who was seated behind an oversized walnut desk with a leather desk pad, and Chick, who was standing behind Roberts, there were three other men in the room. One was Candless. He was standing to one side of Roberts's desk, his tan face drained of blood. Cugat stood in the middle of the room with Jill Maxwell in front of him. The wrestler's big paws were on either side of Jill's throat. Her hair was disheveled and she had swollen lips and a black eye. Her eyes pleaded with me, like those of a frightened fawn caught in the jaws of a wolf. The third man I didn't know. He had a beef-and-bourbon face, black mustache, black hair, pockmarked skin, and a large diamond pinkie ring. He wore a suit that cost about what I spent a year on clothes. The other K.C. hitter.

The dawn was growing through the large window wall behind the dark man, washing the room with a rose cast, painting faces bloody where it touched them.

Morrison and I walked in with our guns pointed. I kept the Browning trained on Cugat's ugly bald head, the shotgun pointed at the belt of the K.C. guy. There were a couple of guns on the floor: one at the feet of the guy with the wardrobe and one near Candless. There were probably more we couldn't see, but their hands were in plain sight. When I thought about Tempestt

I wanted an excuse to shoot Cugat in the middle of his smirking face.

Chick had the long-snouted .22 pointed at Roberts's back, his .357 pointed at nothing in particular in his right hand. Morrison had Candless covered. The renegade DEA man looked surprised and defeated. Roberts was wearing a cream-colored satin robe over silk pajamas. On the desk in front of him was coffee service on a silver-filigreed tray. He had the appearance and demeanor of a man about to drink coffee with his friends.

"Chicory, Storme?" said Roberts, nodding at the silver coffeepot. "I've never gotten over my love of its taste, strong and dark. Reminds me of beignets and mornings in New Orleans, the smell of gulf salt in—"

"Shut up, Roberts," I said. "For two Cheerios box tops and a Captain Marvel decoder ring I'd empty my gun in you and your pet gorilla's heads."

Roberts twisted his head, as if perplexed. "You're mad about something? Why are you taking this personal?"

"You killed Tempestt."

He laughed. "First you accuse me of killing the sheriff, and now it's Miss Finestra. You are wrong both times. I did not—"

I ignored him. "Morrison, take the girl and leave. This doesn't concern you."

"If it starts happening," said Chick, "kill the Sicilian first thing. He's the most dangerous. Cugat doesn't have a gun, and Candless just thinks he's tough. I'll shoot Roberts immediately."

"You are all under arrest," said Morrison. "Kidnapping, conspiracy, and—"

"Forget it, Morrison," said Chick. "They're not leaving here with you. They know it and you know it. Take the girl and get outta here."

Cugat tightened his grip on Jill's neck. Her body stiffened and she raised up on her toes.

I snapped back the hammer on the Browning. "Don't do that, Cugat," I said.

"I'll break her neck," he said. Cugat was the wild card in the deck. He had the manic, moon-shaped eyes of a hard-core speed and steroid freak.

"You do, and you'll never hear the referee count three."

"Seems we have a stalemate, gentlemen," said Roberts. "I'm willing to forgive and forget, though."

I kept my concentration divided between Cugat and the wise guy.

"How you figure?" said Chick. "I'm gonna kill you right off, and all your buddies got their backs to me. Ducks in a pond. Storme's itching to kill something, and me, I do it for the sport of it. After me, you're the most dangerous man in the room and you're already dead. Storme'd rather die than watch you hurt the girl, and that's straight up. This time," he said, his eyes glinting with the pain behind them, "this time, nobody hurts the girl. That's the way it is." I felt my teeth grinding.

Chick continued.

"Storme's willing to die for the lady, Morrison's willing to die for his oath, and I'm willing to die for the hell of it. Who's willing to die for you, Willie? Cugat? Maybe. Candless? Never. And what about you, pasta-breath? You ready to die for Roberts?"

The hood said nothing, just stared at Chick, dully, with hooded eyes. But I think he objected, on an intellectual level, to pasta-breath.

"What's it gonna be, Antonio?" asked Chick. "You want to walk out of here straight up, or die for Roberts? You call it."

"My partner," he said, in a monotone, his black eyes flat, unemotional. "Dead."

"Not your fault. Roberts forgot to tell you about another copy of the formula he wants to sell to your people. He didn't cover you. Roberts's fault, not yours. Bad business decision to die if you don't have to. Capisce?"

He nodded.

"Then leave the gun on the floor and walk out. The one in your boot, too. We got no argument with you."

The dark man reached down, rolled up a pant leg, and removed the small, flat automatic from the ankle holster and laid it on the floor next to the other one. "What about the fed?" he asked.

"Let him go, Morrison," Chick said. "Just keep an eye on him until he's off the property. Don't arrest him, okay?"

Morrison nodded. "He can go."

"Get the girl and go, Morrison," I said. Morrison took a step in her direction.

"Don't let her loose, Cugie," said Roberts. Cugat's grip tightened again and Jill squealed. Morrison stopped. Cugat glowered at me.

"Better let her go, Roberts," said Chick. "Honest to God, you better."

"I think not," Roberts said, a smug smile on his face. "I think I will test your—" Chick's target pistol sneezed and Roberts's right shoulder shivered.

"Damn," Chick said. "Never know when this thing's gonna go off." He prodded Roberts in the back of the head with the gun. "Need another one?"

"Let her go, Cugie," Roberts said, his head down.

"No," said Cugat.

"Dammit!" said Roberts, breathing heavily. "I said let her go!"

Cugat's face twisted into a mask of hate. He shoved Jill at me. When he did, the Sicilian bent over to pick up his gun. I tripped both barrels of the 12-gauge, cutting him in two. The slap of buckshot against flesh was heavy, obscene. The glass wall behind him shattered with a loud crash. Chick shot Cugat with the .22, but it didn't stop him. Later, I realized Chick couldn't use the .357 because the big gun's bullets could go all the way through Cugat and hit Jill or me.

Candless ripped at his jacket to free his gun. Morrison hollered at him to hold it, but Candless drew the gun and snapped off a hurried shot that caught Morrison in the hip just as the FBI man shot him high in the chest.

I dropped the shotgun, grabbed Jill by the front of her blouse, threw her behind me, and tried to get the Browning up to shoot Cugat, but it was too late. With a yell of rage and hatred, the huge wrestler backhanded me. The world tumbled around me and I fell over a straight-backed chair. I felt Cugat's weight on my chest and his hands reaching for my throat. I dug my chin into my chest to keep him from strangling me or snapping my neck. Instead, he lifted me from the floor by the front of my fatigue sweater and threw me against the glass door, which had not been touched by shotgun pellets. My head cracked against the unforgiving glass and I fell to the floor. I tried to clear my head, remembering to hold on to the gun. A reflex. If you're going to get hit anyway, don't let go of the ball.

Cugat started to reach for me, but Jill whacked him on the ear with a heavy crystal ashtray. He bellowed and grabbed her by the hair and slapped her hard across the face. He started to turn on me again, when he was shoved sideways by a flying kick from Chick. I raised the gun to shoot the off-balance Cugat, but Chick stopped me.

"No!" he said. His eyes were flinty and he was in a boxer's stance. "He's mine." He hit Cugat once, then again, with left jabs that flicked out then returned to their original position. Morrison was hurt but had his gun on Roberts now. Both Candless and the K.C. slugger lay still, the K.C. guy forever.

Cugat reached for Chick and Chick hit him twice in the solar plexus, then jumped back and to Cugat's right. Chick backhanded him on the ear and followed that with a roundhouse kick that smacked against the back of Cugat's neck. Cugat pitched forward, recovered, and threw a big roundhouse. Chick ducked it and uppercut the big man to the ribs. Cugat bellowed in pain but still cuffed Chick on the side of the head with a left hand. Chick staggered, and with surprising quickness Cugat had him in a bear hug, lifting Chick from the floor.

Cugat, his face smeared with blood, squeezed, and Chick's face turned scarlet. Then Cugat buried his face in Easton's shoulder and bit down on his neck. Chick made no sound, but his face twisted in agony. Cugat was killing him.

I holstered the gun, stepped up, and punched Cugat in the kidneys as hard as I could, twice. He didn't flinch on the first one, but the second brought a cry of pain and caused his back to arch. I hit him again, and he dropped Chick and turned on me. I backpedaled. Had to keep his hands off me. He swung and I blocked it with my shoulder, stepping inside and hitting him with uppercuts to the body. It was like hitting a slab of frozen beef and my shoulder felt as if I'd been hit with a hammer, but he was starting to breathe hard. I moved right and under his other hand and gave him another body shot. He brought his elbow back and swung it at me. I tried to get an arm up, but his elbow glanced off my shoulder and caught me on top of the head as I tried to duck. My feet came out from under me as if I were on ice. I fell across a table, knocking a lamp off it. When I hit the floor, I rolled away from him.

I looked up from the floor as Cugat swung a right at Chick and missed, grunting with the effort. Chick shuffled sideways and kicked the giant on the side of the knee. Cugat bellowed, and there was a discernible pop from his knee. He fell to one knee and Chick hit him twice, then danced away as Cugat recovered and swung another haymaker. It was like trying to fight a building by throwing rocks at it.

I stood up to help, when Jill yelled, "Watch out!"

Candless, not dead, had crawled and managed to reach his gun. Morrison stepped on his hand and Candless screamed, but Morrison had taken his eyes off Willie Boy, who yanked open a desk drawer and reached in, producing a small automatic pistol, which he swung out of the drawer with his left hand. I jerked the Browning out of its holster and moved right. Morrison swiveled in Roberts's direction but was slowed by his wounded hip. Everything was in slow motion. Roberts shot, and I felt a tug at my sweater, then he swung the gun at Morrison. Even wounded and shooting with his weak hand, Roberts was confident he could one-shot both Morrison and myself.

Roberts's second shot smacked the wall behind Morrison. I fired twice. My first round barked wood from the desk. The second hit him and spun him away from me. Morrison's gun roared and a puff of leather and lining material exploded from the chair.

Cugat, oblivious to the shoot-out, stalked Chick. He was limping and his breathing was labored. The bloodstain on his back from the .22 bullet looked like a Rorschach inkblot. Chick hit him—two short lefts, a right cross, left uppercut, right uppercut, left jab, overhand right, left, a spinning backhand, followed by a front kick. Chick used the momentum of his landing to launch a roundhouse kick, which caught Cugat full on the temple. The big man staggered drunkenly, and his breath made a liquid sound in his chest. His head was bloody. I heard the soft crying of Jill Maxwell on the periphery of my awareness.

Sultan Cugat swayed, put a hand out to steady himself, reaching for support that wasn't there. Maybe he was looking for the ropes. Then he fell heavily to the floor and lay on his back, blood smearing his mouth and nose. One eye was closed, and his nose cast hung by one piece of bloody tape on his cheek.

The room was quiet, save for the rattle of Cugat's breathing and Jill's mewling sobs.

Chick's chest was heaving, his face slick with sweat and blood, his shirt plastered to his chest. "Stick a fork in this turkey," he said, standing over Cugat. "I think he's done."

Chick's lower lip was split and bleeding, one eye was swollen and beginning to shut, and there was an angry red welt on the right side of his neck where Cugat had bitten him. He retrieved his .357 and jammed it back in its holster.

Cugat raised up on one elbow and muttered through bloody lips, "We're not finished yet." He began to get to his feet.

Chick pulled his gun and pointed it at the giant. "Yes we are," he said. "TKO. I'll be damned if I'm gonna go through that again. Sit down." Cugat did so. Chick handed his gun to Jill. "You know how this works?" She nodded. "Okay. If he moves, shoot him."

"How about even if he doesn't?" she said, a fierce gleam in her eyes.

"I think I'm in love," Chick said, smiling at her. He cuffed Cugat with a pair of Morrison's no-deposit, no-return handcuffs.

I walked to Roberts's desk. Willie Boy lay behind his desk with two dark stains on his expensive satin robe and a splinter from the desk lodged in his cheek. He rolled his head to look up at me, blood trickling from the splinter.

"Why?" he asked. "Why'd you get in this?"

"The sheriff," I said. "And Tempestt. They were good people. They deserved to live, and you took it from them. That, and one of your men poached a deer."

Roberts laughed until he coughed. Morrison limped over to use the phone. Roberts recovered from his coughing spell and said, "A deer? You are one crazy bastard, that's for sure." He coughed again. "You know what's funny?" he asked. I didn't say anything.

He said, "I didn't have anything to do with any of that. The girl, the sheriff, not even the deer. Nothing."

I looked at him, chewed my lower lip. "You're lying," I said. Chick walked over and stood by the desk. Jill was with him. He had his arm around her and she leaned against him. Her face was composed. Tears dry. She was tough.

"Why should I lie now? I think you've killed me." He paused to spit a small glob of blood. "No. I've killed my share, me. Crazy that I should die for something I didn't do. It evens out." He spat again. Coughed. "Ask Candless about the girl. He's the one gets hurt by her staying alive. She knew about him. I knew that, so I kept her alive to leverage him. He killed her. Why would I kill her? Could've done that anytime." He rolled his head. "You know, maybe I won't die, after all. Candless's greedy. Him and his friend, that lawyer…you were right, I shouldn't have used amateurs."

"Candless and Winston?" I said. "What's their connection?"

"Old college buddies. Fraternity or something. Candless found out Winston was involved, and Winston cut him in on the deal. Fucked everything up. Cugat tried to tell me. I didn't listen. The girl, she found out things about Candless. He tried to cut himself in on the take. I couldn't whack a fed. Sheriff, either. Too much heat." He took a breath. "Is Candless dead?"

"Not yet."

"Good. I want him to live so he can suffer in prison. Cute little blond boy. They love cops inside."

"What about the sheriff?"

"A stupid thing. You don't kill the law, I said. You buy them. But that sheriff"—he paused to take a breath—"couldn't be bought. Or controlled. Those kind you walk around." He was having trouble now. I reached down and plucked the splinter from his cheek. He winced, then continued.

"Winston and Baxter, they did that. Winston had a thing going with an underage girl. Sheriff found out and was going to blow it up in Winston's face. Bad blood between the two. Winston had Baxter do the sheriff." He coughed deep in his chest and spat blood on the carpet. It made a scarlet stain. He cleared his throat, then ground his teeth together in pain. I tried not to admire him.

What he was saying made sense. He could have killed Tempestt instead of pumping her full of narcotics. She found out about Candless's involvement, so Roberts had Cugat give her the chemicals and hid her out in the motel. Winston must have told Candless she was at the hospital, or Candless had figured that's where I would take her. He knew she might be there, and Chick's and my presence at the hospital confirmed it. I remembered they didn't know what room she was in. We had inadvertently led Candless to her room. He would have no problem circumventing a posted guard. His DEA credentials would gain him access. I had more questions.

"What about the marijuana field?"

"Not mine."

"Whose, then?"

"Never rolled over on nobody. But this bunch…no fuckin' brains. You think about it. Why would Baxter kill Kennedy?"

"He could run for sheriff unopposed."

"Only part of it," Roberts said. "Where was Kennedy going the day he was killed?"

I thought about it. The day I met Kennedy, Baxter kept trying to find out what I knew about it, first, before Kennedy got back, then he tried to worm his way into the office, even with Kennedy threatening to fire him. It was crazy, but I had it. "It's Baxter's marijuana."

"Yes," said Roberts. His eyes looked into mine. "I should've zipped you and this one." He indicated Chick with his eyes, since he was unable to move much else. "But I still never busted a cap on a vet. You understand that?"

I nodded.

"But I was going to have to, this time. And you, Easton. A man like you. Why stick your nose in this? Nothing to gain from it. You're a pro. Why?"

Chick smiled. Shrugged. "Eccentricity, I guess."

"Took the both of you to take the Sultan."

"I got a hangover," said Chick.

"Will you testify against Baxter, Candless, and Winston?" Morrison asked Roberts.

"No."

"Might get a reduced sentence."

Roberts seemed amused. Morrison was wasting his time. Roberts's reticence was his final dignity.

"Will you get Baxter and Winston anyway?" Roberts asked.

"Yes."

"Good."

THIRTY-SEVEN

By eight o'clock Roberts's house was crawling with paramedics, federal agents, and state troopers. Baxter made an appearance but was denied entry, so he was standing outside the house, cursing. Chick was soaking his hands in an ice bucket from the bar and drinking Glenfiddich from the bottle when the police arrived.

The highway patrol questioned Jill Maxwell. A paramedic treated Morrison's wound while the agent talked with a man in a charcoal suit. Candless and Roberts were rushed to the hospital, but there was no help for the Mafia gunslinger. He'd been dead from the moment he'd reached for the gun. Cugat was arrested, then taken to the hospital.

"Place looks like a war zone," said Sam Browne when he arrived. Sergeant McKinley and two other troopers were with him. "You're still alive," said Browne when he saw me. "I was afraid of that."

"Glad to see you, too," I said. "They have to tear you away from the speeders and jaywalkers?"

"Just set up a roadblock for a guy with a broken taillight when the call came in."

Sergeant McKinley walked up and without preamble said, "You clowns got things to explain. There are three corpses outside and one guy out front with a concussion wearing Saran wrappers on his wrists. Got two more guys upstairs. Four of 'em got .22 holes. I've got two Italians from the big city look like Swiss cheese. We found an illegally altered shotgun that has been fired, and I've got an FBI man with a hip wound. Now, for all my trouble I can't find a .22 pistol. And, of course, you guys don't know nothing about it. Everybody's been shot to shit, and all you guys got are cuts and bruises. How'd you manage that?"

"We dodged," said Chick.

"One of them shot my sweater," I said, showing him the hole made by Roberts's gun. "It was brand-new, too."

McKinley's eyes grew large and hot. Browne said, "They think they're comics, Mac."

"Why ain't I laughing, then?"

"Repression?" offered Chick.

"Which one of you smartasses had the .22?"

Chick shrugged, drank some scotch. I said nothing. Morrison had instructed us to make no statements, that he would construct the scenario. We were to give out no information; he would take care of everything, which I hoped he would do soon, since I didn't like the color of McKinley's face. He looked as if he wanted to chain us to the bumpers of two patrol units and head north and south, simultaneously.

"That's the way it's going to be, huh? Okay, fellas, you just bought yourself a load of—"

A fresh-faced trooper bustled up. "Found the gun, Sergeant." He held up the pistol. He had stuck a heavy marking pen through the trigger guard.

"Run prints, though I doubt it'll do any good. Notice you two guys are wearing gloves."

"There was a little nip in the air when we got up, sir," I said. "My mom used to always—"

"Shut the hell up! Sam, if this man opens his head again, shoot him."

"Love to," Browne said, then smiled, but he did so where his boss couldn't see it. Coward.

"Now, which one of you clowns does that gun belong to?"

"I'd never own a gun with an illegal silencer, sir," said Chick. "That would be dishonest."

"Dishonest?" roared McKinley. "We've got B and E, assault with a deadly weapon, homicide, illegally altered hunting weapons—Shit, why didn't you break some real laws while you were here?"

"We were going to set fire to the place, but we couldn't find any matches."

Browne chuckled, and McKinley whirled on him. "You find something funny in all this, Browne?"

"No, Mac," said Browne, but the grin stayed on his face. Just then, the man in the charcoal-gray suit walked up. He was finished talking to Morrison, who was being carried from the house on a stretcher. Morrison raised a hand to me as he left.

"Pardon me, Sergeant," said Charcoal Suit. "May I speak with you a moment?" He pulled McKinley aside and talked to him. At one point, McKinley threw his head back and looked at the ceiling in disgust. Finally, he nodded, and the two men shook hands. McKinley came back to us.

"Well," he said. "Seems the FBI has cleared the Marx Brothers here of everything." He looked at us. "Says you were 'assisting' Agent Morrison. That he received an anonymous phone call that the Maxwell girl had been kidnapped and that Candless was dirty. Apparently, Baxter is implicated. Every one of the dead men has a sheet. Something big was going on here." He turned to Browne. "Sam, go outside and arrest Baxter—suspicion of murder and drug trafficking. And you two get the hell out of my state." He turned his attention to other matters.

Browne said, "We'll impound the shotgun and the ownerless .22. I'll have to take your handgun, Storme, but you can get it back—Hey! Where're you going, Easton?"

"I want to watch you arrest Baxter. Hurry up."

Browne looked at me. "I suppose you want to see this, too?"

"Wouldn't miss it," I said.

"All right, but stay out of the way."

Jill and I followed Browne outside into the morning light. Baxter was stamping around like a horny bull. Simmons was with him.

"I'll be goddamned if I'm gonna take this kinda shit," Baxter was saying. "This is my county and I won't—" He stopped when he saw Chick. "What the—? What the hell is this guy doing here? He should be under arrest. What're you state guys doin', Browne? In there scratching your balls?"

"Baxter," said Browne, pulling his gun from its holster. "You are under—"

"Not yet," said Chick, interrupting Browne and moving closer to Baxter.

"Dammit, Easton," said Browne. "Stay out of this."

"Stay out of what?" asked Baxter, ever the straight man.

"This," said Chick, ramming a fist deep into the breadbasket of the fat ex-interim sheriff. Baxter doubled over and fell to his knees, as he tried to catch his breath.

"That's it, Easton," said Browne. "You're under arrest. Couldn't leave it alone, could you?"

"Worth it," said Chick. "You can put me in a cell with fat and stupid here. Save you the cost of the trial."

"You gonna arrest Baxter?" asked Deputy Simmons.

"Yes. Easton, too. Les Baxter, you are under arrest. Murder and drug trafficking." Then he read Baxter his Miranda rights. Baxter was still on the ground, gasping for air.

"Do you understand your rights as I read them to you?"

Baxter continued to try to suck air into his lungs.

"Sounds like a big yes to me," said Chick.

Browne was not amused. "Same goes for you, Easton."

"What are you arresting Easton for?" asked Simmons.

"You saw it, Deputy. He assaulted a prisoner."

A smile grew on Simmons's face. "Didn't see a thing."

"Me neither," I said.

"I'm a trained journalist," said Jill. "And I didn't see it, either."

"So that's the way it's going to be?" said Browne.

Simmons held up a pair of handcuffs. "May I?" he asked Browne. Browne nodded.

Simmons cuffed Baxter and helped him to his feet. "I'll get you for this, Simmons," Baxter said.

"You bring it right on," said Simmons. "Just anytime. I got a bellyful of you."

Chick walked over and put his arm around Simmons's shoulders. "Louie," he said, his upper lip stretched tight over his upper teeth. "This could be the start of a beautiful friendship."

Browne stood there shaking his head at us. "You two are a couple of jug-butts. Come on, Baxter, you know how it works."

THIRTY-EIGHT

They finally let us go at noon. Morrison was a man of his word. He did take care of everything. We were released into our own custody and told by McKinley to drive under fifty-five for the remainder of our lives. We would probably have to return at a later date to testify.

We hadn't eaten since the night before. I was starved. "I know a place where they serve you a whole fricasseed Clydesdale on a platter," said Chick.

"Good. But I don't think I could eat more than two."

We settled, however, for Burger King. Junk food. It tasted marvelous.

We drove through the pickup window and ordered two of everything, hold the anchovies, then drove to the emergency room at Citizens Memorial to see how Morrison and Jill were. He was in a private room and not allowed visitors, but was all right. We checked on Jill, who was being released when we caught up with her. She had been treated for minor bruises. We sat in the coffee shop and drank coffee that tasted medicinal. Chick and Jill smoked cigarettes.

Jill looked down at her coffee. "You saved my life."

"Wait'll you get the bill," I said.

She laughed. "All I did for you was cause trouble. Bothered you for interviews when you wanted privacy. Stuck my nose in this terrible business and almost got us all killed."

"It's a pretty nose, though. Didn't whine when they had you. Got a good lick in on Cugat. You also uncovered the mystery man, Simmons, and kept digging when another reporter would have quit. You're tough and smart."

"I found out about your visit to Winston's office through his secretary. She must've told Winston I was nosing around, though I'm sure she isn't involved. I also found out that Winston and Candless had old school ties. Apparently, they found out I knew, too. That big goon, Cugat, he grabbed me last night when I was getting into my car in front of the paper. It was late. Nobody around. If I'd stayed put, you could've taken them without any risk."

"There was risk either way," Chick said.

"What's going to happen to Winston?" she said. I wondered myself. There wasn't enough evidence to issue a warrant for his arrest. He had not been at the scene. He'd made sure he kept himself clear. Unless Candless dumped on him he was untouchable.

"He'll walk," I said.

"That stinks," Jill said. She reached out and put her hand on top of Chick's. She left it there. "What about Horton? He's got a thing for Winston. Maybe he knows something. Worth a try. I hate to think about that oily rat getting away with this."

"It's not a perfect world," I said, quoting Sandra Collingsworth. Chick turned his hand over and took Jill's hand in his. It's not a perfect world, I thought, but sometimes we get close.

"What do you think Horton would say if he thought Winston and Candless had something going?" said Chick.

"He'd go nuts," said Jill. "He's got a bad temper."

"You think Horton knows anything about Winston's involvement with Roberts?"

"I doubt Horton's part of that."

"Not my meaning. I'm not asking if he's involved. I'm asking if we could get Horton to tell us anything about Winston?"

"I see what you're getting at," she said. "Horton likes to think he's in the know. But he wouldn't snitch-off Alan."

"Not even if he thought Alan had another boyfriend?"

"Oh. I see." She shook her head and pursed her lips. "That's an interesting thought. A very interesting thought."

"Speaking of interesting thoughts," said Chick. "What are you doing tomorrow night?"

We caught up with Horton at the newspaper office. He was wearing a tapered oxford shirt and a chocolate-and-tan-striped tie. Brown pinstriped slacks with a knifelike crease and tan tasseled loafers. "He looks absolutely scrumptious," lisped Chick.

"Don't start that stuff. I don't want to spook him."

"You're saving him for yourself, you bitch, you," he said, still with the lisp.

"I don't want to talk to you guys," Horton said when asked if there was anyplace private we could talk.

"You'd be surprised how many people feel that way," I said.

"Besides, you look like you've been in a fight and lost. Thought you were rough, tough guys."

"We have been in a fight," said Chick. "And we won."

"I suppose I should see what the other guys look like."

"Some of 'em are dead," said Chick.

He looked at us from thirty-year-old eyes in a fifteen-year-old face. Looked much younger than he was.

"Still not interested," he said.

"It concerns Alan Winston."

His face flushed, like a junior high kid caught with his fly open. "And what is that to me?"

"Come on, Horton," said Chick. "We know Alan's your squeeze. So cut the shit."

A funny look appeared on his face; it was pride mixed with a little heat. "If that were true, and it's not, what would you have to tell me?"

"Not here," I said. "Somewhere private."

"Okay." He led us into the publisher's office. "Uncle Marvin's not here. We can use this." The office was simple and comfortable. Dark paneling. Heavy odor of cigar smoke, couple of chrome-and-leather chairs for visitors, a high-backed fabric swivel chair, large walnut desk. Pictures of fish and game birds on the wall. Several newspaper awards, word processor on a side table. Chick and I sat in the leather chairs. Horton sat in Uncle Marvin's executive swivel. The privileges of nepotism.

Horton assumed a superior air, as if the chair had transformed him into a man of power. "Now, what is it you wish to tell me, and quickly, because I have things to do. Another thing, if you say anything I find distasteful, I will terminate this conversation, and you will have to leave."

Chick looked at me, raised an eyebrow, a playful smile on his lips. "Bet old Horton's real popular around here."

"Hey, Horton," I said. "Time for a wake-up call. Take a look at us, then think about what you just said."

He fidgeted in his chair. "Meaning what?"

"Meaning," Chick said, "we're between you and the door, hoss."

He swallowed noticeably, his cheeks turned blotchy, and he began straightening things on the desk. "I won't be intimidated."

"We're not here to do that, either," I said.

"Yeah," said Chick. " 'Fraid you might like it."

"Maybe you could beat me up," said Horton. "Slap me and kick me around." He licked his lips, warming to it, his voice becoming husky. "Two big guys like you."

"Holy-gee-gosh," said Chick. "You believe this?"

Horton sat back, laughed, and took a deep breath. "If you're going to tell me about Alan and that Bennett slut, I already knew about it." Suddenly, no denials. "Just a fling. She's anybody's. He got over her."

"I don't know about that," I said. "I'm talking about a man. Guy named Dan Candless." I didn't like lying to him, but I needed what he knew. "He's a DEA agent. There's a teenaged girl, too."

It was as if I had stuck a cattle prod under his seat. He sat bolt upright, and his boyish face twisted into an ugly thing. "That bitch!" he screamed. "That cocksucker. He's a liar. He lied to me."

"Be fair," Chick said. "Lawyers get paid for that stuff."

"Do you know anything about a drug called dreamsicle?"

"What?" He stood up and was looking wildly about the room, as if gargoyles were floating in the air. A spooky exhibition. "I don't want to talk to you anymore."

"This won't take long. Just settle down some."

He picked up a coffee cup and smashed it against the wall. Tiny bubbles of saliva formed at the corners of his mouth. He slammed both hands down on the desk.

"*Get the fuck out! NOW!*" he screamed, his voice high-pitched.

We stood up. "Geez," said Chick. "You're going to have to lay off the sugar, Horton."

"*Assholes! Get out!*"

We complied. He was kicking furniture and throwing things about the office when we left.

Getting into the Bronco, Chick said, "Not one of your better ideas, pard."

I now doubted that Winston trusted Horton with information about his operation. He'd surely seen Horton's jealous rages before. Probably when Horton found out about his affair with the Bennett woman, whoever she was. I was also beginning to doubt the rumors of Winston's gay side. Horton was Winston's toy. Right up Winston's alley. He used everybody and everything. Horton was a kept woman, or man, or whatever. There was a tinge of unrequited passion and frustration in Horton's behavior. Winston probably kept him on a string. There's no thirst like that for the water you can't have. But Chick was right, talking to Horton was a waste of time, a mistake of judgment.

"You're gonna like my next idea, though."

"We're gonna talk to Winston's secretary? Ellen Fontaine?"

"Might as well."

"Wyatt, you are all right. She's extra deadly. However, if she asks us to gag her or spank her, or anything weird, I may have to go along with it—that is, in the interest of investigatory tactics."

"Sure are fickle. Thought you had a date with Jill."

"I do. Just trying to be democratic."

"Uh-huh."

THIRTY-NINE

I should have left it alone, packed it in and gone home, but I wanted Winston. There was too much blood on the ground for him to walk away to clink his glass at cocktail parties, secure in the knowledge that he had ridden the tsunami and left everyone else to crash against the rocks—Sheriff Kennedy, Deputy Simmons and his sister—and Tempestt. Mostly, for Tempestt.

We drove to Winston's office, parking the Bronco in Bedford's slot. As we got out of the Bronco, Alan Winston pulled into the slot next to ours. He was driving a silver Mercedes. He avoided looking at us, but it was a studied avoidance. He knew it was us. He got out of the German car. He wore a dark gray power suit, gray tie with narrow crimson stripes, dazzling white shirt, the oxblood tasseled loafers. Very fetching. I felt unclean.

"Hey, Al," said Chick. "How's tricks, man? Defending the scum of Paradise County must be highly lucrative. What do you think of his wheels, Wyatt?"

"Pretentious."

"What do you want?" said Winston.

"We just came by to see if you wanted to turn yourself in and throw yourself on the mercy of the court. Maybe you can get a good lawyer. Maybe even an honest one."

"Bet he don't know any," said Chick.

Winston laughed. "You have active imaginations. Somewhat immature perhaps, but creative." No smile now. "You're too full of yourselves. Don't equate your macho displays with real power."

"We've been talking to Horton," I said. "He's under the impression you're his guy. No accounting for taste, I guess."

"Horton deceives himself. He's a pathetic troll."

"I was talking about his taste, not yours," I said. "He told us some interesting things."

Winston appeared smug. "Horton doesn't know anything. I use him for information. He's helpful that way. There's nothing he could have told you that would interest me."

I believed him. Winston had the earmarks of a classic sociopath. He had Baxter for information of police dealings. He leveraged Simmons with the drug charge against his sister. He had tried to seduce Jill Maxwell, but when she rebuffed him he turned to Horton instead. He had someone everywhere. He always knew what was going down everywhere. Interesting that he wasn't at Roberts's house this morning. Had intuition saved him, or something else?

"People are dead, counselor," I said, then stepped inside his comfort zone, my chin level with his nose. He moved away. Something about him bugged me. I instinctively didn't like him—didn't like Roberts, either, but it was on a different level. I didn't like Roberts because he was a cheap hood with a face-lift. I didn't like Winston because he was a spoiled brat, a small-town bully with a pedigree. Didn't like the way he used people—even Horton. "A lot of people. And you're part of that, no way around it."

"If you're referring to that Marine assault you two overgrown adolescents pulled this morning, I thank you for that. You rid the county of some undesirable imports. I'm very pleased." He smiled and patted the back of his hair. "I almost feel compelled to reimburse you for your efforts, but I'm sure two do-gooders like you would refuse any reward. I don't wish to spoil it for you."

"Adolescents?" said Chick.

"Alan knows all about adolescents," I said. "He prefers them two-to-one over grown women."

"Jealousy is an ugly thing, Storme," said Winston.

"They've got the sheriff in custody," I said. "Maybe he gets nervous and starts talking."

"Baxter?" he said. "That's humorous. I'll defend him and he'll get off. And don't count on Roberts; he won't talk. He has the hoodlum mentality when it comes to that sort of thing. Even if he were to squeal, with his background, I'll get it tossed out first thing. Of course he wishes to implicate the sheriff, I'll say. The sheriff who dogged him and whose unceasing efforts for law and order have made him enemies in crime circles. I'll make a hero out of Baxter and a liar out of both of you."

I stepped closer again. It made him nervous. It was a cheap schoolyard trick, but how much longer could he keep stepping away? "You offend me, Winston," I said. "I don't like you. I'm going to burn you down. Watch me."

He stepped back, adjusted his tie. His face was tight, teeth clenched. "Don't you fuck with me," he said. "This is my town. Mine. I do what I want, and I go where I please. You don't belong here. You think you're players, but you're just a pair of funny little moralists with no voltage. You're nobody."

"Darn," said Chick. "Now I'm going to get a complex. Sorry about Candless, your frat buddy with the microwave tan. But where you're going there are plenty to choose from. Maybe a chainsaw killer, or a Colombian drug lord with bad teeth. Maybe even a child-molester just like you."

A vein twitched under the starched white collar. "Go away, heroes. This is my playpen. My rules. There's not a shred of evidence connecting me with any of this. I'll never spend one minute in jail." He walked away, laughing. I looked at the hole in my fatigue sweater. I was tired and dirty and my head hurt.

Chick whistled, lowly. "Man, you could ice-skate on that guy," he said.

"He's probably right, you know," I said.

"Yeah. Probably."

"He's going to get away with it."

"The way I got it figured, too."

"Oughta be something we can do."

Chick walked over to the Mercedes. It gleamed like a new bracelet. He kicked a saucer-sized dent in the door.

"How about that?"

"It'll have to do," I said. "For now."

Back in the Bronco I entered the flow of traffic, which was heavy for midafternoon. We headed west on the four-lane road. Three blocks up, on the eastbound side, was a red Nissan weaving erratically through traffic, dodging and passing cars as if its driver were late for dialysis. It careened into the westbound lane, passing two cars running abreast, nearly scraping one of them. When it met us I saw the driver's face.

It was Horton.

I slowed the Bronco and looked for a place to turn around, but the traffic was too thick. I knew where he was headed.

"Shit," said Chick, looking back. "He just pulled into the executive park on two wheels. Almost hit a van."

I waited for an opening, my hands tapping on the steering wheel. "Come on," I muttered to myself. I had a sick sensation in my gut. I didn't like Horton, but I didn't want anything to happen to him, especially since I was the one who set him off. And had lied to do so. Finally, an opening appeared, and I rammed the Bronco through it and into a gas station. The pump aisles were full, so I couldn't drive through to turn around. I shoved the gearshift lever into reverse and backed up, tires hopping. I hit first and headed for the highway, just pulling in ahead of a 'vette. The driver made an obscene gesture at me.

I wound the engine tight, shifted into second, then third. The needle touched sixty a block from Winston's office. I leaned on the brakes and came to a full stop, once again having to wait for traffic to thin before turning in. There was no way to go fast through the twisting, landscaped parking lot. After weaving through the maze of evergreens, planters, and late bloomers, I skidded the truck to a halt beside the red Nissan, the nose of which was buried in the side of the silver Mercedes. So much for Chick's dent. We jumped out of the Bronco, leaving the doors open. Winston's secretary, Ellen Fontaine, came running out of the office, waving her arms and crying. She ran up to me, and I grabbed her and held her.

"It's…it's horrible. I…I've never seen anything so…so…" Her chest heaved with her sobbing, and I felt her body trembling.

"Are you all right?"

"Please," she wailed. "Help him. Hurry."

I let her go, and Chick and I ran to the office. The door to Winston's inner sanctum was open. Chick pulled the .380 Colt, which the police hadn't found. There was a strange, animal sound coming from the office, like the low moan of a wounded rabbit.

When we entered the office I witnessed a scene that rivaled anything I'd seen in Vietnam. Lying on the luxurious, deep-pile carpet, facedown in a widening pool of blood, was the late Alan Winston. He'd been shot in both shoulders and through the head. Chick rolled the body over, said, "Shit," in a low voice, then rolled it back on its belly. I started to walk over for a look, but Chick held up a hand, stopping me.

"You don't want to see it," he said. "Castrated."

Horton sat slumped in a chair, a gun in one hand and a bloody tile knife in the other. My head swam. He was shaking his head and muttering to himself. There was white powder caked around his nostrils, and his eyes were glassy and distant.

"He's flyin'," Chick said, his gun pointed at Horton.

Horton rolled his head up to look at Chick as if Chick were a curiosity, then he looked at the gun in his own hand.

"Forget it, Horton," Chick said. "No way you're faster than me. No way."

Horton looked at the gun in his hand as if it had suddenly appeared and he didn't know what it was. "I won't shoot you," said Horton. Then his voice rose a notch. "He shouldn't have done it. He was mine. I cared for him and he treated me…he treated me…like…a thing. A freak!" His face was agonized. My mouth was sour, and there was an urgent tremble at the back of my shoulders. He looked at me. "He shouldn't have used me like that."

"No, Horton," I said. "He shouldn't have."

He smiled wanly and said, "Thank you."

"Come on, Horton. Let's go."

"No. I…I can't." He lifted the gun and put it in his mouth.

I stepped toward him.

"Horton! No!" My voice roared in my ears, and I felt as if I were moving through syrup. I was one step away when the gun exploded. Horton 's head jerked violently and then lolled forward as if there were no bones in it.

The room echoed with silence.

I looked at what was left of Horton. My throat burned with the bitter taste of spent gunpowder and emotion. There was a fine blood-spray on my hands and sweater. I was suddenly more tired than I'd been in a long while. My shoulders sagged and I stood there very still. Horton was also very still. He had been an unhappy man.

I wanted to be away from this room, away from this town, but I seemed riveted, lethargic. I felt a hand on my shoulder.

"Not your fault, man," Chick said.

He used the office phone to call the police.

I heard the sirens growing near as I was throwing up in the wastebasket.

FORTY

The police, and particularly Sergeant McKinley, were less than joyous to find Chick and myself at the scene of another homicide. Ellen Fontaine's account got them off our backs, but not before we spent four hours drinking rancid coffee and reading out-of-date *Newsweek* magazines at the courthouse.

"Why don't you two move to Iraq?" said McKinley. "They'd hardly notice the dead bodies, and Saddam wouldn't last a week with you around."

"I think he likes us," said Chick, as we were leaving.

Later that evening I bought Sam Browne a steak at the Raintree Inn. I paid for it with Prescott's money. Chick ordered a bottle of champagne, which I didn't drink, so he and Browne shared it.

"Roberts died at 5:05 p.m.," Browne said. "He told us nothing. Probably get something out of Candless. Cugat told us some things because he wanted Candless and Winston to pay. And Bedford, Winston's partner, is another person we'll talk to. Bedford has some cash-flow problems. Made a bad investment in a local nightclub and a couple of stores downtown, at Winston's urging. Winston was genuinely trying to revive the downtown area. Bedford also had some gambling debts he couldn't cover but needed to, quickly. That's how he got involved." He took a bite of his steak.

"What we can piece together is this: Roberts was set to sell the formula to the Chicago bosses, and that's where the two shooters come in. They were an advance guard for the buy. Jerry Scalia was the guy we found in the library. Best hitter in K.C. The other spaghetti-bender was Ray Gorbotti, the nephew of Augustus Caravelli, also known as Gus the Horse. Gus controls most of the drug traffic in Kansas City on both sides of the state line. Owns several high-volume discount record stores and a couple of nightspots, some hotels. Runs a string of high-class call girls. You guys rang the bell. That is, if Gus doesn't take your killing his nephew personally. Probably sent the kid to check out the deal before he came to town."

"Why did Winston and Baxter decide to kill the sheriff when they did?" I asked. "And what did the marijuana field have to do with it?"

"That's a story in itself. Apparently, Roberts got out of the marijuana business a year ago, but Killian and Bedford kept it alive. That's when Baxter decided to cut himself in for a share of the take. Roberts didn't know Bedford and Killian were still producing, nor that Baxter had become their partner, but Winston did. Winston knew lots of things. Had ears everywhere. Kennedy found out about Winston's tryst with the girl, which probably wouldn't have amounted to much, but Winston's reputation would have suffered. When Kennedy found out about the marijuana field, Baxter had a double reason to zip him. He couldn't let Kennedy shut down his marijuana operation, and he thought it would get him in good with Winston. Roberts knew none of this until after the fact."

"So then Willie Boy had to cover for them to keep the heat off his dreamsicle sale."

"Looks like it. Roberts didn't like it that the sheriff was killed, so he bumped Killian, then spooked Killian's dope buddy Dexter, hoping we'd take the bait and chase the scapegoat. Either that, or Dexter was killed, too, and his body dumped to make us think he ran. Would have worked, too, if not for you guys. Roberts was never directly involved with Baxter. His involvement with Winston came because he needed a front man. Somebody no one would suspect. Winston had the name and position in the community. Gave Roberts instant respectability."

"Gave him a fall guy, too, if it went bad," said Chick. "Somebody to leave holding the bag after the deal went down."

Browne nodded. "But Roberts hadn't counted on his partners getting big ideas and undermining him. All of them, including Candless, had hidden agendas. Candless got in through his relationship with Winston. Candless got greedy and wormed his way into the inner circle. He could offer inside information about federal movements. I'm sure Roberts had something planned for Candless, but he couldn't afford to do anything until the deal was over. Once it was over, nobody could've touched Roberts. The other principals thought they were going to market dreamsicle, but Roberts had other plans. Roberts had the two K.C. guys set up Prescott's phony suicide, and with the chemist dead, Roberts could sell the formula and disappear, since he was the only one left with a copy of the formula."

I cleared my throat. "There's another copy," I said.

His fork stopped halfway to his mouth. "What?"

I reached into my jacket—slowly, because of the creeping soreness from the fight with Cugat—and pulled out the dreamsicle formula. I handed it to him. He looked at it for several seconds before tearing it into little pieces. He shook his head.

"How'd you get it?"

I shrugged.

He sighed deeply, looked at Chick, then back at me. "When will you be leaving the state?" he asked.

"Soon."

"Good. I've got enough work to do as it is."

Chick and I stayed in Paradise for two more days. Long enough for him to take out Jill Maxwell. Twice. Good for him. Good for both of them.

Tempestt was buried in Overland Park, Kansas. Chick and I attended the funeral before heading to Colorado. Morrison was there on crutches. I shook his hand. Tears in his eyes. Tears in my heart. Where you couldn't see them.

Couldn't wipe them away, either.

FORTY-ONE

It was raining in the Rockies. Into the Little Silver River as I looked out the bay window of my Colorado cabin. I liked the rain. It was a nice break from the snow and reminded me of Missouri autumns when I was a boy. I liked that also.

I had a fire going in the fireplace. Flames licked at the logs, which popped and sizzled, the sparks dancing upward. The fireplace was natural stone. I'd built it myself, selecting rocks at different times, in different places, then fitting them together.

I looked down at the river. Van Morrison sang "Into the Mystic" on the stereo. A fluted glass containing champagne sat in front of me, another glass next to it. The hand of Denver's loveliest anchor-person reached for it.

"I forget how beautiful it is here," she said, smiling. Her eyes were bright, blue as the summer sky. Her hair was the color of fresh cornsilk. She wore no makeup except a small kiss of lipstick. Her teeth were a rich milk-white, the mouth intelligent and able to register anger, disdain, or happiness with a subtle turn of its corners.

I said nothing. I looked down at the river. Watched the rain kiss the window and roll down like teardrops. My shoulder hurt from the fight with Cugat.

"It's not your fault, Wyatt," Sandy said. "That woman, Tempestt. The sheriff, either."

"What about Horton? And if I hadn't been there, maybe Tempestt would still be alive. Maybe the sheriff, too."

"And Roberts and those other creeps would have sold a drug that would have cost more lives."

I looked at the champagne. Watched the bubbles form and drift to the top. There were many bubbles. When they floated to the top, they popped and disappeared.

"Yeah," I said. "I'm the greatest."

"Stop feeling sorry for yourself. You're not the type to put on a pity party."

" 'Pity party'?" I said, brightening. "Sure talk funny for a news personality."

The corners of her expressive mouth turned up, and her eyes sparkled in the pale light of the fireplace. "Loved by millions," she said. She sipped her champagne. "Thousands, anyway."

"At least by one."

"We'll start there," she said.

"Then marry me."

"I can't live up to what you expect."

"You are what I expect."

She looked into her wineglass. "There have been other men," she said.

"None of whom," I said, "are able to bend horseshoes with their eyebrows, I'll bet." She looked at me, searched my face. I said, "I don't care about that. Just you."

"You can't live in the city."

"No. But I want to be with you. I can try. I'm not asking you to give up the things you like. Your career. Your dreams. But I don't do 'progressive' relationships. I want a wife, not a roommate."

"You're an old-fashioned fuddy-duddy," she said. "But a cute one."

"Also rustproof and guaranteed for life."

"Not to mention hardheaded and overconfident."

"I prefer resolute and undaunted."

She laughed. "And, you're a wiseass."

"Then we're a matched set."

"You don't have a job."

"Don't need one," I said. "You have a job and can support me in a manner to which I plan to become accustomed."

"I'm not fooled by that," she said. "You are still the king of the sexist porkers. You'd open a car door for Gloria Steinem."

"Marry me and reform me."

"I'd have a better chance of being struck by lightning while holding a winning lottery ticket."

"But nobody loves you like me," I said. "Nobody."

Her eyes softened. She looked at me for several seconds. Her lips parted slightly. I gave her the hypnotic Storme smile, the one women were powerless against. She cocked her head.

"Yes," she said. "I will marry you."

Actually, it was the first time the old hypnotic smile had worked. Maybe I was on to something.

"Good career move," I said. "I hear this Storme guy is the catch of the century. So, you wanna kiss or something?"

"How about 'or something'?"

"I'm not that kind of guy."

"You're ridiculous. And you haven't touched your champagne."

I looked at it. "I'm afraid if I drink it, you'll take advantage of me."

She laughed. "Nobody," she said, "takes advantage of you."

So I sipped the champagne. Wasn't so bad.

ABOUT THE AUTHOR

W.L. Ripley is the author of two critical acclaimed mystery series, one featuring Wyatt Storme, an ex-NFL star and atavistic cowboy, and the other featuring Cole Springer, an enigmatic ex-secret service agent. Both series are published by Brash Books. Ripley is a native Missourian who has been a sportswriter, a successful high school and college basketball coach, and a well-respected educator. He enjoys watching football and playing golf, spending time with friends and family, and enjoying a good cigar when his wife, Penny, allows it. He's a father, grandfather, and unapologetic Schnauzer lover. Ripley writes daily from his western Missouri home.

Made in the USA
Columbia, SC
22 December 2017